Betrothal Voyage

Cosmic Lovers 2

Leda Palmer

Contents

1

Screaming

Zenda

Where the hell was she?

Heart thumping, I slid down the corridor, hunting for my quarry. The gentle whir of mechanical equipment buzzed in my ears, drowning out the soft padding of the critter's footsteps. A flash of gray darted past my peripheral vision. I whipped around and lumbered after my prey, nearly tripping over my own feet.

I am entirely too clumsy for this. Thank the Gods for food processors.

It seemed someone above was listening. As I neared the end of the hall, I finally spotted the little fuceria, crouched in a corner near the docking bay.

I buried the urge to cringe as I inched closer. But man, even after weeks together on the newly remodeled Verne, I still hadn't gotten used to how ugly Lux's pet was. She looked like a mix between a bunny and cat—only one that had all its hair torn off and was painted a sickly shade of gray.

"Hey, Smudge," I whispered softly, keeping my movements slow and steady. "I know we got off on the wrong foot, but you know me now. Can't we be friends?"

Her eyes bulged as I tentatively reached out, itching to pet her. Warmth bled off her skin, hitting my hand even as I hovered a few inches above her.

Clang.

Smudge darted through the docking bay hatch just before my hand landed.

"Fuck. I almost had her."

Someone started chuckling. I turned my head slowly and aimed a death glare at my friend. "Damn it, Capt, it's not funny."

Arda's laughter cut off as she leaned against the docking bay hatch. "Sorry, Zen. Guess Smudge still hasn't warmed up to you yet?"

"It's pathetic." I crossed my arms, fighting to keep a pout off my face. "You know how much I love animals. And I can't even get the one living with me to let me pet her. I think I've lost my touch."

Arda clapped me on the back. "Maybe you shouldn't have screamed bloody murder when you first met her?"

I shrugged off Arda's hand and adjusted my glasses. "Hey, I heard you screamed at her, too. Why doesn't she avoid you?"

Arda shrugged. "I'm fucking her daddy. Guess that wins me some points."

I rolled my eyes. "Fat lot of good that tidbit will do for me. Lux is so obsessed with you, he wouldn't touch me if his life depended on it. Not that I want him to."

Arda snickered. "Yeah, he's plenty obsessed." Her eyes glazed.

Probably recalling whatever the big guy did last night that made me break out the noise canceling headphones.

Lucky bitch.

I loved Arda like a sister, but I couldn't help feeling a little jealous of her sometimes. Where was my alien royal, ready to crash into my life and sweep me off my feet? Where were my scream your damn head off multiple orgasms? Guess that kind of thing only happened to curvy beauties like Arda, not plain Jane goody-goodys like me.

I sighed, brushing aside my regrets. I'd never been one to linger over things I can't change. 'Make the best of what the Gods gave you,' that was my motto.

I'd long ago given up on being the girl who had men swooning at my feet. I couldn't change my average looks. But I *would* figure out a way to get that little critter to love me.

If I couldn't spend my life surrounded by the beloved animals I used to work with—after one stupid mistake sent me packing—the least I could do was catch myself a consolation prize to study.

And love on, too, of course. I mean, a girl with no hope of finding a man still deserves something to cuddle, doesn't she?

Arda blinked back her dazed expression and met my eyes. "Don't worry, Zen. Smudge will come around. You want me to ask Lux to bring her to your room when he gets back?"

"No, I'll win her over on my own." I scrunched my nose. "I didn't know Lux was out. What's he up to?"

Arda flicked her long brown curls over her shoulder. "He had to go shake some hands down at Subralia. Said it wouldn't take long."

"Oh. That's...nice." My stomach clenched. I had the good fortune of being stuck on a ship with someone constantly going to the one place I couldn't.

Ugh. I can't go a full minute without feeling jealous about something today.

"That's actually what I wanted to talk to you about. You know we've been hunting for an in at Vorillion, right?"

Along with finding a hunky mate, Arda recently discovered a few quirks in her DNA—the illegal, experimental kind. Since then, she'd been on a mission to uncover the truth. She found a clue leading her to a medical research facility on the Vorill's homeworld, and we're hoping it will hold the answers she's seeking.

I frowned. "You haven't gotten approval to land there yet?"

Arda shook her head. "Lux even threw around his family name. We're still tied up in red tape." She sighed, then brightened. "Although it sounds like the mayor of Subralia might have the answer for us."

"Really?" Can't say I was too fond of Mayor Prim after our last interaction. But he was a Vorill... "Will he smooth things over with landing control?"

"Not exactly." Arda jerked her head down the hall and started walking. "Would you mind double checking that everything is set up in the largest traveler's quarters?"

I fell in step beside her. "Sure, I'm on it." My heart sank as I put two and two together. Sounds like I was about to be stuck on a long journey with the man who destroyed my future. I flicked a glance upward. *Really guys? Can't help your girl with Smudge, and now this...* "I'll program the atmospheric controls to Vorillion standard. Does the mayor have any specific instructions?"

"The mayor isn't coming," Arda said.

An invisible weight lifted off my shoulders. "I'll leave the atmosphere alone then, I guess."

"No. We're still going to need to change it. We're bringing a Vorill with us." She grinned. "Apparently, citizens get automatic landing clearance."

"Nice." I stopped in my tracks before turning toward the Verne's new addition with all the passenger cabins. My heart slammed against my ribs. When I lived in Subralia, there were only two Vorills there.

The mayor and—"Wait, if that room's not for the mayor, then who's coming?"

Arda's grin widened, and she rocked on her heels. "A certain friend of yours."

"Nash? No way." I bit back a squeal. *It's too good to be true!* The hell with it, I squealed. "I just talked to Nash yesterday. Why didn't he tell me he was planning to hitch a ride with us?"

"Yeah, that's the thing, Zen." Arda leaned in. "I don't know all the details, but it sounds like your buddy is not too keen about going home." She shrugged. "Mayor Prim arranged the ride with Lux. Something about a contract deadline..."

"Huh. Weird." Whatever Nash's business was, I was glad I'd be stuck with one of my best friends instead of someone I'd do anything to avoid.

Arda patted my shoulder. "You'll have plenty of time to chat about it on the ride to Vorillion."

My stomach fluttered the way it always did when I got a call from Nash. Only this time, we'd be face to face for the first time in nearly two decades. "Yeah. Guess we will."

"Well, I've got some work I need to finish on the bridge. I'll catch you later, Zen."

"Later, Capt."

I lifted my eyes skyward as she walked away. My lips curved into a smile. *Good looking out up there.*

2

Hunted

Nash

I ducked down a hallway, my heart in my throat. An enormous hammerhead flanked me outside the glass windows. One bulbous, laughing eye followed my movements through the underwater corridor.

Yeah, I get it. I'm pathetic. But believe me, she's more of a predator than you are.

The shark shook its head before tearing off into the ocean, leaving me with only the loud clatter of tapping heels drawing ever closer.

Where was it? There. I breathed out a sigh as I eased open a hatch and slid inside. The caustic stench of chemicals flooded the air in the tiny closet, but at least I was hidden.

The *tap, tap, tapping* grew louder before blessedly tapering off in the opposite direction.

There was nothing quite like starting your morning being hunted.

I took a moment to compose myself, quickly licking my face and adjusting my blue-green skinsuit. I only had myself to blame. There was a time when I would've delighted in Stasia seeking me out. Though lately, I'd found myself avoiding the leggy beauty.

Not just her, but all of them. The playboy Vorill of Subralia was getting bored with all the anonymous encounters. You might be asking yourself, why don't you tell them to take a hike? I know that would be the smart play. A kindness even, to let the women of Subralia know I wasn't interested in being their one stop shop for a wild night of no strings attached sex.

Fact was, confrontation was not my strong suit. You might even say I went out of my way to avoid it. So much so that I hadn't spoken to my own parents in years.

Yep, *years*. Don't worry. I'm not missing out on much. They dumped me on my uncle decades ago. Made sure he took me in on a backwater little planet called Earth, so they wouldn't have to deal with me. And I just... went with the flow.

That's me. So easy going, I couldn't stand to see a pretty girl disappointed. So ready to avoid drama, that I would rather hide in a cleaning closet than tell her to take her raincheck and shove it.

At least she was gone, for now. I sucked in a steadying breath and stuck my head out of the door.

Coast is clear.

I shut the hatch quietly behind me and turned.

"Nash. There you are."

I cringed. "Uncle. Good morning." Mayor Prim, the leader of Subralia—Earth's largest underwater city and research facility—stood in the hall, scowling. He, like all Vorill, had green-hued skin and large, round eyes. His bald head shone with sweat, like he'd spent the morning jogging through the entire settlement searching for me.

I cursed my luck. Another person I was hoping to avoid today.

"The shuttle to the U.S. Atlantis left on schedule an hour ago, in case you were curious."

I patted Uncle on his shoulder jovially and flicked a speck of dust off his dark-blue skinsuit. "Is that so? Good to hear the shuttles out of Subralia are running smoothly."

"You were supposed to be on it, Nash," he practically growled. "This trip has been arranged for months."

"Oh, was I?" I feigned distress. "I'm so sorry, Uncle. But c'est la vie."

Uncle rolled his eyes, an act which looked particularly humorous with his large, black orbs. I choked down a chuckle that would only make him more upset. The Terrans were bound to rub off on the guy when he'd lived and worked with them for over two decades.

"You have to return home." Uncle sighed wearily. "Didn't you read any of the paperwork I dropped off?"

I shrugged casually, maintaining a carefree air while all I wanted to do was scream.

Did I read it? Of course, I did. I wished I hadn't.

"If you'd read it, you'd know why you have to return to Vorillion. You can't—"

"Oh, I understand, but it's too late. Decision's already made." I turned toward my quarters. "Now, if you'll excuse me."

Uncle caught my arm. "I had a feeling you would pull something like this. You're going, and that's final. I won't sit back and watch you throw away everything that's rightfully yours."

I gritted my teeth, then forced a smile. "Uncle. If I wanted anything to do with Vorillion, I would have been on that shuttle. Trust me, the day I left was the best day of my life."

Uncle Prim met my gaze and his expression softened. "Be that as it may, I won't stand idly by and watch you throw your inheritance away. It's one trip, Nash. One visit to Vorillion to sort through the conditions of your contract, and you'll never have to set foot on the planet again."

I knew what he really meant, but was smart enough not to mention. The real reason I wanted nothing to do with my home world had nothing to do with the planet. It had everything to do with *them*.

"Listen." I slung an arm around his shoulder. "The thought was nice, but I mucked it up already. I missed the shuttle to the Atlantis. There isn't another space transport heading to Vorillion for weeks. By then, the deadline will have come and gone."

"Oh, that's where you're wrong, my boy." Uncle Prim tugged my arm off his shoulder and linked elbows with me, then began shuffling down the hall, forcing me to keep pace with him. "You're right about the transports. The public ones, at least. Lucky for you, I happen to know a private ship whose captain owes me a favor."

"What?" I shook my head, digging my heels against the tile floor. "No."

"Yes." Uncle tugged mercilessly, dragging me forward. "Your bags are already being loaded into their hopper as we speak."

"Are you insane? I can't spend weeks on a private ship." My mind raced, searching for any excuse that would let me wiggle out of this. "A Terran ship won't have proper atmospheric controls. I'll shrivel up and die before we leave the system."

"They've assured me they have everything you'll need in the passenger quarters. They've been newly renovated to Galactic Standard."

"What about you? Who will fill in for me in my absence?" *I might have him there.* Although my nights were spent entertaining women—or lately avoiding them—my days belonged to the city. I was my uncle's right-hand man, taking care of countless tasks that ensured the underwater settlement ran smoothly.

Uncle, forever a diplomat, answered carefully, "I'll miss your help, that's for sure. But the trip will only last a few weeks, there and back. You deserve an extended vacation after all your years of exemplary service."

So, it's a forced vacation now, is it? I cursed my uncle's ability to spin any situation to his advantage.

"What about the crew? We vetted the people on the Atlantis. How can we be sure this private ship won't be chock full of extremists looking for a quick payday by taking me for ransom?"

A slow, smug grin spread across his face. "That's the best part." Uncle halted in front of a hatch and pounded on the keypad.

"What are we doing at conference room E?" I cocked my head as the hatch swung open.

A tall, golden-haired, hulking fellow wearing a black skinsuit sat in the room alone. I squinted at his back, but it wasn't until he swiveled his chair toward the doorway that recognition struck me. "Luxuth. What are you doing here?" I grinned, taking a step into the room before it hit me. "Wait," I turned to my uncle, "you mean, he's the captain?"

Uncle Prim licked his face. "It's Commander, remember? Although let's not get caught up in semantics."

"It is good to see you again, Nash." Lux rose from his chair and paced toward me, his four fingered hand held out for a shake. Even though neither of us were human, I gripped his fist in the Terran greeting. 'When in Rome,' as they like to say here.

"It's nice to see you too," I muttered on autopilot, while my mind spun.

If Lux was the one giving me a ride, then that meant a certain old friend would be onboard. My stomach flip-flopped, and my traitorous heart beat like mad.

I glared at Uncle Prim. They didn't nickname him "the fixer" for nothing. My uncle just found the one thing that could convince me to return home.

"I hear you need a ride to Vorillion," Lux said.

"Yeah." I sighed. "I guess I do."

3

Stroking My Pretty

Zenda

The door to the med-bay whooshed open. I glanced up from my tablet and adjusted my retro cat-eye glasses. "Hey, Ren," I said brightly.

Our resident mechanic hovered in the doorway, curling a hand nervously through her short blonde curls. "Hey, Zen. You busy?"

I set down my tablet and fought not to purse my lips when I spotted the way she cradled her other hand against her oil-stained green skinsuit. "What happened this time?"

Her blue eyes flitted to the floor. "It's just a scratch," she grumbled.

I waved her forward and grabbed the portable med-bot. If I knew Ren—and after a year together on the Verne, I definitely did—then she was bound to need it. She laughed off scratches that would make me curl into a ball and wail for my momma.

"Give it here and let me do my job." I tugged on a pair of gloves and waited.

Sure enough, the hand she planted on my examination table held a deep gash. It wept blood after I carefully removed the dirty cloth she'd wrapped it in.

"Fuck. That hurts." She turned her head aside, clearly uncomfortable staring at the cut while I prodded at it.

I tutted. "What do you expect when you keep it to yourself this long?" One look at the wound, and I could tell it wasn't fresh. "Did you think it would just heal on its own? A cut this deep used to require stitches."

"Sorry, Zen," Ren said. "I was busy."

Busy meant she was probably stuck so far inside the innards of some machine she couldn't bear to tear herself away. Ren was practically a savant, more in tune with machines than people half the time. But we all have our quirks. Gods knew I had enough of my own, too.

"Uh-huh. Well, you're lucky we live in a universe full of med-bots." I wrapped the device securely around her palm and keyed in the proper sequence to get it working. "You'll be good as new in about ten minutes."

Ren blew out a relieved breath. "Thanks."

"No problem."

"So, I hear we're about to have our first passenger." She waggled her brows. "How's it feel knowing you're about to see lover boy again?"

I rolled my eyes. "He's just a friend, remember?"

"Yeah. So you say. But haven't you not seen each other in person in like, twenty years?"

I shrugged. "Exactly." My stomach fluttered at the reminder. I certainly wasn't the same tiny twig of a teen I'd been back then. I couldn't help wondering what Nash would think of me now, thunder thighs and all.

"What happens when he shows up and you can't keep your hands off each other?"

I cackled. Straight up, cackled like a witch. "Yeah... that's not gonna happen."

"Why not?" Ren frowned. "Is he ugly?" She scoffed. "Guess that's why you stuffed him in the friend zone."

"No, he's not ugly." I twisted my lips. "At least, he wasn't when we were younger."

I flashed back to the last time I'd seen Nash. We'd only spent a few short months as neighbors and friends before I was forced to leave, but I could still picture him clearly.

He was skinny back then too, but he always had the most fascinating eyes. Larger than a human's but beautiful and black, with tiny flecks of purple hidden inside the irises, if you looked closely.

I'd been a little weirded out by the whole face-licking thing at first—I mean, who wouldn't be a bit shocked to see a guy who looked remarkably humanoid flick out a tongue long enough to moisten his entire face? But once he'd explained his species need to stay wet, the action started to intrigue me instead.

And man, his smile—I'm talking about the real one, mind you—not that fake casual grin he painted on all the time. When I got him to drop the 'everything's okay' act he played with everyone else, that smile of his always made my heart race.

Ren interrupted my woolgathering. "Okay then, he's not ugly. All the more reason the two of you are gonna get freaky."

I swallowed down the cackle this time, but laughter still erupted out of me. "Yeah. I don't think so."

"Why the hell not?" Ren asked as the med-bot beeped. "You're both single. You've spent years chatting each other up. Mark my words, it's happening."

"No, it's not." I stepped closer, knowing that beep meant I had to check on the bot's progress. "And I'll tell you exactly why."

I leaned over the med-bot and adjusted a few settings. Ren glared at me when I finished. "I'm waiting. Tell me about how lover boy will keep his hands to himself for all those weeks you two are together out in space."

I shook my head, and my stomach clenched. "It's simple. Nash doesn't want me. He never has."

"Get real, Zen. A guy doesn't call you every few days like clockwork without at least picturing you between the sheets once or twice."

My heart stuttered. She hit that shot a little too close to the mark. I wasn't planning to share how many times I'd pictured us together over the years. Still, we weren't talking about me. Plus, Nash had his chance to be *way* more than friends with me once. Look where we were now. Both single... like he always wanted.

"Nash and I are just friends, okay?" I spit out, trying to hide the annoyance in my tone.

"I'm just saying, don't be surprised if he wants to be more than friendly on this trip." Ren bit her lip and gave me a cool once over. "You're one hot momma, Zenda."

The med-bot beeped three times in a row, signaling the treatment was finished. I sighed, happy for an excuse not to dwell on my looks or more accurately—lack of them.

Fact of the matter was, I'd never be a statuesque blonde with cheekbones to die for like Ren. I'd made peace with the fact that guys like Nash would never look at me twice. But that didn't mean I wanted to get into a heated debate about it.

I peeled the bot off Ren's hand and peeked underneath. She covered her eyes with her hand and cringed. "I can't look. Is it better?"

I pulled it off fully and grinned. "Good as new, just like I told ya. Be more careful this time, yeah?"

"Will do, Zen." Ren shook out her hand and stood.

"If you do hurt yourself, come find me straight away next time," I hollered after her. "Arda didn't hire me as med-officer so I would just sit here and look pretty."

She waved as she darted out the door, turning toward the docking bay. I walked to the hatch, intending on shutting it again, but at that moment a flash of gray bolted across my peripheral vision.

A smile spread across my lips. "Smudge. There you are, girl."

I detoured back into the med-bay and scooped up the green and white flowers I'd spent the morning researching. It had taken me hours to hunt down the code for the Pherian flower and add it to the food processor.

I lifted the pretty bloom triumphantly. "You better work." My research claimed the rare bloom worked like catnip for fucieras. We were about to find out.

"Here, Smudgie, Smudgie."

Maybe I ought to get low, where she can smell it.

I crouched on the ground and crawled down the corridor in the direction I'd spotted her racing. I held the flower out, waving it back and forth.

"Come out pretty," I cooed. "Please? I just want to stroke you. I promise I'll be gentle. You're gonna love it when I stroke you. I'm really, really good at stroking. I swear."

I was so busy swinging the flower and wiggling down the hall, I didn't notice I wasn't alone until it was too late. A door slammed behind me.

"Fuck," I squeaked. From my position on all fours, clearly the smartest thing to do was to lean my head upside down and peek between my spread legs.

My glasses clattered to the floor. *Idiot.* Heat bloomed on my cheeks. Luckily, the damn things were only for show these days, so I had a clear view of the shiny black boots standing behind me in the hall.

Who the hell was that? And how much of that had they heard? *Gods, I wasn't just begging to stroke my pretty, was I?*

"Double fuck," I whispered under my breath. Of course, it was too much to hope that the clang was Ren slamming the door to the docking bay.

I lifted my head and scrambled to put my glasses on before gaining the courage to turn.

4

What in the Universe

Nash

"This is it." Lux landed the hopper in the docking port of one of the ugliest ships I'd ever seen. "Welcome to your home for the next few weeks."

"The Verne." The mid-sized vessel might not be pretty, but the sight of it set my heart racing. It would be fun to explore the ship one of my best friends had lived in and worked on for the last year. I grinned as I followed Lux out of the hopper. "I can't wait to surprise Zenda."

Lux said his mate, Arda, told Zen I was coming, but we'd snagged an early clearance out of Subralia. We'd landed on the Verne a full hour ahead of schedule.

"You want to find her now?" Lux curved a hand through his shoulder-length golden hair. "I have some docking procedures to run through. You don't need to stick around for that. I'll load your luggage on a hovercart and bring it to your quarters once I'm done."

My palms sweated inside my gloves. "You sure?"

"Yeah. Go ahead." He pointed to a hatch on the far wall. "She's probably in the med-bay. Turn left and head down the hall. You can't miss it."

I strode across the docking bay, too wrapped up in thoughts of Zenda to take much notice of the neatly organized tools and equipment lining the walls.

Twenty years was a long time to go without seeing a friend face to face. Technically, it was more like eighteen or nineteen, but close enough.

Would she still wear that bright red hair of hers tied up in a tight bun? She used to be a skinny little thing. Always so prim and proper in her plaid skirts and cardigans with those ridiculous oversized glasses. My lips curved into a nostalgic smile. I'd always secretly wondered what she'd look like with her hair down and that good girl uniform swapped for something more *her*.

A lot can change in two decades. *Who knows, maybe today I'll get my wish?*

The hatch popped open before I could reach for the opening switch. A tall blonde wearing an oil-stained skinsuit darted in, apparently lost in thought. She turned immediately to close the hatch behind her without noticing me standing a few paces in front of her.

"Hold the door," I said, making her flinch. "I'm going out." I flashed my signature casual grin, hoping to set her at ease.

She blinked a few times, then cocked her head, likely noticing the hopper parked in the bay. "You must be Nash." She held the hatch open with one hand but didn't move to shake my hand with the other. "I'm Ren. Zenda's told us a lot about you."

"That's me. Nice to meet you, Ren." I settled for a nod instead of sticking out a hand. "I was just going to say hi to Zen. Have you seen her?"

Ren nodded. "Med-bay. Down the hall to the left." With that, she stalked off into the docking bay and I stepped into the hall.

"Come out pretty," a voice greeted me immediately. Zenda. I'd been looking left as I exited, but my head whipped to the right as I recognized the sultry voice I spoke to over voice-chat on the regular. Zenda really had the sexiest voice—

Hold on a sec...

"Please? I just want to stroke you. I promise I'll be gentle. You're gonna love it when I stroke you. I'm really, really good at stroking. I swear."

What in the universe is she talking about? I bit back a chuckle. And where was she?

My gaze flicked to the floor and my cock twitched. A woman crawled on her hands and knees, her cute little ass swaying as she waved some flowers wildly ahead of her. Was that...

The hatch slammed closed behind me.

"Fuck," the woman squeaked. No, not some woman—Zenda. That voice was unmistakable. And if I'd needed more confirmation, a pair of glasses clattered to the floor as she bent her head low.

Was she trying to look between her legs?

She whispered something I didn't catch and scooped up her glasses. She slid them back on and slowly turned.

My heart lurched at the same time a huge smile split my cheeks. "You know, I've been told I'm pretty once or twice, but the stroking is a new one."

"Nash!" Zenda jumped to her feet and raced down the hall. A heartbeat later, her cheek pressed to my chest and her arms wrapped around me tightly. I hugged her back, sighing at the feel of her in my arms.

How could I forget? She was always a hugger.

She pulled away before I was ready to let go and popped my shoulder with her tiny fist. "FYI, that speech was *not* for you." She backed up, pointing at the discarded flowers. "I've been trying to get Lux's pet to warm up to me."

Her explanation barely reached me. I was too busy staring. Zenda looked amazing. Her hair was still in a bun, making my fingers itch to tear out the meticulously placed pins. But that was where the similarities ended.

Instead of the preppy get-up I remembered, a pink skinsuit plastered to her limbs. The skinny teen was long gone, but damn, the womanly curves looked good on her. She'd even traded her oversized frames for a set of black cat-eye glasses. Her brown eyes sparkled behind the glasses, and they fit perfectly with her face, making the splash of freckles on her nose and cheeks stand out.

I gulped and shook off my reaction as Zenda's cheeks turned bright scarlet.

I must be weirding her out, with all the staring.

"No stroking?" I plastered on a frown. "Really? Not even a little? You know, since you're *so good* at it." I winked, not willing to let the chance to tease her pass me by.

"Gods, you're not gonna let that go, are you?"

I slung an arm around her shoulder. "Have you met me?"

She groaned, but an instant later a smile lit her face. "You're here early, aren't you?"

"Keeping tabs on me already?"

She rolled her eyes. "Please."

"We got an early clearance. Just landed a couple of minutes ago."

"Perfect timing," she grumbled, her gaze landing on the flowers again.

Her cute butt wiggling filled my mind. "Yeah, that was quite the welcome show."

Zenda blushed again, and I decided to change the subject. I scanned the empty corridor. White walls with metal and chrome accents spread down the ship, but no busy-bodies peeking their heads out to see what was going on in the hall. "It's pretty quiet. Where's all the crew?"

Zenda waved a hand. "They're around somewhere."

"And no other passengers?"

She shook her head and patted my arm. "It's shaping up to be a quiet journey. Sorry to say you'll have to cool it with your whorish ways."

"Excuse me." I scoffed. "I can't help it if I'm *pretty*."

Zenda chuckled. "I'm just saying there aren't many options. Lux will kill you if you look at Arda sideways, for one."

"What about the blonde I met in the docking bay?" I wasn't even slightly interested in Ren, but I was curious about Zenda's reaction to me mentioning her.

Zenda stiffened. "Ren? Nope. She's not into dating. Besides, she's far too young for you, old fart."

I choked down a chuckle. *Old fart. I'm thirty-six.*

"I'm the same age as you. What do I get to call you if I'm an old fart?"

Zenda shucked my arm off her shoulder and spun to face me. "No, I think your only options on this flight will be the twins."

"Twins, huh?" I pursed my lips. "Sounds promising."

"Yep. I think you'll have fun getting to know Palmela and Handrea."

I quirked a brow. First, she practically bit my head off when I mentioned Ren. Now she's shoving a set of twins in my face. What kind of mind games am I signing up for on this trip?

"When do I get to meet Pamela and Andrea?" I asked.

Zenda smirked, her eyes shining with mirth. "Oh, you've already met."

I frowned.

She leaned closer and stage whispered, "Make sure you get their names right. I hear they can get a little *slappy*." She grabbed one of my gloved hands. "Here's *Palm*ela" Giggling, she nudged my other hand with her fist. "And *Hand*rea."

Laughter roared out of me. This was why I never stopped calling her week after week, year after year. No matter what stress I was dealing with, Zenda always found a way to make me laugh.

I squeezed her hand tightly. "Have I told you lately how much I love you, Zen?"

She ducked her head, then patted my shoulder. "Love you too, buddy."

Zenda

I opened the hatch to Nash's quarters. "This is it."

He brushed past me as he entered, and my arm tingled from the contact. I followed him into the small room filled with brand new furnishings. The just painted smell still lingered after the renovations.

Gods. Did you have to make him grow up so hot?

The scrawny teen I remembered was long gone. Nash's blue-green skinsuit clung to his body, showcasing enough muscle to make a body builder jealous. He'd grown a few inches, too. The top of my head had fit perfectly under his chin when he'd hugged me in the hall.

He trailed around the room and I let my gaze wander over his muscular back. And even lower. Fuck. His ass was a thing of beauty—perfectly sculpted and enough to make my hands itchy.

I rubbed my jaw, suddenly worried I was drooling. My fingers encountered moisture and for a second, I panicked.

Seriously? I am not drooling over one of my best friends.

Nash lifted his hand and tugged off his slim fitting glove. "You got the temperature controls perfect."

The temperature controls, *right*. I chuckled nervously. "Good. I don't need you in the med-bay everyday complaining you're uncomfortable."

"Hm, too bad. I imagine all that dry skin would need lots of *stroking* with ointments and creams. Maybe a sponge bath or two." His eyes sparkled with mirth, and when he flashed that killer grin of his it nearly took my breath away.

The other glove came off, and Nash folded them together. I couldn't stop staring at his hands.

Vorill fingers were unique. Long and tapered close to their palms and big and bulbous at the tips. Thanks to the Outer Rim's brothels and their Voril model sex-bot, I had a very clear memory of what they felt like inside of me.

"You all right, Zen?" Nash's big black eyes narrowed with concern.

"Yep." I forced a smile and clenched my thighs together. "My mind was just wandering for a moment there. What do you think of the room?"

Nash set the gloves on a tiny desk and sank down on a wooden chair next to it. The mini workstation sat in one corner, with a large bed, fitted with crisp white sheets occupying the other. Except for a closet and an attached bathroom, there wasn't much else to see.

"I like it. It's... cozy." He flicked his long tongue out and licked his face.

My cheeks warmed. I turned aside, nearly ripping the closet door open in my haste to hide my reaction. "Plenty of room in here." Yeah. Plenty of room to hide out when you can't stop picturing that tongue licking something else.

"You're not upset I'm here, are you?" he asked quietly.

I whipped around and crossed my arms. "No. Of course not. Why would you say that?"

He waved a hand in my direction. "You're acting weird."

Ugh, why does he know me so well? I tamped down my raging hormones and rolled my eyes extra dramatically. "C'mon, have you met me? I'm always weird."

He chuckled. "If you say so."

A knock at the door saved me from making even more of an ass of myself. "I'll get it." I hurried to the hatch and threw it open. "Ren. What are you doing here?"

My heart sank. Nash said they already met. Had that single interaction led Ren—the girl who couldn't stand men—to his door?

But Ren jerked her head sideways, drawing my attention to the loaded hovercart sitting beside her. "Lux asked me to bring Nash's luggage."

Nash appeared at my elbow. "Thanks. You can come in."

Ren nodded and tugged the cart inside and set it beside the closet.

"Let me take these off and you can have the cart back." Nash bent to the task, his muscles rippling as he lifted each trunk and placed it on the floor.

Ren spotted me staring and nudged my side with her elbow. I side-eyed her as she waggled her brows.

"Here you go," Nash announced.

Ren grabbed the hovercart. "Thanks. I'll get out of your hair." Her gaze flitted to Nash's bald head. "Er, I mean—"

Nash cut her off. "I get it. After nearly twenty years living with humans, I've grown accustomed to your strange sayings."

Nash's lack of hair had never bothered me. With his chiseled bone structure, he could definitely pull it off.

Ugh, what am I thinking?

As Ren turned for the door, I saw my opportunity to flee. I had to get a handle on these embarrassing thoughts I should *not* be having about a friend.

"I'm gonna head out, too." I waved at his luggage. "Give you a chance to get settled."

"Oh," Nash said. "Here I thought you'd be dying to get a peek at my unmentionables. Maybe get a few strokes in."

I turned for the door so he wouldn't see my damn cheeks turning red—again. "Keep your dirty undies to yourself. I have work to do."

"See ya later, Zen," Nash called, laughter in his voice.

I threw out one last parting shot before the hatch slammed closed. "See ya later, Bobbles."

My face split with a cheeky grin. If Nash wouldn't let the whole stroking thing slide, then it was time to break out his embarrassing old nickname.

"Bobbles? What's that all about?" Ren asked as the hatch to Nash's room closed.

"Oh, just a little nickname I gave Nash when we first met." I leaned closer with a smirk. "He always hated it."

Ren tugged the hovercart behind her. I kept pace with her, wishing I could see the expression on Nash's face when I dredged up that blast from the past. Probably shock mixed with a healthy dose of pissed the fuck off. He deserved it after all those stroking comments.

Ren chuckled loudly, interrupting my musing. "You guys are cute with all your inside jokes. I bet you're rethinking the whole 'we're not gonna fuck' thing now, huh?"

Godsdamn it. My cheeks were just starting to cool down. "Nope. I don't think so."

"Well, I can guarantee he's thinking about it."

I frowned, unable to keep a heavy measure of skepticism out of my tone. "Why do you say that?"

"You didn't see where he was looking when you turned to leave." She added an exaggerated wiggle to her steps. "Friends don't stare at each other's asses like they want to bite them."

My heart fluttered at her words until I remembered an important truth. "That's just Nash showing his normal horn dog nature. If he hadn't looked, then I'd be worried he was sick. It's got absolutely nothing to do with me."

Ren arched a brow. "If you say so."

Arda appeared at the end of the hall, a tablet in her hands. "Hey, how's our passenger? Do you need any help getting him settled?"

"No, he's all set, Capt." I stopped at her side, and Ren passed us both with a nod and a wave, dragging the hovercart toward the shuttlebay. "He's unpacking as we speak. Said the environmental controls were perfect."

"That's good to hear. I'll get the Verne underway, then." She placed a gentle hand on my arm. "Thanks for taking such good care of him,

Zen. I really appreciate it. You know, if we didn't have him with us, we'd still be waiting on that landing clearance."

I rocked back on my heels and stuffed my hands in my skinsuit pockets. "Yep. No worries." Not like I did much more than joke around with him. Unless embarrassing myself counted as helping.

"Can I ask you a favor?" Arda cleared her throat. "I know you usually spend a lot of time on these long-distance trips holed up with your research in the med-bay. Do you think you could spare some time to keep your buddy company instead?"

"Sure." I mean, it's not like it would be a hardship. Nash might be a bit of a slut, but he was always fun to be around.

"It's just... Lux said the mayor tried everything to convince Nash to leave Subralia. But it wasn't until he found out you would be making the trip that he finally agreed."

"Oh." Something warm and fuzzy expanded in my chest.

"I would hate for him to come up with a reason to turn around before we arrive." Arda shrugged.

"Say no more, Capt. I'll keep him so busy catching up on old times, he won't even realize the lightyears are flying by."

Arda's face lit up. "Thanks, Zen. I knew I could count on you." Her eyes narrowed, and she turned with a determined stride for the bridge. "Once we make it to Vorillion, I'll be one step closer to answers."

I shook my head as she wandered off. Maybe I ought to be offended that she was basically sticking me with babysitting duty, when I should be free to pursue my personal interests. After all, that's what attracted me to this gig in the first place. Arda promised me plenty of time to myself when I signed on. Plus, all the medical equipment I needed to pursue my passion—animal science.

But I guess I could let it slide this once. And hey, I would be spending quite a bit of time with an alien species. Nash was no Smudge, but who knows, maybe he'd let me play doctor if I asked nicely.

I chuckled to myself as I ducked into the med-bay. *Wonder what his face would look like after that question?*

5

In The Dark

Nash

I knocked on the bridge hatch. The rumble of voices within halted, then the hatch swung open. Lux peeked out of the doorway. "Thought it was you. No one else would bother knocking."

I grinned. "I'm looking for your mate."

Lux's voice dropped an octave. "Why?" He crossed his arms and glared at me.

Okay... guess Zen wasn't kidding about him being possessive.

The woman in question appeared at Lux's elbow. "Cool it with that crap, big guy." She thrust out a hand, and I shook it. "It's nice to meet you, Nash. Come in and chat for a while."

I aimed a lopsided smile at Lux as I inched past him onto the bridge. Two big black chairs sat amidst a sea of blinking lights, digital readouts, and electronic panels. The viewport was uncovered, showcasing a black starlit expanse with a red planet in the far distance.

I squinted. Was that Mars? "It's a pleasure to meet you as well, Captain. I wanted to introduce myself. I met everyone else already."

"Call me Arda." She sank into one chair and nodded for me to take the other. "We don't give a shit about formalities on the Verne."

"Sure, Arda." I sat, sparing a glance for Lux, who leaned against the open hatch, still glowering. Then I turned my attention to the curvy brunette in the pilot's chair. Despite her penchant for cursing, she was certainly attractive. I could see why Lux was so obsessed, even though her heart-shaped face and blue eyes weren't quite doing it for me. "Looks like we're well underway."

"Yep." Arda leaned forward and keyed up a display. "Here's the flight plan. We're running the sub-light engines until we clear the system, then we'll execute a series of FTL jumps. Of course, we'll need to slow to sub-light again before we arrive, but we should have you back home with plenty of time to spare."

Ugh. The mention of faster than light jumps made my stomach churn. Unfortunately, it was a necessary evil that came with traveling the stars.

Doesn't mean I have to like it.

"Lux says you have a business contract waiting for you on Voril-lion."

"Hm?" I shoved my anxiety aside and concentrated on the conversation again. "Yes. A trivial formality, I'm afraid. I honestly don't understand why I have to return at all, but it appears I've been summoned..."

I trailed off, pursing my lips as my parent's faces flashed in my mind. For nearly twenty years they were perfectly content only communicating through prerecorded messages and the occasional extravagant gift on my name day. Now they expected me to drop everything and come running—like I should be grateful for their scraps of attention. It was just like them to be inconsiderate and completely self-absorbed.

"You okay?" Arda squeezed my gloved hand, her brows furrowed and her eyes swimming with concern. "You want to talk about it?"

I squeezed back and stood, shaking my head. "Don't worry about me, I'll be—what the hell is *that*?" I stiffened, staring at one of the ugliest critters I'd ever seen. The gray-skinned animal strolled through the bridge hatch, coiled around Lux's boots, and started... purring?

"This is Smudge. She's my pet." Lux scooped her into his arms, shaking his head. "Don't listen to him," Lux cooed at her, rubbing her floppy ears. "I've seen how he decorates his quarters in Subralia. No taste at all with those silly figurines. He wouldn't know a proper pet if it pissed in his boots."

I chuckled, ignoring the urge to defend my collection. But then a snatch of conversation replayed in my ears. Was Zenda really crawling around trying to make friends with this ugly little thing? She had always loved animals. Maybe I could give her a hand.

I softened my voice even more than Lux's, talking to the critter like she was a baby. "Sorry, Smudge. I just wasn't expecting you there. Want some belly scratches?"

Lux narrowed his gaze at my outstretched arms. "You want to hold her?"

I swallowed the urge to cringe and nodded. "Of course I do." More baby talk spilled out of my lips. "We're gonna be best buddies, aren't we?"

Arda's head jerked between us. Then she burst into a fit of giggles and waved at the door. "Can you two play pass the pussy somewhere else? I have a ship to fly."

Nash

I strolled down the hall, the purring critter cradled in my arms.

Knock, knock. "Hey, Zen. You in there?"

"Yep. Just a sec." A few bangs sounded beyond the med-bay hatch, piquing my curiosity before she called, "Come in."

I opened the hatch and found the room awash with darkness. *What is she doing in the dark?* My mind swam, bombarded with naughty imagery. Like Zen with her delicate little fingers between her thighs. But the vision only made my balls ache before I shoved it aside.

The light blinked on, and I spotted Zenda. Her hands were nowhere near where my dirty mind had expected. She had one planted on the light switch and the other busy removing the most ridiculous looking goggles.

I chuckled, flashing back to the oversized glasses she used to wear when I first met her. "What's with the eyewear?"

Zenda blinked at me as she pulled them off. "They're night vision lenses. I need them to observe my test subjects."

I scanned the room, quirking a brow. The med-bay was clean and neat, with white walls and all the typical medical gear one would expect. But I didn't see anything living except for her.

"What test subjects?" Zen mentioned her research from time to time when we chatted, but she never got into the details, since she knew science wasn't exactly my thing.

She set the goggles on an examination table and pulled her cat-eye frames off the top of her head. "Earth fish from the deep ocean.

They're hidden behind the cabinets." She slid her glasses on. "I have to keep them in the darkness—" her explanation cut off as her gaze flicked to my arms. "Hey, what are you doing with Smudge?"

I grinned mischievously. "I brought her for a stroking. Someone ought to benefit from your skills."

Zenda rolled her eyes. "Mm-hm. Why am I not surprised you charmed her so quickly?"

I shrugged. "Because you know I have a way with the ladies?"

"Sure. That must be it." She reached for Smudge and frowned when the ugly thing hissed at her.

"Hey," I said to the frightened critter. "Relax. Zen won't hurt you."

Zenda sighed and backed away. "It's fine. You can let her go."

"You sure?" My heart squeezed at the defeat in her tone.

"Yeah." She picked up her goggles and began wiping them carefully with a small cloth.

I set Smudge down, and she wasted no time hightailing through the open hatch into the hall. *Good riddance.* "What did you want that ugly thing for, anyway?"

Zenda sighed again. "It's not every day I get to study creatures from another planet. I thought..." She crossed the room, opened a drawer, and set the goggles inside. "It doesn't matter. I still have my fish."

"So, the fish are from Earth?" My stomach churned.

She nodded, her face brightening. "Yeah. Arda helped me get them when I signed onto her crew." Her expression turned wistful. "I'd almost forgotten how much I loved watching them."

"Oh. You'd be sick of them by now if you were still stuck in Subralia." The churning increased, spinning through my gut like a whirlpool.

"Funny, I didn't feel stuck there." Zenda shook her head. "Too bad I'll never get the chance to return." She chuckled dryly, her brown eyes downcast and a tiny frown on her lips at odds with her laughter. "I thought I'd be running the research facility by now. I always thought working with ocean creatures would be my calling. Not much of a need for it on Mars."

"Yeah." My gaze flicked to the door, and I fought the urge to heave. "I didn't realize you still wanted to go back."

"I never wanted to leave in the first place." She waved a hand. "But you can't always get what you want."

I gulped down the bile in my throat. "Um, I forgot. I promised my uncle I'd call him once I settled in. I better go..."

Zenda smiled benignly. "Oh. Okay. Talk to ya later."

I hurried out of the med-bay like my ass was on fire, but it was better than standing there listening to Zenda go on about her family's banishment.

All the years we'd spent chatting over the phone, she'd never let on how much she missed living under the sea. Sure, she'd made a comment here or there, but seeing the depth of sorrow and longing in her eyes when she talked about Subralia... it nearly killed me.

I sucked in a shaky breath. It would be all right. I just had to keep her mind on other things until we reached Vorillion. And no matter what, I had to keep my mouth shut about what *really* happened back then.

If Zen ever finds out that I was the one who got her kicked out of Subralia, she'll never forgive me.

6

Giggling Like an Idiot

Nash

19 years earlier

The captain threw an arm around my shoulders, helping tug me to my feet. My eyes fluttered, and a giggle spilled out of my lips. "Really now, I don't need help. I'll be just fin—" the word cut off as I tilted sideways, nearly slamming into the hatch.

"Nash?" A booming voice bounced around my skull. "What in Jiklion's moons?" My uncle rounded on the poor fellow struggling to keep my gangly limbs from spilling all over the hard concrete in the landing bay. "How did my nephew end up in this state?"

The gruff voiced captain shrugged and dumped me into my uncle's arms. "Environmental controls gave out after our last jump. He insisted he'd be fine."

"And you just took the word of a teenager? Can't you see he's clearly not fine? He's giggling like an idiot."

"Hey!" I bit out around a round of chuckles. Could I help it if this whole situation was hilarious?

"How am I supposed to know what passes for *fine* in your species?" The captain crossed his arms. "I look like a doctor to you?"

"Your parent company will be receiving a complaint." My uncle threw up a hand, nearly sending me tumbling again. Then he twisted me sideways and shoved me down a hall, grumbling all the while. "Some humans. I swear they drive me crazy."

"Funny you'd come to a planet full of them." My laughter increased, rumbling through my chest and making Uncle Prim's shoulders stiffen.

"Come on, my boy. We need to get you in some water, fast."

"Oh. That would be lovely." My eyes refused to land anywhere but on my feet. I shuffled along at Prim's urging, unable to cut off the laughter even as my stomach rolled. "I don't feel so good."

"No kidding," Uncle replied dryly. He halted beside a hatch with Lab E stenciled on the door. "Come on." After he punched a code into the keypad, the hatch slid open and I sighed. The cool chill of moisture hit my skin like a balm and the trickle of water soothed my ears like the sweetest serenade, finally calming my manic laughter.

Uncle Prim held me steady and helped me shuck off my blue skinsuit. He shook his head as he took in the sickly yellow pallor of my skin. "You idiot. Why didn't you tell them you needed more water?"

"I didn't want to cause a fuss," I mumbled. After all, look where speaking up had gotten me. The last time I spoke my mind—regardless of the drama that might arise—I'd ended up on the first ship off of Vorillion.

Uncle Prim loosed a weary sigh. "It's fine. Come on. You'll be back to normal after a few good soaks." He grinned at me. "The water here is quite refreshing. I dare say it's even better than back home."

"Really?" I clambered over to a low pool set into the floor.

"Wait, not that one." Prim stopped me before I hopped into some of the bluest water I'd ever seen. He grabbed my elbow and spun me toward a pool in the back of the echoey chamber. "This one is empty. Go on."

He didn't have to tell me twice. I dove into the cold, salty pool. The second I was completely submerged, the haziness in my mind lifted. I let the water flow around me and wash away the stench of that awful spaceflight.

Though I wanted to linger underwater for much longer, I popped up after only a minute. "Thanks, Uncle Prim. I needed this." I swam to the edge, finally clear minded enough to take more than a cursory look at my surroundings. "Where am I, exactly?"

I treaded water as I scanned the vast room. Wetsuits and breathing masks lined the walls behind my uncle. Buckets full of odds and ends hung below it. And beyond that, a massive desk stood behind a glass wall. A corner office perched there, looking out over the enormous pools.

Curiosity burned inside me. What was in the other pools? Whose office was that, and what was the purpose of this place?

Uncle Prim rocked on his heels. "This is the research lab of one of our most promising professors. He lets me use that pool when I need a soak—while it's empty, of course."

I cringed, peeking down at my naked body beneath the water. "Oh. Where is he?"

Prim glanced at his watch. "Teaching class. Don't worry, no one will disturb you." He turned for the door, but seemed to think better of it, and changed course for the office instead. He walked inside and scrawled something on the desk before returning to show me.

I squinted, not understanding the strange handwritten letters. "What does that say?"

Prim frowned. "I thought you were studying English while you were en route?"

"Didn't seem necessary." I shrugged. "I already had my translator upgraded for spoken language."

"Not necessary?" Prim pinched the bridge of his nose. "You do recall you'll be finishing your schooling here, right?"

This again? I frowned. "I thought since I'm only a few months away from graduating, we could call it done and good enough."

My uncle glanced at his watch again. "Look, Nash. We'll discuss this later. I have a meeting I'm running late for." He shook the paper. "If you could read this, you'd see it said 'No entry. Do not disturb.' I'll tack it to the hatch and leave you to it. By the time my meeting is over, you should feel much better."

I waved lazily and forced a smile. "Sure, Uncle. See you later." My heart twinged as he opened the hatch and left me alone. I shouldn't be surprised to be abandoned to my own devices. As Mayor, Uncle Prim was a busy man. Even so, his easy dismissal stung.

He couldn't even be bothered to take a full afternoon off to ensure my arrival went smoothly. Guess I was trading in one set of absent guardians for another. *Lucky me.*

Then again, it's not like I wasn't weeks away from turning eighteen. Children generally stayed with their parents well into their twenties on Vorillion, but here on Earth it was the age of majority.

Still, I wasn't completely alone. And for now, at least, I had this strange indoor pool all to myself. I smiled and sank below the surface again. With the cold water buoying me, I could almost fall asleep.

Vorill were made for the water. Our species couldn't breathe underwater, but we could hold our breath much longer than the Terrans. My lungs wouldn't start screaming for nearly an hour. One benefit of our unique skin was that we could absorb small amounts of oxygen through it. It also meant we were reliant on water to keep us healthy, far more than most creatures in the galaxy.

I was actually lucky Uncle Prim was here, and so quick to spot the signs of my dehydration. If he'd sent an underling to collect me from the landing bay instead, I might've collapsed and ended up on a gurney in the med-bay.

I guess I should give him points for that. There's no way Mom and Dad would ever deign to dirty their hands by collecting me off a shuttle. The ghostly echo of my mother's voice reverberated in my mind, 'That's what drivers are for.'

I shook my head below the water and pushed off the pool wall. Now that I was feeling a bit better, it was good to work off some of this nervous energy. There'd been little chance for exercise in the spaceship. And who knew what it would be like here? I'd barely glimpsed anything of my new home, with my brain so foggy.

Perhaps I should climb out of this pool and go for a quick tour? The idea had barely formed in my mind when a loud bang gave me pause. Was that Uncle Prim, back from his meeting already?

I rose to the surface and craned my neck, searching for whatever made that sound. And when I spotted a feminine profile hunched over the desk in the office, a smile slowly spread across my lips. That definitely wasn't my uncle.

Things are about to get interesting.

7

Bobbles

Zenda

19 years earlier

"Thanks a million, Zen." Stasia dumped a stack of workbooks in my outstretched arms. "You know we all appreciate it."

I buried the urge to scowl at the tall redhead, and the circle of classmates ringed behind her. "Well... I am headed there, anyway."

I shuffled out of the classroom, doing my best to balance the wobbly pile of paper. Professor Mueller asked us to drop our completed assignments on his desk in the lab, but somehow, I ended up elected to take them all.

Damn Stasia. She might hide it behind a too bright smile and a layer of pleasantness, but I *knew* she hated me. She never missed a chance to heap extra work on my shoulders and the other girls were happy to allow it, if it made their days easier.

My stomach boiled as I hurried down the glass halls of Subralia. A school of yellow fish hovered outside, doing nothing to lighten my mood. Just because my mom worked in the kitchen and not as a researcher, didn't mean they should force me to play maid.

It's not my fault I'm doing better than most of them in our classes. Maybe if they actually studied, instead of drooling over our biology professor, then they'd be doing well too.

I sighed as I approached the hatch to Professor Mueller's research lab. I get that the man was hot—and yeah, I was the only one he'd invited to have extra lab hours—but did that really have to make me the subject of their jealousy? Stasia liked to act like I was *so* lucky, when the truth was, I'd worked my ass off for those extra hours. And *not* because I wanted to ogle Professor Mueller.

It was all about the animals for me. A smile crossed my face even as I struggled to hold the papers while inputting the hatch code. Professor Mueller researched all kinds of sea life. Sharks, fish, and turtles. But more than anything, I loved the dolphins. That's why I was headed to the lab. I'd taken over afternoon feeding duty, even though it cut into my lunch break.

Paper crinkled as I pushed the hatch open with my shoulder and nearly dropped the stack in my arms. I hurried to the corner office and kicked the door open. The bang of my Maryjane's colliding with the door echoed in the lab while I shuffled to Mueller's desk and dumped the stack on top of it.

"Whew." I straightened the stack and turned, looking out of the glass at the lab. Water sparkled in the pools. My chest swelled with lightness as I left the office and strolled to the wall where my wetsuit hung.

I whistled like Professor Mueller taught me, doing my best to approximate dolphins' calls. We'd been working with this pod for months. I ran my fingers along the wetsuit, considering my options as a splash sounded behind me.

I could grab some fish and get the feeding done quickly. Or I could suit up and go for a swim. The latter meant I'd miss my lunch entirely.

Hm. I tapped my chin. *Swim with dolphins, or eat overcooked fish in the mess? Duh.*

I grabbed my wetsuit and set it on a bench. Then I shucked off my sweater. I'd just tugged the bottom hem of my button-up blouse out of my skirt when a throat cleared loudly behind me.

"Hello?" I whipped around, a hand on my chest and my cheeks flaring with heat.

"Sorry to interrupt, but it didn't feel right letting you strip in front of me."

My gaze flashed to the pool in the back. The one that was supposed to be empty—but currently had a bald, lanky Vorill swimming in it.

"T-thanks." I wandered closer, dropping my hands to my sides. "I didn't realize anyone else was here." I don't know what it was. Maybe the fact that he'd stopped me from stripping when he could have been a creeper and watched. Or maybe it was the easy grin he sent me as he floated there. Something about the guy had me liking him instantly, despite my embarrassment.

"Yeah. I figured. I'm Nash. Nice to meet you."

"Zenda." I crossed my arms. "What are you doing bobbling out there, Nash?"

"Bobbling?" His brow crinkled adorably. "That what they call swimming on Earth?"

I giggled. "No. You just remind me of a bobblehead, the way you're floating out there."

Nash shook his head, making him look even more bobblehead-like. I couldn't still the laughter that erupted from my chest.

"Can't say I know what that even is, but okay." He swam to the pool's edge and folded his bare arms over the lip.

I gulped as the action brought more of his green-hued skin into view. Enough for me to realize he wasn't wearing a wetsuit. My gaze flicked to the floor, and I spotted a discarded blue skinsuit laying in a heap.

Is he naked in there? The thought made tingles spread through my stomach.

"So, it's kind of a crazy story. I just got here, and I was so dehydrated, my uncle forced me to go for a swim." He shrugged. "He told me he'd put a 'do not disturb' note on the door. I'm guessing you missed that."

I toed the floor with my shiny black shoe. "My hands were kind of full when I got here."

"No harm done." Nash grinned and pushed off the wall. "Don't let me stop you from whatever you're here for. Did you want me to turn around so you can get changed?"

"Gods no." I grabbed my wetsuit and rehung it on the wall. "I think I'll skip the swim today."

"I am in your way, aren't I?" Nash darted to the lip of the pool and hoisted himself halfway out. "I'll go."

"No!" My cheeks burned as I stared at his naked chest. He'd lifted himself enough I could see the sexy divots in his stomach on either side of his belly button. *Gods.* I tore my eyes off him and turned aside. "You're not in my way at all. I just have to feed the animals in the other pools."

"If you say so." Water splashed as he sank further into the water. "I'll be over here floating, then."

"Okay, Bobbles." I opened the mini-refrigerator set into the wall and pulled out a bucket of fish just in time to hear Nash groan.

"Oh, please tell me that's not going to stick. I finally escaped one terrible name. I don't need another one haunting me."

"Terrible name?" I sent him a mischievous smile as I lugged the heavy bucket slowly across the room. "Do tell."

"Nope. That monstrosity will never leave my lips." He met my smile with one of his own, and I nearly swooned. Wow. That smile... it was stunning.

"Well, I guess you better get used to being Bobbles then." I set the bucket down and dug my fingers into my lower back. *Did the stupid thing have to be so damn heavy?*

"You're killing me, Zenda." Nash swam to the edge closest to where I rested, and lifted a brow, his large black eyes narrowing. "What do I need to do to get you to keep that little nickname between us?"

I sighed. *I should really let the guy off easy and tell him I won't call him that.*

"How about I come help you lug that bucket tomorrow?" He flexed his skinny arms, showing off some mildly impressive muscles. "Looks like you could use a hand, huh?"

"While I would love some help with the manual labor, you'd need clearance from Professor Mueller, not me."

"I don't think that will be a problem."

I rolled my eyes at his cocky grin. "Uh-huh. We'll see, Bobbles."

"Shh." He flicked a glance nervously at the walls, and I bit back a giggle. "What do you say, Zen? If I get the clearance, will you drop the Bobbles?"

"Sure." I lifted the bucket again and shuffled closer to the dolphin pool. "Though I don't see why you care so much. It's just a silly name."

He shrugged. "Haven't you ever wanted a fresh start?"

I frowned. The other girls could be a pain sometimes, but I loved being part of the research team. Honestly, I'd be happy to stay here forever. "Nope. I like it here."

Nash sighed and pushed off the edge, treading water easily. "Well, I do want one. And this is it. I don't want everyone here thinking I'm some joke on day one."

That made sense, I suppose. I'd had fun joking around with Nash, but I wasn't planning to tease him in public when he seemed so uncomfortable about it. I made up my mind not to call him Bobbles, except for when we were alone—clearance or not.

My heart raced at the possibility of being alone with him again. If he pulled off the clearance, then we'd be together again tomorrow. He'd be out of the water then—close enough to touch. Stomach fluttering, I settled down to feed the dolphins and tried to concentrate on the task and forget about the cute alien watching my every move.

Nash

I emerged from a long dive underwater. My party crasher was still perched on the edge of another pool, humming and whistling to the creatures she fed. Her voice was incredibly sexy—smooth and husky all at once. She'd be more at home recording audio than spending her days feeding fish in a lab.

I treaded water, watching Zenda work out of the corner of my eye. She went about the task with methodical precision. That and a quirky grin interrupted with the occasional giggle.

I couldn't help feeling like I wanted to be in on the joke. But that would have to wait—until I wasn't naked.

My new friend wasn't classically beautiful by human standards. She was too skinny for one, with half her face hidden by an oversized set of thick-framed glasses. All the same, there was something about her that made me want to learn more.

Once she'd tossed all the fish out of the huge bucket, I swam to the pool's edge. "So, tell me about yourself, Zenda."

She startled slightly, like she'd forgotten I was there, then lifted a shoulder in a lopsided shrug. "There's not much to tell."

I couldn't resist teasing her a little. "Let me guess. You're Subralia's resident bad girl."

She snorted and her cheeks pinked adorably. "Right. Where'd you get that idea?"

"Well, you blatantly ignored the 'do not disturb' sign on the door."

She dumped the bucket next to a floor drain and started rinsing it with a hose. "I didn't ignore it. I *missed* it."

"Hm. Sure, but then you blackmailed me into hard labor within minutes of meeting me."

"Blackmail?" She dumped the water out and stacked her hands on her hips. "You offered."

"Only to stop you from destroying my reputation." I grinned.

"Puh-lease." She glared at me. "You're one to talk. Skinny dipping in the research pool." She shook her head slowly and pursed her lips.

"Is that not allowed?" I gasped dramatically. "And you can't peel your eyes off me, you naughty girl."

I thought she'd avert her gaze for sure, but Zenda surprised me. She strode closer, keeping her big brown eyes glued to me the entire time. "Why should I? You climbed into the research pool. I wouldn't be a good student if I didn't take the opportunity to study a new species."

She was a student? *Uncle Prim's insistence that I continue my schooling might need a little more consideration.*

I backed away, giving her a clearer view of me hovering at the water's surface. "So what's the verdict?"

Her gaze popped up from my chest and zeroed in on my face. A chill ran down my spine as she examined me like a lab specimen.

"Your stamina for swimming is impressive. And the length of time you can hold your breath as well." She tilted her head and adjusted her glasses. "It's quite—fascinating."

Guess she hadn't forgotten I was there. Sounded more like she'd been keeping tabs on me all along. A tingle replaced the chill, thrumming through my veins and making my nerve endings crackle. "Yep. I knew it."

She cocked a hip. "What?"

"You *are* a bad girl. Hitting on someone you just met." I flashed a playful smirk.

Zenda rolled her eyes and stepped away. "You caught me. I'm *so naughty* skipping my lunch break to work." She paced toward the door. "Don't get it twisted. That wasn't a come on. I find eels and sea slugs fascinating, too."

"You leaving already?"

Zenda spun around before she hit the hatch. "Yep. Not all of us can lounge in the pool all day. I have a class I need to get to if I want to graduate. See you around... Bobbles." She waved once and disappeared into the hall.

I chuckled to myself as the door slammed behind her. The whole Bobbles thing was kind of cute. I wasn't planning to tell her that, though. It was more fun acting offended.

Normally, I couldn't stand conflict. I went out of my way to avoid drama of any kind. Yet for some reason, sparring with Zenda didn't make my skin crawl like an argument with anyone else would. Maybe it was the little teasing smiles curving her lips when she lobbed a comeback at me. Or the fact that she gave as good as she got. Hell, for the short time we'd spent together, I'd forgotten about my family issues.

I climbed out of the pool and pulled on my skinsuit, feeling reinvigorated. I'd just finished lacing my boots when the hatch swung open again.

"Nash, my boy." Uncle Prim sauntered in, a stack of pamphlets in his hands. "Good to see you looking more like yourself. I brought you these." He thrust the papers at my chest. I shuffled through them, quickly noting a pattern. Each one featured a class offered in Subralia.

"I don't need these." I tried to hand them back, but he crossed his arms and words spilled out of mouth, one right on top of the next.

"No. Look through them. There has to be something of interest to—"

"Uncle Prim, you're not listening. I've already decided to finish my schooling."

"You have?" Prim smiled widely. "Wonderful. What changed your mind?"

A glimpse of red hair and too big glasses flashed through my mind. I shrugged. "I don't know. Seems like it might be fun."

8

Deliciousness

Present day

"Hold still," I demanded, tilting the portable med-bot to the correct angle to fix Arda's knee—again. She was stretched out on the examining table in the med-bay with a banged-up leg. "If you keep wiggling around, we'll be here all day."

"Sorry. It's not my fault Lux is determined to make sure I never sit right again," Arda grumbled.

I wiped invisible tears off my face. "Woe is me. My hunky alien lord's enormous peen is just *too big*." Crossing my arms, I glared at her. "You realize that's what you sound like, right?"

Arda had the audacity to giggle. "What? It *is* big." She shrugged unapologetically.

"Please tell me you don't need me to fix your bruised vagina." I shuddered. "I know it's my job and all, but—"

"No, my pussy will be fine in a few hours." She started pulling up the fabric of her skinsuit on the leg I wasn't working on. "You might want to take a look at this knee too, though."

She finished rucking the gray cloth up, and I scanned the mark. It was oddly similar to the one on her other knee. I hadn't questioned her yet about where the first scraped knee originated. We were on a working spaceship, after all; small cuts and bruises were practically an everyday occurrence. But seeing two nearly identical marks on her knees... I had a sudden intuition that I knew exactly what had caused them.

"Where was it this time?" The med-bot beeped, and I moved it to the new scrape.

Arda's eyes glazed, and a tiny smile curved her lips. "The engine room." She blinked, then leaned closer. "I don't recommend it. Those floor grates are murder on the knees."

"I can see that. Maybe you should stick to your quarters? That giant bed you put in looks pretty comfy."

They'd had to knock down a wall to fit Lux's bed into Arda's quarters during the remodel—*my* wall. But I wasn't too mad about having to relocate to the new traveler's addition. Those two were so loud I still kept my noise canceling headphones on my nightstand.

Arda sighed. "I know we should. But Lux is very... spontaneous." Her grin shifted to a coy smile, and I knew she was likely recalling something sexy the big guy had done when her eyes lifted to the ceiling dreamily.

My stomach twisted—that twinge of jealousy returning to plague me. I did my best to shake it off as a knock echoed behind me.

"Sorry, am I interrupting?" Nash asked from the doorway.

The med-bot chimed again, and I sent him a grin before turning back to Arda. "We're just finishing up." I cocked a brow at her. "Unless there's any other injuries I haven't looked at yet?"

"Nah." Arda waved a hand and hopped off the examination table. "I'm all good. Thanks." Shaking her pants legs down, she turned to Nash with a wide smile and nodded back at me. "Zen's the best, isn't she?"

Nash smiled at her. "I can't argue with that."

Arda whipped around as she breezed through the hatch and winked at me.

I rolled my eyes at Arda's blatant attempt at matchmaking. "See ya later, Capt." I turned to the exam table and fiddled with the med-bot. "Hey, Nash. I didn't think I would see you for a while. How'd your call go?"

Back for another embarrassing edition of Zenda's host of regrets? He'd run off so fast earlier, I'd barely had a chance to catch up. Not that I was planning to spill more details about my failed first choice of career after how uncomfortable it clearly made him.

Not that I was surprised. Nash was great fun, but try talking to him about anything heavy, and he always changed the subject. Or just bolted. I was more than halfway convinced that call he needed to make was invented on the spot.

What made him so skittish about his emotions? It wasn't the first time the thought had crossed my mind, and it likely wouldn't be the last. But I buried it away with all the other unanswered questions I had about Nash's past. I'd learned pretty quickly to avoid asking him about his parents, and any of his family besides his uncle.

"It was fine." Nash cleared his throat. "I thought maybe you'd want to grab something to eat in the mess? It's about time for dinner."

My stomach fluttered. If any other man as gorgeous as Nash asked me to dinner, I'd be dancing a happy jig. I sighed internally. But Nash didn't want to date me. Never had and never would. I had to stop thinking of him as anything more than a friend.

Maybe it's hunger making my belly rumble. "Sure. Dinner sounds great."

It didn't take long to walk from the med-bay to the mess. Stopping at the food processor, I plugged in one of the meals I ate on the regular, collected it once the machine spat it out, and sat at the table to eat.

Lifting my fork, I pushed the chicken and veggie stir-fry around on my plate, biting back the sigh that fought to spill out of my lips. The overhead lights in the mess hall shone down on my plate mockingly.

"That all you're eating?" Nash wrinkled his nose as he sank into the hard plastic chair across from me. "Doesn't look very filling... or appetizing."

"I'll have you know this is an optimal meal for a Terran. Nutrition-ally balanced and delicious." I stabbed a piece of broccoli with my fork and crunched into it loudly. I mean—delicious was a bit of a stretch, but it's not like I could get away with eating chocolate cake for every meal.

"Okay, doc. I believe you." Nash held up his gloved hands in sur-render, then bent over his plate. He scooped up a bite of fish, popped it into his mouth, and grimaced. "I forgot how bland food processor meals taste."

I shrugged. "You get used to it."

Of course, Nash was right. I'd stopped grabbing planet-grown food when we docked to avoid overeating all the deliciousness.

Nash watched me pick at my plate. He lifted another forkful of fish to eye level, but set it back down. With a grin, he hopped out of his chair and stalked back to the processor.

I swallowed a mouthful of bland chicken. "Forget something?"

"Yep. Flavor."

I tried not to stare at his broad shoulders and round ass as he punched in another order. Luckily, I tore my gaze away before he spun around and caught me. Lifting my eyes from my stir-fry, I cocked a brow as he settled back down with a fragrant cup of yellow liquid clutched in his hands. My mouth watered at the unmistakable scent.

"Is that garlic butter?" I asked, though I already knew the answer before he started nodding.

"Yep." Nash dumped the steaming butter all over his plate. He picked up the fork again. This time, when the morsel hit his tongue, he let out a husky moan that made my stomach clench.

Gods! Does he have to make that sound so orgasmic?

"Oh yeah. That's much better." He speared another bite on his fork, then thrust it toward me. "Here, you have to taste this."

I couldn't stop myself from instinctively licking my lips as the scent of garlicky heaven wafted around me. "No thanks. That butter will go straight to my thighs."

Nash held the fork stable but ducked his head so he could slide his gaze down my crossed legs. My skin tingled like he'd traced his fingers over them instead. His eyes flicked to mine, full of heat. "Not a problem from where I'm sitting."

My cheeks warmed, and I scoffed. "Okay. All the same," I nodded to the fish, "I still don't want it." I stabbed a hunk of carrot on my plate.

Nash shrugged and popped the delectable bite in his mouth. He groaned dramatically. "Mm. You don't know what you're missing." He scooped up another piece and held it out. "Come on, Zen. Screw your diet. Be bad with me. You know you want to."

His taunting words skittered across my skin and ignited a fire in my belly. When we first met, I had always been a good girl. But with Nash staring at me with that teasing grin, I wanted to be bad just to prove him wrong.

Because I wasn't a good girl anymore. Nash just didn't know it yet. *Maybe it's time to show him.*

9

Classy

Nash

Zenda glared at me, and for a second I almost regretted taunting her. It was clear she had some hangups about her weight—not that she had any reason to. I'd barely stopped myself from panting when I'd checked out her curvy thighs a minute ago.

Zenda uncrossed her legs and lifted out of her seat. Her gaze shifted from my face to the bite of fish hovering on my fork between us. Garlic butter glistened, threatening to drip onto the table. She leaned forward and opened her mouth, locking eyes with me as her tongue darted out. Then her lips closed over the morsel and her pupils dilated.

Fuck. My cock twitched as her seductive mouth claimed the bite. I couldn't stop images from flooding my mind. Of her on her knees, with those sexy lips wrapped around my dick. Her big brown eyes lighting up with pleasure... like they were right now.

The throaty moan she released set mine to shame. Blood zinged through my veins and my fingers itched. *Is that what she sounds like when she comes?* I was dying to find out.

What the hell was I thinking? Zenda's friendship was too important to treat her like some sexual conquest. If I lost her because I couldn't keep my dick in my pants, that would be a tragedy I'd never recover from.

Blinking furiously, I snatched the fork back and stabbed another bite of fish. "It's good, right?"

I waited for her to nod and settle back down. Only she didn't. She rounded the table with her plate and stopped right beside me. Her arm brushed mine as she stole my plate and fork, then cut a big hunk of my fish with it. She dumped it onto her plate, with a good portion of my garlic butter, too.

Eyes widening, I opened my mouth wide, feigning shock. "Hey. You don't have to take mine. The processor's right there."

Zenda shrugged. "It is, isn't it? Why don't you order yourself some more?" She grinned mischievously and popped a butter coated finger into her mouth, sucking hard enough to hollow her cheeks.

I groaned, tearing my eyes off her tempting little mouth. "I know I told you to be bad, but I think you're taking it too far."

She chuckled as she circled the table and sat. "You don't know the half of it."

"Oh, really?" I leaned back in my chair. "Do tell."

Zenda popped another bite of fish into her mouth and hummed appreciatively. "I'm not the same goody-goody I was back in school."

"Is that right? You mean with your job healing people?" I gave her a cool once over, ending my perusal on her perfectly-in-place hairstyle. "Not to mention, that school teacher bun."

Zenda patted her hair, and her voice turned icy. "This is a chignon. It's classy."

A wide grin crossed my face as the word sparked a memory. "I bet you still read those *classy* novels, too."

"Yes, historical romance is still my favorite genre. There's nothing wrong with that." She crossed her arms.

"Is that your confession? That you still have an obsession with naughty books?" I smiled, remembering the first time I'd spotted her collection. She'd been so embarrassed. It was cute that she thought she had to hide her addiction to smutty books from me back then—a teen male infatuated with porn in all its forms.

At least now she wasn't ashamed to admit it freely. Score one point for bad girl Zen. But she wasn't convincing me with that alone. Or the way she kept moaning as she ate, teasing me with that sexy voice of hers.

She swallowed her last bite and nodded at my plate. "You done with that?"

I shoveled the last piece in my mouth and nodded. She scooped up both of our plates and dumped them into a bin on the counter.

"Are you ignoring my question, then? If you think that makes you bad, I hate to break it to you..." I stood and leaned close to her ear, stage whispering, "it's just annoying."

She whipped around and shoved my shoulder playfully. "Shut up. I'm not ignoring you. I'm going to *show* you." She grabbed my hand and tugged, setting my heart racing. "Come with me."

My skin tingled beneath my glove as Zenda hauled me out of the mess and down the hall. I expected her to pull me into the med-bay, but she hurried past the hatch without pause.

What could she possibly want to show me? And where?

My pulse sped when we turned down the hall that led to my quarters. Was she planning to throw open my door so we could use that bed? That would certainly be a bad girl move. No. That wasn't Zenda at all. There had to be another explanation.

"Are we going to my quarters?" I blurted when the anticipation became too much to bear.

"No." Zenda stopped at the door next to mine and keyed a code into the hatch opening mechanism. "We're going to mine."

"I didn't realize we were neighbors." A rush of jitters spread across my skin. I'd be sleeping right next to her, with only one flimsy wall separating us.

"Yep." She pointed to the door on the other side of hers. "Ren's over here." She flicked a glance at my face and frowned. "Don't worry. You've got the best room out of all of us."

Yeah... that's not what had me worried. Not even close. If those walls were as thin as I suspected, then I'd be requesting a new room before long. I don't know if I could handle listening to her puttering around at night. Wondering what she's doing in her bed.

The hatch opened, and I forced the thought aside. Zenda jerked me inside, then dropped my hand unceremoniously beside the doorway. She strode across the small room to a narrow dresser stationed next to her single bed and turned her back to me while digging through the top drawer.

It gave me a perfect opportunity to examine the space. She'd decorated the white walls and uniform tan furnishings with bold colors. Patterned throw blankets draped the bed and the single desk chair. But the posters on her walls nearly did me in. Every one featured bright fish and gorgeous blue water.

My stomach clenched at the evidence all around me. Zenda's love for the ocean went far deeper than I'd realized.

And I could've—I gritted my teeth and buried the thought before it fully formed. The past was better left alone.

"Ah!" She snapped the drawer closed and spun on her heels, clutching something to her chest. "Found it."

I lounged against the doorframe, quirking a brow. "One of your romance novels?"

"No." She slowly paced closer, keeping whatever she'd grabbed hidden beneath her hands. "I do love those books. I guess a part of me relates to the lonely spinsters who eventually find love—wish fulfillment, I suppose."

"What are you talking about?"

She shrugged. "I'm thirty-six and single, with little hope of ever landing a husband. In Regency England they called—"

"I know what a spinster is," I cut in as something uncomfortable washed over me.

Zenda smirked. "Right. Well, do you know what I realized?"

"What?"

"It's not Regency England anymore. And husbands are overrated." She handed me a black plastic card.

"What's this?" I frowned, twisting the unassuming rectangle in my hands. Both sides displayed the same etching of a couple embracing, their silhouettes vague enough they could be any of a dozen different species.

"That's my VIP card for the outer rim brothels." Zenda leaned back on her heels with an arrogant grin plastered across her face.

And me? My lungs burned like I was one second away from drowning.

"Your what?" I barked.

Her delicate eyebrows furrowed. "Don't tell me you're gonna be a prude about it. You practically have a different girl every week." She snatched the card back and glared at me.

My stomach churned. Why did it have to be the damn bots? "That's different."

"How?" she demanded.

"At least they're alive."

Her face drained of color. "I won't apologize for taking what pleasure I can get. Not all of us can be lucky like you."

"What's that supposed to mean?"

"Please." She jabbed a finger at my chest. "You live on a planet overflowing with women and you look like a damn underwear model. Of course you're swimming in pussy."

I licked my face nervously. How did this silly, flirty conversation go off the rails so quickly?

"Don't worry," Zenda continued, her voice cracking. "I'm sure you'll never run out of willing women and have to settle down. I know how much you don't want that."

"Zen." I sucked in a deep breath, but before I got out another word, her desk chimed insistently.

"That's my comm alert. I have to answer it." Zenda smacked the hatch controls.

"Wait, Zen."

"We'll talk later, Nash, kay?" She forced a smile and shoved me through the door. As the hatch slammed shut, I stood there reeling.

What the hell just happened?

10

Secrets and Monstrosities

Zenda

I fought to compose myself as the hatch slammed closed. Gods-damn Nash. Where the hell did he get off acting all offended?

Sucking in a deep breath, I marched to my desk. "Verne? Route my call through my room, please."

"Of course," a masculine, computerized voice answered. "Task complete."

"Hello? Zenda speaking." I sank into my desk chair, nerves coiling in my stomach. Besides Nash, only two people normally called me. Who would it be today?

"Zen? It's me."

The anxiety drained out of me when I recognized my little sister's voice. "Kar. Hey, I wasn't expecting your call." A tiny sliver of discomfort returned. "Everything all right?"

"Yeah. Everything's fine."

I exhaled shakily. "That's good. So, what's up?"

"I have some news to share." Karsen's voice practically hummed with excitement.

It must be good. "I'm listening."

"Do you remember how I was considering upping my class load so I could graduate faster?"

Karsen was only eighteen, but she'd always been crazy smart. So smart that it wasn't high school she was talking about. It wasn't even college. She'd finished both ages ago. Karsen was already one step away from earning a doctorate in medicine.

"Yeah, I remember. I thought you decided to take it slow?"

"I did originally. But you know how bored I get being idle."

Only Kar would describe a normal class load as idle.

I chuckled. "Sure do. You wouldn't even nap as a baby."

"Well, I did it, Zen. I graduated."

"Seriously? Congratulations! That's incredible." Warmth spread through my chest. It still floored me that my baby sister had followed in my footsteps to study medicine.

"Thank you. I just had to share the news with someone who gets it."

"Let me guess. Mom patted the back of your hand and said 'that's nice, dear,' then tried to set you up with some rando in the next breath."

Karsen exploded with laughter. "Almost exactly! It's like you were there."

I sighed. Fact is, I had been there. Karsen and I could show up with any number of degrees and accomplishments, but the only thing that would make Mom truly happy was becoming a grandmother. And she never let me forget it.

I didn't want to turn Karsen's good news into a bitch fest, so I bit my tongue and laughed along with her. "So, what's next?" I asked once our laughter tapered off naturally. "Are you signing up for more school?"

"Actually, I was thinking about applying for a few postings like yours. I could use a bit of adventure exploring the stars." She paused. "You like it, right?"

"Yeah. Most of the time." I couldn't hide the hint of annoyance in my tone.

"What happened?" Karsen's voice softened. "Are you okay?"

I twisted the black card in my hands. "I'm fine. Just... you remember my friend Nash?"

"Sure. How is he?" She gasped. "Oh no. Is he sick? Did he die?"

My stomach roiled. "No, nothing like that. He's onboard as a passenger and we got into a big fight." Saying it out loud after Karsen's dire assumption made me feel a little silly. Was I really that worked up over a dumb argument?

"Aw, I'm sorry. What was it about?"

Shit. We were close, but I wasn't about to spill all those details to my barely legal little sis. "It was something stupid, really," I deflected. "What's upsetting me most is the fact that we argued at all. Nash and I never fight."

When I really thought about it, it made no sense at all. Nash had never been a puritan, and he clearly had an active sex-life. Why did he get so rattled over me visiting a brothel?

"Well, if it was so silly, why don't you just apologize and make nice?"

I tugged off my glasses and rubbed the bridge of my nose. "I guess I did kind of blow up at him." Still, something about apologizing rubbed me the wrong way. After the judgmental way Nash looked at me, he ought to be the one begging me for forgiveness. "I'll think about it, Kar."

Ugh, how did the conversation turn to my pathetic issues? We should be celebrating—as much as we can over a comm line. I shoved my problems aside and said cheerily, "Enough about me. Tell me about your graduation ceremony. What are you wearing?"

Zenda

I avoided Nash for almost twenty-four hours. Did I feel guilty for ignoring Arda's request to keep him company? Sure did. But not enough to seek him out. Not with his stupid assumptions about my sex life ringing in my ears.

Still, the ship wasn't exactly the easiest place to hide. I'd skipped the mess hall for breakfast and lunch, certain he'd be there. But the old protein bar I'd scrounged out of my desk and choked down only went so far. Once dinner had come and gone, hunger drove me out of my quarters.

After peeking out of the door, my gaze wary like a kid up past their bedtime, I stepped into the hall. My stomach growled so loudly I jolted and whipped around, certain I'd stepped on Smudge's tail.

Of course, the hall was empty. *Hunger's driving me stupid, apparently.*

My pulse pounded as I tiptoed to the mess. The hum of chatter was absent. No scrape of utensils, chewing, or smacking lips. A smile creeped across my face.

Looks like I waited long enough—fuck.

I bit back the urge to utter the curse aloud somehow, but I couldn't stop my smile from disappearing. Nash sat in the mess, his gloved hands wrapped around a mug with a pensive stare on his handsome face.

I took a step back, prepared to duck away before he spotted me.

Growl. I winced. My stupid stomach gave me away.

"Zen," Nash said. "I thought you were planning to avoid me forever."

A sigh spilled out of me as I walked into the mess. I hurried to the food processor and punched in an order before turning to face Nash. "Yeah, well, you know me. I can't stand being fake. And you really pissed me off."

Nash frowned. "I'm sorry."

I cocked a brow and crossed my arms.

"Fuck, Zen." Nash rubbed the back of his neck. "Can't you just accept my apology and we forget it happened?"

"I shared something personal, and you made me feel like a freak. Friends don't do that." I turned to the processor as it beeped and scooped my plate out.

I plunked down at the table across from Nash with another chicken stir-fry. He eyed it like he wanted to say something, but he was smart enough to keep his dumb comments to himself—this time.

"I am sorry, Zen. Truly." Nash leaned forward as I scooped up a big bite and chewed. "It was idiotic of me to react like that. You do deserve to have pleasure." He paused, and the way his gaze flicked over me after that loaded sentence nearly had me choking on my meal. "It's the sexbots that struck a nerve for me."

I forced the bite down my throat. "Really? Why would bots bother you?"

Nash twisted his mug. "It doesn't matter."

"You're seriously not gonna tell me?" I rolled my eyes and shoved another bite into my mouth. Silence spread out, punctuated by the crunch of my chewing. After two more bites, I had enough of waiting. The damn stir fry tasted like sawdust, anyway.

My half-empty plate clattered as I dumped it in the wash bin. "Keep your secrets. I don't know why I'm surprised. Not like you shared anything personal with me before."

Nash jumped out of his chair and into my path, blocking me from the hatch. "I've told you more than anyone."

"If you say so." I waved him aside. "Do you mind?"

Nash sucked in a breath, a panicked look in his eyes. "You want personal." His face lit up. "How about my name?"

I flashed back to our first meeting. I still remembered that day so clearly. He'd been so insistent he'd never tell me his full name. I'd needled him dozens of times over the years to try to get it out of him. Was he really about to spill it?

"All right. Go for it."

Nash hung his head and mumbled something.

"Doesn't count if I can't hear it."

He lifted his head and met my eyes. "Anashclitis."

My eyes bulged. "Gods! What were your parents thinking with that monstrosity?"

He chuckled humorously. "It's a family name. Belonged to my great grandfather."

"He should've kept it." I nudged him with my elbow playfully. "That wasn't so hard, was it?"

Nash flashed me a lopsided smile. "Now I just have to listen to you tease me about it for the rest of our lives."

His statement sent a riot of conflicting emotions zipping through me. Pleasure raced up my spine, knowing he trusted me enough to share something that clearly embarrassed him greatly. And then the bit at the end, about the rest of our lives. Nash was in this friendship for the long haul, and I couldn't be happier about that.

But the hint of vulnerability I glimpsed in his eyes made my stomach clench. Who hurt him so badly that he kept his own name locked away for decades? I wanted to find whoever was responsible and wring their stupid neck.

Yet another feeling rose above all the rest. Hurt welled in my chest, deeper and darker than the ocean's depths. "Don't you know me well enough by now? I would never joke around if I knew it would hurt you. I swear I won't tell a soul, Nash. Ever."

His eyes widened at the fierceness in my voice. Then his smile transformed, lightning up his face and stealing my breath. He slung his arm around my shoulder and squeezed me in a side hug. "You're incredible, Zen. Have I ever told you that?"

"I'd rather you told me about the bots."

Nash dropped my shoulder and backed away. "I can't..."

"You can't or you won't?" I crossed my arms and lifted a brow. Seconds ticked by as we stood in silence.

So much for trusting me. I turned for the hatch, shaking my head. "Goodnight, Nash."

I walked away, trying to ignore my heart breaking.

11

The Mistake

Nash

Zenda stalked away, leaving the mess hall without a backward glance.

Idiot. The hurt on Zenda's face when I refused to talk flashed in my mind. I couldn't stand to see her like that. But I'd kept the truth about what happened on Vorillion secret for so long. I'd worked hard to forget it, not allowing myself to remember that awful day when everything changed.

Emotions bombarded me. Anger. Shame. Humiliation. I didn't want Zenda to experience that, too. At the same time, I couldn't watch her walk away, thinking I didn't trust her.

"Zen, wait!" I hurried out of the mess, desperate to catch her before she reached her door. I caught up to her just as she crossed into the new addition. "Hey. Stop."

"What, Nash?" She whipped around before I could grab her elbow to stop her and let out a weary sigh.

"I'll tell you, okay?"

She gazed at me, cocking a brow. "Good. I was beginning to think you'd made the whole thing up to avoid telling me I'm a dirty slut."

Fuck. My dick twitched hearing that final phrase uttered with her throaty purr. "I don't think that at all." *Does she really think I see her like that?*

Zenda's lips twitched, and I got the impression she was biting back laughter. "Go on, then. I'm listening."

I gulped and my gaze shot down the hall. "Can we go to my room, at least?"

"Sure." Zenda fell in step with me, and soon we'd reached my room. I ushered her in and gestured to the bed. Zenda settled on a corner, her legs dangling off the edge.

I shut the door and sucked in a steadying breath. My skin rejoiced at the cool moisture in the air, but the rest of me wound tight at the thought of reliving that day. I paced nervously, wringing my hands. "I haven't told this to anyone."

Zenda's expression softened, her eyes filling with compassion. "You can tell me. I won't tell a soul."

I nodded once, my stomach churning. I knew that. Zenda always kept her word. Still, I couldn't help worrying that she'd look at me differently after this.

I sank down on the bed beside her. "One day, just before I moved to Earth, I made a mistake that ruined my life."

Zenda grabbed my hand and tugged it on her lap. The heat of her flesh seeped through my glove as her little fingers stroked soothingly.

"I'd skipped school that day. I don't remember why. Some test I wasn't prepared for, maybe. Or just to have a break." I shrugged. "Guess it doesn't really matter. The mistake was spotting my mother."

Zenda frowned. "Your mother? Did she punish you for missing school?"

"She didn't see me." I blew out a shaky breath. "If I'd just ignored her, then nothing would have happened. But she was dressed strangely, in this huge overcoat, even though the weather was beautiful. And she kept darting glances around, acting even weirder. So, I followed her."

"Where did she go?" Zenda's hand tensed.

I attempted to send her a crooked smile, but my heart wasn't in it, and it probably ended up more like a scowl. "A brothel. One with sexbots."

"Oh."

"I was livid." I squeezed her hand and met her eyes, wanting her to know I meant what I said next. "*Not* that she was going there. I don't have a problem with sexbots. It was because I assumed from her sneaking around, she was doing it behind my father's back."

"I gather they were together, back then?"

"They still are."

Zenda's eyes bulged behind her glasses. "What did you do? Did you confront her?"

It might have been better if I had. I shook my head. "No. I went straight to my father. Walked right into his office in the middle of the workday." My eyes pinched closed as the memory washed over me. Bile stung the back of my throat.

"What happened?" Zen inched closer and burrowed against my side, no doubt sensing I needed a hug more now than ever.

I rested my cheek on her head, the light floral scent of her shampoo invading my senses. It made it a bit easier to admit the truth. "I found my father doing something even worse."

Zenda clutched me tightly, her hand gently trailing down my back. I could sense what she was thinking. What could be worse than catching your parent entering a brothel? But she didn't press. She just sat there, letting me soak up the comfort of her embrace until I was ready to spill the rest.

It all flew out in a rush. "He was fucking his assistant." I cringed. "No, actually, his assistant was fucking him. His *male* assistant."

Zenda's arms tightened around my middle. "Gods, Nash. That must've been awful to walk in on."

"Tell me about it." I shook my head, trying to dislodge the image from my brain. "The outer door to the offices was locked, but I knew the code. I should've suspected something was off then. But when his assistant wasn't there to greet me, I figured they were out to lunch. I barged right in to my father's office to wait."

"Then you saw them." Zenda rubbed my back. "Did they see you, too?"

"I wasn't exactly quiet when I threw open the door. They tore apart and fumbled for their clothes with me standing there frozen like an idiot." I tugged Zen closer, wrapping my arms around her waist. "My dad kept screaming at me. Like *I* was the one in the wrong."

"Seriously? *He* yelled at *you*?" she asked, her voice dripping with indignation.

I nodded against her head. "Yeah. After his assistant slinked out of the room, he really laid in on me. But the more he accused me of spying and harped on me for showing up unannounced, the angrier I got, until I finally snapped."

"What did you do?"

"I screamed right back at him. Told him he was a coward for cheating on my mother, and an even bigger one for stringing her along when he really wants to be with men."

"Good. He deserved that. I hope you told your mother, too."

I chuckled humorously. "I would agree with you if not for what he told me next."

Zen pulled away far enough to meet my eyes. Her cheeks were flush, her eyes teary. "What did he say?"

"He said she already knew, and she didn't care. Apparently, they had an arrangement, and it wasn't any of my business."

Zenda gasped. "That was why she was at the brothel."

I shrugged. "Probably."

"You never asked her about it?"

"I didn't get the chance to. My father ordered me a ticket on the first ship leaving for Earth. He told me to pack my bags. When I got home, my mother was there, holed up in her bedroom. I banged on her door, but she refused to talk to me. I guess my dad called her first and told her what happened. Since then, it's practically been radio silence, except for a card on my birthday with money stuffed inside."

"Nash, I'm so sorry." Zenda clutched me tighter. "I can't believe they abandoned you like that."

My heart thundered as the horrible truth settled in my bones. They didn't want me. Didn't love me enough to keep me around after I learned their sick little secret. Even now, so many years later, it made my gut clench and a wave of heat spread up my neck.

"I'm sorry I didn't want to tell you before. Honestly, I don't like to think about it. It's not fun knowing my dad prefers his secret lover over his son. And my mom didn't even try to fight him on it. I guess she'd rather have a machine around than me."

"Oh, Nash." Zenda pulled back and stared at me with fire in her eyes. "Fuck them. You're better off without them. The way I see it, they did you a favor."

I quirked a brow. "How do you figure?"

"If they never sent you on that ship, you'd still be living on Voril-lion." She pursed her lips. "You know I'm not crazy about your uncle after what happened with my mom, but he's a good man. Aren't you happy working for him?"

I nodded. "I am. And I like living in Subralia, too."

"See. Your mistake didn't wreck your life. It just transformed it." She patted my chest and grinned. "Anyway, I'm glad you came to Earth. I doubt we would've met otherwise."

"That's true." The thought of never having known her—hell, of losing her—I knew without a doubt that would wreck me completely.

"Thank you for telling me." Her eyes shone and her voice rang with sincerity before a teasing smile curved her lips. "Now that I know, I promise not to regale you with more stories of my brothel visits. I can see why that touched a nerve."

My heart started pounding for an entirely different reason. "Hey! I didn't agree to that. How about a story for a story?" I waggled my brow, and she giggled, inching away.

"Nope. Not gonna happen," she declared. I lunged for her, but she darted off the bed, the bubbly sound of her laughter chasing away the ache in my chest. Until her gaze snagged on something over my shoulder. "Shit. It's late. I better call it a night."

"Stay with me," I blurted, the invitation rolling off my tongue be-fore I'd even considered it. Once it was out in the open, I realized how much I meant it. After spilling my guts about my past, I didn't want to be alone with my thoughts. "Please, Zen."

Zenda froze, her gaze darting away from the clock and back to me. I was sure she was a second away from cracking a joke and disappearing into the hall. But my desperation must have been written on my face. "Okay," she said finally. "But you better not keep me up all night. I have work in the morning."

I shoved aside the wicked fantasies that fought to surface when I pictured keeping her up all night and grinned. "Deal."

12

Give It To Me

Zenda

My heart raced as Nash stared at me with a jaw-dropping smile and those big black eyes. "Well..." I inched closer to the door. "I'll pop over to my room and get changed."

"No," he shouted, hopping off the bed. His wild gaze darted from me to the door, almost like he was afraid I'd leave and never return.

"You don't expect me to sleep in this, do you?" I tugged the front of my skinsuit. Wearing a skinsuit was pretty common, even for people who weren't space travelers. The Vorill manufactured the special fabric. It maintained the perfect balance of temperature and moisture for whatever species wore it. But skinsuits weren't exactly comfortable for sleeping.

"Course not." Nash brushed past me and headed for the dresser. He dug inside, then thrust some folded clothes into my arms. "This should work."

I nearly shoved his clothes back at him until I caught a tiny twitch in his hands. I'd never seen Nash look so… desperate.

"Okay." I clenched the soft fabric to my chest and slipped inside his washroom. Then I closed the door and leaned against it.

Nash's story replayed on a loop when I closed my eyes. His parents—the fucking bastards. I couldn't believe they'd sent him halfway across the galaxy rather than fess up to their deception.

My chest ached for him. For the lost boy I once knew who hid his pain behind a carefree smile. And the man out there now, who guarded his heart so cautiously.

He hadn't hidden from me… I shivered, clutching the bundle tighter. A burst of freshness and something spicy reached my nose. I glanced at the fabric in my hands before dragging it up to my chin. I breathed deep, inhaling a mix of Nash's detergent and his cologne.

The hell am I doing?

Nash was upset after reliving his past. Desperate for a friend. And there I was, sniffing his—I unfolded the clothes and fumbled, nearly dropping them—was that his *boxers*? My eyes bulged.

Yep. He'd given me a plain cotton t-shirt and boxers to sleep in.

It's just clothes, Zen. Don't be weird about it.

No matter how much I told myself that—repeating the thought over and over as I wiggled out of my skinsuit and slipped the silky shorts up my legs—I couldn't stop picturing what else that fabric had touched. I slid the tee over my head, giggling when it fell to just above my knees. I hardly needed the boxers. They were too big, forcing me to fold the band twice so they wouldn't fall down my legs.

My pulse roared. I pictured walking out there brazenly in only a t-shirt, with nothing on underneath but my little cotton panties.

Yeah… not happening.

I folded my skinsuit, hiding my sports bra inside the bundle, and set it on a shelf beside the sink. Nash's toiletries rested inside the mirrored cabinet. Sliding my glasses on top of my head, I helped myself to his face-wash, frowning at my reflection as I toweled off my cheeks.

I took two steps to the door and shoved it open, rubbing the towel across my wet forehead and eyelids. "Hey. I don't suppose you have an extra toothbrush, do—"

The question died on my lips as I slid the towel off my face and spotted him. Nash stood with his back to me, his skinsuit gone. A pair of boxers identical to the ones hanging limply off me molded to his sculpted ass. His muscles rippled as he finished tugging a black t-shirt on, covering all that delicious green skin.

"Hm?" He spun around, a crooked smile tugging up the corner of his mouth as he noticed me wearing his baggy clothes. "Oh, yeah. Let me give it to you."

Give it to me... yeah, you can give it to me, all right.

He stalked toward me and my mind blanked. All I could see was him prowling closer. His muscled arms swayed, those long, thick fingers swinging by his side. Liquid heat pooled in my belly and raced through my veins.

I licked my lips as Nash halted beside me in the washroom doorway. He leaned in, making me crane my neck to meet his eyes. My heart rattled my chest. Then his hand disappeared behind me. I waited for his fingers to clamp on my back. My ass. My hips. Anywhere so he could drag me the last few inches to his smirking lips.

But his hand reappeared a heartbeat later. "Here."

I blinked at the plastic wrapped toothbrush in his hands. "T-thanks." I snagged it and quickly turned back inside. Before I could snap the door closed, Nash sauntered in.

"What are you doing?" I tugged my glasses down, slipping them back on. I glanced at Nash in the washroom mirror before he swung the cabinet open.

"I need to brush, too." Nash plucked a toothbrush off a shelf and shook two pill-sized toothpaste tablets out of a jar. He handed me one before popping his in his mouth and crunching down on it.

I followed suit, biting the tablet to activate the cleanser. Then we stood there—side by side—the *scritch scratch* of the bristles loud in my ears.

It was so—domestic. So mundane. Brushing teeth next to a man, about to head to bed. I don't know why sharing the simple task sent a rush longing straight through me.

This is what it'd be like to have a husband. Despite all the denials I fed to my baby-crazed mother, I couldn't deny how much I craved this simple companionship. Sure, I had Arda and Ren. My sister. But this... I wanted this more than anything.

Maybe it was wrong of me to allow it. Sure, playing house with Nash, even in this limited capacity, would be fun while it lasted. Except tomorrow when he was feeling more himself, I'd be back in my own little bathroom.

Brushing my teeth alone—like always.

Sleeping alone—like always.

Shoving the depressing thoughts aside, I snuck a peek at Nash in the mirror and found him staring back at me. He winked before leaning over the sink to spit. I watched his throat bob and clenched my thighs together.

I took my turn spitting, then Nash held out his hand for my brush. "Go climb in bed. I'll join you in a minute."

My heart beat even more erratically. *Was I really about to do this?* I glanced at my reflection as I handed him my brush. Well, one thing had to go if I had any hope of sleeping. I inched closer to the mirror as Nash turned on the sink.

"Go ahead, Zen. I'll rinse."

"Just a sec." I lifted my hands into my hair, tugging out the first pin in my chignon.

Nash froze with our toothbrushes under the stream of water. But he wasn't looking at the sink. His gaze stayed glued to my head.

I tugged out the second pin. A tendril of red slipped down my neck. Nash tracked the movement, biting his lip.

My fingertips closed on the third pin. "I think they're wet enough, Nash." I pulled the pin and my hair cascaded around my shoulders in a fragrant cloud.

"What's wet?" Nash croaked, his eyes bulging.

I nodded at the sink. "The toothbrushes." I giggled.

"Shit." Nash wrenched the knob. The water cut off.

I strode out of the washroom and stopped beside the bed. It was twice the size of the little twin-sized mattress in my cabin next door, but Nash wasn't exactly tiny. Was I really about to spend a whole night wrapped up in his sheets? Inches away from him. Wearing his stupidly comfy clothes.

The hurt on Nash's face as he talked about his parents flashed in my mind again, and I sighed. What kind of friend would I be if I practically demanded he spill his guts, then left him all alone wallowing in the past?

Just go to sleep, Zen. A few hours rest and he'll be ready to face tomorrow. He needs you. He needs his friend.

I climbed under the sheets, praying I'd be able to keep my itching fingers to myself as I comforted my *friend*. If only that word didn't scald my throat like acid. But friends were all we'd ever be. No matter how much I wished we could be so much more.

13

Down

Nash

That hair. I groaned, grabbing the sink with a death grip. Staring in the mirror, I watched Zenda sashay out of the washroom with those long red locks swinging across her back.

How many times had I wondered what she'd look like out of that prissy school teacher bun? The reality was better than I could have imagined. With those soft curls framing her face, she was every man's wet dream. She pulled out those three little pins and went from looking so damn cute swimming in my clothes, to making my dick hard in an instant.

I slowly tugged the door closed, taking a minute to compose myself. Glaring at the bulge tenting my boxers, I whispered, "Down, idiot."

Maybe this was a mistake. I should send her back and spend the rest of the night... I let the thought trail off, knowing exactly what I'd do if she left.

I'd spend about five seconds picturing those silky strands dangling in my face with my fist wrapped around my cock. And after I came, I'd be awake the rest of the night, unable to erase the memories I'd dredged up from the past.

No. She was staying. Zen would keep me company. That's all there was to it.

I blew out a breath and splashed some water on my face. Then I steeled myself, shoving images of those long curls wrapped around my fist to the back of my mind.

With the lights out, I can forget she even let it down, right?

Inching the door open, I slipped out. A small lump topped with red lay under my sheets. Tingles erupted, racing across my skin and colliding in my stomach with all the force of a supernova. I shook off the nerves.

It's just Zen. We'll crack a few jokes and curl up to sleep.

She met my eyes as I peeled the sheets down on my side. Her glasses were gone too, folded neatly on the small bedside table. With the blankets tugged to her chin, she was back to looking adorable.

"What?" she asked.

"Just wondering how much you can see right now."

Her gaze slid down my body, and my skin burned wherever it traced.

"Huh?" her nose crinkled. "Why do you ask?"

I hopped in bed and pulled the blankets up my chest before my dick betrayed how much I liked her staring at me. "Without your glasses, I mean."

Zenda's cheeks flushed. "Oh. I can see fine. I had laser surgery years ago. But I wore glasses so long as a kid, my face doesn't feel right without them."

I chuckled. "Really?" I leaned over her, the move making my upper body hover above her, and snatched her glasses off the table. "So, what's in these, then? Just regular glass?" I looked down, meeting her wide eyes, her frames dangling off my fingers.

She gulped. Nodded.

I slid them on my face, blinking at the view. Except for a tiny smudge, I could see perfectly. I waggled my brows. "How do I look?"

Zen burst out laughing. "Ridiculous." She choked out between giggles.

I gave her my best affronted look and sat up. The door to the washroom stood open. If I leaned a little, I might—

Laughter spilled out of my chest when I spotted my reflection. Zen was right. The frames were clearly not designed with Vorill eyes in mind. I looked like a cartoon or—

I faced Zen, jiggling my head like the Earth toys she'd introduced me to. "Now I get it. I *do* look like a bobblehead."

Zenda howled, clutching her stomach. "B-bobbles," she gasped out. "Told you!"

Her laughter was contagious in the absolute best way. By the time we'd both run out of steam, my stomach muscles burned.

Zenda jerked up and leaned on one knee. Her fingers stretched out, aimed at my temples. She was still smiling, a huge grin stretching from ear to ear. That gorgeous hair floated around her shoulders, making my breath catch. "As much as I'm tempted to let you keep those, I don't think I can. I'd probably die of laughter before we reach Vorillion."

Her soft fingers whispered across my cheek as she slid her glasses off. Although her mention of my home world sobered me enough that I barely registered the light touch.

Zen set the glasses down and turned back to me. Her smile faded, replaced with a tiny frown. "Hey. What's wrong?"

What's wrong, she'd asked. *Where do I begin?*

Though it pained me to think about my parents and how they tossed me out of their lives, telling someone—telling Zen—had actually been freeing. Still, decades of conflict avoidance made me say, "Nothing. I'm just tired."

Zenda pursed her lips and slid under the sheets. "Guess we better get some sleep, then."

I joined her, laying on my back and tugging the blanket up my chest. "Computer, cut the lights."

Blackness descended. I blinked as my eyes adjusted. Vorill had better night vision than most species—an evolutionary necessity when swimming in the deep, often-murky waters on Vorillion. Normally, I was fond of the skill. But not when my keen eyes picked out the tiny frown painting Zenda's lips as she stared blankly at the ceiling.

Say something, dummy.

"I don't want to go back," I admitted. "I hate that they're making me."

Zenda shifted, rolling on her side to face me. "Why did you agree to go in the first place?"

"It's complicated." I picked at the comforter, bunching and releasing the thick weave.

A warm touch landed on my hand. Zenda slipped her fingers beneath mine and squeezed.

"Have I told you about how my family is involved in manufacturing on Vorillion?"

Zenda nodded. "Sure. You mentioned it once or twice."

"Well, I may have downplayed how deeply we're involved." I sighed. "Long story short, my family's loaded. My father's the head of the company right now, but he's about to retire."

"Okay... and he's calling you home for what, exactly?"

"To inherit. To take over as the company head."

Zenda's voice wobbled. "You're not moving back to Vorillion, are you?"

I shook my head. "Not if I can help it. The company is pretty self-sufficient. I'll have to sign a lot of paperwork from now on, and I'll get the final say in any major decisions, but we have a team who runs the day-to-day operations."

"You didn't say no. Is there a chance that you'll have to stay on Vorillion?"

I flipped her hand over and traced lazy circles on her wrist with my thumb. "There's a tradition in our family. When the power is handed down from one generation to the next, the man retiring leaves his son a final request. If he's not willing to honor it, then the company passes to another."

A small gasp spilled out of Zenda's lips. "So, your father... what will he ask you for?"

"No clue." My stomach churned. My father might as well be a stranger now, for how well I knew him. "It could be anything. His father, my grandfather, required his charitable foundations to live on and be generously funded."

"Somehow, I doubt your father's request will be that honorable."

Leave it to Zen to say exactly what I'm thinking.

"What are you going to do?" she asked.

I shrugged. "Hear him out, I guess. Hope he doesn't ask me to do something abhorrent."

"Gods. That's insane, Nash. But you can always say no." She squeezed closer and her warm breath tickled the side of my neck. "Who will inherit if you refuse?"

"My cousin, Purkour." I shuddered. "I'd rather swallow a live gilat than see that idiot at the helm. But I suppose, if it comes down to it, I'll give it all up."

Admitting it out loud made a fiery rush pour through my veins. My family's legacy shouldn't be held hostage by the whims of one cruel man. But it was. And I had no choice except to follow through with whatever he demanded—or be cast out of the business for good.

"Whatever happens, I'm here if you need me." She lowered her voice. "Arda found this cute little blue planet where we can dump your cousin. I bet he'll fit right in with the microbial life."

I chuckled. "Careful, I might take you up on that."

Zenda stretched, kicking me in the shin. "Sorry. I'm not used to sleeping with anyone."

"It's fine. Me either."

She scoffed. "Yeah... okay."

"You think the women of Subralia are lining up to sleep in a room set with Vorill temperature controls?"

"Hm. I can see that. I'll be waking up with damp hair tomorrow."

"I can adjust—"

"Don't. It's not a big deal. I always shower when I wake up, any-way."

Of course, my brain conjured an image of Zen in the shower. All that long hair sticking to her breasts. Her smooth skin slick with water. My cock twitched, and I scrambled for something to say to knock the vision out of my mind.

"I wouldn't have wanted to sleep with them, anyway."

"Why's that?" Zenda asked.

"Sex is one thing, but when you start inviting women over for the night, they want more. I'm not looking for a relationship." I winced as the words spilled out. *But it's the truth, isn't it?*

I'm not sure what I was expecting Zen to say in response. Maybe that she'd crack a joke. Or that she'd simply roll over and say goodnight. What happened had my eyes bulging out of my head and my heart pounding.

Like a sloth climbing a tree, she curled against me, one arm and leg tossed over mine and her torso flush against my side. It happened slowly enough I had every opportunity to stop her—but I didn't. "Good thing you have a friend to snuggle with, then." She rested her head on my chest and sighed contentedly.

"Yeah." I gulped, begging my dick to behave as the sweet scent of her shampoo enveloped me. "Lucky me."

"Goodnight, Nash," Zenda whispered.

"Goodnight," I whispered back.

Zenda's breathing evened out quickly, but I lay awake for ages. With her body wrapped around me—giving me comfort even in her sleep—I had to admit what I'd known for years but tried so hard to ignore.

The feelings I have for this woman are not friendly. They're so much more.

14

Crazy Observant

Zenda

19 years earlier

I sighed, walking down the hall to the research lab. Another day of tests and droning lectures, halfway over. Just a few more months and I'd graduate and be able to start my career in research.

I ignored the tingle in my belly as I approached the lab. It was just another day. Yeah, I might have spent most of it on the edge of my seat, waiting to see if a certain boy would appear in any of my classes. Spoiler alert—he hadn't.

He wouldn't be at the lab either. So what if he'd promised to help me yesterday? Chances were, he'd forgotten about our awkward meeting the second I'd left the room. No guy had ever gone out of his way to befriend me, and Nash would be no exception.

Face the facts, Zen. You're pretty forgettable.

The wayward thought made a scowl cross my face as I pushed open the lab hatch.

"Yikes. I thought you'd be happy to see me," a familiar voice announced.

Eyes widening, I spun sideways. Nash stood next to the fridge, a bucket of fish at his feet. Thankfully, he was clothed this time, a turquoise skinsuit covering his lanky frame, along with matching gloves. "You came."

"I said I would." He smiled widely, though I couldn't help feeling like his grin seemed a little forced. "Can't have my reputation dragged through the gutter now, can I?"

I scoffed. "Okay, Bobbles."

"Hey! We had a deal." He hefted the bucket and carried it to the dolphin's pool. "I help you, and you forget—"

"Yeah, sure. I remember." I hid a smile behind my hand as I followed him to the pool. Suddenly, it was like I'd swallowed a school of fish and their fins were tickling my belly uncontrollably. I hadn't been imagining it after all. If Nash was back, then he must want to be friends.

I'd been so sure Nash wouldn't be returning, and it wasn't just from doubts about my lack of likeability. Professor Mueller was notorious for keeping access to his lab tightly restricted. I opened my mouth to ask Nash how he'd swung an invitation when a door banged loudly behind me.

I whipped around, a hand flying to my chest. "Professor Mueller. I didn't realize you were here."

Stalking out of his office, Professor Mueller raked a hand through his unruly brown hair. "Running late. Oh good, Zenda. I see you've met Mayor Prim's boy. He'll be using the back pool for swimming while it's empty." He rubbed his hands down his khakis, and his distracted gaze flitted from Nash to me and back again. "See to it that you don't disturb any of my research, hm?"

"I wouldn't dream of it," Nash replied cheerily, flashing a distracting smile that didn't quite reach his eyes. "Thank you for being so accommodating."

Professor Mueller nodded curtly and turned to leave. "Yes, of course. Carry on." The outer door slammed behind him, the bang echoing in the cavernous lab and making me wince.

"The mayor's boy? And here I'd assumed you must be exceptional at groveling to get lab clearance from Professor Mueller."

"Grovel? For him?" Nash shuddered. "Luckily, Mayor Prim's my uncle. I left the clearance to him."

I whistled for the dolphins before tossing the first fish into the pool. "Hm. Too bad. I bet you'd be good at groveling." I barely kept a straight face while I continued feeding the dolphins.

"Seriously?" Nash drew back, his big black eyes popping even wider than usual. "How do you figure?"

I blinked innocently, enjoying teasing him when he reacted so dramatically. "Well, you've got the fake smile down pat," I deadpanned.

I thought he'd try to play it off. Maybe crack a joke about nothing about him being fake. Instead, his smile fell completely. "You're pretty observant, aren't you, Zen?"

I shrugged, my heart twisting at the hint of sadness in his tone.

Great job, Zen. Make your new friend depressed. That'll make him like you.

I cleared my throat, an idea forming. "I am *crazy* observant, actually." I leaned close and gave him my best goofy grin. "In fact, I can prove it." I held my breath, waiting for his reaction.

Gods, you sound like a lunatic, Zen. He's gonna tell you to get lost.

Miraculously, my strange boast intrigued him instead. He smirked, crossing his arms. "Yeah? Let's see this proof, then."

I giggled. "I was hoping you'd say that. Help me clean up, and I'll show you."

"Why can't you show me now?" he asked, arching a brow.

"Because my proof isn't here." I rolled my eyes when I spotted a petulant pout painting his face. "Come on. You're gonna get a kick out of this. I promise."

Nash

"Where are we going?" I asked.

"You'll see," Zenda replied with a smirk.

Figures she would make me wait. Judging by the dozens of people we passed so far idling around, it seemed that life under the sea moved at a slow pace.

"What is it with all the women here?" I trailed Zenda down the glass encased halls of Subralia. Fish drifted past, and I licked my face.

Zenda's curious gaze tracked my tongue. "Didn't you bother to learn anything about the planet you were moving to before you came?"

I bristled. "It was kind of a spur-of-the-moment decision."

"Okay..." Zenda adjusted her glasses. "Have you heard about the Terran civil war?"

"Vaguely. It ended recently, right?"

"A few years before I was born. That's why there's so many women. And not just here in Subralia, but the entire system."

"Do Terran females not fight?"

"Some women volunteered. But men were conscripted when they came of age. They accounted for most of the casualties."

I studied a group of youngsters giggling among themselves as we passed. Even the children appeared to be mostly female. My brow furrowed. "That explains the lack of older men, but what about kids?"

Zenda lowered her voice. "Half a century ago, a new medical procedure popped up. It allowed mothers to choose the sex of their babies. Authorities discouraged its use, but it didn't stop billions of women from choosing not to birth boys. Even after the war ended, tensions between planets lasted for so long, most played it safe and kept having girls."

Guess I better get used to being surrounded by women. "Thanks for the history lesson."

Zenda shrugged. "Just doing my part to keep your reputation intact."

I quirked a brow. "How do you figure?"

She halted in front of a hatch. "If you asked anyone else that question, they'd have pegged you for a simpleton."

"A what?" I sent her my best glare, and she waved a hand dismissively.

"Everyone knows about the wars. Even children. Stick with me. I'll make sure no one realizes grade schoolers are smarter than you." Zen input a code and the hatch swung open.

I bit back a retort as she ushered me inside a cramped living room. A small floral-patterned couch and desk-sized table and chairs took up most of the space.

"Is this where you live?"

Zenda walked toward a door in the corner. "Yeah. Me and my mom. Come on, the proof is in my room."

Tingles spread across my neck. What could she have in there she wanted to show me?

She opened the door, revealing an even smaller bedroom. One wall held a narrow bookcase. A single bed draped with decorative throws was wedged across from it, with a tiny walkway in between.

"How do you sleep in here?" I asked from the doorway. "It's like a closet."

"This is what you get when you're the help." Zenda shrugged. "We're actually lucky. Mom snagged one of the few two-bedroom units allotted for cafeteria workers a couple of years ago. We used to share."

They shared a closet? Being the only person on that tiny cot would be hard enough to manage. I couldn't even contemplate how cramped they must have been with two of them sharing one room. And Zen still managed to climb to the top of her class while living in a shoe-box—that was pretty impressive.

She stopped at the back wall and slid open a small closet door. Turning sideways, I shuffled in after her and sat on her bed while she rummaged inside her closet.

I studied the bookshelf while I waited. Textbooks dominated most of the rows. A quick scan of the spines revealed the majority were about marine life or the ocean.

A smile spread across my face as I spotted the top row. Paperbacks, their spines creased in dozens of places, were lined up neatly. I stood and plucked one off the shelf. A shirtless man stared up at me, his arms wrapped around a woman in a flouncy lace dress.

Zenda spun around just as I flipped to the back cover. "Put that down!"

"Interesting literature you have here." I read enough to discover the story was about a young lady and a roughish duke before the book was rudely snatched out of my fingers. "Hey! I wasn't finished."

Her cheeks a pretty pink, Zenda stood on tiptoe and shoved the book into place. "That's my mom's shelf."

"But you've read them, haven't you? Tell me, does the duke repent his roughish ways in the end?"

Zenda's cheeks turned even redder. "Shut up." She thrust something hard into my chest. "Here. This is for you."

I snagged the item before it fell and stared at it curiously. It was a figurine with a gigantic head and a tiny body. "What is it?"

"An alien," Zenda announced. "Or, I guess it's what humans thought aliens looked like before we met any. More importantly," she plucked the figurine out of my hands and set it on the bookshelf, "it's a bobblehead." She flicked the toy, and the head started jerking like crazy. "It's like looking in a mirror, right Bobbles?"

The ridiculous thing looked nothing like me, but I couldn't help it—I laughed—longer and harder than I'd laughed in ages. I probably sounded like a madman. Every time I'd almost stopped, I caught sight of the silly thing bobbling, and I burst out with a new round of chuckles.

Zenda laughed right along with me. Finally, the toy stilled, and our laughter stopped with it.

"Thanks, Zen. I needed that."

She smiled shyly and grabbed the bobblehead. "Happy I could help. Here, you can keep it."

My heart sped up as my fingers closed around the goofy figurine. "You sure?"

Zenda nodded. "Yeah. I want you to have it."

When was the last time anyone had given me something just for fun? The gesture brought the tingles back, shooting across my chest and making my skin prickle.

Bang.

Zenda winced, her gaze darting over my shoulder through the open doorway behind me. "Mom? Shouldn't you be working?"

Her mother was here? My heart hammered. Was I about to be thrown out of their quarters?

I turned and spotted a small woman saunter in and drop an armload of cloth on the couch. She flicked her curly brown hair over her shoulder and spun to face us. "I could ask the same of you. Skipping classes with a—new friend?" Her brown eyes trailed across me before she beamed, looking much more pleased about finding her daughter with a boy in her room than I would've expected. "Come out and introduce yourself."

Zenda clicked her tongue and nudged my back. I stepped into the living room and flashed my most winning smile. "Hello. I'm Nash." I stuck out a hand, thanking the stars I recalled enough about Terrans to extend the proper greeting.

"I'm Portia." Zenda's mother ignored my hand and wrapped her arms around me instead. "And we're huggers," she explained, squeezing me in a tight embrace.

Portia released me and hugged Zenda next. "I can't stay. I had a break, and I wanted to drop these off."

Zenda extracted herself from her mother's arms and approached the mound of clothes. "What is all this?" She picked up a tiny pink shirt off the top of the pile and held it aloft, lifting a brow.

"Oh, Nora gave them to me. Aren't they adorable?" Portia sighed, her eyes going soft and her smile wistful.

"But why, Mom?" Zenda's voice quivered, her fingers clenching around the fabric. "Is there something you need to tell me?"

Portia grabbed the crumpled shirt out of her daughter's hand and smoothed it out, placing it atop the pile. "No. Not yet, at least. Still, I figured it wouldn't hurt to be prepared. You know I'm on the list for donations." She smiled brightly, splitting a glance between us. "And you're getting older, too."

Zenda stiffened. "Mom..."

"Oh, dear." Portia threw up her hands. "Look at the time. I have to get back. Finish my shift." She squeezed her arms around Zenda tightly, but swiftly. Then she turned and wrapped me in her arms again. I barely had time to pat her back before she released me and hurried to the door. "It was lovely to meet you, Nash. I hope we'll be seeing a lot more of each other."

The door slammed behind her, and Zenda let out a weary sigh. "Sorry about that. My mom is a little much."

"It's fine." I smiled. "I like her." Sure, I wasn't used to parental affection—my family were definitely *not* huggers—but I could get used to it.

Zenda frowned, lifting the tiny shirt again. "She's always been baby crazy, but this..." she shook her head.

"What? You don't want another sibling?" I sat on the couch.

"It's not that simple." Zenda sank down beside me. "There aren't enough men, remember?"

"Well, sure, but one man could impregnate a lot of women. With science to help, they don't even have to meet."

Zenda tossed the shirt back on the pile. "Yeah. Except most of the men left were exposed to toxic amounts of radiation during the war. It's not as easy to get usable sperm as you might think." She shrugged.

"Mom's been on that list since the day she weened me. I doubt she'll ever get a second donation."

My chest tightened. "What about you? Are you itching to sign up for a donation?"

"No. I've told her already a dozen times I want to focus on my career." Zenda's gaze flicked around the little room. "Mom was in such a rush to have me, she never finished school. I have plans that don't involve a baby anytime soon." She turned to me. "What about you? Being a man in a world crammed with women is sounding more appealing by the second, I bet. You can have your pick of beauties to marry."

I clenched my jaw. "Nope. I'm never getting married."

"Wow." Zenda adjusted her glasses. "That's a pretty bold claim." She smirked. "I bet you'll change your mind when you meet the right girl."

She was wrong on that count. I'd seen what madness marriage brought to my parent's lives, and I wanted no part of it. "Never gonna happen." I stared into her eyes and spoke with conviction. "I'm never getting married. Mark my words, Zen. It'll *never* happen."

Eyes widening, she inched away, making me wonder if I overdid the sincerity, just a smidge. "Okay, okay. I got it." She stood, grabbed my hand, and tugged me up. "Come on. This was fun, but I have to get back to class."

Then Zenda wrapped her arms around me, mirroring the tight squeeze her mother had given me a few minutes earlier. *Yeah... I can definitely get used to this.*

"See ya later, Nash."

"Later, Zen."

15

Nothing To See Here

Zenda

Present Day

Zipping my skinsuit, I tiptoed out of Nash's washroom and quietly slipped across his quarters. I spared a glance at his strong profile in the dark chamber. He still slept peacefully, sprawled out on the bed. When I woke up in his arms a few minutes ago, I'd almost ignored my internal alarm clock. But as much as I wanted to pretend the fairy tale where Nash wanted me sleeping in his bed was real, I just couldn't.

I snagged my boots off the floor, worked the hatch controls, and snuck into the hall. At least I was the only one privy to my early morning walk of shame. Since our rooms were right next to each other, it would be easy enough to slip back into my quarters with no one the wiser.

With a few long strides, I made it to my door. My fingers landed on the control panel just as Ren's door flew open and she stepped into the hall.

Don't notice me. Keep walking. Nothing to see here.

"Good morning, Zen."

Shit.

"Morning." I sent Ren a wobbly grin, praying she'd be distracted enough by whatever machinery she needed to fix today that she would breeze right past me.

Her gaze caught on my damp, disheveled hair. "Where's your bun?"

I curved a hand through my curls. "Oops, did I forget to fix my hair? Silly me." I pounded on the hatch controls. "I don't know what's gotten into me this morning."

Ren snickered. "I know what's gotten into you. Or should I say, who?"

"What?" I whipped around and spotted her staring at my boots tucked beneath my arm. I gulped. "It's not what it looks like."

"Sure," Ren replied casually.

I sighed wearily. "Look, I need a shower and about a gallon of coffee. Meet me in the mess in fifteen and I'll spill."

Ren grinned. "Deal." She turned on her heel and sauntered down the hall without a backward glance.

I dumped my boots beside the door and dove into my morning routine. Soon, warm water cascaded on me, unknotting the tension in my shoulders. I had half a mind to linger in there, remembering how perfect it felt waking up with Nash's strong arms wrapped around me. But that would be foolish.

Nash doesn't want me. Besides, his moment of weakness wasn't likely to happen again. Sleeping with him was a stupid idea. One that I'd be foolish to repeat, even in my memory.

I hurried through my shower, threw on a new skinsuit, and pinned up my hair. Before I knew it, my boots tapped down the hall on the way to the mess.

Ren glanced up as I entered, but didn't slow eating. She shoved a bite of her breakfast burrito into her mouth and nodded to the steaming cup of coffee on the table. "Ordered for ya," she added after swallowing.

"Thanks." I sat across from her and took a fortifying sip of the bitter brew.

"So, what's the story? You still gonna tell me you two are just friends?"

"We are."

Ren rolled her eyes. "I stopped having sleep-overs with my friends in grade school."

I set the cup down, but kept my hands wrapped around it, soaking up the heat. "Nash has always been kind of closed off about certain topics. I may have pushed him to share more than he wanted last night. After he did, he didn't want to sleep alone."

"Huh." She tilted her head. "And nothing happened while you were comforting him? In his bed... all night long."

My core clenched at the image her words planted in my mind. Nash and I curled up in that bed. Our bodies tangled and writhing. If only that were the truth, instead of the pathetic dream of a lovesick woman pining over her very uninterested friend.

"Nope." I shrugged. "I passed out pretty quick. Left while he was still sleeping."

Ren frowned and tore another bite out of her burrito.

"What he told me though…" I sighed. As much as I wanted to lay out the entire conversation for her, I'd promised to keep it to myself. But that didn't mean I couldn't talk about the way it made me feel. "I've always wondered why Nash acts the way he does. Why is it always a different girl every other week? Now, I think I get it. I'm glad he finally trusted me enough to share his past with me."

Ren set down the mangled remains of her burrito. "Well, that's good, I guess. I still hope he pulls his head out of his ass and sees what a catch you are."

My brow furrowed. "That's funny coming from you. What happened to the 'you don't need men' advice you gave Arda?"

"It was different with her. She and Lux just met. But you and Nash, you've been friends for ages. It's the whole insta-love nonsense I don't trust. There's nothing worse than some big oaf declaring his love for you when you just met." She shuddered dramatically, and her eyes went a little hazy.

The diehard romantic in me recoiled at her declaration. What made Ren so leery of love at first sight?

Footsteps echoed down the hall. I straightened in my chair, cradling my mug against my chest. What if that was Nash? What will he say about me leaving without a goodbye this morning?

I blew out a sigh when Arda entered the mess. "Good morning, ladies."

"Morning, Capt," I said.

Arda strode straight to the food processor and punched in an order. "Head's up. Get everything strapped down this morning. We'll be making our first FTL jump today."

"Got it." Ren stood, taking her empty plate with her.

Arda turned to me. "You mind filling our passenger in on jump protocol?"

"Sure." I settled my cup on the table, suspecting the warmth pooling in my belly had more to do with the prospect of seeing Nash again than the coffee. "You can count on me, Capt."

Nash

I yawned, stretching out in bed. I'd slept like the dead last night. When was the last time I'd slept without waking a dozen times to toss and turn? I honestly couldn't remember.

I needed to thank Zen for staying with me. My eyes snapped open, and I found myself alone. Disappointment hit me hard and fast, pinging through my chest like a meteor shower.

Well, she did say she had work to do this morning.

I sat up and flung my legs out of bed. I'd have to hunt her down in her lab and issue my thanks there. Just not in my pajamas.

After rushing through my morning routine, I strode to the door.

The desk picked the perfect time to chime. I marched over to it, brow furrowing when I didn't spot any controls. "Computer, what's with the ringing?"

"You have a call from Earth. Shall I put it through to your quarters?"

I sighed. "Yes. Go ahead." I knew even before the call connected exactly who it would be. There was only one person who knew what vessel I'd left on.

"Nash, my boy. How's the flight?"

"Hey, Uncle. To what do I owe the pleasure?" I sank into the desk chair.

"I have good news. I've arranged for a lawyer to meet with you when you land on Vorillion. He'll have a copy of the contract waiting for you. You'll have time to discuss the minutia before meeting with your father to sign."

"Thanks. I appreciate that." Uncle Prim knew me too well. All bets were off when it came to seeing my father again. I was liable to sign as quickly as possible to escape his presence. It was smart to get the contract in advance.

"Listen, I know I said I'd get on fine without you, but there's a few loose ends I could use some help with, if you don't mind working remotely?"

A grin split my cheeks. "Well, well. I told you that you'd be lost without me."

"Rightly so, my boy." Uncle chuckled. "What do you say?"

"No worries. I'm on it." We hung up shortly after exchanging a few more pleasantries and I got to work. It was the least I could do after everything Uncle Prim had done for me over the years.

When I'd shown up on Earth as a neglected teen, I'd gotten into all kinds of mischief, but my uncle always stood by me. He'd shown me the love I'd never felt from my own parents. He'd given me a job and a purpose. If skipping breakfast to help him cross some t's and dot some i's would help his day run a little smoother, then I was going to do it.

By the time I finished, my lower back ached from sitting on the tiny chair and my stomach growled non-stop. I left my room, stopped in the mess to order a protein shake, and wandered down the hall toward the med-bay.

A wonderful sound wrapped around me as I approached the open hatch. Zenda hummed loudly, her sexy voice making the notes of some unfamiliar tune sound deliciously sultry. I halted in the doorway, delighted to see her swaying to the beat. She faced the back wall, bent over a notebook, leaving her behind on full display as she hummed and sashayed in another skin-tight skinsuit.

I leaned against the doorframe and took a sip of my shake. For a second, I felt a little slimy. Here I was leering at her ass like some kind of voyeur... but who was I to turn down a show with my meal?

Of course, good things don't last forever.

"Gods!" She twirled around, a hand flying to her chest. "How long have you been standing there?"

"Not long." I pushed off the door frame and stepped into the room. "Do you always hum while you work?"

Her cheeks flushed. "I-I... sometimes."

"Don't be embarrassed. You have a beautiful voice."

The pink stain on her cheeks darkened to a deep red. "Did you come here for a medical reason, or just to harass me?" Her hand fell to her side, and she started to turn back to her notebook.

I caught her elbow, stopping her. "Actually, I was coming to thank you."

"Thanking me? For what?" Her brown eyes stared at me, suspicion swimming in their depths.

I knew what she was thinking. That I would turn my thank you into some kind of joke, like I usually did. But not this time.

I stepped closer, drawn into her orbit. "For last night. I haven't slept that well in ages."

"Happy to help," she replied cheerily. Zenda tugged her elbow, but when I didn't let go, her gaze shot to mine. She licked her lips, and my blood pumped furiously through my veins.

An alarm blared, breaking the spell.

"What is that?"

"Oh." Zenda tugged her arm free. "We're jumping today." She grabbed the cup out of my hands and frowned at the half-filled protein shake. "That's the five-minute warning. We need to get strapped in. Come on. The mess seats have straps."

My stomach churned as I followed Zen to the mess. I'd only experienced a handful of FTL jumps in my life, but every time they made me feel awful. Still, there was nothing to do but grin and bear it. Faster than light travel was a necessary evil if you wanted to travel between the stars.

Zenda stashed my cup inside a hidden dish sanitizer, then plopped down on a chair at the table. Ren appeared just as I sat beside Zen and she took a seat across from me.

"Where are the straps?" I asked, running my hands along the bottom of the seat and feeling nothing.

"Verne," Zenda barked. "Strap us in."

Elastic bands shot out from the seat-back and wrapped around my shoulders, disappearing beneath the seat and pulling snug across my chest. I breathed deeply, doing my best to avoid panicking.

The alarm chimed again.

"That's one minute. You ready?" Zen asked.

I nodded and closed my eyes. *A minute and a half, and it'll all be over.*

I gritted my teeth as the jump began and conflicting sensations slammed into me. It was like my muscles decided to take a run at super speed, while at the same time, my bones slammed on the brakes. I bit back a scream at the sickening feeling of being ripped in two. Just as I felt like the scream was about to break free, the jump ended.

"Verne, remove the straps," Zen ordered. She stood. "That wasn't so bad, was it?"

I plastered a carefree grin on my face. "Nope, not bad at all." I stood and wobbled as all the blood in my body rushed to my feet. I was still smiling when I fainted.

16

Doc's Orders

Zenda

Nash collapsed to the floor, smacking his head on the mess table on the way down. Ren gasped, her eyes wide with horror. I leaped into motion, crouching at his side and assessing his condition. Unconscious, but breathing.

Gods, what happened, Nash?

"Ren, run to the med-bay and grab my med-pack."

"Got it." The slap of her boots quickly faded as she sprinted down the hall.

My heart slammed against my ribs, but I ignored the traitorous organ, relying on my medical training to guide me.

This is why you're not supposed to treat family and friends.

But out in space, there was no avoiding it. Nash was in trouble and I'd be damned if I didn't do everything in my power to help him.

Blood leaked out of a deep gash on the side of his head. I snagged a clean towel out of a nearby cabinet and applied pressure to the wound.

Nash groaned, coming to.

"Shh. Don't move. You have a head laceration."

"What happened?" His voice was thick with panic, his gaze darting around the room.

"I'm not entirely sure yet. But don't worry. We'll do some tests and figure out what's happening."

Nash's wild eyes landed on me. "Thanks, Zen." He snagged my free hand and squeezed it tightly. I squeezed back, but pulled my hand free when I heard Ren's footsteps pounding up the hall.

"Have you ever fainted before?"

Nash grimaced. "No. Never."

Ren skidded to a stop and thrust my med-pack at me.

"You mind opening it for me?" I nodded at my hand, clutched around the now bloodied towel above Nash's temple.

Ren paled, looking slightly queasy. She kneeled down and unfastened my bag. I dug out a portable med-bot, punched in a command, and covered Nash's wound with it.

I smiled at Nash. "Let's take care of the bleeding, then we'll move you to the med-bay." I cleared my throat. "Verne, open a channel to the bridge."

"Captain Arda has set a 'do not disturb.' Emergency communications only."

I clicked my tongue.

"That sounds serious. Better not disturb—"

"No," Ren cut Nash off. "That just means her and Lux have another room to sanitize."

Normally, I'm not one to cock-block, but desperate times... "Verne, this *is* an emergency. Disturb them."

"Is it really an emergency, though?" Nash winced as he tried to adjust his head to meet my eye.

I leveled him with my best stern glare. "I need to get you back to the med-bay without dropping you on your head again. Have you seen how big you are?"

Footsteps echoed down the hall. Soon, Arda and Lux arrived in the mess. From the wild tangle of hair and bee-stung lips on our captain, I could guess what act we'd interrupted.

"What in Dral's name happened?" Lux thundered. His eyes widened as he stared at the blood on the floor.

"Nash fainted after the jump. I need your help to move him to the med-bay as soon as the bot is done repairing this gash."

"Are you all right, Nash?" Arda bent beside him and grabbed his hand. "Do you need me to contact anyone?" She glanced at me. "Should I start hunting for a medical facility along our route?"

"No contact is necessary," Nash insisted. "Zen can take care of me. Surely, it's not that serious."

"I think he's right. I'll know more once I run some tests, but the preliminary scans from the med-bot tell me his health isn't in immediate danger."

Arda nodded, her gaze drifting to the blood splattered on the floor. Her entire body froze except for her tongue, which darted out, licking her lips.

I wrinkled my nose. Maybe I should've waited until the blood was cleaned to call Arda and Lux in to help. "You okay, Capt?"

Arda shook herself out of her daze and cleared her throat. "I'll get the sanitizer. Mind helping me clean up while they move him to the med-bay, Ren?"

"Sure, so long as you sanitize the bridge when we're done." Ren smirked and trailed after Arda, presumably to help gather cleaning supplies.

The med-bot chimed three times, signaling its completion. I gingerly removed it, grinning at the repaired skin that greeted me.

"Is my head fixed?" Nash asked.

"Yes, good as new." I stuffed the bot in my med-pack. "Lux, help me move him?"

Nash scrambled to sit. "I can walk on my—" The jerky motion caused the exact effect I was hoping to avoid. He wobbled in place, and if not for Lux shooting out a hand to stabilize him, he would've likely slammed into the floor again.

"Easy," I said. "Until we know what caused the fainting, I don't want you walking anywhere without assistance. Doc's orders."

Lux flashed a rare grin at Nash. "Hm, guess it's your turn to owe me one."

Nash groaned as Lux tugged him to his feet. "You got it, big guy. Just don't drop me."

I followed them out of the mess, darting ahead to get things set up in the med-bay. By the time Lux led Nash inside, doing his best to steady his staggering steps, I'd prepared a cot. I lined up the testing supplies I'd need on a rolling tray table beside it.

Lux dumped Nash on the cot. Nash took one look at my supplies and cringed. "Do we really need the needles?"

Men. I swear they can be the biggest babies sometimes.

"Don't worry." I softened my voice, like I would to soothe a frightened child. "There's a lolly with your name on it when we're finished."

Lux chuckled, retreating to the doorway. "You need me again, have the Verne hail me."

"Will do. Thank you, Lux." I turned to Nash. "I need to draw some blood, then we'll get to the bottom of this."

Nash closed his eyes. "All right. I trust you, Zen."

My heart warmed. Now to prove to my friend that his trust was well deserved.

I don't care how long it takes; I'm going to find out what's wrong with Nash.

Nash

I pulled the cherry-flavored candy out of my mouth with a loud pop. "You know, these aren't half bad."

Zenda chuckled, pushing her glasses up the bridge of her nose. "Yeah, I figured you liked them after you stole a second—then a third." She bent over her tablet, her fingers flicking across the screen.

She'd set up a portable vid-screen to keep me occupied in the long hours since my fall, but I found myself mesmerized by Zen more than the old action flick. The sure way she handled her equipment. The steely concentration furrowing her brow as she focused on my medical scans. I had to admit, watching her in her element was a major turn on.

I had half a mind to snag her when she breezed past my cot and haul her on top of me. *But friends don't do that.* I shook the thought from my mind, wishing I could wipe away the lingering wooziness so easily.

Zenda gasped. She sat up straight, her gaze dancing across the tablet's screen.

"What is it?" I asked.

"I think I may have it." Her face lit up. "I just need to check the data again."

She wheeled her chair to the end of my cot, her attention laser focused on my readouts. I grabbed the vid-screen remote, pausing the old film. "Well? Give it to me straight, doc. Am I dying?"

Zen rolled her eyes. "No. But you have a diagnosis." She sucked in a big breath and all the humor drained out of her. "It's called jump sickness."

"Jump sickness?" My brow furrowed. "I've never heard of it."

"It's extremely rare. Only .0001 percent of FTL travelers are diagnosed with it."

"So, it *was* the jump that caused me to faint." I'd been assuming that was the case all along, but hearing confirmation calmed a bit of the unease swirling in my gut.

"Yes. I'm afraid you have a sensitivity to faster than light travel. I'm surprised it's taken you this long to realize it."

"You know, it actually makes a lot of sense. I only traveled by FTL once before this, when I moved to Earth. I got stupidly sick on that journey, too, but I thought it was because of the lack of environmental controls in my suite."

Zenda leaned back, her gaze turning pensive. "Hm. Dehydration and jump sickness can cause similar reactions."

"Well, what's next? Is there a treatment?" I shifted, inching my feet off the cot, but Zenda shot out a hand to stop me.

"Not so fast. Now that we know you have J.S., we can mitigate the symptoms in the future. It will mean taking a nutrient shot before every jump, and taking it easy after."

"That doesn't sound too bad." I grimaced. "Except for the whole needle part."

"You haven't heard the bad news." Zenda frowned. "I'm afraid I can't do much for the symptoms you're feeling now. If you withstand a FTL jump without prepping, then you'll experience dizziness and stomach upset, for a while after."

Guess that means the wooziness is sticking around. "How long is a while?"

Zenda shrugged. "A few days, maybe a week."

"Great." I sighed.

"I think the best course of action is for you to stay in bed, in your environmental-controlled suite, until the symptoms pass. And I'll talk to Arda about cutting down the number of jumps we need to make it to Vorillion."

"Wait!" My stomach somersaulted. "I have to get there on time. If I don't, the contract will expire before I even learn what my father's demands are."

Zenda grabbed my hand and squeezed. "I understand how important it is that you arrive on time. But you need to take this threat to your health seriously, too. Don't worry. I'll make sure Arda knows to cut the number of jumps, while still getting you home on time."

"Okay, Zen." I sank more firmly into the plush pillow and closed my eyes. It helped slow the ferocity of the room's spinning. "I trust you."

"Good." I could hear the grin in her tone, even though I couldn't see it with my eyes closed. "Let's get you to bed."

I swallowed a groan. If only Zenda said that for an entirely different reason...

Nope. Get that thought out of your dirty mind. Zen just wants to heal you.

But that didn't stop my head from filling with a dozen doctor jokes. *It's gonna be a long trip.*

17

Only Bad Options

Nash

Zipping up my suitcase, I took a last look around my room for anything I missed. Chances were I'd hitch a ride back to Earth on the Verne, but it was better to be prepared for anything. After all, who knew what my father would ask from me?

I sighed. It had been a long, boring journey to Vorillion. The jump sickness meant I spent almost all of it stuck in my quarters.

Zen came to visit, but the nausea and dizziness were slow to fade, making me poor company. She assured me a day or two of planetary gravity would be just the thing to kick it completely.

Honestly, I was ready for the trip to end. And not just to get better. I was sick of wondering what that contract would say. With the extended delay, at least I wouldn't have to wait long. The signing deadline was tomorrow. I'd sent word to the solicitor to collect the documents, and would meet him soon after debarking.

Tugging my luggage into the hall, I ran straight into Lux.

"Hey." He stopped short, his face betraying no emotion. "Need a hand with that?"

"Pfft." I jerked the bag away from his grasping four-fingered hands. "I can handle carrying my own bag."

"If you say so." Lux trailed me down the hall, shaking out a sheet of paper.

It wasn't long before my curiosity got the better of me. I mean…I was just cooped up in a single room for what felt like a lifetime. I was starved for entertainment in the worst way. "What ya' got there?"

He held it out to me readily. "It's a map. Just somewhere we're hoping to visit while we're on Vorillion."

I leaned closer, scrutinizing the map. "Huh. I think you better change your plans."

"What? Why?"

"That's outside of the capital." I jabbed a gloved finger at the map, tracing a line around the city borders. "No off-worlders are permitted without special clearance. Unless you want to end up expelled from the system, I'd find somewhere else to sightsee."

Lux's brow furrowed, and he leveled me with such an angry stare, you'd have thought I'd kicked Smudge down the hall.

"Look, don't shoot the messenger." I held a hand up in defeat. "I don't make the rules, I just abide by them."

"How do we get clearance?" Lux barked.

"I don't know. You want me to ask my lawyer?"

That finally chased away the dark clouds in Lux's silver eyes. "Yeah. Can you? It's pretty important we get there. For Arda."

"Say no more. I'll let you know what my guy has to say. I'm meeting with him in a few hours."

"Communication from Vorillion for passenger, Nash," the computer's masculine robotic voice rang through the hall.

"Speak of the devil." There was no one else who'd be calling me from Vorillion.

"Devil?" Lux asked.

I waved a hand. "Nothing. You hang around Earth for twenty years, you'll pick up some choice phrases, too." I shot him a lazy grin. "I better take this. Maybe I can get your answer now."

Lux nodded and punched a code into the door we'd just passed. "You can take your call in here." He cleared his throat. "Verne, direct Nash's comm to the exercise room."

"Thanks." I leaned my suitcase beside the door and weaved between the stationary exercise equipment to the comm panel in the back corner. The nausea and dizziness didn't exactly leave me begging for a brisk jog on the treadmill, or a ride on a bike, so this was my first time inside. It was a nice addition, even if the lingering odor of sweat made my nose wrinkle.

"Hello? Nash speaking."

"Nash. It's your lawyer, Durzo."

"Hey. We're gearing up to land in a few. Did you need to push our meeting back or something?"

"No. Actually, I need you to meet me sooner. Your father's solicitor sent me the papers finally, and—well, let's just say you'll want to be sitting down for this."

My heart pounded, so much sweat pooling in my gloves that the state-of-the-art fabric couldn't wick it away fast enough. "That bad, huh?"

"Depends. Honestly, there are a few ways we can play this. That's why I need to meet you sooner. Discuss your options."

Well, that didn't sound too bad. Options are good, aren't they?

Verne's voice blared over the ship wide speakers. "Landing commencing in five minutes. All crew and passengers strap in."

"Hey, did you hear that? I have to go."

"Yeah. I heard. Meet me right after you land. Same address I arranged with your uncle. I'm heading there now."

"Okay, thanks Durzo. See you soon."

I canceled the call and raced for the hatch, snagging my bag on the way out. *Let's just hope the options aren't only bad ones.*

Zenda

"Nash." I hurried into the docking bay. "I know you're itching to bask in planetary gravity, but were you seriously about to leave without saying goodbye?"

He hovered beside the outer hatch. He clutched his suitcase in his gloved hands, one boot tapping repeatedly as the creaking docking gear descended. "Sorry, Zen. I have a meeting with my lawyer straight away. Want to meet me after?"

"Sure." I sent him a grin, wishing I could do something to displace his nervous energy. Well... there was one thing. I threw my arms out wide. "C'mere. I need a hug."

Nash's big eyes bugged out slightly, but that didn't stop him from dropping his luggage and snaking his arms around me.

Gods. I shivered at the first contact. I'd given hundreds—more like thousands—of hugs in my life. They'd never felt remotely sexual. But somehow, this one lit up every synapse in my body. I reveled at the strength of his arms wrapped around me. All those hard muscles flush against my curves. I had the sudden urge to rub my face against Nash's pec and purr.

Down, girl. I pulled away, hoping the heat in my cheeks wasn't betraying my wayward thoughts.

Nash met my eyes, his flat stare replaced with a wobbly smile. "Thanks, I needed that." He squeezed my elbow gently. "See you later, okay?"

"Yeah." I cleared my throat. "Later."

The gangplank slammed down, and the hatch hissed open. Nash snagged his suitcase and bolted outside, moving so quickly he was practically jogging.

I lifted my nose toward the hatch, taking my first breath of Vorillion's air. It was similar to the conditions we set in Nash's chamber, wet and heavy with humidity, but with none of the sterile scents onboard. Instead, the rich aroma of plant life abounded, redolent with fragrant notes that stood out even here in a shipyard.

"You ready to do a bit of exploring?"

I whipped around, flashing Arda a grin. "You know it, Capt." Lux strolled at her elbow, wearing his normal mask of indifference. I frowned. "What about Ren?"

Her blonde head peeked out from under the hopper's hood. "What about me?"

"You coming to check out Vorillion?" I asked.

She shrugged. "Do I have to?"

Arda slammed the hood closed. "Yep. Capt's orders." She slung an arm around Ren's shoulders, avoiding the big oil stain on the neck of her skinsuit. "Lux found a cantina nearby. We're getting some proper food for a change."

Ren grinned. "And drinks?"

"Definitely. First round is on me," Arda answered.

We stepped off the Verne, and I took my first look around Vorillion. A pang of disappointment spread through my chest. "Huh. Not exactly what I was picturing."

Arda cocked a brow. "What were you expecting?"

"I dunno. More nature, I guess." My gaze flitted over the modern skyscrapers and neatly paved roads. Sure, there were bits of green layered in between. Spindly flowering trees perched on the roadsides. Mossy purple-tinted grass covered the ground where there wasn't pavement, but still, it was like any other big city back home.

"I doubt you'll find much nature in the Capital," Arda replied.

"Look on the bright side," Ren piped in. "There are drinks."

"Fuck." Arda slicked her brown curls off her forehead. "I could do without the humidity, though. How much you wanna bet my hair frizzes in this? I'm gonna look like a goddamn chia pet."

I cackled, patting my chignon with a smirk. "Have fun with that."

"Chia pet?" Lux asked.

Arda patted his shoulder. "Old earth relic. Not important."

"I'm thankful the sun is not so strong as on Earth." Lux tipped his face up. "Compared to Pheria, the weather is most pleasant."

I shuddered. Lux's world was covered in snow and ice. Certainly not my first choice to visit. I could see why he'd think Vorillion pleasant. Honestly, compared to Earth, it was a little gloomy.

Still, the people here seemed to enjoy it. As we exited the shipyard and strolled down the city streets, we passed countless Vorill. Few of them wore skinsuits or gloves, like I was so used to seeing Nash and his uncle don on Earth. Most wore short sleeves and shorts, leaving their arms and legs exposed to the moist air.

"Ooo, here it is!" Arda clapped her hands and shoved open the door to a quaint building wreathed in flowering ivy, bearing a sign I couldn't read. Luckily, it also sported a handy image of an overflowing flagon.

I followed Arda inside, pleasantly surprised by the familiar aroma that greeted me. I licked my lips and hid a smile as I recalled the last time I had roasted fish drenched in garlic butter.

A huge bar spread along one long wall of the rectangular room. Round tables perched in neat rows on the other half. Arda ignored the bar and the few patrons who lifted their heads from their meals to stare at us. She strolled to a table in the back and pulled out a chair.

Soon we all joined her and took turns punching in our drink order from the electronic console on the tabletop. We spent a short time sipping our drinks and shooting the shit before the conversation turned serious.

"Arda," Lux announced. "I'm afraid I have some bad news."

"What bad news?" Arda asked.

"Nash saw me looking over the map to the research facility earlier. He said there's no way we'll be allowed to visit the site. Off-worlders aren't permitted to leave the Capitol without clearance."

"Fuck." Arda dragged a hand through her hair. "What is it with this place? Landing clearance, traveling clearance. How do they get anything done?"

I frowned. It was rather peculiar, but this was their world. If they wanted to require visitors to jump through a million hoops and wade through an ocean of bureaucratic red tape, they could. All we could do was deal with it, or give up. From the glint of steel in Arda's eyes, I knew what option she'd chosen.

I patted her hand. "Maybe Nash can help."

Lux leaned back in his chair. "He already offered to bring up the clearance with his lawyer. Only maybe we should find someone else."

I adjusted my glasses. "Why would we do that?"

"I couldn't help but overhear a bit of his call with his lawyer." Lux steepled his hands. "Sounds like Nash is going to be dealing with some problems of his own."

My stomach churned. That didn't sound good. What if his father was planning to ask him to do something awful? And I promised to help him, no matter what.

"You all right?" Ren asked, her brow furrowing.

"Yeah." I stood, pushing my chair in. "I just need to find the washroom." I spotted a door by the front entrance bearing the usual sign.

First, I needed a minute alone. After that, it was time to find Nash. *I'm a woman of my word and my friend needs me.*

18

Cut To the Chase

Nash

I sank into a cushy armchair, my gaze flicking around the small, neat office. Official looking plaques hung on the wall, but I barely spared them a glance. Uncle Prim would only hire the best.

"Thank you for waiting," the middle-aged secretary repeated. "Durzo will be right with you."

"Of course." I shot her one of my best carefree smiles. "It's no trouble."

She smiled back and shut the door softly behind her, leaving me with my intrusive thoughts. What the hell did my father want? Sure, Arda had followed Zenda's instructions to the letter. We'd arrived much closer to the deadline than originally planned. Still, what would require me to meet with my lawyer immediately? My mind raced, flinging "what if's" at me like supernovas, each one more destructive than the last.

It could be anything. What if Father wanted me to run for government? Hell, he could ask me to chop off my toes—my hand involuntarily fell on my lap—or something more precious. The stupid tradition left it all on the table, no holds barred.

What if he wanted me to leave Earth for good and stay here? The very real possibility thrummed through my brain on repeat. What would I do if faced with that choice? After twenty years, Subralia was home. I'd made a life there with my uncle when my family ousted me. Sure, it wasn't perfect, but I was comfortable. Content. Yet with everything at stake, I honestly couldn't say what I would choose.

I had to know what was in that contract. Where was Durzo?

As if summoned by my thoughts, the door flew open. A disheveled Vorill in a brown, three-piece suit hurried inside, slamming the door closed behind him. He plunked a briefcase on the table and stuck out a hand. "Nash, I presume? Sorry to keep you waiting. Catching a transport at this hour was harder than expected."

I rose from my seat, clasping his forearm and giving him a quick once over. He was slimmer than me, the lack of muscle no surprise if he spent a good amount of time in an office. His clothes, though crumpled, were well made—a good sign for a prosperous lawyer. And most importantly, his eyes were as sharp as I'd expected when he met my gaze with a curt nod.

"It's no trouble. I've only just arrived." I squeezed his arm in the typical Vorill greeting, belatedly realizing I should probably lose the gloves when his gaze caught on my hands for a second too long.

"Please, have a seat." Durzo circled his desk and sat behind it. "I'll dispense with the pleasantries. I'm sure you're curious why I called you in early."

I sank down in the chair. "Durzo, I'm gonna say this once and only once. I might have more money than most of your clients, but

I promise you, I'm nothing like them. You can throw all the normal pomp in the trash with me. Tell it to me straight, or find me someone who will."

"Understood." Durzo didn't flinch at the bald statement. In fact, I may have spotted a glimmer of admiration in the lawyer's eyes before he leveled me with a business-like stare that gave away nothing.

He spun a numerical code into the briefcase lock before snapping it open and slapping a thick, stapled pamphlet on the table. "Your father's demands are simple, but personal in nature. I thought you'd appreciate being apprised of them before meeting to sign the agreement." He lifted a slim wrist, glancing at his watch. "Which, due to your late arrival, is scheduled to happen shortly."

I grabbed the papers, sliding them in front of me and scanning them greedily before coming to a swift conclusion. The damn thing might as well be written in Pherian for all I understood of the thick legalese. I dropped the papers on the desk and tugged off one glove, then the next. "And those demands are...?"

Instead of answering immediately, Durzo's gaze flitted to the ceiling, and he sucked in a deep breath. My already roiling stomach trembled like a battered moon after an asteroid storm.

Durzo met my eyes. The look he speared me with made me feel like I was about to face a firing squad. "He wants you to marry and produce an heir, to ensure the company lives on."

I leaned back in Durzo's cushy armchair, feeling like my world was imploding.

How had he known? How had my father discovered the one thing I swore to never do—get married.

"Fuck." I cradled my head in my hands.

Durzo cleared his throat. "I hope it wasn't presumptuous to assume that this would be a hard sell for you."

"No. You assumed correctly. I'm not a damn pet he can order to breed on his command." I slapped a hand on the papers. "What the hell kind of stipulation is that? Is it even legal?"

"Yes, I'm afraid so." Durzo shook his head slowly. "I've pored over this document and the original agreement drafted by the founding father of your company. This stipulation is legal and will be binding, should you agree to sign."

Rubbing my temples, I sighed. "And the alternative? What happens if I tear this contract up and send you to that meeting with a suitcase full of confetti?"

"Purkour gets everything. Final say over company decisions. Oversight of all the money." Durzo leaned forward, dropping the bomb that detonated in my stomach like a Gilboni nuke. "All the charities, too. You'll be out. Entitled to a generous bi-yearly stipend but—"

I groaned. "Ugh. The charities, too?" I'd hoped that my father wouldn't think to include them in the deal. They were an expensive investment that he only grudgingly agreed to continue. Now, their fate was as much at risk as everything else.

"I'm sorry, sir, but yes."

"There's no way that idiot Purkour will keep funding them." If Grandfather's charities lost their funding, I'd never forgive myself. And not just because of the billions of lives across the universe that benefited from them.

No. There was one person in particular whose life would be upended. And that was an outcome I refused to accept. Even if it meant doing the unthinkable.

"All right. I guess I'm getting married." I fanned through the papers. Maybe it wouldn't be so bad. *I can hire a wife, can't I?* I'd treat it like a business transaction. Set her up in a comfortable apartment somewhere and get a divorce before things got complicated. "What does the contract require, exactly?"

"Well, you have to remain married for at least a full Vorill year, living together. You must have a traditional Vorillion mating ceremony, held at Whitemist Estate." Durzo paused, the fingers of one hand drumming lightly on his armrest. "Tomorrow evening."

"Tomorrow evening!" I jerked out of my chair, toppling it over. "That's insane! How will I find a wife by then?"

Durzo winced but remained seated. "They have a willing bride lined up for you."

"They thought of everything, didn't they?" I threw up my hands, then leaned on the table. "Who is it?"

"Just a second." Durzo snagged the contract and leafed through it. "I ran a background check. She comes from a well-respected family. No criminal record. They even included a physical with the contract. She's in peak health and very bright, too."

"Her name?" I barked.

Durzo flipped faster, stopping on a page in the middle. "Kristla Convay"

A desperate sound filled the room. It took a second for me to realize it was slipping out of my lips.

"I take it you're acquainted."

I drew a steadying breath, praying I didn't puke. "You could say that."

"The good news is, you have options."

"Options..." That's right. The whole reason we were here was to discuss my options. I grabbed the sliver of hope the word planted in my mind and asked, "What are they?"

"The contract allows for a divorce after the year has passed, if certain conditions have been met."

Like marrying a practical stranger wasn't enough. What else did he want from me? "What conditions?"

"You must have an heir, either in the flesh or in the womb, and past the dangers of the first two trimesters."

My stomach twisted. It was as bad as I thought. "I can't believe this. An heir? I can't produce an heir in a year!"

"Ah," Durzo smiled; a big smug grin that I itched to slap off his face, "but there's a loophole you can use, should you choose to."

My heart pounded. "What loophole?"

Durzo leaned back in his chair, his smug smile stretching wide. "There's nothing to stop you from adopting an heir. By Vorillion law, adopted children are afforded the same rights, so long as the adoption is legal and binding. And there's no stipulation in the contract to prevent it."

"Yes." I laughed, noting the manic way my chuckles bounced off the walls, but doing nothing to still them. "That could work. So, I adopt an heir, spend a year living with,"—I choked down the urge to gag—"my wife, then I'm in the clear to divorce?"

"Almost. Both parties must agree to the divorce. But a man of your means should have little trouble arranging a suitable settlement."

I groaned, my stomach sinking. "Damn. He's got me."

"What do you mean?" Durzo waved a hand. "For the right price, anyone—"

"No, you don't understand. Kristla's not just anyone. Once she has her claws in me, she'll never let go."

Durzo frowned, then flicked a glance at his watch. "Oh no. We need to go. The meeting with your father and his solicitor is almost started."

"What? I can't go. Not until we find a solution. Please, Durzo. I can't marry Kristla."

Durzo stood, brushing his hands down his legs. "I'm sorry, sir, but I'm afraid you don't have much choice. If you don't marry someone at Whitemist Estate tomorrow, then the deal expires. Unless you have another bride waiting in the wings, or a betrothal I don't know about, I'm afraid you're stuck."

I followed him numbly, barely registering as we left the office and turned onto the city streets.

"Look on the bright side," Durzo added. "A year is a long time. You'll have plenty of time to think up something to get Kristla to agree to the divorce."

Oh, if only he knew. Kristla would never divorce me. She was cut from the same cloth as my mother. The perfectly bred daughter of a senator. The only thing worse for women like them than never marrying was a failed marriage.

"Where are we going?" I asked. My absorbing thoughts finally abated enough for me to notice we'd left the drab offices and high-rises of the financial district and turned down a narrow road.

Durzo stopped in front of a quaint brick building covered in Ivy, bearing a sign dubbing it the Mellow Drum Cantina. "Your mother requested a lunch date."

"My mother is here?" My voice came out so squeaky I had to clear my throat. "I thought I just had to sign and be on my way?"

"Well, considering what you'll be signing, I believe she thought it appropriate to introduce you to your wife."

My *wife*. This wasn't happening. I'd stepped into an alternate reality. I was not about to sign away my future, my freedom, hell, my very loins, to a debutante I haven't seen in over twenty years. One who made my life hell every chance she got when we were kids. Back then, Kristla had been the definition of a mean girl—always quick to lob a cruel word at anyone who stepped out of line or was slightly different—and I had a hard time believing her personality changed that drastically while we were apart.

The urge to turn and run smashed into me. *It's not too late. I still have a chance.*

But my uncle's hopeful face rose in my mind's eye. If I ran, his life would be ruined. How could I live with myself, knowing I could've saved everything he held dear, only to let it slip through my selfish fingers?

I couldn't.

"All right. Let's do this."

Durzo nodded curtly and pushed the door open.

The scent of garlic and fish lingered in the air of the modern restaurant. I guessed from how crowded the place was, the food had to be good. But right now, eating was the last thing on my mind.

At the front table, they sat waiting. They were so much older than I remembered, but it was impossible to miss the familiar scowl my father wore. That and the wary flick of my mother's weary black eyes, assessing me like always.

My parents sat with an old man I didn't recognize, his wrinkled hands clenched around a pack of papers.

And Kristla. She pinned me with a perfectly polished smile, her hands folded before her, her willowy frame sheathed in a demure dress that fit her like a glove. She was everything a man like me was supposed to want. Trained to know her place. Effortlessly beautiful. But when I looked into her eyes, it was as if my future was sucked into a black hole. I couldn't breathe. Couldn't escape.

Then, like a sign from the gods she held dear, Zenda appeared. "Nash. Hey, I was about to go hunting for you." She popped out of a side door, and I silently thanked the stars that fate had led me here, at this exact moment.

Zen was the answer!

My hand flashed out, grabbing her and hauling her close. "Play along, please." I whispered in her ear.

She nodded instantly, a blush staining her cheeks. "Okay. Sure. Whatever you need."

I spun us to the table and crossed the room, Zen tucked close to my side.

"Mom. Dad. This is Zenda. Meet my betrothed."

19

Defective

Zenda

I stared at Nash, frozen, trying desperately to comprehend what he'd roped me into. Did he just announce to a table-full of Vorill, including *his parents*, that we were betrothed?

What the hell is he thinking?

Apparently, he wanted me to speak, if the not too subtle nudge in my side was anything to judge by.

Luckily, when I froze, my smile had frozen, too. I couldn't say the same for the rest of the table. Everyone present sported bugged out eyes and slack jaws.

Another nudge poked my ribs. I needed to say something fast, before the mildly awkward introduction morphed into a creepy smiling mute girl who couldn't stop staring.

"Hell-lou!" *Holy mother of God, what just came out of my mouth?*

I blamed Nash. The idiot knew I wasn't good at faking shit. And springing it on me without warning? It was no wonder I couldn't string a simple greeting together. The least he could do was come to my rescue... but no. His damn eyes were sparkling, and he bit his lip, looking like he was barely holding back laughter.

He can choke on it for all I care.

There was nothing for it but to brazen forward.

I cleared my throat dramatically. "Pardon me. It's a pleasure to meet you."

Nash slid a chair out for me, and I sank down on it. While he strode to a nearby table to fetch another chair, the Vorill in the suit who'd arrived with Nash thrust out a hand. He clasped arms with the other suited fellow and began making introductions.

I scanned the cantina, fighting the urge to melt into the floor. If I could catch Arda's eye, she'd come save me. Hell, I'd even welcome Lux or Ren. But my bad luck struck again. Our tables were too far apart and a huge party was seated between us, blocking them completely.

The new chair scrapped the floor as Nash dragged it over and parked it next to mine, close enough for him to sling an arm around the back of my chair possessively. As all eyes turned to him, I studied the table.

The suits were clearly lawyers. That made sense, seeing as Nash only traveled to Vorillion to sign a contract. I never expected to be present at the signing, but here we were. Nash was going to have some serious explaining to do once this meeting was over.

Nash's dad was dressed more casually, in a freshly pressed, collared shirt. He looked like an older version of Nash—if he were slightly pudgy around the middle, and wearing a scowl. It was hard to keep my cool as I recalled Nash's story. But I doubted Nash pulled me over here to pick a fight, so I stayed silent.

The two women at the table sat side by side, wearing sharp dresses and modest makeup. They were as bald as the male Vorill, but the lack of hair didn't detract from their femininity. I pegged the older woman as Nash's mom, and despite everything he'd told me about her neglect, I found myself drawn to her more than anyone else present. It was probably the fact that she was the only one who looked pleased with how the meeting was going. Once she'd shook off her surprise, she hadn't stopped smiling.

The same couldn't be said of the woman beside her. If not for her pinched expression, her nose scrunched like she'd sniffed something rotten, she'd have been a stunner. As her black eyes narrowed, ping-ponging between Nash and me, my stomach roiled.

"This is a joke, right?" the stunner asked, her voice dripping with scorn. "You're betrothed to *her*?"

I frowned. Who was this haughty bitch and why was she at this meeting? I seriously hoped Nash wouldn't be stuck working with her at his family's company.

"This is no joke." Nash grabbed my hand and the slick brush of his bare skin against my fingers sent a shiver up my arm. "Right, love?" He squeezed gently, prompting me to nod emphatically.

In for a penny...

"Of course. Who would joke about being in love?" I chuckled lightly and threw in a wink for good measure.

"I can't believe this!" The stunner shoved back in her chair, glaring at Nash's parents. "After everything you've put me through, you're going to allow him to marry a human? All the interviews. The medical scans." She waved a hand in front of her eyes. "Just look at her! She's defective."

My jaw dropped. Did she seriously call me defective because of my glasses? Fury burst through my veins, burning so hot I'm surprised steam didn't blast out of my ears. Before I could scoop my mouth off the floor and tell that bitch to get lost, Nash beat me to the punch.

He slammed a fist on the table. "Get. Out." He breathed in deeply, tempering the venom in his voice. "You're no longer needed or welcome at this negotiation. And if I ever hear you speaking about my future wife again, you'll live to regret it."

I blinked repeatedly, my pulse pounding. Nash's normal reaction when things got tense was to crack a joke and extract himself from the situation. But he hadn't hesitated to stand up for me. Even if it this whole engagement was a farce, seeing that made me determined to put on the best damn show this cantina had ever seen.

"Buh-bye!" I cuddled against Nash's shoulder and flashed my brightest smile. The sour-faced bitch launched out of her chair and bolted for the door.

Nash's mom pushed her chair back calmly. "I'll have a word with Kristla. Don't worry, I'll remind her of the non-disclosure agreement she signed." As she circled the table, she paused beside me. "It's lovely to meet you, Zenda." A sweet smile lit her face, and a pit formed in my stomach. "Congratulations on your betrothal, son," she added, meeting Nash's gaze briefly before heading to the door.

That left us with the lawyers and Nash's father. He sat still as a statue, that scowl so firmly in place it might as well be painted on.

Nash's lawyer cleared his throat. "Well. Considering the betrothal, I'd like to request a short extension to have the names changed to reflect the new parties involved."

"Then you'll sign?" Nash's father finally spoke, directing the question to Nash.

Nash stiffened. "I will."

"Then have your extension." Nash's dad stood. "We'll meet for dinner at Whitemist." He shifted, eyeing his lawyer. "Arrange the travel clearances."

"We'll need clearances for our guests as well," Nash cut in smoothly. "Three of them."

"I'll take care of it," the older lawyer insisted.

"And I'll draft a new contract," Nash's lawyer said.

I smiled like an idiot as they murmured goodbyes and left. As soon as the door shut behind the last lawyer, I spun to Nash with a hard glare.

"What the hell was that? You owe me big time for that performance. Do you realize how hard it was for me to restrain myself? I was itching to tell your parents off the whole time. And I swear, I almost murdered that bitch when she made fun of my glasses."

Nash chuckled nervously. "I know. I'm sorry." His expression shifted, those big black eyes going all soft and pleading. "I'm going to need another favor, Zen."

I crossed my arms. "What favor?"

"Will you marry me tomorrow?"

Nash

I stared at Zen, waiting for her answer. The blank expression on her face wasn't exactly the reaction a guy hoped for after popping the question. But it wasn't like this was a normal proposal.

"You can't be serious," she spit out finally, her gaze darting across my face.

I shook my head. "Believe me, I wish I wasn't."

She glared at me. "What happened to you never getting married?" She crossed her arms. "And asking me, of all people. After what happened the day I left… you have some nerve." Zenda bristled in her chair, looking angry enough to slap someone.

Me. She definitely wants to slap me.

"Does it look like I'm happy about it?" I cringed inwardly, realizing that was probably the stupidest reply when Zenda's eyes bulged. I lowered my voice and leaned forward. "It's what he's asking so I can take over the company. That I marry and have an heir."

Zenda paled. "Excuse me?" She blinked repeatedly. "A *what*?"

I waved a hand. "Don't worry about the heir. Durzo found a loophole. He assured me I can adopt an heir and still fulfill the contract."

"Isn't that just peachy?"

"I don't know. It could be fun."

Zenda jerked, looking like she'd been the one slapped. "Fun? Really?"

"You've been wanting to go back to Subralia, haven't you? You can once we're married. Just think of it like business arrangement. We both get something we want out of it."

She shook her head and let out a humorless chuckle.

"It will only be for one year. Well, a Vorill year, which is about a year and two months in Earth days." I glanced at her and spotted her grinding her teeth. "Anyway. Once the year has passed, we'll be free to go our separate ways."

Zenda rubbed her temples. "A year." She stared at me directly. "You know I love you, Nash, but do you hear yourself right now? You're asking me to give up an entire year of my life for this lie. What about my job? Did you even consider that?"

"I know it's a lot. I wish I had another choice, but I don't." I reached across the table and grabbed her hand. "Zen. Please."

She met my gaze. I stared at her, focusing all my energy into pleading with my eyes.

"No." She tugged her hand free. "I can't."

"Don't say that. Zen. I need you."

"Find someone else."

"There is no one else. If I don't marry someone at Whitemist Estate tomorrow, then the contract will be broken."

"Then let it be broken." Zenda crossed her arms. "You're happy on Earth, aren't you? Why go through with this charade?"

I sighed. "For my uncle. If I don't gain control, his life will be ruined."

"How?" Zen's brow creased.

"Remember those charities my grandfather set up?"

She nodded.

"Well, did you know Subralia is almost entirely funded by grant money from an anonymous donor?"

Zenda gasped. "No..."

"'Fraid so."

From the way her eyes widened, I knew I had her. It seemed the one thing that would sway my friend was losing the place she grew up in and longed to return to.

"So you're telling me," Zenda fiddled with her glasses, "if we don't get married tomorrow, Subralia loses its funding."

"All the research will stop. Hundreds of people will lose their jobs. Maybe they'll scrape together enough funds to keep the lights on, but it won't be the same." I shook my head sadly and my stomach clenched. "Uncle Prim will be devastated."

"Stop." Zenda pressed her hands into her temples. "Fine. I'll do it. But I need something from you, too."

My heart lifted. "Anything."

"First, I need to make sure Arda's okay with me taking a year-long sabbatical." She pinned me with a hard glare. "And you have to help her find what she's looking for here on Vorillion."

"Agreed." I still wasn't sure exactly what Arda was hunting for on my home planet, but if it got Zen to agree to the marriage, then I'd find it. After the wedding, I'd have the funds to move mountains.

Like the conversation had summoned them, Arda, Lux, and Ren appeared from the back of the cantina.

"Hey." Arda stopped at our table and leaned against one of the empty chairs. "There you are Zen. We were just coming to look for you."

I cleared my throat. "I have good news. I arranged that clearance you were looking for, Lux. Only you three will have to add another stop to your sightseeing tour."

Zenda cringed and buried her head in her hands.

"Where?" Lux asked.

"How do you guys feel about attending a wedding?"

A bright smile spread across Arda's face. "A Vorillion wedding? Sign me up. Whose party are we crashing?"

I slung my arm around the back of Zen's chair, tugging her close. "Mine and Zen's."

Arda laughed, clearly thinking the announcement was a joke. Lux's silver gaze darted between us, his frown deepening.

Only Ren seemed unsurprised. She quirked a crooked grin and slapped Zen's shoulder. "What did I tell you? I knew he was going to pull his head out of his ass. Congratulations, you two!"

I ignored the pained groan spilling out of my betrothed and answered with a grin. "Thank you, Ren." Not sure what she was talking about, but I wasn't about to complain. Even if that statement made me extremely curious to learn what exactly Zenda and Ren had been

saying about me. "The wedding's tomorrow. Let's talk travel arrange-
ments."

20

Appearances

Nash

I stepped out of the transport onto the Whitemist Estate grounds. The family manor looked exactly the same as I remembered. The manicured lawn spread out, complete with all the flamboyant statues and topiaries one would expect from a family in *our station*.

Zenda and her friends *oohed* and *ahhed* as we walked down the winding path to the front door.

Me? I wasn't so easily impressed. This was just another reminder that all my father cared about was appearances. It seemed the years hadn't changed that in the slightest. So, it didn't surprise me to find my lawyer waiting in the foyer after Bosegs, my father's valet, ushered inside us.

"I have the updated papers ready for you to sign," Durzo announced.

I sighed. I hated to leave Zenda's friends immediately upon our arrival, but it seemed there was little help for it. "Bosegs, can you show my companions into the music room and arrange for some refreshments?" I smiled apologetically. "This shouldn't take long."

Arda, Lux, and Ren followed Bosegs down the hall. I snagged Zenda's hand when she tried to leave with them.

"You need to sign, too," I whispered in her ear.

Zenda shivered. Or was that a shudder? I shook off the question and tugged her with me.

"Follow me." I waved a hand. "Let's get this over with."

I led them into the sitting room, hiding my surprise at the bright green wallpaper that greeted me. Not everything was exactly the same. The pang in my chest hit me out of nowhere. When had they redecorated? I buried the feeling and sat on a fluffy brown couch, pulling Zenda to sit beside me.

We spent the next fifteen minutes signing here and initialing there while Durzo patiently explained the contract, line by line.

"That's it." Durzo stood, holding out his hand. "If you need anything else, don't hesitate to contact me."

"Thank you." I walked him to the door.

The door closed firmly behind him with a *click*. I returned to Zenda's side and found her staring at the papers, a stunned look on her face.

"Are you okay?"

She glanced up, then went right back to staring. "Yeah. It just didn't feel real until now."

I sank back down beside her. "I get it. For what it's worth, I'm really sorry I had to drag you into this mess. If I had any other choice—"

"It's all right." Zenda shook her head and plastered on a smile. "I'm glad you chose me to be fake married to. If you'd picked that snooty bitch instead, I'd need to disown you as a friend."

"That right?" I chuckled.

"Yep." Zenda stood. "Now, let's go get some of those refreshments. I'm starving."

We left to join the others in the music room. Laughter spilled out into the hall, easing some of the discomfort in my stomach. At least they were enjoying themselves, even without me playing host.

I held open the door for Zen, and my gut clenched. "Mom?"

"There you are, dear!" She sat on the piano bench, all smiles, an enormous book open on her lap and Zenda's friends crowded around her, peering at the pages. "I was just showing your friends some of your baby pictures."

Seriously? I blinked repeatedly, sliding the door closed behind me.

"Ooo, I have to see those!" Zenda darted across the room, and Mom slid over, patting the bench beside her.

I frowned. What was this? Just Mom putting on the act of doting mother? Then why did the smile she sent Zenda look genuine?

My stomach flip-flopped, and even though the platter of food on the side table smelled amazing, I knew I wouldn't be able to choke down a bite. I headed for it anyway and grabbed a plate, piling it high with everything I thought Zenda would like.

I handed it to her a moment later, groaning when I spotted the picture my mom was showing off. "Bath pictures? Are you kidding me?"

Mom grinned, smoothing the page. "What? I covered your little bits with a washcloth. There's nothing to be ashamed of."

"Little bits." Arda chuckled under her breath.

"Look at how cute you were, Nash!" Zenda cooed, her eyes all warm and gooey. "I wish I was there so I could pinch your cheeks." She shoveled a bite of Vorillion stew into her mouth and moaned. "Wow, this is good!" She turned to Mom. "My compliments to the chef. Is this going to be on the wedding menu?"

I buried a chuckle. There was no way Father would ever agree to serving such a simple dish for a family wedding.

Mom patted Zenda's knee. "If you want it to be, then I'll make sure it is."

"Thank you." Zenda beamed, popping another forkful into her mouth.

I'll believe it when I see it.

"So, tell us about the wedding," Zenda said. "What should we expect?"

Mom cleared her throat. "It will be a beautiful ceremony. Everything is set up, so you two just need to be there. I'll take care of greeting the guests, so you both have ample time to dress and prepare."

Zenda set down her fork. "I didn't realize there'd be guests. Will there be many?"

"Of course. No one will want to miss a wedding at Whitemist. But don't worry about that." Mom patted Zenda's knee again. "I have it all taken care of."

Zenda's left eye twitched. I sensed the panic washing over her. "Well," I interrupted. "Now that everyone's had a bite, how about showing us our rooms?"

Mom snapped the photo album closed. "I'm sure you're all eager for a short rest after the long drive from the capital. Follow me. We'll talk more over dinner. I'll have the chef prepare more dishes for you to sample, Zenda."

"That sounds wonderful. Thank you." Zenda handed me her half empty plate and followed at my mother's side.

I sighed as I set down her plate. At least they weren't at each other's throats. Honestly, I couldn't ask for more than my mother and bride-to-be getting along swimmingly.

If only I could trust it. But of course, I couldn't. Even if my mother's act wasn't fake, Zenda's and mine was. If only that weren't the case. Because with each moment that passed, I regretted it more and more.

The huge guest list was just another reminder that appearances were all that mattered to my parents. They didn't care about my happiness. And here I was, dragging my friend into this flawed family.

I should've never made Zenda agree to this marriage.

Zenda

I trailed Nash's mom up the stairs of the most opulent mansion I'd ever set foot in. Sure, Nash told me he was well off, but honestly, this house was a little insane. The place had literal wings spreading off the central staircase, topped with an enormous sparkling chandelier. Don't even get me started on the immaculate grounds. Or the music room. Who the hell has a whole damn music room? Whitemist Estate was something else. It was like I'd died and woken up inside the pages of one of my historical romances.

I tore my eyes off the pretty decoration dangling overhead and returned my attention to my soon to be mother-in-law. "Your home is incredible. Thank you so much for letting us stay here. I know it must be hectic to prepare rooms on top of all the wedding preparations."

"It's no trouble at all." She smiled, her big black eyes full of warmth. "You're family now, and always welcome here at Whitemist."

My stomach twinged. I didn't want to minimize the pain she'd inflicted on Nash in the past, but it was a struggle not to like his mother. She'd been nothing but kind to me and my friends since we'd arrived. It was hard to equate the indifferent mother who had abandoned her only son with the warm, welcoming woman beside me.

While here I am, lying to her face.

Nash's mom turned at the top of the stair, leading us down a long, carpeted hall. Enormous canvases of alien landscapes hung on the walls, bordered with tasteful crown molding. "This wing will be entirely yours while you're here." She stopped at the first door, her hand resting on the doorknob. "Nash. We kept your room—"

"A guest room will suit me fine." Nash stopped at my elbow.

I bit back a scowl when his mother's face fell. But she plastered a new smile on a second later. "Very well." She strolled down the hall, opening doors along the way. She stopped once she'd opened four of them. "You can have your pick of the rooms on this wing. These have been aired out already, but if you'd prefer another, just let me know which."

"Thank you..." Arda trailed off. "Sorry, Mom, I don't think you told us your name yet."

"Mom is perfectly fine." She chuckled sweetly. "Or you may call me Siara as well."

"Siara. Thank you." Arda ducked into one of the rooms. "Wow! Dibs," she shouted from the doorway. "Lux, get in here!"

The big, golden-haired alien shook his head, but followed Arda inside. Ren shuffled down the hall and peeked into the room beside it, her eyes widening before she cautiously stepped inside.

"I'll leave you to get settled." Siara smiled again and turned on her heel.

"See you at dinner!" I called after her.

She peeked over her shoulder, a twinkle in her eye. "I'm looking forward to it."

Nash rolled his eyes and grabbed my elbow, hauling me through one of the open doors.

"What?" I planted my feet just inside the door, crossing my arms. "Did you want me to be a bitch?"

My jaw nearly dropped when I flicked my gaze away from Nash and got my first look at the room. The color scheme was full of blues and ivories, with subtle silver accents. A massive four-poster bed dominated one wall, and there was still enough space left for a loveseat and rocking chair in one corner, and a huge antique desk in another. The windows were thrown open, revealing a balcony overlooking a gorgeous lake, with—was that a fountain?

Nash snapped his fingers in front of my face. "Zenda." He smiled crookedly. "Did you just hear a word I said?"

"You were talking?" I shook my head. "Sorry. I was blinded by all,"—I waved a hand around me—"this. Gods, Nash. What does your family company do, print money?"

"I know it's a lot." Nash frowned and grabbed my shoulders. "Look, Zen. I know I begged you to do this, but if you really don't want this, I'll figure something else out."

My gaze darted across his face. It was sweet he was giving me an out, but he really didn't expect me to leave him in the lurch, did he?

"What, and miss out on the butlers serving me hand and foot?" I let a wicked grin spread. "I bet your butlers have butlers, don't they?"

Nash squeezed my arms and tingles shot up my spine. "I'm serious, Zen."

The humor drained out of me when I heard the slight tremble in his voice. "It's all right. *I'm* all right, I promise. It's only a year. We'll make it work." I smoothed my hands over his chest, frowning when I felt the frantic beating of his heart against my palms. "I'm doing this for Subralia. You're right. We need to save it. Let's make sure your idiot cousin doesn't get his greedy hands on it, okay?"

Nash sighed. "Okay." The thudding beneath my hands slowed, and the panicked urgency washed away from his eyes.

I pulled out of his arms and turned away, sucking in a calming breath before I blurted out the real reason I was doing this. Yeah, Subralia deserved to survive. And all the other charities Nash's grandfather's grant funded across the universe did, too. But if I were being perfectly honest with myself, neither of those things swayed me.

When I dug deep down into the pits of my soul, there was only one thing that made me say yes. Nash. I wanted more of what I felt the night I fell asleep in his arms. The chance to play house, not for a single night, but an entire year. Because the sad truth was, even though it wasn't real, it was the best I was ever going to get.

Let's just hope Nash doesn't realize how pathetic his stand-in wife is.

Zenda

Knock knock.

Who could that be? Nash left me to go unpack his things about an hour ago. I'd whiled away the minutes since then staring out the balcony window, too lost in thought to even touch my suitcase. I strode to the door. When I slid it open, my pulse went haywire.

Nash stood on the other side, looking good enough to lick in the casual shorts and polo shirt he'd changed into. A wry grin curved his lips as he caught me staring. "You busy?"

I nearly shook my head before thinking better of it. *No need to let on to exactly how pathetic I am.* "Actually, I was just about to check in with Arda. You should come."

Nash shoved his hands into his pockets. "You sure? I can find something else to do."

"Nope. No way." I grabbed his elbow, pulling him down the hall. "You owe me now, remember? It's time to collect." I waggled my brows and stopped in front of the door to the room Arda and Lux claimed, then knocked firmly on it.

"Come in," Arda called. Arda, Lux, and Ren stared at the door as we entered, the three of them—oddly—lined up in a row. "Oh. It's just you." Arda cocked out a hip. "Where've you been hiding?"

"Just getting settled," Nash offered.

The room was decorated similarly to mine, only in pale pink and burgundy with a touch of gold.

Lux and Ren shifted, and I spotted a flash of wood and paper behind them. "What ya' got there?"

"It's the map." Arda stepped away, revealing the wrinkled paper spread across another antique desk. "We were hiding it; in case it wasn't you guys knocking."

"Great. Just what I brought him for." I grabbed Nash's elbow again, pulling him toward the desk. "C'mere. Take a look at this."

Nash frowned at the paper. "Lux showed me once before." He traced his finger across the page, landing on the building someone had circled. "We're a lot closer now than when we were in the capital."

"Yeah?" Arda grinned. "That's good, right? Should be easy to sneak away and have a look-see."

"I didn't say that," Nash replied.

"What do you mean?" Lux asked, his voice all gravel.

Nash swiveled to face him and leaned against the desk. "For one, considering off-worlders are basically unheard of in these parts, you're bound to draw suspicion."

"Even with the travel clearance?" Ren asked.

"Yeah. Especially if you don't have a Vorill escorting you." Nash scratched his bald head. "I'll have to go with you. No way around it."

"So when do we go?" Arda asked.

Nash shrugged and turned back to the map. "Depends. What is this place exactly? The map doesn't say."

I grinned. Nash was being incredibly helpful so far. How helpful would he be when he learned the truth? "Would you believe it's a secret medical research facility?" I leaned close as his eyes bulged. "Because, it is."

"O-kay." I have to give him credit; Nash shook off his surprise quickly. "I'm guessing they don't have normal business hours."

Arda chuckled. "No surprise there." She walked to the bed and unzipped a suitcase laying on top of it. "I've done some digging. I couldn't get much. Not enough to know what's inside, but I managed to snap some shots of the exterior when we were in orbit." She offered Nash a folder.

He flipped it open, and I peeked inside. Even from afar, it was clear the place was falling apart. "Are we sure it's not abandoned?"

Nash squinted at the picture. "Wait. I know this place. The Old Foundry. Even back when I was a kid, no one had used it in ages. There was talk of tearing it down, but some folks had it declared a historical site." He shook his head. "That might make sneaking in a bit more complicated."

"Strange." Lux shot a look at Arda. "Makes me wonder if there's someone out there who didn't want the secrets inside destroyed."

Arda pursed her lips. "Maybe. Either way, we need to get inside. I can't rest easy until I know I did everything in my power to solve this mystery."

"Don't worry, Capt." Ren curved a hand through her short blonde curls. "We'll figure out something."

Nash nudged me with his elbow and lifted a brow. "Mystery, eh?"

Another knock pounded on the door. "Your presence is requested at dinner," a masculine voice spoke through the door.

"We'll be right there, Bosegs. Thank you," Nash replied. He lowered his voice and placed the file on the bed. "Guess you better fill me in later. We don't want to keep them waiting."

21

Dinner

Zenda

"Ugh, I don't think I can eat another bite." I dropped my fork, wincing as it clattered against the fine pottery. "Everything was delicious. Thank you for another wonderful meal." I wasn't just saying that to be polite, either. It was lucky Nash didn't need to stay here for good, or I wouldn't last the year without gaining a hundred pounds.

The dining room was as impressive as the spread. The long black table gleamed, polished so shiny the twinkling lights from another striking chandelier glittered across the surface. We perched around one end of the table, barely using a quarter of its surface.

"You're welcome, Zenda. I'm so pleased you enjoyed everything." Siara smiled at me for about the hundredth time since we'd met.

If only a bit of her happiness could transfer to Nash's father, then we'd be in business. I spared him a quick glance, spotting his scowl locked in place. If the man hadn't opened his mouth to eat, I'd have wondered if the damn thing was painted on.

Nash hadn't been much better. In fact, none of the men had done more than grunt and chew. If not for the women at the table, we'd all be eating in tense silence.

Arda folded her napkin in her lap. "So, Siara. Tell us more about the wedding. I've never attended a Vorill ceremony before. What can we expect?"

"Well, Nash and Zenda will perform the traditional Vorill mating ceremony, of course."

Panic clawed at my throat. "The what now?"

I speared Nash with a hard glare, mad enough to wring his neck. I was getting sick and tired of things being sprung on me out of nowhere. When exactly was he planning on telling me I had to put on a show?

"Don't worry, dear. It will be mostly Nash doing the performing." Siara patted my hand. "Here on Vorillion, males are expected to publicly woo their chosen mate. You'll just need to accept his hand when he gives it to you."

"Oh." My speeding pulse slowed. "That doesn't sound too bad." The whole *public* part I could do without, but who was I to deny their customs?

Nash at least had the sense to blush before clearing his throat. "I promise, I'll be quick." He aimed a grin at me, and the bastard was so devilishly handsome I forgot my plans to strangle him.

"Don't rush on my account, *love*. You can woo me anytime." I smiled back at him, adding an extra dose of syrupy sweetness to my voice.

Ren snorted, then tried to cover the noise with a cough that I doubt anyone bought.

"What happens after the ceremony?" Arda leaned back in her chair. "On Earth, they usually hold a reception after, with dancing, and cake."

"I would kill for a slice of cake right now." Ren glanced at her empty plate forlornly.

I shook my head. Ren was one of those lucky women who could eat a horse and still zip up her skin suit in the morning. Not me. If I even looked at a slice of cake, I might need to go up a pants size.

"Our customs are not so different. There will be a grand feast to follow," Siara explained. "After the meal, we'll confine the lovers to their suite, but the festivities will continue until morning."

I blinked, and my hand froze on its way to grab my drink. "Confine the lovers? What do you mean, confine?" I forced my hand to move, and lifted the glass of crisp wine to my lips, taking a sip.

"It's tradition. The wedded pair are allowed to retire together early." Siara stared at me like I had two heads. "Human couples mate on their wedding night, don't they?"

Holy shit! Is she seriously asking if I intend to bang her son tomorrow night?

It's a miracle I didn't spray wine all over the table when I heard that question. "Yes. They do." I choked out. "Only, they don't typically do it while under lock and key."

"Don't worry, *love*." Nash smirked. "They'll be no shortage of wooing then, too."

I bit back a groan. The cheeky bastard. Heat rushed up my neck. I had to get out of here before I said something stupid.

"Well." I forced out a yawn. "It's getting late. I'm sure tomorrow will be busy, busy."

"Yes, of course. You'll be needing plenty of rest." Siara pushed her chair back. "Breakfast will be served here buffet style, tomorrow morning. Pop on down whenever you'd like. Goodnight, everyone."

Soon, we all piled up the stairs and down the hall to our wing. Arda and Lux ducked into their room quickly. I paused outside my door, "I guess this is goodnight—"

"Not so fast." Ren slid past me, turning the knob and shoving her way inside. "I came up with the perfect plan to get into that research facility."

"Really? That's great." I frowned as I followed her inside. "But shouldn't you be telling Arda, not me?"

"Nope." Ren leaned sideways and jerked her hands at Nash, waving him in. "I'm going to need both of you for this to work."

Nash hesitated in the hall, his gaze finding mine. I sighed, nodding for him to enter.

Did I want to get involved in what was no doubt bound to be something either incredibly stupid or insanely dangerous? Not really. But I didn't want to go to bed either.

I cracked a smile as the door shut with a *click*. "All right, Ren. What's the plan?"

Nash

I tossed and turned in the guest bed. No matter which way I rolled, I couldn't fall asleep. Too many questions weighed on my mind.

That or the worst case of pre-wedding jitters in the universe.

To be fair, Ren hadn't exactly helped with her little *project* for tomorrow night. What she'd had me and Zenda do definitely wasn't soothing before bed. Though, I had to admit, her plan was pretty genius.

I threw off the blankets with a sigh. Stuffing my feet into slippers, I left the room and trailed down to the kitchen. Maybe a warm drink would help calm my mind... and a few other wayward organs.

The house lay dark and empty. The fine furnishings sat there looking picture perfect, yet lonely, with no one there to enjoy them. It reminded me of my childhood. I always had to look the part, stand still, toe the line. But what had that obedience gotten me? A deserted house with parents who couldn't be bothered to notice me most of the time.

I balled my hands into fists at my side. With the wedding looming, I hadn't given much thought to the second part of my father's request. But now...

This life will never be mine. I refuse to treat my heir like an accessory.

As the vow entrenched itself in my heart, my steps felt lighter. Maybe this wasn't—

I froze in the doorway. She sat at the kitchen island, cradling a mug and staring out the window blankly. "Mom. I didn't know anyone else was awake."

At the sound of my voice, her demeanor brightened. "You're no bother, dear. Come. Sit. Would you like a warm cup of melo to help fall asleep, too?"

"Sure." I approached warily and slid atop a stool. "Thanks."

Mom pulled out a mug and spooned a bit of powder from a tin into my cup. I licked my lips as she added hot water from the kettle and the distinctive aroma filled the air. Melo was a Vorill staple, one I'd not had in years.

"Here you go." She slid the cup in front of me.

I lifted it to my lips, heedless of the steaming temperature, and sucked in a tiny sip with a sigh. Melo tasted a bit like tea, only fruiter, and with none of the caffeine. I took a longer pull, wincing at the heat.

"I see some things haven't changed." Mom chuckled. "You never could stand waiting for it to cool off."

I set the mug down a bit too roughly. A loud *clunk* reverberated in the quiet room.

"Anashclitis," she began, until I glared at her. "Nash, dear." She smiled and blinked quickly, banishing the tears gathered in the corner of her eyes. "I missed you so much. I'm so glad you've come home."

"Don't get used to it. I'm returning to Earth as soon as this farce of a wedding is over."

Her face crumpled. "Farce? But Zenda's so lovely. I thought…"

I shook my head, realizing what I'd almost admitted to. "I'm not talking about Zen. This is about father's demands forcing my hand. I shouldn't be rushing to get married at Whitemist. I shouldn't be here at all."

"Don't say that." Mom's voice trembled. "This is your home."

Eyes narrowing, I bit out, "No. Subralia is my home. The best decision you ever made was sending me away."

My stomach wobbled. This conversation was morphing into an argument. Wasn't that just the ultimate way to top this wretched day? I chugged the rest of my melo, ignoring the burn in my throat. "Goodnight."

I stood, but Mom stilled me with a hand on my sleeve. "You get that from me, you know."

"What?" I turned back, staring at her.

"Avoidance." Mom ducked her head before lifting her gaze to meet mine. "My therapist helped me see that my coping mechanism isn't healthy. Don't make my mistake, son. Fight for what you love." She dropped my sleeve and folded her hands in her lap.

I nodded curtly and walked away.

Should I have proved her wrong and stayed? Maybe. But even if leaving proved her right, I couldn't bear to stand there another minute.

Fight for what you love. I scoffed as my slippers scraped across the stairs. Please. Mother grew up the sheltered child of a politician, then moved onto an arranged marriage. She never fought for a single thing in her life.

Maybe I am just like her.

If that was true, then how could I go through with this wedding? I just vowed not to subject my child to this life, but I was willing to put Zen through it?

No. It wasn't the same. Besides, this was only for a year. I could do better, be better, for a year, couldn't I?

Zenda was already different. Special. I just had to make sure I didn't let my cowardly nature come into play where she was concerned. If she wanted to talk, no matter what it was about, I wouldn't avoid her.

Still, as I slipped back into bed, one thought kept flitting through my mind, keeping me awake despite the melo warming my belly.

I rescued Zenda from one trapped marriage only to trap her myself. What is wrong with me?

22

Open Minds

Zenda

I emerged from the shower, wrapped in a big fluffy robe. I plunked into a seat in front of the antique vanity Siara sent to my room after breakfast and slid on my glasses.

It was morning on my wedding day. I stared at my reflection in the mirror.

My *wedding* day. I still couldn't get over how bizarre that sounded. "Am I really getting married today?"

Arda chuckled. "Fucking weird, isn't it? Lux keeps hinting he wants the whole shebang when we visit Pheria, so I get it." She trailed her hand across the rack of clothes taking up half the free space in my room—another gift from Siara. Arda and Ren still hadn't selected anything, but with a few hours left until the wedding, they weren't in a rush to change out of their skinsuits.

"Better you two than me." Ren sat on the bed, picking at her nails. "But hey, at least it's only for a year."

I nodded blankly. I'd shared the whole truth with my shipmates before we boarded the transport for Whitemist. They knew the pathetic sham for what it was. I could slap on a borrowed dress and take Nash's hand in that ceremony, but that didn't make it *real*, did it?

My wild eyes found Arda's in the mirror's reflection. "You're sure you're okay with me taking a sabbatical?"

Her easy grin calmed a little of the roiling in my gut. "My answer hasn't changed. And when you're ready to come back, there'll be a spot waiting for you on the Verne."

I blew out a shaky breath as an idea popped into my head. "You know, I might know someone who can replace me." I swiveled in the chair, meeting her gaze directly. "How would you feel about taking on someone fresh out of school as your medical officer?"

"I'm not opposed." She shrugged. "Assuming they're qualified."

"She's extremely qualified. Over qualified even."

Arda's grin widened. "Fancy. All right. Have her contact me, if she's interested." She waggled her brows. "After the honeymoon, of course."

I scoffed and rolled my eyes. "Right."

"Hey, you never know." Arda sank down beside Ren. "Maybe this whole arranged marriage thing will turn into something more. Seems like you two are in each other's pockets already."

"And then there's all the eye fucking," Ren chimed in.

"Is not," I replied sourly with all the wit of a five-year-old.

"Is too," she shot right back.

"Puh-lease." Arda narrowed her eyes at my face. "Do you need new glasses, Zen? Because you'd have to be blind to miss the eye fucking."

I scowled.

Ren erupted into giggles. "Told you so."

Arda's expression softened. "Look, I'm not telling you to jump his bones if you're not interested. But if you are interested…" she let the words trail off, and winked.

"Just have an open mind," Ren added. "See where things go."

I sighed. They made it sound so easy. But they didn't know Nash like I did. They weren't there two decades ago when he tore out my heart and stomped on it. I couldn't jump his bones. What if he rejected me again on our wedding night? Then I'd be stuck living with him for a year, knowing exactly how much the thought of touching me repulsed him.

A knock rattled the door, pulling me from my dark thoughts. "Come in," I called.

Siara poked her head inside, her big black eyes blinking owlishly. "Are you sure you don't mind? I don't want to intrude."

"You're not intruding." I waved her in, flashing my brightest smile.

"Ooo, I'm glad you're here!" Arda popped up from the bed and strode to the clothes rack. "We need advice on what to pick." Her brow furrowed as she pushed the garments apart. "It looks like there's two distinct styles here."

"You're right." Siara pulled the door closed and hurried to the rack. "You'll want one of these." She shuffled through the silky dresses on the back half of the rack before sliding to the other side. "These cozzies are for Zenda, for during the ceremony." She glanced at me with a smile. "You'll want to choose a dress as well, to change into after."

I stood, wandering over for a closer look at the peculiar garments. They reminded me of skinsuits, but with long skirts attached to hide the pants, only the fabric was different. If I didn't know any better… "Are those wetsuits?"

My eyes widened. *What the hell kind of ceremony are we having?*

Siara chuckled. "You're quite right. This is for the performance. Traditional wooing always takes place underwater."

"O-kay." I gulped, my pulse racing at light speed. Nash said he'd be quick, but I couldn't help freaking out inside. "Exactly how long does this wooing last?"

"Don't worry, dear." She slid a small device out of the pocket of her yellow sundress. "That's one reason I came to see you. This is a breather. I suspected you'd be more comfortable with one."

I think what she meant to say was alive and not drowned, but I didn't bother to correct her. "Thanks." I took the horseshoe-shaped device and turned it over in my fingers. "How does it work?"

Ren perked up. "I've heard of those. You just shove it up your nostrils, right?"

"How romantic," Arda teased.

I blatantly ignored her quip and turned to Siara. "What was the other reason you wanted to see me?" I held my breath, praying she wasn't about to detonate another missile on my head. *Who the hell gets married underwater with plastic shoved up their nose?* I eyed her pocket suspiciously. "Please tell me you don't have anything else that needs inserting hiding in there."

Siara's eyes bulged.

I cringed. My stupid mouth.

But after half a second, Siara laughed uproariously. I joined in, drawn in by the pure joy of her laughter, so different from the restrained chuckles she'd graced us with so far. Ren and Arda couldn't help giggling, too.

Siara wiped her eyes. "No." She chuckled once more, but then her expression turned serious. "I just wanted to tell you how happy I am that you're joining our family."

My chest twinged. "Oh. Thank you." I offered a pinched smile.

She stepped closer, meeting my eyes. "I know Nash and I haven't been exactly close." She sighed. "He doesn't know this, but I've always watched him from afar, so I know you two have been friends for ages." Saira smiled radiantly. "I'm glad he chose someone to marry who's been part of his life when I couldn't. Someone who loves him, and truly gets him." She squeezed my shoulder gently. "I'm glad he chose you, Zenda."

Tears pooled in my eyes. With the way Siara's smile softened and she tugged me into a hug, I'm sure she thought they were tears of joy. They weren't.

My heart twisted. *If only this were real.*

Nash

I can't believe I'm about to get married.

There'd been a swarm of activity out back all morning. The event planner arrived just after dawn with a crew of workers. They'd transformed Whitemist's grounds into an elaborate wedding venue worthy of a fairytale. Twinkling lights and flowers dotted rows of seats facing the lake. Hours later, I stood in the shadows on the guest room's balcony, watching the backyard fill with guests.

Vorill streamed in by the dozens, decked out in their finest clothes. Servers balancing trays of appetizers wove through the crowd of guests, who chatted and laughed at each other's stupid jokes. Some I could vaguely place, but after nearly two decades on Earth, most were strangers.

A pair of guests stopped below me, and their conversation drifted to my ears.

"Lovely setup, wouldn't you say?" a man asked.

"I see Laytun has spared no expense," the woman replied. "But I suppose that's to be expected when his wayward son is marrying the Convay girl."

"Haven't you heard? That was just a rumor."

"No!" The woman sucked in an aghast breath. "Then who is he marrying?"

The man leaned in, a smug grin on his face. "A human."

"Oh my. Well, I guess it makes sense. That's what happens when you send your children to alien worlds." She snickered cruelly. "At least he brought home a female. Not like—"

"Shh." The man cut her off, whipping his head around as if confirming they were out of earshot of the rest of the guests. "Talk about rumors! You know that's never been confirmed."

"Yes, you're quite right. It's poor taste to disparage Laytun's reputation on his son's wedding day." The woman lifted a glass to her lips, hiding her sour expression. "Ah, I see my business partner. Do excuse me."

I frowned as the pair separated and drifted away from me. My gaze flicked across the crowd.

It was easy to forget how things were on my home planet after such a long absence. Especially when I'd spent so long living somewhere where love was celebrated in all its forms. Had this wedding been held on Earth, there would surely be a few same-sex couples in attendance. Here, all the pairs holding hands, or strolling with their arms linked, were clearly heterosexual. A sick feeling spread through my gut.

Knock, knock.

I left the balcony, strolled across the room, and opened the door. "Lux. Come in."

Lux walked inside and sat on the couch. Then he stared at me without saying anything.

I shut the door. "To what do I owe the pleasure of this visit?" I plunked into the seat across from him.

He cleared his throat, and if not for the stone-like expression on his face, I'd have guessed he was nervous. "Arda said your ceremony will be similar to a Terran wedding."

I sighed. "Some of it is, I suppose."

"I've researched Terran weddings. The grooms usually have someone stand with them."

A slow smile spread across my face. "Lux, did you just offer to be my best man?"

Lux grunted. He nodded.

"I'm touched." I rubbed the corner of my eye and threw in a fake sniffle for good measure. "You *really* like me."

Lux pushed to his feet. "Forget it."

I popped up. "Nope, you can't take it back now, bestie." I slapped him on his rock-hard shoulder, grinning like an idiot. "You're off the hook for the ceremony, though. We don't do the whole best man and maid of honor thing."

"Good." He strode across the room.

"Wait, where are you going?" I followed him to the door.

"To find a seat outside." He paused with a hand on the handle. "You coming?"

I wonder who sent him to make sure I wasn't planning to become a runaway groom? Funny how the idea hadn't crossed my mind until that second. Strangely enough, even though getting married was the last thing I ever saw myself doing, a sense of calm enveloped me. *Maybe because it's not real?*

"Yeah, I'm coming. Will you hold my hand on the way down?"

Lux chuckled, eyeing my outstretched hand like he wanted to slap it away. "Your sense of humor is twisted." He shoved his hands in his pockets.

"That's why you like me, right?"

Lux narrowed his eyes. Together, we made our way down the stairs, through the house, and out onto the lawn.

Most of the guests had taken their seats, but conversation still buzzed in the air as they stared toward the lake. I followed the path of their gazes, and my heart stalled. Zenda's sultry laughter sliced through my chest. She smiled at my mother, and turned, meeting my gaze across the crowded lawn.

She'd chosen a dark pink cozzie for the ceremony. Sure, the dress was one step away from a wetsuit, but she looked stunning in it. And her hair. She'd left her hair to cascade down across her shoulders. My fingers clenched on empty air as a light flush spread across her cheeks.

At that moment, I knew I had it all wrong. It wasn't that this wasn't real filling me with comfort. It was Zen.

I smiled at her just as a big hand clamped on my shoulder.

"Go get your girl, Nash."

My new bestie could use a few pointers in eloquence. But luckily, I didn't need a pep talk to get me moving.

"Thanks. I think I will."

23

Are You Ready

Zenda

Nash stretched out a hand. "Are you ready?"

What a loaded question. My pulse raced, and I could feel all the eyes resting heavily on me. *Why the hell did they invite so many Vorill?* It made me itchy knowing this crowd of strangers would dissect any wrong move I made.

Still, I'd signed up to help my friend. Not just Nash, but Arda, too. And after today, we were leaving this planet for good. Any missteps I made would be long forgotten by the time we arrived in Subralia. Or at least, only remembered by these strangers I would never see again.

Time to get the show on the road.

I stared at Nash's hand for a heartbeat before slipping my fingers into his. Maybe if I concentrated on him, I could forget the spectators.

That certainly wouldn't be a hardship. He wore a fancy wetsuit like mine, only without the skirt attachment. The midnight-blue fabric molded to his muscles in the most delicious way. I bit back a sigh as he shifted to lead me to the lake and I got a close-up view of his ass.

Cool it, Zen. I tore my gaze up before I started drooling. Or worse, my face turned pink enough to match the outfit I'd chosen.

We stopped on the lake's edge next to a Vorill decked out in a long, rainbow striped robe. "Anashclitis. It's so nice to see you again."

Nash coughed. "Please, Parson Renic. Call me Nash." He gripped the Vorill's forearm. "This is Zenda."

"Zenda." Renic smiled kindly. "It's lovely to meet you."

I reached out and squeezed Parson Renic's arm. It had been a bit of an adjustment remembering to clasp everyone's arms instead of their hands. Vorill didn't shake either. They gave a gentle squeeze instead. They tended to hold on a hair longer than I was used to with Terran handshakes, and the experience was altogether wetter, due to their uniquely moist skin. Still, I resisted the urge to wipe the slickness on my clothes once Renic let go of my arm.

Not like I'm about to stay dry much longer. I glanced at the lake, anxiety pinging through my stomach like a meteor shower.

"Are you both ready?" the parson asked.

"Almost." Nash's palm landed on the small of my back. "Do you need a breather?"

I dug into my pocket. "I have one. Your mother gave it to me."

"Good. Put it in."

I cringed inwardly, but stuck the device into my nose. After a second where it felt ridiculously awkward, the breather inflated, suctioning into my nose perfectly. I took an exploratory breath, pleased to find air flooding into my lungs like normal.

"We're ready," Nash announced.

Parson Renic's grin widened. He lifted his hands, palms outstretched toward the sky. It must've been some silent signal the guests had been waiting for. A hush fell over the group instantly.

"Nash. Zenda." Renic's voice boomed. "Have you entered this agreement to share your lives willingly, and with love in your hearts?"

"Yes," Nash replied. "I have."

Well, at least I don't have to lie when I answer.

I gulped. "Yes, I have."

"Then let the ceremony commence." As Parson Renic's hands slowly fell, my eyes widened. The water rose out of the ground, forming into a sphere that hovered over the lake bed.

Fascinating. How was that possible?

I peeked over Parson Renic's shoulder, and spotted two Vorill operating big, metallic devices on opposite sides of the lakeside. I had no clue what exactly the big boxes were, but I had no doubt they were the source of the sphere. Mystery solved.

Nash cleared his throat, and I spun to face him. He took a step away from me and held out his hand.

This was it. Siara had said all I needed to do was take his hand. But then what? Fear crawled up my spine. Was he going to pull me into that hovering sphere? How would we even stay inside without falling out and smashing into the lake bottom?

Excited murmurs erupted behind me as I stood there, hesitating.

You can do this. I brushed aside my doubt and grabbed Nash's hand.

Nash's smile brightened. With his free hand, he slipped my glasses off my face and handed them to Parson Renic. Then he pulled me forward, and we stopped below the enormous water ball. Enough water remained in the lake that it splashed against my ankles. Still, I didn't see how—

"Don't worry." Nash squeezed my hand. "The grav-ball won't collapse. And we won't fall out. Just keep holding my hand, okay?"

Of course, Nash knew what to say to calm me. I wasn't entirely sure what was about to happen, but I knew he'd keep me safe. "Okay." I squeezed back, clenching his fingers in a death-grip. "Let's do this."

"We need to jump in. Ready?"

"Ready," I echoed.

We jumped. The water sucked us in, the grav-ball somehow keeping us floating within the sphere easily. My heart slammed to life as the water enveloped me. But after a few panicked breaths filled my lungs without problem, and Nash squeezed my hand again, reminding me he was still there, a wash of wonder spread through my chest.

Multi-colored fish swam before my eyes. It wasn't just the water that'd been sucked into the ball. All the creatures within the lake had, too. In the distance, I spotted a green critter with big black eyes that seemed oddly familiar.

Nash tugged on my hand, spinning me into his arms. I giggled, making water bubble up and tickle my nose.

The skirt of my dress fanned out, whipping through the water. Nash wove around the sphere, twisting and turning and spinning in a way that left me breathless. At the same time, it was exhilarating—and just downright fun. I grinned at him, helpless to do more than trail after him. He was a far stronger swimmer than me, but with his tight grip on my hand, I wasn't afraid.

Before I knew it, the elaborate dance ended. Nash tugged me out of the sphere, and we landed on the lakeshore. Deafening applause rang out. Everyone clapped and shouted well wishes. Parson Renic slapped Nash's shoulder and handed me my glasses, then swiveled around, directing the men with machines to shut them off. The water splashed back into the lake behind us.

"That's it?" I asked.

Nash nodded and smiled at me. "Yeah. That's—"

"Kiss her!" someone shouted.

I whipped around, my cheeks heating. That voice sounded awfully familiar.

"Yes. Kiss the bride." Siara rushed forward. A hush fell over the guests. "Isn't that one of your Terran customs? Go on, son."

Oh, my Gods... I could feel the heat spreading now, washing all over my neck and face. I was probably red as a tomato. "It's okay. We're on Vorill—" The word cut off on a gasp.

Nash gripped my waist and bent me backward, then planted a kiss on my lips. Shock reverberated through me. I stood still as a statue, afraid to move. *Am I dreaming? Is he really kissing me?*

After a half a second, the shock wore off. His lips were still on me, making my heart pound and my stomach flutter.

Hell, this might be the only kiss I ever get. I'd be damned if I was going to lie there like a cold fish. My hands snaked around his neck, and I pulled him closer, moving my lips against his.

The crowd hooted and hollered, but their voices faded away in my mind. I gave my all to the kiss, heedless of who was watching. Tingles spread across my skin, and my belly clenched. Nash's fingers tightened on my waist. It felt so fucking good. Nash was kissing me! I wanted nothing more than to stay there all day. But after a few seconds, I pulled away, fighting to draw breath into my lungs.

Nash stared at me, and I'd be lying if I didn't admit I was a little pleased at the stunned look in his eyes.

"Let me be the first to say congratulations." Siara clapped her hands, a huge smile on her face. She raised her voice. "Please, everyone, head inside. We have a meal prepared in the dining room." She smiled at us. "Why don't you two get changed out of your wet things, hm?"

I nodded quickly, happy for the chance to escape. Nash and I walked silently across the lawn and into the house, where a servant handed us warm towels. Tension pooled in the air, so thick it was cloying.

"Sorry," I blurted as we trailed up the stairs, "about the whole 'kiss her' thing. I think it was Arda who yelled that."

Nash chuckled. "It's all right. I'm sure we'll need to get comfortable with a bit of P.D.A. now that we're married." He frowned. "Unless—was that awful for you?"

Gods, couldn't he tell I was in heaven?

"No." I shook my head. "It was nice."

"Good." He stopped in front of my door. "I'll see you downstairs, Zen."

"Yeah." I slipped into my room, shut the door, and slammed my forehead against the wood. "Nice. What a crock of shit."

That kiss was mind-blowing. Too bad it was likely the only one I'd ever get.

24

Locked In

Nash

"Get in there you two!" yelled a rather enthusiastic Vorill I didn't recognize. "And don't come out until morning!"

Zenda ducked under my arm as I swung open the door. "We won't." I replied, flashing my best smile at the crowd. Then, with a wave, I followed her inside, slamming the door closed behind me. Giggles erupted in the hall, and a series of bumps and bangs rattled the wall.

"I guess they weren't kidding about the locking us in part." Zenda stared at the door, her brow furrowed.

"Sadly, no." I sighed. "I'm sorry, I—"

Zen shook her head. "No, don't be. The wedding,"—she waved her hands at the lavishly decorated bedroom, equipped with candles and flowers—"this room, hell, even the whole lock them up thing, it's like I'm a character in one of my books."

I scoffed. "That didn't really happen in one of your swoony romances, did it?"

"Actually, it did." Zen plopped on the bed and gazed dreamily out the window. "I can't remember the name, but I once read a book just like this. After they were locked up together, the groom had to show proof that they did the deed. His bride was too scared with all the people listening at the door, so he cut his hand to bloody the sheets."

"Yikes." I sank down beside her. "Is that a hint?" I waggled my brows. "Need me to disguise what a bad girl you've been?"

Zenda shoved my shoulder roughly. "Shut up." She stood and pinned me with a glare. "No one better come around examining our sheets. That wasn't part of the plan."

I chuckled. "They won't. If it makes you feel better, I'll throw them in the wash myself before we leave."

She stalked across the room toward the attached bathroom. "Good. It would."

"Happy wife, happy life," I mumbled under my breath.

"What was that?" She peeked over her shoulder.

"Nothing." I stood, brushing a wayward flower petal off my pants. "Are you going to get changed in there?"

Zen wore a figure hugging dark pink dress to the dinner party. Honestly, I wouldn't mind if she kept in on forever. She looked so damn good in it. But it wasn't exactly appropriate attire for sneaking into an abandoned medical facility.

"Yeah. I won't be long." She bent and scooped her luggage off the floor.

"Okay. I'll get changed out here." I waited until the washroom door closed to grab my things. Then I quickly exchanged the formal suit I'd worn to the party for a navy-blue skinsuit and boots.

I had to admit, Zen was right about one thing. The wedding had been worthy of a storybook. My parents pulled out all the stops. Much to my surprise, they'd included every dish Zen had requested at dinner, even the Vorillion stew.

And me? After I spotted Zen waiting for me, I didn't even have to fake my smiles. The joy radiating out of her was infectious. Don't even get me started on that kiss...

When I tipped her back, I'd only been planning to give her a little peck. The second she started reciprocating, I swear I almost dropped her. I'd probably still be down there with my tongue in her mouth if she hadn't pulled away. Fuck *nice*—it was the best damn kiss of my life.

The entire meal, I couldn't stop staring at her lips. I was dying to kiss her again. But would she want that too? Nice. I shook my head. Who the hell wants their wife to think their kisses are just *nice*?

The door creaked open. I spun around, swallowing thickly as Zenda emerged. She'd changed into a black skinsuit and boots, and pinned her hair into her signature bun.

"Do I look all right?" She smoothed a hand down her sleeve and bit her lip.

All right? More like a fucking snack.

I cleared my throat and grinned. "Hottest damn thief I've ever seen."

Zenda rolled her eyes, but I didn't miss the light flush that spread over her cheeks. "Did you set up the thing from Ren?"

"No. Just give me a sec." I dug into my suitcase and pulled out the tiny recorder, then flipped the power switch.

"Is it on?" Zen cocked her head, staring at the square box I settled atop a pillow on the bed.

"Yeah. She said she gave it a slight delay before the playback starts." My heart raced. I knew exactly what I'd recorded. I couldn't help wondering what Zen's contribution sounded like, but I guess I'd have to wait to find out until we got back. "You ready to do this?"

Zen dragged in a deep breath, then she squared her shoulders and nodded firmly. "Yeah. Let's go."

Nash

"Is this it?" Zenda asked.

"Yep." We stood beside the Old Foundry, sheltered in a deserted alley separating it from the much more modern building beside it. Vorillion's twin moons shone brightly in the cloudless sky, giving us enough light that we hadn't needed to pull out our flashlights yet.

We'd decided it made the most sense for Zen and me to do the breaking and entering. After all, we had a wedding full of alibis who would swear up and down they knew exactly where we were all evening. It had been simple enough to sneak out of the window on a retractable ladder. And borrowing a nondescript transport from my parent's garage wasn't any trouble either.

Now for the tricky part... finding a way in.

"Help me look for an open door. Try the windows, too." Zen bent beside the first window she spotted, grunting when she couldn't force it up. We worked our way down the alley, trying each of the first story windows.

"I don't know if this is going to—" Footsteps echoed, coming closer. "Someone's coming," I whispered frantically, grabbing Zen's hand.

What were we going to do? If we got caught, who knows what would happen? I wasn't in the mood to spend my wedding night locked in a cell. Or worse, expelled from the planet on the first ship leaving the system.

My gaze flicked around the deserted alley. It was practically barren, with no handy dumpsters or crates to hide behind. Wait—there!

I pulled Zen with me into a tiny alcove, hiding a door to the building beside the Old Foundry. We crammed into the narrow opening, and I tugged Zen tight against my chest. She trembled in my arms, her heart beating so fast I could feel it pulsing even with the layers of her skinsuit and my gloves in between us.

My pulse wasn't exactly slow either. Especially not when whoever those footfalls belonged to reached the entrance to the alley. They shone a light down the dark corridor. It lit the space enough that I had the perfect view of Zen's big brown eyes staring at me.

My breath caught in my chest. She was so close. I could lean down and taste her lips again. She wouldn't even be able to stop me. Not without getting us both caught. I almost gave into the urge, but then the light swung away, washing us in darkness again.

The footsteps faded, and I shoved the thought of mauling my unsuspecting wife away. "I think we're safe," I whispered in her ear.

She backed away slowly. "C'mon. We better hurry. Who knows if that guy will be back again?"

Zen darted into the alley and bent beside another window. Stopping beside her, I frowned. "I don't think we'll have any luck on the first floor." I lifted my gaze to the second story. "Maybe we should try one of those?"

"How are we supposed to do that?" Zen stood, crossing her arms. "You want me to stand on your shoulders?"

The thought of Zen climbing me like a tree, her curves rubbing all over my body, made a jolt of lust rush straight to my cock. My tongue flicked out, and I licked my face quickly before shaking my head. "No. I brought the retractable ladder."

She smiled brightly. "That's perfect! Let's try it."

I pulled the knapsack off my back and dug out the lightweight ladder.

"It's lucky you found that. I thought for sure we'd have to scale the trellis back at Whitemist," Zen said.

I shrugged. "I may have used it to sneak out of my bedroom once or twice when I was a teen."

Zen chuckled quietly. "Why does that not surprise me?" She leaned closer as I placed the ladder on the ground below the closest second-story window. "And it was still in your bedroom all these years later?"

"Yeah." I hit the button that made the ladder begin to slowly stretch out. "It was like a shrine in there. Everything exactly the way I left it."

"Don't you see what that means?" Zenda rubbed my shoulder. "Your parents still love you."

I shrugged off her hand as I stood. "How do you know they just couldn't be bothered to clean out the room?"

Zen clicked her tongue. "They could have ordered a servant to do it the day you left without having to lift a finger."

I leaned on the ladder when it finished extending, testing the fit. "It's ready." Just like I was ready to be done with this conversation. Zenda wasn't right about them. My parents weren't harboring a secret longing for the son they'd abandoned.

Not everything works out the way it does in Zen's romance books.

Thankfully, she took the hint and clambered up the ladder. All thoughts of my parents fled my mind as I watched her round ass jiggle. She stopped at the window, and I held my breath while she pushed.

"Yes!" She let out a tiny squeal and disappeared inside.

I hurried up after her. Once I'd squeezed through the small opening, I hit the button to retract the ladder to the top and pulled the device inside, then closed the window firmly.

Zen flicked her flashlight on, illuminating the space. I frowned. It was as barren as the alley.

"C'mon. This building is huge. We better get busy." Zen breezed through the door and into the hall.

After dropping the ladder into my bag, I grabbed my flashlight and followed. "How do you want to do this?" I caught up to her in the hall. "Should we split up?"

Zen shuddered dramatically. "Are you crazy? Have you ever watched a horror vid, like ever? You *never* split up inside creepy abandoned buildings."

"Are you sure about that?" I glanced down the hall. Doors spread out, dotting the corridor every few feet—and this was just one floor out of four. "We might be here till morning."

"No, we won't." Zen adjusted her glasses. "I know exactly where to go."

I scoffed. "How could you possibly figure that out already?"

"Didn't you know I'm psychic?" She smirked and lifted her flashlight, illuminating a sign on the wall. "I can't read Vorillian, but I'm guessing one of those says something about medical research."

My face lit up as I spotted it. "Good find. We need to go to the basement."

I trailed Zen down the dusty stairwell to the Old Foundry basement. As far as wedding nights go, this was probably one of the strangest in the universe. But Zen was right. I owed her a million favors after what she'd done for me.

"So, tell me. Why are we doing this, exactly?" I still hadn't gotten a clear explanation about what was so important in this old building.

Zen glanced at me, but didn't slow her descent. "A little while back, Arda discovered something strange in her DNA after she used Lux's med-bot. She always assumed she was human, but it turns out, she has a bit of Vampherian in her genetic code."

"Really?" My brows shot up. "Isn't it illegal to tamper with genetics?"

"Yeah," Zen agreed. "We traced it to her grandmother, who—get this—was one of the most notorious serial killers of her generation. They called her the Bathing Butcher."

The name struck a chord. "I think I watched a true crime vid about her once. Didn't she like to bathe in her victim's blood?"

"Yep, that's her." Zen frowned. "Now, it's pretty clear the Vampherian DNA played a part in her crimes. Once Arda found out, she vowed to learn all she could about what happened. The only clue we found that her mother hadn't explored already led us here."

"Wow. I had no idea." We arrived at the bottom floor and Zen pushed open the hall door. "But why are you so eager to help her? I get that she's your friend, but I mean, there aren't a lot of friends I'd steal for."

"You mean, except for me, right?" Zen sent me a cheeky grin, but then her expression turned serious. "Arda isn't just my friend. She's like family. If she hadn't shown up on Mars and given me a job, I'd probably still be stuck on that stupid rock, miserable and bored out of my mind."

I flinched. "Was Mars really that bad? You never mentioned being bored and miserable when we'd talk."

Zen shrugged. "Talking to you was always the highlight of my week. I didn't want to wreck that by droning on and on about being depressed."

A wave of shame struck me, ripping through my core like a supernova blast. Zen was depressed? She was on Mars for almost two decades. Had I really been that blind I never noticed?

More than that, it was all my fault. If I'd never—

Zen gripped my sleeve, bouncing on her toes. "I think this is it!" She shone her flashlight through the window on the door beside us, and I spotted what looked like medical equipment inside.

Her hand shot out, and the door banged open.

"Quiet." I whispered harshly. "We don't need anyone outside wondering what that noise was."

"Sorry." Zen hurried inside. "I'm just excited." She scanned the room and, after only a second, she rushed over to a filing cabinet in the corner and opened the top drawer.

I walked more slowly to join her and shone my light inside.

"Thanks." She leafed through the files, frowning. "You better look. This is all written in Vorillian."

I handed her my flashlight. "What am I looking for?"

Zen bit her lip. "I'm not sure. I guess, anything to do with Earth, Terrans, or Cora Jenson."

I scanned the files carefully. The first drawer yielded nothing, so I shut it and moved onto the next.

Zen sighed. "You know, I don't think I thanked you yet, Nash."

My chest squeezed. "For what?"

She whacked my shoulder. "What do you mean, for what? For this, dummy." She wobbled the light over the file cabinet. "I would've never found this room on my own, much less made sense of these files. Arda wouldn't either. This really means a lot to her. And me, too. So, thank you." Her voice rang with sincerity, making me feel even more like a fucking ass.

She was seriously thanking me... *me*, the idiot who wrecked her life on Earth. And here I was, doing the same thing, once again. Upending her life. Taking her away from the job that saved her from a depressing existence on a planet she hated. Dragging her away from the friends that she loved like family.

I don't deserve her thanks. Not one little bit.

"Zen..." I sucked in a deep breath, working up the courage to come clean. But then my fingers trailed across a file marked *Cora Jenson*. I plucked it out. "I think I found it."

25

The Show

Zenda

I climbed the rungs of the collapsible ladder up to our wedding suite with a huge smile on my face. We'd returned without a hitch, and I had a feeling the electronic diskette tucked safely in my skinsuit pocket would be exactly what Arda was looking for.

Of course, there was no way to tell now. The few papers we'd found inside the file were deteriorated to the point of being illegible. Plus, with the power out in that old research lab, we'd had no way to check exactly what information was on the stolen diskette. But that was a worry for tomorrow, when we were safely back on the Verne.

I pushed open the window, and my smile disappeared fast. Moans reverberated off the walls. *My* moans.

Gods, this is so embarrassing! I scrambled inside the room, but not before stubbing my foot on the sill.

"Fuck!" My toe throbbed. I hopped on one foot, slowly working my way to the bed.

"Fuuuccckk," recording Zenda echoed.

My cheeks burned, and I shot a glance back at the open window. Nash still hadn't climbed through. There was time to stop the recording before he heard my sex voice. Ignoring the pain, I hobbled across the room.

Almost there...

"Zennn," Nash's voice stopped me in my tracks. My body lit up, fire blazing through every cell like the hottest of suns. "Come for me."

Holy. Shit.

If that wasn't the sexiest thing—ever. Images burst through my mind. Both of us, naked in that big bed. Nash hovering over me, holding my ankles at his shoulders, his dick splitting me open. Then he'd slip one hand down, down, tracing a moist finger over my throbbing—

"What are you doing?"

I squeaked and leaped for the mattress, just as recording Zen lived out my fantasy.

"Yes! Yes! Gods, yeeeeesss! Don't stop. Don't sto—" I slammed the off switch, and buried my face in the pillow. My glasses rammed into my nose, but I didn't dare move. Not when I knew my cheeks were bound to be flushed so badly I looked like a stoplight.

"Damn." I registered the quiet *whoosh* of Nash shutting the window. "Was that good for you, wife?"

I picked up the pillow and threw it at his stupid face. "Fantastic." I sent him my best stern glare after he chucked the pillow aside. Then I swung my legs over the edge of the mattress.

Nash chuckled, walking to the bed. He lowered his voice as he sank beside me. "I have to admit, Ren wasn't kidding. I wasn't sure how convincing that thing would be, but it sure sounded real."

Too real. How the hell was I supposed to sleep with the memory of what we'd sound like fucking fresh in my mind?

I sighed. "Ren knows her shit." She'd promised us the program she used would randomize the moans and phrases we recorded the other night. That way, if any of the wedding guests listened at the door, they'd get quite the show. Sure, it made our alibi a lot stronger, but right now I almost wish we'd gotten caught instead.

Nash's palm landed on my thigh. I stilled, staring at his hand as he stroked my leg. What was this? Was he just as turned on by that act as I was?

"Hey, you okay?" The kind concern in his tone doused the lust boiling in my veins.

"Y-yeah." I stood, knocking his hand off. "Just worked up." My eyes widened. "From the robbery, not the—" I shook my head, gulping down the rest of my embarrassing words. "I'm gonna wash up for bed."

The door slammed closed behind me, and I sucked in a deep breath. *Thank fuck that's over.*

After taking my time changing into a loose nightgown and finishing my nightly skincare routine, my face had returned to its normal pale hue. As I began pulling the pins out of my chignon, weariness stole over me. It had been a long night, and an even longer day.

Maybe I can get some sleep after all.

I pushed open the door just as a yawn split my lips. "All yours." I crossed the room and traded places with Nash. He shut the door quietly while I slipped under the covers.

Wow. This bed is amazing. There were definitely a few benefits to being completely loaded. I snuggled into the mattress, feeling like I was one step away from floating.

Nash slipped into bed a few moments later. "Should I turn off the lights?"

I nodded. "Would you?" The room darkened enough that I could only see the shadowy outline of his body next to me. My pulse pounded and suddenly, sleep was the last thing on my mind.

I mean, it was our wedding night. Sure, it was fake, but what if...

Nash shifted, and my breath caught in my throat.

"Can I ask you something, Zen?"

My Gods, what is he going to ask me? Want to cuddle? Can I kiss you? Can I fuck you?

My pussy tingled, but I swallowed thickly, forcing my racing thoughts to slow. "Sure."

"The contract said we had to live together for a year, but it didn't say where."

Wait, what?

"Do you want to keep your job on the Verne? We could stay there instead of in Subralia. I'm sure my uncle would understand..."

From the way he trailed off, I got the feeling that statement wasn't totally true. Still, the fact that he would give up his job for me made a rush of warmth spread through my chest.

"Don't be silly. You love your job."

"I know, but—"

"Plus, you have jump sickness. What kind of friend would I be if I forced you to live on a spaceship for a year when every jump makes you sick?"

"I'm sure I could manage."

I rolled my eyes, though surely he didn't see in the dark room. "Nash, no. I don't want to live on the Verne." I reached across the bed and grabbed his hand. "You know I've always wanted to go back home."

His hand tensed beneath mine. It was really sweet he wanted to give me a choice. I appreciated it more than I could put into words.

"You know Arda already approved my sabbatical, right?"

Nash sighed. "Yeah."

"Well, that's all there is to it. We're going back to Subralia."

"Okay." Nash flipped his hand over and starting drawing lazy circles on my wrist.

With him silent again, and his tickling touch sliding across my skin, all those questions from before came racing back.

"I think we should set up some rules," I blurted.

Nash stilled. "What kind of rules?"

I shrugged, pulling my hand free only to tangle it in the blanket. "Well... we'll be living together for an entire year, pretending to be married. It would be nice to know what to expect. What lines not to cross."

"Okay." Nash's voice took on a hard edge that hadn't been there a moment ago. "I have one for you."

"You do?" I turned sideways and stared at his shadowy profile. "What is it?"

"No brothels."

My jaw clenched. I almost snapped at him with an emphatic *no*. Didn't we hash this out already? There was nothing wrong with me having a healthy sex drive. And using a sexbot was a hell of a lot safer than sleeping around with half the women in Subralia like he did.

But then I remembered his story about finding his mom sneaking off to a brothel. I supposed it made sense he wouldn't want his wife doing the same thing. And it would only be for a year.

"Fine. No brothels," I agreed.

Nash's chest sank so much the blankets shifted. It seemed he was perfectly happy with that arrangement. But me... I was just reminded of something that I absolutely needed to be comfortable with this charade moving forward.

"I have one for you. No other women. I don't care how discreet you are, I don't want—"

"Done." Nash cut me off. "I'm not a cheater, Zen. I *never* will be." He spit out the last with so much venom I suspected he was thinking of his father.

My heart clenched. Poor Nash. They really put him through the wringer.

I scrambled for something to say, hoping to break the tension. "Glad that's settled. Man, no brothels for me, and no randos for you. Sounds like we signed up for a year as monks."

Nash chuckled. "I don't know about that. We *are* married."

I gulped, my whole body vibrating. *Is he saying what I think he's saying?*

Do it. Say yes! A part of me screamed.

Another part of me answered. The pissed off part who was still thinking about all those women he was happy to service back on Earth. "If you think just because we're married..." I sucked in a deep breath, fighting to tamp down the burst of anger raging inside of me. "You really can't keep it in your pants, can you?"

26

The Bet

Nash

My mind raced, Zen's words ricocheting around my head like a bomb blast.

"What kind of friend would I be…"

"No brothels for me, no randos for you…"

"You really can't keep it in your pants, can you?"

"You wanna bet?" I growled, my voice so low I barely recognized it.

Zen dragged a hand through all that gorgeous hair of hers. "W-what?"

"I bet you I can keep it in my pants longer than you."

"Really, Nash?" She giggled. "Sure, you can."

"I mean it, Zen. You don't think I can control my sex drive, but I most certainly can. I think you're the one who'll be begging me for release."

"Oh-kay…" She spun in bed, turning away from me. "Let's just get some sleep." She sighed and nuzzled into her pillow, clearly done with the conversation.

Me? Nope. I was *so* not done. I'd been worked up from the minute we got back into this room, and I heard her sultry voice on that recording. My cock had hardened so fast I almost didn't make it off the ladder. I wanted to hear it for real. I needed to swallow those moans while they spilled out of her lips.

But no. Zen was too busy thinking the worst of me.

I don't know what was worse, that she thought I'd cheat on her while we were married, or that she still only thought of me as a *friend*.

Fuck, Zen. Can't you see we're so much more than friends?

Maybe it was time to show her.

I scooched across the mattress and snuggled against her, tugging her back to my chest.

"W-what are you doing?" she asked.

"Spooning my wife." My nose filled with her decadent scent, those long red waves tickling my face. I breathed in deep, snaked my arm around her waist, and splayed my hand flat on her warm, curved belly. Damn, she felt so good. And when the tiniest of sighs spilled out of her lips, I swear my dick jumped in my pajamas.

"Mmm, you're a good snuggler." I let my hand trail across her belly, maddeningly slow and feather light.

"Am I?" She tipped her head back, like she was trying to get a look at my face in the dark.

I nodded. "So good." My pinky traced down. So far, I could feel the faintest indent of her panties under the thin nightgown. I toyed with the line for half a second, then started a trail back up her belly. "I bet you're good at a lot of things." I dove deeper into her hair until I knew the heat of my breath would wash over her neck. "Do you want to know what I'm good at?" I whispered against her skin.

Zen's chest heaved, her breath escaping as hard pants. "Tell me."

I traced back up her stomach, keeping my touch whisper soft until my thumb brushed the underside of her breast. "Vorill have one part of our anatomy that's more than double the size of humans."

Zenda shifted, her chest inching closer to my questing digit.

"I bet you know already, don't you?" I let my thumb linger on the bottom of her breast for half a heartbeat before angling my hand down in another slow sweep.

"Well, I am a doctor." Her reply lost a bit of her usual snark when it came out so breathless.

I nuzzled against her ear. "So, you know we're very, very good at licking." I opened my mouth and traced the smallest of licks across her earlobe.

Zen groaned, and her hips canted back, rubbing her soft ass against my cock.

Fuck! That one little move nearly had me spilling in my pants. I lay stock still until the urge to grind against her passed.

My hand had made it back down her belly again. I took it further this time, inching over the top of her panties until my pinky hovered just above her mound. Her hips rocked forward, relieving the pressure on my aching cock.

"I'd love to show you how good I am. Would you like that, Zen?"

"Mmm," she moaned, tipping her sweet pussy closer to my finger.

I was dying to rip that nightgown away and feel her skin on mine. But not before I heard her admit it. I needed to know she was as crazy about me as I was about her. "Tell me. Just tell me you want me and I'll show you everything."

Instead of moaning, *yes, I want you,* and putting us both out of our misery, Zen froze. Then she jerked her head away from me and rolled out of my arms.

"Go to sleep, Nash," she mumbled into her pillow.

I rolled away too, escaping to the opposite edge of the bed. How the hell did that go wrong? One second, she was grinding against me and panting. The next...

Shit.

That stupid bet. Zen just didn't want to lose. But I'd show her. I *can* keep it in my pants. *She'll see I'm not a slave to my sexual urges. Even if it kills me...*

Zenda

After the sun rose the next morning, I jumped out of bed and tiptoed to the washroom. I'd spent a mostly sleepless night tossing and turning. That and trying to forget the way Nash's hands felt on me. And all those naughty things he'd whispered in my ear.

My clit pulsed as his words washed over me for the thousandth time. *I'd love to show you how good I am. Would you like that, Zen?*

Gods, I'd been so ready to say yes. Then he had to remind me about that dumb bet. The one I never even agreed to in the first place...

Of course Nash didn't want to touch me for real. He was just proving a point. If I'd given in and begged him to fuck me like I was dying to, he'd have laughed and responded with a breezy, "Told ya so."

The way he rolled over and went to sleep only proved it. As far as I could tell, he hadn't moved the entire night. I shook my head as I finished my shower and changed into my skinsuit. For a second there, I could have sworn I felt his hard dick rub against my ass. It was probably just his knee. Or my hopeful imagination.

Get over it, Zen. He's just your friend.

After pinning up my hair, I was ready for the day. I pushed open the door and gasped. "Nash. Good morning."

He stood on the other side, frowning, fist raised to knock, his bare chest dewy in Vorillion's humidity. My mouth went dry as I slid aside, making room for him to enter.

"Morning," he grumbled before brushing past me and shutting the door.

Wonder what crawled up his ass and died? I rolled my eyes and started gathering the few things I'd left out, stuffing them back into my suitcase.

By the time I'd finished, Nash exited the bathroom, dressed in his usual blue skinsuit. "You ready?" he asked grumpily.

"Just about. Are we heading down for breakfast?"

He shook his head sharply. "I booked a transport back to the capital." He glanced at a clock tacked to the wall. "It should be here shortly."

"Oh." I sighed. Guess he wasn't planning on having any heart to hearts with his parents, then. Not that I could blame him. Still, my intuition kept telling me there might be more to the story than even Nash knew. That if he'd just talk to them, maybe...

I shook off the urge to bring up the subject. He was already in a bad mood. Besides, it wasn't like I was his *real* wife. *I should probably keep my opinions to myself.*

We left the room, and I paused in the hall. "Should we knock for Arda and Ren?"

"No need. I told them about the transport last night. They're likely already waiting outside."

I shrugged and followed Nash through the house. Before we made it to the front door, two pairs of footsteps clattered toward us.

"Zenda. Nash. Wait!" Siara's voice reached us just before she popped out of the dining room. Her short-sleeved yellow sundress swished around her knees as she halted before us. "I hope you weren't planning to leave without saying goodbye."

I smiled and crossed the hall to greet her. "Of course not. Thank you so much for the wedding. Everything was beautiful."

She ignored my outstretched hand and dragged me into a hug. "Not as beautiful as you were, dear." Siara pulled back, her smile soft and her voice ringing with so much sincerity my cheeks warmed. "You'll take good care of my Nash, won't you?"

I gulped. "Sure."

Siara let go of me, and turned to her son, her arms outstretched.

Nash hefted our suitcases higher in his arms, backing away. "Another time. I need to drop these off at the transport. Goodbye, Mother." He nodded curtly to his father, who lingered in the dining room doorway. "Father." With that, Nash turned on his heel and left the house.

My heart ached as I watched the door swing closed behind him. I glanced at Nash's father in time to catch the longing look he aimed outside before his features smoothed into his signature scowl.

"Goodbye, Mr.—"

"Nonsense. Call me Laytun. We're family now." Nash's father cut me off gruffly, smoothing his hands down his freshly pressed khakis. "Farewell, Zenda."

With a small wave, I followed Nash out the door. *Wonder if that's the last time I'll see them?* If it were up to Nash, then I bet I knew the answer to that question.

Nash's mood improved with every mile our transport put between us and Whitemist Estate. By the time we pulled into the shipyard and climbed aboard the Verne, he was back to his usual easy-going self.

"All right." Arda rounded on us as soon as the hatch door slammed closed. "Hand it over."

I pulled the stolen diskette out of my skinsuit pocket. We'd agreed to pretend the evidence didn't exist until we were safely back on the ship, but it appeared Arda couldn't wait a second longer. "Here ya go, Capt."

Arda plucked the slim piece of plasticide out of my fingers like it was the finest gem, her eyes gleaming. Then she strode swiftly across the hold.

"Aren't you forgetting something?" Nash slung a beefy arm around my shoulders. "When you interrupt your wedding night and turn thief, the least you can expect is a thank you."

I punched Nash's chest. "Cool it, idiot."

Arda spun on her heel. "No. He's right." She met my gaze with an enormous grin. "Thank you, Nash. You too, Zen. You're the fucking best."

I giggled and ducked out from under Nash's arm, then followed Arda's lead. "Do you think the Verne can read what's on that?" Nash, Ren, and Lux trailed behind us, everyone seeming eager to discover what secrets the diskette held.

"Only one way to find out." Arda strode onto the bridge and we crammed in after her. The small flight deck was really only meant for two, but with Arda and Lux seated in the pilot and co-pilot chairs, the rest of us were able to squeeze in behind them.

Arda inserted the diskette into the appropriate slot. A holographic display materialized, hovering in the air in front of her. I held my breath, scanning the readouts over Arda's shoulder. But the strings of letters and numbers made no sense to me. "What's it say?"

Brow furrowing, Arda glanced at me. "I don't know. Do any of you know what language this is?"

Her question prompted a round of 'no's' and shaken heads.

Arda raised her voice. "Verne. Can you translate this, please?"

The computer's male monotone answered, "Negative. This language is not in my database."

"That's strange." Ren scratched her head. "Think it's a code or something?"

"Shit." Arda's shoulders slumped.

My heart plummeted. *Don't tell me we went through all that for nothing...*

Lux leaned forward. "Don't worry. I'll send it to Elys. She dated a linguist a few years back who prided himself on figuring out obscure messages like this. I'm sure he can crack it."

I swear I spotted hearts in her eyes as Arda swung toward the copilot's chair. "Really? That would be amazing."

Lux's stoic stare softened as he met her gaze. "I can think of a few ways you can thank me."

I rolled my eyes. "Get a room, you two." Sure, they were in love or whatever, but did they have to rub our faces in it?

Arda laughed. "We will. This one." She shooed the three of us out. "You guys need to strap in for takeoff, anyway."

Ren, Nash, and I shuffled down the hall and into the mess. Within minutes, we'd strapped in, and the Verne shot into motion. The craft shook as we picked up speed and fought to escape from the planet's gravity.

I shot a glance beside me. Nash's eyes were pinched shut, his gloved hands gripping his seat's armrest tightly.

"You okay?" I asked quietly.

He didn't answer until the Verne evened out—a sure sign that we'd reached open space. "Yeah. I'm all right." He flashed a wobbly grin. "Maybe a bit queasy."

"That reminds me," I unbuckled the straps holding me down as the ship chimed an all-clear bell over the loudspeakers, "we need to get you to the med-bay for your pre-jump shot."

I didn't imagine it was possible, but somehow Nash's skin turned even greener with that announcement. "Do I have to?" He released his straps and followed me into the hall.

"Yeah. Unless you want to spend the return trip in bed like you did on the way here."

"That might not be so bad." He smirked. "This time I have a wife to keep me company."

My cheeks warmed as my traitorous imagination conjured a dozen different ways I might keep him company in that big bed. But I buried the tempting visuals and shoved open the med-bay hatch. "Come on, don't tell me you can't handle a tiny little needle." I grabbed his arm, and pulled him forward, when it was clear he didn't intend to walk in himself.

"Fine," he grumbled. He stopped in the doorway with me, wedging his muscular body so close my skin tingled from the proximity. "As long as you promise to give me something to lick afterwards."

I bit my lip, flashing back to his boast last night. *You know we're very, very good at licking.* I gulped, fighting to dislodge the echo from my mind. Nash certainly didn't help when he leaned back and trailed a leisurely look down the length of my body.

"W-what do you want to lick?" I asked, unable to stop my voice from sounding hoarse, but needing to know all the same.

A smug smile painted his lips at the same time he stepped into the med-bay. "Another one of those lollys. You have more, don't you?" He walked straight to the drawer where I kept them.

I raced over and slapped the drawer closed before he pulled it open more than an inch. "Excuse me. Didn't anyone ever tell you to keep your sticky fingers to yourself?"

Nash chuckled. "Nope. I haven't had any complaints where my fingers are concerned."

Gods! Could the man turn anything into an innuendo? "Lucky you." I planted a hand on his chest and shoved him toward the exam table. "Let's save the licking for after the pricking, shall we?"

Nash laughed uproariously. I shook my head, turning for my supplies. Still, our exchange put a tiny smile on my face. Yeah, I was crushing on him—hard—when it was the last thing I ought to be doing. And he made that idiotic bet. But if we could still joke together like this, then maybe there was hope for our friendship after all.

I flipped around, holding the needle aloft. "You ready, Bobbles?"

27

Filling In

Zenda

My heart thrummed as I sat in my quarters, waiting for the comms to connect. There was only one long distance unit in my family's tiny quarters on Mars. I had a fifty-fifty shot of reaching my sister.

Let's just hope she's home instead of Mom.

"Hello?" My sister's voice spilled over the speaker and I blew out a huge sigh.

"Hi, Karsen. How's the job hunt going?"

"Nothing, so far. Every job I apply for seems to want someone with experience." I could picture the frown painting her overachiever face. "I'm thinking about applying for some on planet placements instead."

"Don't. I have a job you'll be perfect for."

"Really?" Excitement leaked into her voice. "What is it?"

"You said you want a job like mine, right?"

"Exactly. I'm dying to get out and see the universe."

"Great." I grinned. "You'll get plenty of travel filling in for me on the Verne as medical officer."

"Seriously?" She squealed, but the joyful sound cut off abruptly. "Wait... if I'm filling in for you, what are you doing?"

"I'm taking a year's sabbatical." I sucked in a nervous breath, knowing exactly what she'd ask next.

"A sabbatical? For work, I'm guessing. Where are you going?"

"Subralia."

The comm went silent for a full five seconds. "But the banishment... I thought the only way you could—" She gasped. "What did you do, Zen?"

I cringed. "I kinda... got married."

"How do you *kinda* get married? And to who?"

"Are you sitting down? It's a long story." I drew a deep breath and filled her in, leaving out a few of the more intimate details. Like how hot and bothered my fake husband got me in bed last night.

"So after a year, you'll get divorced and return to the Verne?" Karsen asked after I finished.

"That's the plan." I sighed. "Listen Kar, can you do me a favor? I'm not planning to tell Mom. You know how she is. She'll hear the word *married* and start sending me baby clothes every chance she gets."

"Don't worry. She won't hear about it from me."

"Thanks, sis. So what do you think about the job? Should I give Arda your contact info?"

"Oh, definitely. A year to travel and see the universe will be perfect for me and give me the experience I need to land a permanent posting."

"Good." I leaned back in my chair, pleased to have one thing working out the way I envisioned it.

Karsen cleared her throat. "Can I ask you something, Zen?"

"Sure."

"What happens if you don't want to come back after a year?"

I scoffed. "Weren't you listening? It's not real."

"Yeah. Only what if it turns into something more? You'll be living together, day in and day out, for a whole year."

It was my turn to go silent. Honestly, I wanted that more than anything, but I couldn't bring myself to say the words out loud.

"Just keep an open mind. Yeah?" Karsen added.

"Sure. I can do that." I reached over the desk, my hand hovering over the comms. "I gotta go. You'll be hearing from Arda about the job soon. I promise." We said our goodbyes, and I cut the call. Then I sat back in my chair and rubbed my temples.

Arda and Kar would get along just fine. Hell, they both had exactly the same advice about Nash.

Am I being too closed off with Nash?

Maybe...

I immediately assumed his advances were a joke, but what if they weren't? What if, on some level, the bet—maybe even him choosing *me* to marry—what if that was brought on by underlying interest?

We'd been friends for so long. We were compatible on so many levels. In a way, getting physical together would be a natural extension of that. Especially under the circumstances.

The analytical part of my brain ran with the notion, cataloging pluses and minuses at rapid speed. But all too soon, I forced my mind to quiet. If any of this happened, it wouldn't be solely up to me. I needed to sit down with Nash and hash it out with him—logically and in the bright light of day, where his talented hands couldn't distract me.

I left my quarters and wandered down the hall. I stopped at his room first, but after knocking and getting no answer, I moved on. There were only so many places to search on the Verne. Before long, I heard the clatter of weights being lifted ringing out in the hall. Then voices coming from the exercise room.

Guess he's not alone. Maybe I should come back later...

I'd just spun on my heel when someone grunted, and a masculine voice asked, "How's married life treating you?" Definitely Lux.

I paused, even though I know I should've hightailed it out of there. Eavesdropping in the hall was not cool. Still, I couldn't deny the urge to hear Nash's answer.

His rich voice rang out a second later. "It's been... frustrating. In more ways than one."

My heart stalled. Frustrating? I could guess one of the ways he was referring to had to do with last night, but what about the rest?

Lux grunted again, and more metal banged. "Funny. I assumed from your reputation you wouldn't have that problem. If you need any pointers—"

"Keep your pointers. I don't need them with Zen."

What the hell was that supposed to mean? I pressed a hand on my belly, suddenly feeling like a black hole opened up and sucked out all my insides.

"Suit yourself. But if you ask me, you'd have a much happier marriage if you—"

Nash cut off his statement with a humorless chuckle. "Marriage. How the hell did I end up married? I never wanted this."

I'd heard enough. My pulse pounded so hard I'm surprised it didn't explode out of my skin as I stalked back to my room.

I slammed the door closed and leaned against it. *What am I doing? I'm so stupid.*

Tears burned the corners of my eyes. How did I allow myself to get sucked into Nash's orbit again? I promised myself the last time he broke my heart, we'd only ever be friends. I had to stop imagining things that didn't exist, or this year would be a torture I'd never recover from.

Nash

I stepped out of the shower, rubbing my sore shoulders. It was good to be back en route to Earth. I couldn't wait to put this strange trip behind me.

I tugged on a skinsuit and left the washroom, frowning as I caught sight of the time. Where was Zen? I'd spent so long lifting with Lux, I thought I'd find her fast asleep when I got back to my quarters. Then it would be simple enough to slip in with her and pick up what we started last night.

My fingers itched at the memory of her soft curves. Those breathy little moans that left her lips when I touched her echoed in my ears. I was dying to feel her writhing against me again. Maybe tonight I could even convince her to lose the nightgown.

But alas, my room was still empty.

Guess I'd have to get used to having a workaholic wife. I slipped into the hall and wandered to the med-bay, expecting to find her poring over some research. Yet, when I arrived, the hatch was closed, and the room was awash in darkness.

I peeked into all the open hatches on my way back to the passenger quarters, but I didn't spot her anywhere. My stomach clenched as I halted outside her door.

Bang, bang, bang. "Zen? You in there?"

Footsteps pounded behind the door, and I sighed as the hatch swung open. Zenda stopped in the entryway and adjusted her glasses, another one of those thin nightgowns swishing around her shapely thighs. My mouth went dry and my cock took notice, instantly hardening.

"Hey. What are doing in there?"

"What do you mean?" She crossed her arms, dragging my attention to her perky breasts and the hard points straining against the worn fabric. "It's my room."

I gasped dramatically, pressing a hand to my chest. "But we're married. Shouldn't we be sleeping together?"

She scoffed, the harsh sound dragging my gaze up to her flushed face. "Give the fake indignity a rest. I know you don't want to be married. I know you don't want *me*. Let's save the pretending for Subralia, okay?"

What in the universe had gotten into her? When I'd left the med-bay that afternoon, she'd been all jokes and smiles, but now she was practically fuming, and dark circles shadowed her eyes. It was clear she was hurting—why, I honestly couldn't say—but there was no way I could let her go on thinking I didn't want her. My eyes bulged as she reached for the hatch. I stepped onto the threshold before she could slam the door in my face.

"I do want you, Zen," I blurted.

She shook her head sharply. "No, you don't."

I tore her hand off the door and slipped her palm on the sizeable erection tenting my skinsuit. "Does it feel like I'm pretending?"

Her eyes widened before she shot a dazed look at her hand. Then her mouth fell open, and her fingers trembled within my captured grasp, making me bite back a groan. She sucked in a shaky breath as

I stepped even closer. Her hand froze on my dick, but the heat of her skin soaked through the fabric, setting my blood blazing. I grabbed her waist and hauled her against my chest. Then I leaned down to her ear. "I've always wanted you, Zen. Tell me you want me, too."

Zen shivered in my arms.

I held my breath. *Just admit it, Zen. Please.*

She ripped her hand out of my hold and shoved my chest so hard I stumbled back into the hall. "You're just trying to win that dumb bet, aren't you? Go to bed, Nash." The door slammed closed an instant later, barely missing my nose.

I retreated to my room, cursing under my breath. That fucking bet. I never should've made it. *Now, Zen will never believe me.*

Worse, would she even talk to me after I forced her to grope me? I'd always been so careful to keep her at arm's length. I cherished her friendship more than anything. My own parents had dumped me, but not Zenda. She'd always been there, even when we were separated by thousands of light-years. But now... my heart shattered, spreading shards of ice through my veins and leaving me numb. The sad fact was, it was all true.

I do want her. I always have. And now that I've admitted it out loud, I can't even lie to myself about it any longer.

28

Saucy

Zenda

19 years earlier

I stared at the poster tacked to the wall. The Grad Dance. As a child, I used to sneak down to the cafeteria while my mother prepped meals for the school's end of the year event held in Subralia. It signaled the end of the school year for some, and graduation for others.

I could never resist peeking in at all the teens, dancing, laughing, and celebrating. They looked so happy and carefree. I couldn't wait to be one of them.

Once I was old enough to attend, the dance's luster had faded. By then, my classmates resented me—the daughter of *the help* who outshined them. I never even bothered to step foot in the dance, knowing I'd spend the evening stuck on the outskirts, watching everyone celebrate but not included in the fun.

Still, my insides vibrated as I stared at the poster. *Maybe this year will be different. Now that Nash is here.*

A tiny smile lit my lips. We'd become friends in the last few months. Well—I guess it was more accurate to say he'd made friends with everyone. He was so easy-going and fun to be around; it wasn't long before everybody liked him. But while all the other students barely tolerated my presence, he went out of his way to include me.

Nash wouldn't let me spend the whole dance as a wallflower. I could picture him now, a hand outstretched and a goofy grin lighting his face as he pulled me onto the dance floor.

How would it feel to have his arms wrapped around me? We would sway to the beat of some soft ballad, his hands on my hips. My skin tingled as I lingered over the fantasy until a bubbly voice broke the illusion.

"Look at that. They put up posters for the Grad Dance." Stasia flicked her long red hair off her shoulder, then tugged her companion's arm, spinning her.

The second girl flipped around, and I recognized the tall blonde as a sophomore named Penny. "Oh. I'm so excited! My mom had a dress special ordered from the mainland. It's so gorgeous!"

My stomach clenched. I tried on a hand-me-down sundress yesterday and felt pretty cute in it. It would have to do. There was no way we could afford anything new on Mom's salary.

"Same." Stasia smirked, giving all her attention to her friend, but talking loudly enough for me to overhear. "My father picked up my gown last month. It's designer." Her smile turned sly. "I can't wait to see what Nash says when he sees me in it."

I nearly rolled my eyes. With so few men in Subralia, I wasn't surprised most of the girls had thrown themselves at Nash. Stasia was one of the most brazen about it.

"You never told me what happened the other day." Penny tilted her head, a coy look in her eye. "Weren't you going to see him... alone?"

My heart dropped to my feet.

Stasia's gaze swept the mostly empty hall. She clearly saw me glaring in their direction. I knew because I hadn't taken any steps to hide and they were only a few feet away. But she turned back to Penny and merely lowered her voice a tiny fraction, not nearly enough to keep me from hearing what she said next. "We kissed."

My jaw clenched, and heat seared my cheeks.

"You didn't!" Penny gasped and slapped Stasia's arm weakly. "I've never known anyone who kissed a Vorill before. What was it like?"

Stasia preened, lifting her nose in the air and puffing out her chest. "It was great." She flicked a quick glance in my direction before leaning in conspiratorially to Penny. "He clearly liked it, too. He called me *saucy*."

I couldn't help it. I snorted.

Stasia sent me a death glare. "Rude much?" She grabbed Penny's arm and tugged her down the hall, out of earshot.

"I'm gonna kill him," I muttered under my breath.

One of my mom's racy historical romances went missing from my bookshelf a few weeks ago. I'd assumed Mom was rereading it, but now I had a sneaking suspicion I knew where it'd ended up.

I'd read that book before. The hero had a scene or two where he called his love interest *saucy*.

I never would've guessed Nash was a thief. What was he reading it for, research into Terran's dating expectations? I sniggered to myself. He would've been better suited picking something a little more contemporary.

Still, it wasn't long before all the humor drained out of me. Did he really kiss *her*?

Stasia was nothing like me. She was tall where I was petite. Drop dead gorgeous, while I was as plain as they come. *If Nash has girls like that to kiss, then what chance do I have?*

I sighed, leaving my spot frozen in front of the Grad Dance poster. It wasn't worth dwelling over. Nash and I were just friends. And I had bigger things to look forward to than a silly dance.

Professor Mueller had requested to see me later. I'd done everything he asked and then some, working diligently all semester. That research job was so close I could taste it. I suspected that was why he wanted to see me. He was going to offer me a position. I just knew it.

But first... I spared a glance at my rumpled school clothes. I had to change into something more professional. Then it was off to the lab, and the job that I'd worked so hard to earn.

29

Filthy Lying Pond Scum

Nash

19 years earlier

Cool salt water flowed around me in Professor Mueller's research lab. I'd been at Subralia for months now, and was long past the need for daily swims to cure my dehydration. Nevertheless, I still enjoyed the occasional soak.

Today more so than most...

I groaned as I treaded water, flashing back to my unexpected visitor last night. I'd just gotten home from spending the afternoon with Zen and settled down for a little reading, when a knock pounded on the door. My heart had fluttered, hoping I'd find Zenda standing there, adjusting her glasses.

Imagine my surprise when I found Stasia instead. She'd pushed right in like she owned the place and barely said a word before she jumped me.

I never knew Terran women could be so *forward*. It would've been rude to shove her off immediately, not to mention hurt her feelings. My stomach somersaulted at the thought. So, I kissed her back. Even though I couldn't help wishing it was a different redhead in my arms.

After a few tiny pecks, I'd spouted off some nonsense about my uncle coming home. I could barely even remember what I'd said, but it did the trick and got her to leave without picking a fight.

I still felt slimy about it. That was why I hid out in the lab, rather than face my classes where I'd be forced to see her. And Zen.

A needle of anxiety pricked my spine. She was bound to hear about my visitor, eventually. Stasia was the queen of gossip. What would Zenda think? Would she dump me as a friend?

Zenda had made my transition to Earth tolerable. She'd always been there to whisper in my ear when I was about to make a social blunder. Her door was always open when I was lonely and needed a place to hang—which was more often than not with my workaholic uncle as my guardian. I honestly don't know how I'd have managed without her as a friend.

I'd lost count of all the times I'd pictured kissing Zen over the last few months. I'd always held off, not wanting to lose what we had. Besides, it's not like it would go anywhere. I was still determined never to marry, and Zen was the kind of girl who lived and breathed happily ever afters.

It's not fair to string her along... right?

The lab door banged open, interrupting my musing. I peeked out of the back pool, and was just about to lift a hand and wave hello to

Professor Mueller, when I glimpsed the person following him into the lab.

What is Zenda's mom doing here?

I made the split-second decision not to alert the pair to my presence. Dropping my hand, I sank lower in the water and silently swam to the pool's edge, where I'd be hidden unless they walked to the tank and stared directly down.

The door closed, and Professor Mueller spoke first. "I'm glad you could meet with me, Portia. I have good news about that matter you requested I look into for you."

"You do?" Portia's voice rang out, full of excitement. "Oh, thank you Professor! I knew you'd be able to pull some strings for me."

My brow furrowed. I'd never known Mueller to be particularly helpful. In fact, he was a pretty big dick. Zen knew it too, but she was so determined to get that research job, she put up with his crappy attitude with a smile. It honestly drove me nuts.

"You understand this was not exactly legal?" Mueller asked.

The plot thickens. I listened intently. Maybe I could use whatever I heard next to finally convince Zen to stop working with Mueller.

"I do. I swear I won't tell anyone you were involved," Portia insisted vehemently.

"Good. I have a favor to ask in return."

"Anything! Just ask and it's yours."

My heart sped up as Professor Mueller paused. What could he be giving Portia that would make her so eager to help him?

"It's about your daughter. I've asked her to come here today. I have a proposal for her. I'd like your help to convince her to accept."

"What proposal? If you're talking about the research position, I don't think she'll need any convincing."

"It's not that." Mueller cleared his throat. "I'm planning to ask Zenda to be my wife."

Shock lit my synapses, reverberating through me so strongly I barely bit back a gasp. I couldn't have heard that right. *That creepy old fuck wants Zenda to marry him?* My mind raced, throwing sickening images at me. The two of them standing at the altar, saying vows. Him stripping her out of a white dress.

No. I shook my head, only for more images to bombard me. Professor Mueller coming onto Zenda in the lab. Him shucking off his white lab coat, bending her over his desk.

Murderous rage washed over me. If he took advantage of her—his barely legal student—I would rip his dirty dick off.

It seemed Zen's mom was just as shocked, and thinking along the same lines. She sputtered before replying, her voice hard. "Why? Has something happened between you two?"

"No. Nothing like that."

I blew out a shaky breath.

"Are you in love with her? Is she in love with you?" Portia sounded hopeful. My stomach clenched.

"No." Mueller chuckled. "I'm certainly not in love with her. And if she felt that way, I'd hardly need your help to convince her to say yes."

I frowned. *If he's not fucking her, and not in love with her, then why in the universe does he want to marry her?*

Again, Portia echoed my thoughts. "Then why marry at all? And why my Zen?"

"It's simple, really. I'm sure you're aware of the lack of men in this facility. I've wasted countless hours fending off advances from Subralia's female population. It's time for me to settle down, take myself off the market."

I rolled my eyes. What a dumb reason to get married.

"And Zenda?" Portia asked.

"She's a bright girl and an excellent researcher. She's already proven to work well with me in the lab. I have no doubt those skills will transfer to domestic life as well."

My gut burned. I'd witnessed the way he bossed Zen around. How he overloaded her with work. And she put up with all of it, assuming it would lead to a job. But that greedy bastard couldn't be content just to have her easing his work life. He wanted her to slave over him after work hours, too.

"Besides," Mueller continued. "Zenda has an excellent work ethic, and her moral character is beyond reproach. Having a wife with those qualities will be a boon to my reputation as a superior scientist."

I wanted to gag. He didn't care about Zen at all. The guy wanted a doll he could boss around and who would make him look good to his peers. What a joke!

"Okay…" The acceptance in Portia's voice chilled my blood. "I assume she'll still be working with you in the lab, too?"

"Of course." He coughed. "Though if she turns me down, I don't know that I could bear to keep her on. It would be too… painful."

That filthy, lying pond scum!

"Well, in that case, you have a deal. Zenda can't stop talking about this job. I wager she'd be happy to do just about anything to keep it forever."

No! I fought the urge to burst out of the pool and talk Portia out of this insanity. Couldn't she see this wasn't right? Zenda shouldn't be forced to marry that pervert to keep her job. She deserved it already. She'd proven it with her hard work and dedication, time and again.

"Perfect," Mueller said. Footsteps echoed. I dared to peek over the pool's edge, desperate to see where they were headed. Professor Mueller stopped at the fridge Zenda used to feed the dolphins. But he didn't pull any fish out. He removed a small box about the size of a book. "Everything you need is in here. Do you remember what to do with it?"

I froze, praying Portia would open the box where I could see. What was so important she'd betray her own daughter for it?

"How could I forget?" Portia took the box with a huge smile, but instead of opening it, she tucked it under her arm. I cursed internally as she turned for the door, only to pause just beside it. "Can I ask you one more thing, Professor?"

"Certainly."

"What's your first name?"

"Adam," he answered.

Portia smiled and placed a hand lovingly on her belly. "If the baby is a boy, I'm naming him after you."

I gulped, staring at the box with trepidation, suddenly certain of what it contained.

Professor Mueller *tsked*. "Please, don't. I never gave that to you, understand?"

Portia giggled. "Oh, I suppose you're right." She sighed. "Thank you again. Goodbye."

The door closed behind her, and Professor Mueller retreated to his office. I sank to the bottom of the pool. Unless I wanted to get caught, I'd have to wait for him to leave. There was no way I could sneak out of the water without him seeing me through the glass window separating his office from the lab.

What was I going to do? One thing was certain. I couldn't let Zenda marry him. No fucking way.

She deserved it all. Not just the job she'd worked so hard for, but a husband who was devoted to her. Who loved her and wouldn't dream of forcing her to do anything.

Finally, I heard the office door open. I resurfaced slowly, careful not to make a sound.

Or not. Fuck!

Mueller's head cocked, and he turned toward my pool. I froze, my heart racing. If he found me, I was screwed. He'd know that someone was onto him and have time to cover his tracks.

He took a step closer. My pulse pounded.

Whistling pierced the air, and in the tank beside mine, an injured dolphin bobbed to the water's surface.

"Oh. It's just you." Mueller frowned at the young dolphin's bandaged fin, then slowly backed away. "Zenda will feed you soon, you greedy little thing." He straightened his lab-coat and turned for the door.

It felt like it took ages for the hatch to slam closed. I climbed out of the tank and dressed in a rush. Then I tore down the hall, determination fueling me. I'd made a decision while I was underwater and nothing was going to stop me from seeing it through.

I threw open the door to Uncle Prim's office. "Please, I need your help."

30

The Miracle

Zenda

19 years earlier

I pushed open the door to our quarters, expecting to find them empty. I nearly jumped out of my skin when I spotted movement in the living room. "Mom? Is that you?"

"Yes. It's me, love." Mom popped her head out of the closet, one of the tiny onesies she'd refused to give away clutched in her hands and tears shining in her eyes.

"You scared me. What are you doing here?" My gaze flicked to the clock and my belly tightened. "Don't you have a shift? Is something wrong?"

"No. It's the opposite, in fact." She beamed, hugging the baby outfit to her chest. "You won't believe what just happened. It's a miracle!"

My brow furrowed, and I opened my mouth, but before I could ask her what was so miraculous, the walls rattled and a series of knocks flooded my ears. I flipped around, staring at the door. Besides Nash, hardly anyone came to visit us. Who was slamming their fist into the door so hard it was like they wanted to knock it off its hinges?

I crossed the room and threw open the hatch. My eyes widened. Three women in khaki uniforms stood on the other side. We didn't have a police force in Subralia—per se. Instead, we had Peace Officers. Since I stayed out of trouble and kept my head down, I had no reason to get to know them personally, but that didn't stop me from recognizing who they were.

"Officers. How can I help you?" I asked politely.

A male voice cleared, and the trio of officers broke apart, shifting enough for a skinsuit-clad Vorill to stride through their midst. "Mayor Prim." I swallowed thickly. I'd only met Nash's uncle from afar, but his presence at my quarters instantly put me on edge. "What's this about?"

Does this have something to do with Nash? I'd noticed he'd been absent from classes today. Was he sick? Or hurt?

"Zenda. I'm sorry, but I must request you let these officers inside."

I shrugged and threw the door open wide. "Okay." It wasn't like we had anything to hide. "Is this about Nash?" I asked quietly as the officers elbowed past me into our small living space. "He's not here. I haven't seen him all day."

"I'm sorry, but I'm afraid it's not." Prim stared at me, creases wrinkling the green hued-skin around the corners of his eyes.

"I found it," one officer announced a second later. I whipped around and spotted her striding out of the washroom, holding an evidence bag filled with what looked like a bunch of trash.

"It's too late," Mom said, a proud smile on her face. "I already used it."

I frowned. "What's going on?" I directed the question to Mom, but she didn't answer. She just kept smiling, a dreamy look in her eyes. "Mom... what did you do?"

Mayor Prim waltzed in and gave the evidence bag a long once over. "We've had reports of stolen property. Now that we have proof—and your confession, Portia—I'm afraid you and your family must face the consequences of your actions."

My head reeled and my skin grew clammy. That didn't sound good. "Consequences? For what?" I shot another glance at the evidence bag. "Stealing a bunch of plastic?" The officer shifted the bag, and my gaze caught on a curious sight hidden among the wrappers and empty containers.

What was that? A turkey baster? *Oh no...*

"Mom? What did you steal?" The baby clothes clutched against her chest suddenly made sense. "Are you insane? It might not even work!"

Mom lifted her chin defiantly. "It will. I know it will."

Mayor Prim shook his head slowly. "The crime of theft is very severe. You understand how exclusive this community is. According to the Subralian charter, the punishment is banishment for you and your entire family."

My heart shattered. All my studies. My work in the lab. It was all about to be ruined because my baby-crazed mom stole sperm.

"Portia." Prim's voice gentled. "I don't see how a cafeteria worker could arrange this without help. If anyone else is complicit in this act of thievery, you must report them. Perhaps we could even forgive your daughter's punishment in exchange."

He was right. There was no way Mom pulled this off by herself. "Tell them who helped you. Please, Mom."

Mom finally met my gaze with her lips pressed together and her chin lifted stubbornly. I knew in that instant my hopes were useless. "I would if I could, love." She turned to Mayor Prim, steeling her spine. "But I can't. No one helped me. I did it all on my own."

No. This couldn't be it. My dreams of a life spent working with dolphins were so close. How could it end like this? Snatched out of my grasp just when I'd been about to earn everything I deserved. "I can't believe this..." My voice was strangled, choked out of a dry throat. "How could you, Mom?"

I flew out the door, scrubbing my cheeks violently. Maybe there was something I could do...

I refused to give up without knowing I'd tried everything.

Nash

I raced down the hall, my heart in my throat. Uncle Prim just returned to our quarters and told me what happened with Zenda and her mom. I cursed under my breath.

It's not supposed to turn out like this!

I'd been sure Portia would give up Mueller to save Zenda from banishment. Mueller would be fired, saving Zen from a forced marriage and getting that perv kicked out of Subralia. Maybe she'd even get to take over his research. I never suspected Zen's mom would stand by the man when her daughter's future was on the line.

I punched in the code to Mueller's lab, suspecting that was where Zenda would run off to. It was her happy place, after all. Though it looked like it wouldn't be for much longer…

My stomach churned. *How had it come to this?*

Still, even if Zenda had to leave Subralia, surely it was better than the alternative. She could start a new life, far away from Mueller's stupid proposal. She'd never have to know that her dream job was about to be denied to her, unless she gave into his sick demands. Zen was smart. She'd find another position she loved—with people who appreciated her for the right reasons.

I choked down my fury as I entered the lab and spotted that bastard standing next to her. I wanted to rage. To scream at him for everything he'd done. But—I couldn't.

Uncle told me to keep quiet. He assured me that the officers would do everything in their power to find evidence we could use against him. Portia's confession would've been ideal, but Mueller could've left some other clues behind that would help us prove he was complicit in the theft. For now, it was just my word against his. That would never hold up. And with Mueller's work contract, the only way we could give him the boot was with cold, hard evidence.

So, I had to play it smart, which meant acting like I had no clue what he'd said and done with Portia earlier.

I knocked on the office door, my heart clenching when Zenda lifted her face from the big book spread on Mueller's desk. Her eyes were puffy and bloodshot. A sure sign she'd been crying. "Zen? I heard what happened. I'm really sorry. Can I do anything to help?"

"Yes." Zenda flew across the room. "I need a hug."

I captured her in my arms, not missing the frown Mueller flashed before swiftly schooling his expression. "It's okay." I rubbed her back soothingly. "You're okay."

She pulled away much too soon and sucked in a shaky breath. "Thanks." She returned to the desk and bent over the book again, flipping a page.

"What are you doing?" I asked.

"It's the Subralian charter," Mueller explained. I flinched at his voice, wishing I could throw him out of his own office. "Zenda is searching for a loophole that will allow her to stay."

"Have you found anything?" I inched closer.

"No. But there has to be..." Zenda gasped. "Wait." A huge smile spread across her face. "This is it!"

"What?" I leaned next to her, scanning the page.

"Right here." She jabbed a finger at the words. "The banishment applies to family members, but look at this addendum. The family member in question must be part of the same household. It doesn't apply to relatives in different households."

"I don't get it," I admitted.

"If I want to stay, I can, as long as I marry into another household. I have to get married."

Zenda's words rocked me to the core. This played right into Mueller's hands! I shot a glance at his slimy face, certain he would pull a ring out of his lab-coat and drop to one knee.

Mueller shook his head sadly. "That's unfortunate. I doubt you'll have much luck finding a husband here. No researcher worth his salt would want to be associated with thievery. It would be disastrous for his reputation."

I blinked, the rest of my body frozen. *What?* Mueller got her into this mess, and now he wouldn't man up and get her out of it? Not that I really wanted him to, but the fact that he'd done a one-eighty over his precious *reputation* made fire scorch my veins. My hands shook, and I was one step away from planting my fist in the dick's face.

Mueller's watch chimed. "I have a meeting I must attend. Zenda, please, use my office for as long as you need." He crossed the room and fled. Spineless coward.

"What if it's not a researcher..." Zenda turned to me, and my heart stalled. "Nash, I wouldn't ask if I wasn't desperate." She bit her lip, looking so damn hopeful I wanted to cave so I'd be the one to save her... but I just *couldn't*.

Fuck, fuck, fuck. I gulped. "You know my thoughts on marriage."

Devastation flashed in her eyes. She held my gaze for a few seconds, and I felt like the universe was imploding. Then she turned back to the desk and flipped the page, her shoulders sinking. "It's fine. I get it. That's too much to ask." She sighed. The exhale was so full of defeat it made my heart ache. "I'll keep looking. If there's one loophole, maybe there'll be another."

"I'll help." I sat next to her and pretended to read alongside her, but the words bled into one another on the page.

I'm doing the right thing, aren't I? I wasn't equipped to be anyone's husband, much less Zen's. She deserved the best—not a guy who was so unlovable his own parents couldn't stand him.

But if that was true, then why did I feel so awful?

This was all Mueller's fault. I had to hope that the officers found some proof. If not...

I'll make that bastard pay for what he did to Zen. Even if it takes me a lifetime.

31

Straight Up Pitiful

Zenda

Present day

I shoved another skinsuit into my suitcase, my stomach fluttering with nerves.

Arda chuckled from her spot beside my bookshelf. "Fuck, Zen. You need to settle down. What did that outfit do to you?" She placed another one of my novels into the box at her feet.

I sighed. "I know. I'm just anxious about leaving."

It had been a long trip back to Earth. I'd managed to successfully avoid my husband's stupid face for most of it. But now that I was leaving, I wouldn't have my girls to run interference any longer.

"Sure you aren't nervous about patching things up with Nash?" Ren tore the sheets off my cot and began folding them.

"Maybe..." I admitted. I'd spilled the beans to them after the night Nash knocked on my door, trying to con me into losing the bet. I'd shared everything. Including what happened when we first met, to the state of my marriage today. The sad story was enough to convince them to keep Nash busy—and more importantly, away from me—while I got a handle on the anger and heartache he'd inflicted on me.

"You know, he hasn't stopped asking about you," Ren added.

I rolled my eyes.

"He shuffles around looking like a kid whose candy was just stolen." Ren giggled.

"No, that's not right." Arda shook her head. "He's more like a dog who shit in his master's boots and knows he's about to get punished. Straight up pitiful."

Ren snorted. The corner of my mouth lifted at the image that planted in my head.

"You know, I've been thinking..." Arda's brow scrunched. "What if it wasn't an act?"

I abandoned my attempt to straighten my suitcase and gave her my full attention. "What wasn't?"

"The other night. When he shoved his dick in your hand."

My cheeks heated. "I told you, he just wanted to win."

"You sure about that?" Arda popped out a hip.

"She has a point," Ren chimed in. "You were arguing with him, weren't you? I don't know a lot about men, but I doubt it's easy to keep a stiffy when they're being yelled at. Maybe he wasn't lying when he said he wants you."

"I might consider it, if he hadn't claimed he'd *always* wanted me." I scoffed. "I think it's pretty obvious from how he rejected me way back when that wasn't the case."

Arda grabbed another book, twisting it in her hands. "I'm not so sure. Didn't his parents basically abandon him?"

"Yeah." My heart twisted. I might be a little ticked off at Nash, but it didn't stop me from feeling for him.

"It sounds like when he got to Earth you guys got tight really fast," Arda continued.

"We did."

"Well, he was probably afraid to lose you, too. I bet that's what made him too chicken-shit to admit he wanted in your pants."

Was Arda right? Could that be why he never tried to take our relationship farther?

"I'm not sure I follow your logic." Ren lifted a brow. "If Nash was terrified of losing Zen, why wouldn't he jump at the chance to marry her?"

Arda scratched her head. "I mean, that makes sense to me, but for a guy who's decided never to marry, maybe not so much." She shrugged and speared me with a glare. "You know an easy way to find out, right?"

"Yeah, yeah." How couldn't I? Arda hadn't failed to suggest it about a thousand times. "I need to talk to him."

"So, are you ready for this?" Ren set the folded sheets into a box.

"If you're not, you can run away with us." Arda patted the wall. "Got the perfect escape, right here."

I sensed from the hard gleam in Ren's eyes she felt the same. They wouldn't hesitate to secret me away if it was what I wanted. I was really gonna miss them.

I shook my head. "I'm good. It's only a year. Besides, you know I've been itching to see what's happening under the sea."

Arda sighed. "Well, for what it's worth, I hope you figure out what's really going through Nash's head."

"Me too." I forced a smile. *Ain't that the truth?*

Nash

The Verne's docking port slammed into place. I sucked in a deep breath and waited for Zenda to finish her last round of hugs with her friends.

"Call if you need anything. I mean it, Zen," Arda yelled with a wave.

My stomach clenched. Arda was certainly adamant about reminding Zen she had other options. Not that I could blame her. From the amount of time we'd spent together during the trip to Earth, any outside observer would likely think my wife hated me.

The entire trip Zenda avoided me, always finding some excuse to duck out if we were in the same room. And she'd refused to be alone with me, making it impossible to talk to her.

I miss her.

At least now that we'd arrived at Subralia, she'd be forced to talk to me eventually. I wasn't planning to push her, but it would be kind of hard to avoid talking once we were living together. I was desperate to apologize properly, and for her forgiveness.

Whatever feelings she was hiding didn't stop her from approaching the hatch with cautious steps. My arms ached, feeling empty. But I didn't throw them out wide for a hug. Not when I was terrified of spooking her.

I settled for a small smile instead. "You ready?"

Adjusting her glasses, she nodded.

I opened the hatch and led her into Subralia's docking bay. Zen paused beside the Verne, sending the ugly ship a long glance.

What was she thinking? Did she regret leaving already?

"Shouldn't we help move our luggage and whatnot?" she asked.

I blew out a relieved breath. "No need. I called my uncle, and he arranged to have it moved."

"Oh." Zenda fell in at my side. "That was nice of him."

"Nash, my boy!" a familiar voice boomed across the bay.

"Speaking of... there he is." I turned to Zen, noting the nervous way she twisted her hands together. I frowned.

"Nash!" Uncle Prim stopped in front of us, wasting no time before pulling me into a big hug. "It's good to have you home, son."

"Good to see you, Uncle." I returned his hug eagerly, smiling widely.

"I hear congratulations are in order?" Prim released me, and turned to Zenda, moving to hug her as well.

Zenda took a step back and thrust out her hand instead. "Mayor Prim," she said icily. "You look well."

My heart twinged. Zenda hugged *everyone*. She clearly held some animosity toward my uncle. I could understand why. I'd likely not want to be chummy with the man who'd forced me to leave the home I loved.

A little voice in my mind whispered, *If she knew the whole story maybe she wouldn't hold her family's banishment against him.*

I shook off the urge to come clean. It wasn't the right time. Zen was barely talking to me already.

Luckily, Zenda's cool welcome didn't faze my uncle—or at least he didn't let it show. He smoothly shifted out of a hugging stance and took Zenda's hand, shaking it firmly. "I can say the same to you, dear. You look radiant! I hope my nephew is treating you well."

I held my breath, waiting for her to answer sarcastically. She'd lob some clever joke, putting me down subtly—only to lift the corner of her mouth to show me she didn't *really* mean it...

Zenda merely nodded, tugged her hand free from Uncle's, and inched closer to the docking bay doors. My stomach twisted. Was she too distracted by her discomfort with my uncle to act normal? Or was this just another sign that she wasn't ready to forgive me yet?

"Well, I won't keep you. I just wanted to welcome you both home. I'm sure you're eager to take your wife on a tour, Nash."

I smiled at Uncle Prim. "I am. Thanks for the welcome."

"Of course, my boy. See you soon. You too, Zenda." He waved at her.

She returned the gesture halfheartedly and stepped away. I hurried to catch her.

"So, do you want to see your new quarters first? Or would you rather go on a tour?" I asked.

"The tour, please," Zenda answered.

I sucked in a shaky breath. Polite and detached. Not how I wanted Zen to act with me, but it was a start.

"No problem." I grinned casually, deciding not to let her glimpse my inner turmoil playing under the surface. If she wanted a tour, I was going to be the best damn tour guide there ever was.

"There's been a lot of changes to the community in the last two decades." I pushed open the door, leading us out of the docking bay and into the hall.

A tiny gasp spilled out of Zenda's lips as she entered the glass tube. "Not this. It's exactly how I remembered," she whispered, her voice filled with awe and a delighted smile painting her lips.

"Actually, the halls have been replaced at least half a dozen times, so you're not entirely accurate."

Zen shot me a glare. "Okay, mister stickler." She focused on the walls again, staring at a school of brightly colored fish swimming beside us. "I wasn't talking about the halls. I was talking about *this*." She threw her arms out to her sides and spun slowly. "It's like living inside an aquarium." Her smile widened, and my pulse raced. "It's *wonderful*."

No... you are. I kept the cheesy line to myself, though my tongue burned to say it out loud. After what happened on the Verne, I doubted she'd believe me.

We spent the next few hours touring Subralia. The tension in Zenda's frame slowly dissipated with each new place I showed her. By the time we arrived at my quarters, I hoped she was ready to listen to my apology.

"Here's our last stop on the tour." I halted in front of the hatch. "Are you ready to see your new home?"

Zenda blinked a few times, seeming to steel herself before she nodded. "Yes. I'm ready."

I threw open the door, my heart in my throat. This was the first time Zen saw my quarters. Would she see it as somewhere she could be happy, or would she be instantly filled with regret?

Zenda stepped inside—and she gasped.

32

The Centerpiece

I sucked in a shaky breath and stepped inside. The spacious room was furnished smartly, with a big cushioned couch and loveseat sitting in the center. At first glance, it seemed perfectly ordinary. A comfortable living space for a man who might be expected to entertain the mayor's guests.

It wasn't until my gaze trailed along the shelves on the cream-colored walls that a breathless gasp escaped my lips.

Is that what I think it is?

"Something wrong?" Nash pushed through the doorway, his brow furrowed.

Heart pounding, I pointed at the rows of tiny figurines with enormous heads sitting on the closest shelf. "What's that?"

Nash followed my finger and grinned sheepishly. "My bobblehead collection."

I gaped at him, my mouth hanging open so wide I probably looked like the fish we'd watched swim past. "You have a bobblehead collection?"

"Well, yeah." He shut the door. "See, there was this girl who gave me one once. When she moved away, I started collecting them. Then whenever I had a bad day, I'd come home and give one a little jiggle." He wandered over to the shelf and tapped the head of a bobblehead shaped like the Statue of Liberty, setting it bouncing gaily. "It always made me think of her and smile."

Oh. My. Gods.

I picked my jaw up off the ground and joined Nash at the shelf. My eyes widened as I spotted the alien I'd given him so long ago, sitting up front and center. I lifted it with shaky fingers, making the silly thing jerk around without even trying.

"In case you were wondering, that one's my favorite." My gaze rose in time to catch Nash winking. "I bet you're thirsty after that long tour. I'll grab us a drink."

Nash wandered off, heading for what I assumed must be the kitchen. I didn't follow. I couldn't. My legs were frozen and I couldn't stop staring at the goofy toy wobbling in my hands.

I'd been so sure Nash was messing with me. That he'd only wanted to be with me to satisfy that bet. But now... maybe he truly *had* harbored feelings for me all along.

My fingers trembled as I carefully set the alien back in its place. I hadn't thought about my old bobblehead in years. Probably not since I'd given it away. But Nash built a collection and set it up as the centerpiece.

Didn't that mean something?

What does it say about me if I desperately want it to mean everything?

I tore my gaze off the shelf before the tears pricking the corners of my eyes fell. I walked away slowly, giving the room another once over. Lovely landscapes of swamps topped with vivid rainbow sunsets hung on the walls. One corner held a holovid-screen, like the one we'd set up during the Verne's renovations.

And—a bookshelf. I strode to it, beyond curious to see what Nash thought of as suitable literature. It wasn't long before I spotted a theme. Thrillers and spy novels seemed to be his preference. Except...

My brow furrowed, and I bent down to trace a familiar spine. I knew it! He *was* a thief. My mother's stolen historical romance sat wedged between two hardbacks, the spine creased so much I barely recognized it.

Why hadn't he thrown it away? Nash could've easily dumped it when he was through reading it. It clearly didn't fit with the rest of his books. Hell, for that matter, he could've tossed the bobblehead I'd given him, too.

Why didn't he?

"I hope you weren't expecting spirits. I only have juice and water at the moment." Nash emerged from the kitchen, carrying two glasses filled with purple liquid.

"Juice is fine." I met him halfway and took the glass, fighting to ignore the tingle that spread up my fingers when he brushed against me. I gulped the sweet liquid, barely tasting it.

Nash finished his just as quickly. "Did you want to watch an old vid together? Or I could put on some music?" He grabbed the empty glass from me, a brow lifted.

"Maybe tomorrow. I'm actually kind of tired," I admitted.

And overwhelmed. Confused as hell. Yeah... there was that, too.

"Okay." Nash lifted the glasses. "Let me get rid of these and I'll show you the bedroom."

My mind raced as he disappeared into the kitchen again. The bedroom—not *your* bedroom. Did he expect me to sleep with him again? The thought made my stomach tingle. If I were being entirely honest, another organ a bit lower started tingling even harder.

I clenched my thighs together. *Down, girl. We're mad at him still, aren't we?*

Nash strolled out, flashing a soft smile. "Come on. It's this way."

I gulped, following Nash into his bedroom. He'd decorated it in deep blue tones that went well with the mahogany wood furniture. The closet doors hung open, and one side had already been cleared out. My suitcases sat in front of it, ready to be emptied.

"Did your uncle clean out the closet for you, too?" I buried a wince at the annoyed tone I couldn't seem to contain. Mayor Prim had been nothing but welcoming. Still, I wagered it would take a long time for me to forgive him for the role he played in my banishment.

Nash chuckled. "No, but he let in the maid service for me. I hired them after the wedding to get everything ready for your arrival."

That was incredibly thoughtful. I turned away from the closet and spotted a piece of plastic lying on the wood floor next to the bed-frame.

My cheeks flamed. *Please tell me that's not a condom.* Suddenly, I couldn't stop picturing all the women who must have slept in that bed with him. All the women who weren't me. Stooping down, I picked it up. "Looks like they missed something." The thin sheet crumpled in my hand, making my brows draw together. "What is it?"

Nash plucked it out of my fingers. "I'm not sure." His face brightened. "I bet that fell off the new mattress. Don't they usually cover them in plastic when they're transporting them?"

"You bought a new mattress?"

"Yeah." Nash met my eyes. "I wanted something just for us. I haven't even slept in it yet." He waggled his brows. "You want to be the first to try it out?"

Guilt flashed up my spine. Here I was thinking he left evidence of an old flame for me to find, instead he'd gone out of his way to make sure I was comfortable. I really needed to stop immediately thinking the worst.

I grinned and face planted into the mattress, not caring that my glasses smashed into my face. "Oh, yeah." I turned my head with a sigh. "This is nice. Might even be better than the beds at your parent's house."

Nash's smile fell for a second, but then his eyes swept down the length of my back and a smirk lifted his lips. "Looks like it." I could almost feel his gaze trailing across my skin and lingering on my ass. "I bet it feels amazing."

Is he still talking about the bed? My pulse kicked into overdrive.

I shifted onto my side and propped my head up with a hand. "Aren't you going to try it?"

Nash inched closer. "Are you sure you want me to?" He hovered at the edge. "I don't mind taking the couch."

Was he serious? I searched his face. Yep. He was really willing to give me his brand new bed, and sleep on a couch that he wouldn't be able to fully stretch out on.

Maybe I ought to let him. Who knew what might happen if he climbed under the sheets with me? Would he keep his hands to himself, or would it end up like last time? I shivered, unsure which way I wanted that question to be answered.

"Don't be silly." I patted the bed. "This thing is huge. We can share."

The grin he flashed took my breath away. Nash spun on his side and jumped on the bed so hard I bounced in the air when he landed.

I giggled manically. "Are you trying to launch me to the moon?"

"What if I was?" Nash chuckled, bouncing again and making the bed heave me into the air.

I grabbed a pillow and whacked him with it, laughing all the while. "Quit it, you weirdo."

Nash stilled, and his expression sobered. "I missed this, Zen." He grabbed my hand. "I missed *you*. The trip back to Earth was pure torture. Seeing you day in and day out, but knowing you wanted nothing to do with me—it drove me crazy."

My heart clenched. I'd just needed some time to myself, but seeing the hurt in his eyes now, and remembering the way he grew up neglected, I realized ignoring him was probably the worst punishment I could've arranged for him.

I met his eyes. "I hated it, too."

"I'm sorry about that stupid bet. It was a mistake. I never meant to make you uncomfortable. I was such an idiot." He squeezed my hand, his voice so sincere my chest ached. "Will you forgive me? Please?"

I nodded, tears pooling in my eyes. "I do." I closed the space between us and snuggled against his chest. Nash wrapped me in his arms, sighing. "I'm sorry, too. I shouldn't have shut you out. I promise if we argue again, I won't disappear on you."

We lay there for a long while, neither of us moving. I might have fallen asleep on his chest if my bladder hadn't protested.

"Where are you going?" Nash asked grumpily as I started to pull away, tightening his arms.

I giggled. "I need to pee. You better let me go unless you want to christen your bed in the grossest way possible."

Nash snapped his arms apart. "Go. But you better get back here when you're done."

I hopped out of bed, cocking a brow. "Of course I'm coming back. That's *my* bed you're hogging."

A pillow flew at my head. "Them's fighting words," Nash declared, in an awful western-American accent.

I squealed and ducked into the washroom, shoving the door closed breathlessly. My heart was lighter than it'd been in weeks. We'd put aside the hurt feelings and now we could go back to being friends. It's exactly what I wanted.

Then why does it feel like something is missing?

33

Talk About Confusing

Zenda

Consciousness creeped up on me slowly. I'd had one of the best nights of sleep in my life in my new bed.

Scratch that—*our* new bed. My belly fluttered as I noticed the other occupant, currently lying behind me, one corded arm slung around my waist.

Last night had been... interesting. I'd been sure Nash would pull something like the last time we slept together. As soon as the lights went out, I'd mentally prepared myself for more of his sensual torture. When he immediately reached for me, spooning against my back, I'd tensed. But Nash's hand didn't trail across my belly. And the only thing he whispered in my ear wasn't anything close to the sexy boasts he'd fed me on our wedding night.

Still, I'd practically swooned. *You feel perfect in my arms, Zen. I never want to fight again.*

Then he proceeded to promptly fall asleep. Talk about confusing.

I'd spent a few minutes wavering between crying and fighting the urge to wake him and demand he show me how perfect I was—preferably with his dick. Although it wasn't too long before the amazing bed and his gentle embrace lulled me into a dreamless sleep.

Who knows what today would have in store for me? Hopefully, it would be less perplexing. I stretched, wanting to move but not ready to leave the warmth of my fake husband's arms. That's when a steel rod poked my ass.

I guess one part of Nash still wanted me. My body heated, and my pulse throbbed in my clit. I couldn't deny it felt nice. Better than nice. His hard flesh dug into my softness, giving me the urge to roll my hips.

My hands tingled, recalling how big he'd felt when he slipped my palm over his skinsuit. As lust pooled in my belly, I had to admit the truth. I was sick of lying to myself. I wanted to touch him again. And I wanted him to touch me. Kiss me. Fuck me.

If he let me touch him once, he won't mind if I do again, right? I was a heartbeat away from squeezing my hand between us and cupping his length when an alarm blared.

Nash rolled away from me and slapped blindly at the bedside table. The sound cut off. Nash rolled back in my direction just as I flipped around to face him.

"Good morning." I smiled sweetly and snuggled against his chest, slinging a leg over his hip. Maybe he'd make it a great morning by doing some of those things I was just fantasizing about.

Nash groaned, pulling me close. "Morning."

"What's with the alarm?" I scooched even closer, trailing my hand slowly across Nash's arm. "Got somewhere to go?"

"Unfortunately, I do." He sighed, pulling away far enough to meet my eyes. The sleepy smile on his face made my heart twinge. "Think you'll be all right on your own while I go check in with work?"

Disappointment hit me like a torpedo blast. I smiled benignly. "Sure. Guess I'll unpack." I tried one more time to entice Nash, dragging my toes lightly down his leg.

Nash pulled me close again and planted a kiss on me. Right on the forehead.

Ugh. *That's so not where I want him to kiss me.* I bit back a groan as his moist lips lifted off my skin.

"I'll stop back before lunch. We can go to the mess together. I've got some of those protein bars you like in the kitchen if you get hungry while you're unpacking."

"Sounds like a plan." I forced another smile.

Nash hopped out of bed, grabbed some clothes out of the closet, and disappeared into the washroom.

I lay in bed, thoughts hammering me one after the other, hard enough to give me whiplash.

Who the hell was I kidding? Nash didn't want me. I couldn't take his morning wood as evidence. He was probably dreaming about someone else.

I'd practically thrown myself at him when he woke up, just for him to kiss my *forehead*. You'd think I was his little sister. Or some pathetic girl whose heart he couldn't bear to break.

I sighed as I heard the hallway hatch slam closed. Then I slowly dragged my horny ass out of bed. I spotted my suitcase and the pout I was wearing shifted into a smirk.

Yeah, I'd told Nash no brothels, but I happened to have the next best thing packed away in my suitcase. I tossed the bag on the bed and unzipped it. Within seconds, I located the big pink box I'd carefully hidden among my skinsuits.

I quickly unlatched it and pulled out my favorite dildo. "Guess it's you and me today." I told the toy. "I hope you're in the mood for a shower, big guy."

Nash

I cursed under my breath as I ducked into the hall. What was up with Zen this morning? A part of me still couldn't believe I'd woken beside her when yesterday she was barely talking to me. And the way she'd touched me... shivers raced down my spine. It could have been innocent. She'd only stroked my arm and leg. But something inside me wondered, what if it wasn't?

Too bad I couldn't turn around and find out. Now that I was back, I had a schedule to uphold and a job that needed me. I'd see Zen for lunch. I could gauge how she was feeling while we shared a meal.

She wasn't coming onto me, was she? It was probably just wishful thinking. I wanted it so badly I was taking every innocent touch as a sign that wasn't there. She wouldn't go from blatantly ignoring me, to wanting to fuck me so fast. Right?

I was so caught up in my own thoughts, I didn't notice my uncle until he was practically on top of me.

"Slow down, Nash." He slapped my back, wheezing slightly. "I called your name three times already. I wasn't sure if I was going to catch you."

I flipped around. Uncle Prim cradled a fruit basket in his arms, a huge smile on his face despite his labored breathing.

"Good morning." I arched a brow. "What are you doing here? Shouldn't you be in your office already?"

He chuckled. "I realized I forgot to tell you to take the day off yesterday. I'm sure you'll be wanting a little time to get your wife settled." He thrust the basket into my hands. "Here. This is for you both. A welcome home present."

"Thanks, Uncle." I smiled, my pulse racing. It's what I'd been hoping for. A bolt of unease spread, threatening to overwhelm the excitement blooming in my chest. "Are you sure you don't need me?"

Uncle scoffed. "I survived without you during your trip. What's one more day?" He shoved my shoulder, forcing me to take a step toward my quarters if I didn't want fruit spilling down the hall. "Go on, now. I'll see you bright and early tomorrow."

"Okay," I agreed. Another pang assaulted me. Uncle Prim still didn't know that my marriage to Zen wasn't your typical love match. I couldn't help feeling guilty about letting him go on assuming it was. But I didn't feel bad enough to spill all the details immediately. Not when there was likely still a warm, snuggly Zen cuddled up in my sheets. "See you tomorrow."

Bright citrus filled my nose. I carted the huge fruit basket back to my quarters, feeling a burn in my arms before I completed the short journey. "No wonder Uncle was wheezing," I muttered under my breath. "How much fruit does he think we need?"

I balanced the basket atop my knee with one arm so I could open the hatch. Once the monstrosity was safely perched on the living room coffee table, I blew out a sigh.

That's when a curious sound made my heart drop. Thanks to that recording Ren made, I instantly recognized it.

Why is Zen moaning like she's about to come? Panic slammed into me. Was Zen deceiving me? Did she—No. I shoved the thoughts aside. There was no way. Zen was *not* a cheater. There had to be some explanation...

Another moan bounced off the walls, making my cock jerk.

I don't know what she's doing, but I'm about to find out.

34

Fun in the Shower

Nash

I crossed the living room, a symphony of Zen's moans making my pulse race. *What is she doing? And where?*

I inched open the bedroom door, half-expecting to find her writhing in bed, one delicate hand working between her spread thighs. But the bed was empty. Well, not completely. Zen's suitcase lay atop it, the lid unzipped, giving me a glimpse at her skinsuits folded neatly inside. That and—I gulped—a pair of tiny lace panties.

I sucked in a deep breath, fighting to wash the image of her wearing those—and nothing else—out of my mind. I managed to shake it off, only to wonder, *If she isn't in bed, then where is she?* My brow scrunched until another moan sounded and my gaze shot to the partially open washroom door. Steam curled in the air, and the light pitter-patter of water falling registered in my mind.

Having a little fun in the shower, is she? I stalked across the room until a pink box half hidden in the sheets caught my eye. I paused, lifting the box. It was so light; I suspected it was empty, but curiosity still blazed within me. *Should I open it?* I started to set it down—opening it would be an invasion of her privacy. But then again...

Another moan made the decision easy. I flipped the lid off. My instincts were right. There was nothing inside. Nothing except for the plastic liner that was clearly meant to keep the item from jostling around when inside the box. A wicked grin spread across my face.

Seems my instincts were right more than once this morning. Zen did wake up horny. But instead of telling me she wanted me, she waited for me to leave and took matters into her own hands.

A war of conflicting emotions bombarded me. I wanted to march into that bathroom and show her what she was missing. But I couldn't help worrying, what if she hadn't told me because she didn't want me? What if she was just itching for me to leave so she could be alone?

"Gods," Zen moaned again, louder than ever. "Gods, Nash. That feels so good."

Something inside me snapped the second I heard my name. The box slid out of my fingers and bounced on the bed. I crossed the room in a few swift strides and stepped into the washroom.

Fuuuccckkk.

My dick turned to granite, and I scrubbed a hand across my face. Zen was in the shower, bent over, her bare legs and ass pressed against the glass. A suction cup hid most of her pussy from view. One I know wasn't there the last time I took a shower.

I slammed the door closed.

Zenda yelped and jerked forward. Then she stood upright and whipped a towel off the wall faster than I thought possible. "N-Nash? What are you doing?" She wrapped the towel around herself but couldn't cover the bright pink flush staining her skin.

I tore one glove off. "I heard you call my name."

Her eyes widened. "B-but I thought you had work?" She backed up, hissing when the spray drenched her towel. I couldn't help admiring the way the wet fabric molded to her curves like a second skin.

I shook my head slowly, keeping my eyes glued to hers as I peeled off the second glove. "I got the day off." It fluttered to the tile. I toed off a boot next. Then the other. Zen's gaze flicked around nervously, jerking to each article as it dropped, then returning to stare at me incredulously. "You just couldn't wait for me to leave, could you? My bad girl."

"What are you doing?" Zen's tone hardened. "If this is about that bet—"

"Fuck the bet." I slid down the zipper on my skinsuit. "I want you, Zen."

She gulped, her gaze lifting from my bare chest. "You do?"

Instead of answering, I continued stripping. Zenda's gaze zeroed in on my cock and she licked her lips, watching my length bounce as I released it. She didn't take her eyes off my dick even when I walked across the room and slipped open the shower door.

I spared a glance for the monster dangling off the glass shower stall wall. Was that a Vorill model dildo? I couldn't stop the smile from spreading when I realized Zen's toy was a pretty decent replica of my anatomy.

My wife is full of surprises. Well, so am I.

"Where are my manners?" With one hand, I reached down and stroked my cock, not bothering to hide my satisfied smile at the little groan that echoed in the back of Zen's throat. Then I lifted a finger and hooked it on Zen's towel. With one hard jerk, it fell, pooling around her ankles. She gasped, covering her breasts with one arm and cupping her pussy with a hand. "I've clearly interrupted you."

"W-what?" her voice cracked.

"Don't let me stop you. Be bad for me, Zen."

Zenda

I couldn't stop staring. Nash's hand was wrapped around his cock, slowly stroking. And I was standing in front of him, warm water cascading down my naked body.

I'm dreaming... I had to be. Nash didn't really walk in on me fucking a dildo in his shower. He didn't hear me call out his name. That would be so mortifying I just might die. No. I was still in bed—and this was all a figment of my very naughty imagination.

"Go on," Nash demanded gruffly.

What is he asking? My mind was dazed. I couldn't think straight while his hand worked up and down his beautiful cock.

Gods, he's so fucking sexy. His muscles glistened, giving his green skin a healthy sheen even without the shower spray hitting him. *And don't even get me started on his cock...*

Vorill men weren't equipped the same as humans. The first time I'd chosen a Vorill sexbot, I'd been hooked on their unique anatomy. The minute I'd left the brothel, I'd hunted down the trusty suction cup model currently dangling on the wall.

Nash's cock was slightly bigger than my dildo, but it had all the same ridges I'd become obsessed with. I caught my lip between my teeth as his rounded fingertips slid across the horizontal ridges that lined his shaft. Then his palm slid over his cockhead, giving the bulbous tip a squeeze before his hand slid down, starting the process all over again.

"You just gonna stand there?" he asked. "Not that I don't mind the view."

I tore my gaze off the hypnotic stroking and focused on Nash's face. His eyes were half-lidded, and his gaze was glued on *me*. Nash was jerking off and staring at the water slipping down *my* body.

Yep. I'm definitely dreaming.

"So, I guess all that bad girl talk was a boast, then."

I clenched my thighs together. *Bad girl.* Gods, if those words didn't sound incredible rolling off his tongue while he worked his length in his hand. And he was right. I was just standing there. Suddenly, I wanted nothing more than to prove him wrong. I wasn't some prissy little good girl anymore.

I dropped my hands, letting him see all of me. Nash sucked in a huge breath, and his hand stilled on his dick. I stepped forward, reaching for him.

"Nope." He backed away until his shoulders hit the shower stall door. "Not until you show me." Nash aimed a pointed glance at the dildo.

He couldn't mean... "Didn't you see enough already?"

He cocked a brow. "Have you met me?" His hand returned to stroking, leisurely rolling up and down his cock.

Nash wanted me to fuck the dildo while he watched. And not from across the room. He wanted to see it up close and personal. The thought was enough to make my clit throb.

I couldn't... *Who the hell am I kidding? Yes, the fuck I can.*

"You mean like this?" I smirked and bent over. The plastic cock slapped my bare ass.

"Mm, yes." Nash stroked his cock faster. "That's my good little bad girl."

Fuck! My pussy clenched.

I reached behind me and grabbed the dildo. But instead of putting it in immediately, I slid it through my folds, rubbing my clit over the rounded tip. Nash groaned. I slid the dildo across my pussy, moaning as each ridge caressed my sensitive flesh.

"I bet that feels good." Nash shifted in the shower, angling his body for a better view of the dildo rubbing my pussy.

"So good." I tilted my hips and lifted one leg as much as I could without falling, wanting him to see.

Nash stared straight between my legs as I slipped the dildo inside. "Fuck, Zen."

I planted both hands on the wall and rocked back. My pussy was so wet, the dildo slid inside easily. "Mmmm." I locked eyes with Nash again. "Is this what you want to see?" I leaned forward, then back, using the opposite wall as leverage, and fucked the dildo with long smooth strokes.

"Yes," he hissed, watching intently.

My pussy was on fire and it had everything to do with Nash. I'd fucked that dildo dozens of times, but nothing compared to how it felt with him watching. I rolled my hips, putting on a show.

Nash's hand stroked in time with my thrusts. He shifted again, moving so close the shower head sprayed him. I licked my lips, watching the water trickle down his muscular chest. I reached for him again, and this time, he didn't move away. He let me maneuver him even closer. Once I pulled him where I wanted him, I wasn't leaning on the wall for support anymore. I grabbed onto Nash's hips and moaned, fucking the dildo harder.

He dropped his cock in favor of rubbing my breasts. For half a second, self-consciousness assailed me. With me bent over fucking the dildo, my breasts hung at a strange angle and jiggled more than usual. But then my hand closed over Nash's cock and the strangled moan he unleashed made every self-conscious thought flee my mind.

Nash pinched my nipples, and I cried out. It wasn't just my pussy on fire now. His rough caresses combined with the water pelting my back and made my whole body tingle.

Two can play at that game.

I leaned over even further and sucked Nash's cockhead into my mouth.

"Fuck!" Nash's hips jerked, then stilled. I gazed up at him with my lips wrapped around his length and swirled my tongue around the tip. "Mm. You're good at that." His fingers tangled in my wet hair, and he started guiding my movements. He leaned forward each time I thrust back on the dildo, chasing my mouth but never pushing far enough to make me gag.

It wasn't long before I was ready to explode. The dildo caressed my pussy, and Nash's eyes never left me, amping me up even faster.

"You look perfect like this," Nash said gruffly. "Does my bad girl like being fucked in her mouth and cunt at the same time?"

Holy shit... I wasn't expecting *that*. My pussy throbbed, confirming how much I fucking loved it. And his dirty mouth, too.

I met his eyes and nodded, not wanting to release his dick to reply. Nash groaned and pushed me back faster, urging me to work my hips in a hectic rhythm. Within seconds, my body combusted, and an orgasm ripped through me. Pleasure zinged through my body, so intense I tore my mouth off Nash's cock and screamed incoherently.

"That's it." Nash caught me when my legs gave out. "Zen. That was so fucking hot." The dildo slid out, and Nash lifted me in his arms, urging me to wrap my legs around his waist. I buried my face in his neck as the last aftershocks of my orgasm faded.

When he shut off the shower and threw open the shower stall door, I lifted my face. "Where are you going?"

Nash grinned. "Did you think we were done?" He strode across the room and planted me on the bathroom vanity.

I gasped as the cold marble chilled my skin. "We're not?"

"Not even close."

Nash

Zenda gazed up at me, her brown eyes wide open and pupils dilated. I tugged her to the edge of the vanity, making her gasp and lean on her hands for balance. The move exposed her neck and chest. I licked my lips and stared at the freckles dusting her creamy skin.

I wanted to taste them all. Connect the dots like constellations in the night sky. I bent down, trailing my tongue across her collarbone.

Zen moaned and reached between us, but I knocked her hand away before she grabbed my length. "Hey, no fair," she whined.

"So greedy." I lifted my tongue off her skin and chuckled. "Just give me a minute to cool down. I don't want to come until I'm inside you."

There was no way I would last if we fucked now. Not after the show she put on in the shower. I'd never seen anything sexier than her bent over with my dick in her mouth and that dildo splitting her open.

Zen tried to clench her legs together, but I didn't let her. I slid my hand between her thighs instead and groaned. "Mm. You're so wet." I backed away enough to get a clear view of my fingers slipping up and down her tender flesh. Zenda quivered, her arms shaking as she fought to keep herself steady on the vanity.

She looked so gorgeous, spread out for me. Her long red hair was wet and sticking to her shoulders. Her chest heaved, making her perfect tits bounce. I could've watched her come all day long and not tired of it.

But I couldn't ignore the question burning on the tip of my tongue. "Do you always think of me when you play with that toy?"

She mewed as I dipped a finger inside her. "I-I..." The prettiest pink flush spread across her chest.

"Tell me."

She gulped, then met my eyes. "Yes."

Holy hell. "I think about you, too. All the time." I stepped closer, hooking my finger up and hitting a spot that had her panting. "I can't tell you how many times. Hundreds. Thousands." She cried out as I thrust my finger inside her pussy. But it wasn't enough. No where near it.

I pulled my hand out, grabbed my cock, and lined it up with her clit, rubbing my length up and down her hot flesh. "You feel amazing, Zen." Her juices slicked the underside of my cock and pleasure coiled inside me. My balls tingled and my cock throbbed.

"Nash." She let go of the vanity and wrapped her arms around my neck. "Please. I need you inside me."

Hearing my name in her throaty purr nearly did me in. Zenda was begging me to fuck her. *My* Zen. I felt like I'd been waiting for this moment since the first time I locked eyes with her in that research lab all those years ago.

And I was done waiting.

I thrust inside her fast and deep. Zenda wailed, and for half a second, I feared I hurt her. But then her nails dug into my back and she slammed her hips down even harder. I groaned, feeling so fucking incredible with her wrapped around me like a vise.

"Gods, Nash," she breathed. "Don't stop."

"Never." I shifted, taking one hand off her hips and cupping her cheek. A smile crossed my face as I stared at her lips. I bit back a laugh.

"What?" Zen asked between moans. "What's so funny?"

I leaned my forehead against hers, continuing to thrust my hips. "I just realized we still haven't kissed." She'd had my dick in her mouth, and I had my cock inside her, but our lips had yet to lock.

Don't know why I'm surprised. Zen and I seemed to have a knack for doing things backwards.

"Did you forget about," she moaned, her eyes squeezing shut, "our wedding?"

"No, but that doesn't really count." I slid my hands to her thighs, and lifted her off the vanity, making us both groan when my cock slid even deeper in her hot pussy. "It was under duress."

Zen rolled her eyes. Then she gasped as I flipped her back against the wall. The new angle brought her higher, lining our mouths up perfectly. "Kiss me, Zen," I whispered against her lips.

She smirked. "Who's greedy now?"

"I'll always be greedy for you," I answered, meaning it from the depths of my soul. It might be early—hell, I still hadn't even come yet—but I could already tell I'd never get enough of this. I'd never get enough of *her*.

Zen's lips crashed down on mine. *Yes.* I plunged my tongue into her mouth, groaning. She kissed me feverishly, making my heart pound and my cock ache. I timed my thrusts with our dueling tongues, and it wasn't long before I felt Zen's pussy fluttering around me.

She tore her mouth off mine. "Yes. Gods, yes! Nash! I'm coming!"

I exploded with Zen, waves of pleasure slamming into me as my dick spasmed inside of her. Her eyes rolled back in her head, and her thighs clenched around my waist. I groaned, feeling aftershocks of her orgasm pulse around me long after I was sated.

Breathing heavily, I pulled out and set her on the ground. "Fuck, Zen. That was incredible."

She smiled widely and patted my chest. "Yeah. I had fun, too."

Fun? I scowled, grabbed her waist, and hauled her against me, ready to show her exactly how much fun I could be. *It's not too soon for round two, right?*

Zenda's stomach rumbled, the sound so loud it echoed off the tile walls. *Guess round two will have to wait...* I chuckled. "Hungry?"

She nodded. "Starving."

I grabbed a towel off the rack and wrapped it around her shoulders. "You're in luck. My uncle dropped off a fruit basket big enough to swim in."

Her stomach growled again. "Sorry, but I don't think fruit is gonna cut it. I need protein." She snagged the towel and patted her hair dry. "Especially if you want to fuck again."

Can't argue with that. "Sounds like we need to make a trip to the mess."

What wifey wants, wifey gets.

35

Claimed

Zenda

A barrage of smells bombarded me, setting off an avalanche of memories. Growing up with a mom who worked in the mess meant I'd spent more time there than most. I could picture Mom's smiling face behind the serving line so clearly. But of course, she wasn't there.

Still, strolling into the mess was like coming home. The yeasty perfume of freshly baked bread made my stomach rumble. Huge buffet tables held steaming platters of fish and vegetables. Bowls overflowed with fresh fruit and yogurt.

I tore my gaze off the delicious food and spared a glance at the smaller tables surrounding them—and immediately wished I hadn't. The amount of curious eyes staring at me was almost enough to make me lose my appetite. Hell, if I hadn't been famished from that fuck fest, I'd have turned tail and ran back to our quarters.

Nash squeezed my hand. "Why don't you go grab a plate?" He let go and pointed to an empty table in the far corner. "I'll grab us each a drink, then get a plate, too. Meet me there?"

He wanted to grab me a drink? My heart fluttered. "Sounds like a plan."

We split up, heading for different buffet tables. I didn't waste time before piling my plate high.

"Zenda?" a feminine voice squealed. "Is that you?"

My heart stalled. That voice. *Is it too late to go back for the fruit basket?*

I turned slowly. Judging by how Stasia's smile fell, my resting bitch face was on point. But I wasn't about to plaster a fake smile on for the girl who made my high school days miserable. "Hey. Yep. It's me."

"I thought so!" Stasia flicked her long red hair over her shoulder.

I shot a quick glance heavenward. *Seriously? You guys couldn't even have the decency to make her grow uglier as she aged, could you?*

Stasia was as pretty as ever, all long legs, curves for days, and perfect skin. But just because she was here didn't mean I had to pretend to like her.

I turned back to the buffet, hoping the dismissal would be enough to get her to leave.

"Wow, I never thought I'd see you in Subralia again." Stasia elbowed in next to me, plunking a tiny piece of fish on her mostly empty plate. She raised her voice. "Weren't you banished because your mom's a thief?" Her tinkling laughter filled the air, attracting even more attention than her practically shouting had.

My cheeks blazed, and I nearly dropped my plate. I placed it on the buffet carefully and sucked in a deep breath.

"You know—" I flipped around, my voice dripping with venom.

"There you are." Nash swooped in and pulled me into a tight hug. "What's taking you so long? I'm getting lonely at the table without my snookums."

Snookums? I bit back a giggle.

Stasia cleared her throat.

"Oh, Stasia. Sorry, I didn't see you there." Nash released me, only to scoop up my plate and click his tongue. "This can't be all you're eating." He pinned me with a look that made my toes curl while piling so much food on my plate it was going to be a bitch to carry without spilling. "I have plans for you later. You need to keep up your strength." Then the idiot *winked* at me. And the whole time, he barely spared Stasia a glance.

She fumed, arms crossed and scowling. "Nash." She choked down her annoyed tone when he didn't answer and tried for sugary sweet. "Oh, Nash?"

"You need something?" Nash shot back, his words clipped.

Stasia blinked owlishly, then shook her head and leaned in, planting a manicured hand on Nash's biceps. "I just wanted to know when I can collect on that raincheck you owe me."

My blood boiled. Stasia's sultry tone left me positive of what she expected for that *raincheck*. She couldn't even wait to get Nash alone before propositioning him. I stepped forward, ready to rip her greedy hand off of him, but Nash saved me the trouble.

"Consider it expired." He stepped back, shaking off her hand while somehow managing to balance everything on my overloaded plate. "I'm married. You remember Zenda, don't you?"

"You're married... to Zenda?" Stasia's jaw dropped.

"She recently did me the honor of becoming my wife at my family's ancestral estate on Vorillion." Nash threw an arm over my shoulders and turned toward our table. "Now, if you don't mind, we worked up quite the appetite this morning. See you around, Stasia."

Or not. I held back the petty remark, but I did nothing to hide my smile. It felt good to put that bitch in her place. I hope she enjoyed watching me gobble up my huge breakfast while Nash stared at me like he couldn't wait to eat something else.

"What's that look for?" Nash asked as we took our seats.

"Just appreciating having a friend who sticks up for me."

Nash frowned, brandishing his fork in the air. "Husband." He leaned close. "Get it right or no more orgasms."

I slapped his fork down. "You wouldn't."

He lifted a brow. "Try me."

"Fine. Husband."

Nash flashed the sexiest smile and planted a firm kiss on my lips. "That's better." Then he bent to his meal, not the least bit flustered.

And me? I just sat there, trying not to swoon. He claimed me. Publicly. Not just in front of Stasia, but in front of the whole mess.

Maybe he didn't notice the perplexed stares lobbed at us. Or the venomous glares a few of the women shot me. The people of Subralia clearly didn't know what to think of us, but that didn't matter. I had Nash, my *husband*, and nothing was going to ruin this day.

I shoveled a huge forkful of food into my mouth and smiled.

Zenda

I stepped into the washroom, carting an assortment of products in my arms. It was just before bed, and I was finally getting the last of my things put away.

Nash followed me in, carrying my robe and a stack of towels. He tugged open a small closet. "These okay over here?"

"Yeah. Thanks." My heart warmed. "I could've gotten that."

"Figured I owed you the help." Nash smirked. "You'd have finished hours ago if I hadn't kept distracting you."

"I didn't mind." Who would when the interruptions inevitably led to both of us naked? Every time I thought he'd need a break, he just kept going and going... like a damn camel in the desert. I've never had so many orgasms in my entire life. "Still, it's probably good you have work in the morning, or I won't get anything accomplished."

"Oh? You got big plans for tomorrow?" Nash stopped beside me at the vanity.

"Yep." I arranged the last of my lotions on the hidden shelves behind the mirror and closed it. "I'm planning to visit Professor Mueller and see if I can get my old job back."

Nash stiffened. "What?" He shook his head. "Why do you want to work for that old prick again?"

Old prick? Nash was being a little dramatic. I blinked and faced him. "He wasn't that bad."

Nash picked up his toothbrush. "He has a reputation for working his assistants into the ground, Zen." He flicked on the faucet and wet his brush. "Don't you remember how much he made you do when you were still a student? It'll be even worse if he's paying you."

"But the research was *amazing*. Mueller was so close to figuring out how to communicate with dolphins when I... left. I've been keeping track of his work over the years and the progress he's made is fascinating." I shrugged. "I'm used to working hard. I can handle it."

Nash shifted from foot to foot before snapping open the mirrored cabinet. "He hired a new assistant right before I left. Unless the guy quit already, I think you'll be out of luck. Mueller doesn't have the grant funding for more than one employee."

"Oh." My heart deflated. I wanted my old job back more than anything. Working with dolphins had been so much fun, it almost didn't feel like work. Well, except for all the paperwork, cleaning, and dozens of other tasks Mueller heaped on me.

"Don't worry." Nash grabbed the toothpaste tablets and shook two out of the jar. "I'll take you to meet Professor Davis in the morning. She heads the research division. I'm sure she'll know where there's an opening."

"Okay." I grabbed the tablet and crunched down on it, then lifted my brush. It wouldn't be exactly the same, but with any luck, I'd still get to work with sea animals.

Nash swung the cabinet closed and met my eyes in the mirror's reflection. "It will be much better working for someone who understands the difference between professional and personal time." By the time he finished, his voice was so icy I had the urge to shiver. Then his tone lightened, and he nudged me with his elbow. "I can't have my wife spending more time at the office than I do."

A chill coursed down my spine as I stared back at him in the mirror. Then a weird sense of déjà vu stole over me. Was it just a few weeks ago that we were brushing our teeth together on the Verne? Now here we were again. Only this time it wasn't pretend.

Except that wasn't entirely true. Sure, Nash just called me wife. And yeah, we spent most of the day together in bed. But our relationship still had an expiration date.

And I'm starting to realize how much I wish it didn't.

36

The Interview

Zenda

"Stop fidgeting." Nash tugged me aside outside Professor Davis' office and rubbed his hands soothingly down my arms. "You have nothing to be nervous about. You're amazing. She'll find the perfect job for you."

I nodded and sucked in a deep breath. It was really sweet of Nash to give me a pep talk. Hell, he'd arranged the meeting and walked me here, too, even though it meant taking time out of his workday.

Still, I couldn't help being nervous. I didn't know this woman at all, and my work history didn't make me the ideal candidate for a research position. At least Mueller would have been a familiar face.

"Ready?" Nash asked.

"Yes."

He knocked lightly on the door.

"Come in," a voice called.

A middle-aged woman wearing a kindly smile and her dark brown hair in a ponytail sat at an enormous oak desk. She rose from her chair as we entered and extended her hand. "Nash. Good to see you."

Nash shook her hand. "Always a pleasure. I won't be staying. I just wanted to introduce you to Zenda." He nodded to me, and I stepped forward to shake Davis' hand next.

"Nice to meet you, Zenda."

Gods, why are my hands so sweaty? "Nice to meet you, too." I had to give the lady credit for not immediately wiping her hand after I let go of hers.

"Please, take a seat."

I seated myself while Nash said a polite goodbye and shut the door.

Davis sat and speared me with a direct stare. "I hear you'd like a job in the research division."

I adjusted my glasses. "Yes. I'm excited about the opportunity. Do you have any openings?"

Davis lifted a sheet of paper off her desk. My resume. I gulped.

"I see." Davis pursed her lips and set down the paper. "The work we do here is very specialized. Most of our employees have studied in their respective fields for their entire career. I'm afraid you'll be at a disadvantage. Are you sure you'll be able to catch up?"

"I will. I'm a very hard worker, and I promise I'll do whatever it takes to get up to speed so I can handle the workload." My knees trembled, and I pressed my feet into the ground to keep them from jerking up and down, betraying my nerves. "I promise you, I've maintained my interest in science my entire life. Even when I wasn't employed in research, I read scientific journals and conducted my own experiments."

I feared from the hard glint in her eyes that I hadn't swayed her. Before I could come up with something else to convince her, a knock pounded on the door.

The door flew open. "Davis. I need your help," a man stated gruffly.

I flipped around in my chair, my eyes widening. His hair was splashed much more liberally with gray than when I knew him, and he'd put on a few pounds, but I instantly recognized my old professor.

Davis sighed. "I'm afraid I'm conducting an interview. Can this wait?"

Mueller's gaze landed on me, and he did a double take. "Zenda? Is that you?"

"Yes. Hello, Professor." I smiled politely. "It's nice to see you again."

Mueller's gaze darted between me and Davis. "An interview, you say?" His face brightened. "Do you know Zenda used to be my student intern? This is wonderful timing. That dolt I just hired gave his notice today. I came here to ask you to find me a new research assistant." A huge grin split his cheeks. "I'll take her."

Professor Davis' brow furrowed. "Jonathan quit already? I thought he'd be such a good fit."

Mueller waved a hand. "He was lazy. Sloppy, too." He turned to me. "What do you say, Zenda? Do you want to be my new research assistant?"

My pulse felt like it sped up to light speed. *Did I want to? Hell, yes!*

"Of course! I would be honored to accept." I glanced at Professor Davis. Nash said she was the head of the department. I'd been so sure she was about to send me packing before Mueller showed up. Would she approve of me now?

After a moment's silence, she steepled her hands and smiled. "I think a temporary contract will be prudent. One month, then we'll evaluate your performance and offer you an extension if Professor

Mueller is satisfied with your work." She pushed her chair back and stretched out a hand. "Welcome to the team, Zenda. I'll have HR send you the onboarding paperwork."

I grinned and rose from my chair, then shook her hand so hard she flinched. "Thank you, Professor Davis. Thank you so much!"

"You're welcome. If you have any questions or concerns, my door is always open."

Mueller and I left Davis' office together. "I'm delighted to have you back, Zenda." He clasped a hand on my shoulder. "Get all your paperwork sorted out today. You can start tomorrow morning. You remember where the lab is, don't you?"

"Yes, I do. Thank you for taking a chance on me, Professor. You won't regret it."

"I'm sure I won't." Mueller squeezed my shoulder and his hand trailed down to my elbow before he stepped away. I buried the urge to wince at the forward gesture. "See you tomorrow, Zenda."

I walked away, floating on cloud nine. I couldn't wait to tell Nash I got a job. And not just any job—my *dream job*. The same one that had been unfairly stolen from me so long ago.

It was like all my wildest dreams had come true. I had a husband. The job I'd always wanted. An enormous smile spread across my face.

Until I turned a corner and my hands curled into fists at my side. That bitch! *Looks like I have a skank to slap.*

Nash

My back pressed against the glass hallway wall. Cold spread up and down my spine, but at that moment, I wanted to sink into it rather than deal with the fiery demoness in front of me.

"I can't believe you got married without telling me!" Stasia fumed, hands on her hips.

She'd cornered me on my way out of the office. I'd returned after Zen's interview only for my uncle to insist I take the rest of the afternoon off. He was certain she'd land a job and want to celebrate.

Instead of finding a smiling Zen, I'd run into Stasia. And this time, there were no handy cleaning closets for me to duck into. It was just the two of us, in the middle of the hall, where anyone might walk by and wonder what I'd done to make her wail like a wounded vorhound.

"I don't understand why you're so upset." I forced a casual grin, even though her shrieking was making my skin crawl. "We never dated. We haven't even slept together in months."

"And whose fault was that?" She jabbed a finger in my chest. "Not mine. You've been dodging me." Her lower lip quivered. "It's almost like... you never wanted me at all."

Oh, no... *Please don't start crying.*

"That's not true," I blurted, hoping my confession would be enough to dry her eyes. "We had fun together, Stasia. But it's over now."

Stasia's gaze snapped to mine and the sadness in her expression washed away so fast it was like I'd imagined it. She stepped closer and planted her hand on my chest. "If that's the case, then why do we have to stop?" She licked her lips. "I won't tell if you don't."

"Absolutely not." Disgust blasted me, making my stomach lurch. "I'm *not* a cheater." I don't know if it was from the look on my face or the venom in my tone, but Stasia's eyes widened and she froze.

"If you don't take your hands off my husband, I'll take them off for you."

I tore my gaze off Stasia. "Zenda." She marched up the hall, sneering and looking mad enough to slap someone. *And for once, it wasn't me.*

Stasia stepped back before Zen reached us and flashed a cruel grin. "Relax. I was just leaving." Her heels tapped quickly in the opposite direction, but she apparently couldn't resist lobbing a final insult. Before she turned the corner, Stasia looked over her shoulder and said, "When you get bored with playing house, you know where to find me."

Zenda lurched in her direction, but I grabbed her waist, hauling her against my chest. "She's not worth it." Her gaze snapped to mine, and I swallowed thickly.

I might have been wrong about the slapping.

Zen's eyes burned with fury. "What the hell was that?" She shoved me roughly and stepped out of my arms. "Do I need to get used to tearing women off of you? Why didn't you tell her to get lost?"

"I-I tried..." I rubbed the back of my neck. "And I didn't touch her. She had her hands on me!"

That was clearly the wrong thing to say. Zen stormed off. I followed, my stomach sinking.

"Look, I'm sorry. You know I don't handle confrontation well."

Zen sent me a sideways glare and picked up her pace. I raced to keep up, feeling like the world was crumbling around me. If Zenda shut me out again... I shuddered. It took me forever to get her to talk to me again after that idiotic bet. Now that we were closer than ever, I couldn't handle her cold shoulder. Not when I was dying to hold her in my arms and wipe that hurt look off her face.

"Please, Zen. I'm not a cheater. I would never take her up on that offer."

Zenda said nothing. She just kept walking, her footsteps thumping in time with the maddening beat of my heart.

"You promised not to shut me out, Zen," I pleaded. "Talk to me."

She stopped in front of a hatch and pounded in the control's code. My brow furrowed. I'd been so intent on getting her to listen, I wasn't paying attention to where she was headed. The door opened, and Zenda grabbed my arm, hauling me inside our quarters.

"You want to talk?" She slammed the hatch closed and crossed her arms. "Talk."

"So, you aren't shutting me out?" My shoulders slumped, and I scrubbed a hand over my face.

Zen finally softened. "No. I just wanted to get out of the hall, so the people walking past weren't eavesdropping on our business."

I grinned sheepishly. "That's smart." Honestly, I couldn't even say if we'd passed anyone on the way back. I was so worried about Zen, so keyed into her every move—it was like nothing else existed. "I'll say it again. I'm sorry. I want you to know I didn't say anything to lead Stasia on. That was all her."

"Why am I not surprised?" Zenda pursed her lips and walked past me, taking a seat on the couch.

"I know I still didn't handle it well. It's just that arguing with anyone... causing a big scene." I shuddered. "I hate it. Sorry, Zen. I didn't mean to hurt you by letting her off easy. I just didn't want to deal with her drama."

"Life isn't always easy. Sometimes you have to be uncomfortable," Zenda said softly.

Glancing up, I spotted what I hoped was compassion glimmering in her eyes. "I know. I'll try harder next time." I sucked in a deep breath. "Will you forgive me?"

Zenda rubbed her chin. "I don't know yet."

My heart stuttered. She couldn't mean that. I cocked a brow, wondering if I would spend the night on the couch after all. "Come on Zen. You have to forgive me. I've already apologized twice. What do I have to do next? Do you need me to grovel?"

Uh-oh.

Zenda's eyes lit up. "You know what... I think I do." A lopsided smirk curved her luscious lips. "Go ahead. Let's see what you've got."

She can't be serious. As I watched her lean back on the couch and get comfortable, I realized there was only one way I was getting back into my wife's good graces tonight. Lucky for her, I wasn't afraid to get down on my knees for my woman.

In fact, this was going to be fun. I'd make sure of it.

37

Groveling

Zenda

My eyes widened as Nash sank to his knees on the living room floor. Yeah, I'd told him to grovel, but I hadn't really expected him to do it.

This ought to be interesting.

He bowed his head. "I was wrong. You..." He snuck a peek at my face. "You're the moon, and I'm just a... rock floating past."

"That's what you're going with?" I giggled. "I can't believe I thought you'd be good at this."

Nash scowled, but his shoulders firmed. His eyes flicked around the room for a moment, like he was trying desperately to think of something less lame. Until they landed on the bookshelf and a tiny smile crossed his face. "Forgive me, my queen."

"Ooo, that's more like it." He knew me too well. How many times had I wished I could disappear into one of my romance novels?

"Yes. You're my queen, and I'm just a lowly servant." Nash grinned flirtatiously. "Please, your highness. Tell this unworthy wretch how I can earn your forgiveness."

I stared into his eyes. Despite Nash's playful tone, I sensed the sincerity lurking within. I could tell him to do anything, and I had no doubt he would. Hell, this little act pretty much proved that. And honestly, I believed him about Stasia. It was clear from their body language back in the hall who'd been the pursuer. I wasn't planning to make him suffer.

But that didn't mean we couldn't have a little fun first.

I smirked. "You really want my forgiveness?"

Nash nodded. "More than anything, my queen."

"Good. Come here." Nash shifted, but before he got close to standing, I barked out, "No. Stay on your knees. I want to watch you crawl."

Nash's gaze shot to mine, his eyes full of so much heat, I felt it all the way to my core. He planted one hand on the floor. Then the other.

I licked my lips, admiring the long lines of his body. From my vantage on the couch, I had a perfect view of his strong back and round ass. Shockwaves of lust raced through me. Then when he started to crawl...

Fuck. This is the stuff fantasies are made of.

His gaze stayed glued to me with every liquid movement. He prowled closer, and my breath quickened. He approached the coffee table. I was sure he would simply crawl around it, but he thrust out an arm instead. The table skidded away, making fruit spill out of the basket, and roll across the floor.

I gasped, my pulse pounding at Nash's predatory stare. He certainly didn't look like a servant anymore. Not that I was complaining.

He drew close enough to touch, and I could tell from the hunger in his eyes he wanted to. Yet, just as he leaned back on his heels, I planted my boot in his lap, dangerously close to his growing bulge.

"Remove your queen's boots," I demanded in my best regal tone.

"As you wish, your grace." He lifted a gloved hand to my calf, caressing the muscle gently before he slipped my foot free.

His fingers pressed into my sole, massaging so perfectly I almost gave up the act and groaned with pleasure. But I wasn't ready to be done. Nowhere near it.

"Now, now." I tore my foot out of his grasp and planted the other boot on his chest firmly. "Don't make me reprimand you for leaving the job half finished."

Nash smirked. "Never, my queen." He made a show of tugging free the laces, moving slowly. "I'll see that you're well satisfied."

Oh boy... is it getting hot in here? My second boot hit the floor.

I thrust my chest toward him. "My zipper."

Nash slowly unzipped my skin suit. By the time he'd reached the bottom, my breathing was shallow.

"Take it off," I ordered.

His gloved hands peeled the fabric off my body, leaving me in my bra and panties.

No. That wouldn't do.

"Lose the gloves," I demanded next.

Nash leaned back on his heels and pulled off his gloves without watching what he was doing. The whole time he stared at me, and I got the distinct impression he was undressing me in his mind.

I smirked. Not just yet.

He reached for me with his bare hands, but I backed away. "Don't be insolent, boy," I said sternly, lifting a brow. "Did I say you could touch me?"

Nash's lips twitched like he was hiding a smile. "No, my queen."

I crossed my arms and ran my gaze down his body. "Strip. Now."

"As you wish." Nash tore off his clothes, his patience clearly at a breaking point.

Fuck. I clenched my thighs together and nearly gasped when I realized how damp my panties were. Clearly, having such a sexy, powerful man willing to follow my every command really got me going.

"Lie down." I waved a hand at the floor. "On your back."

Nash obeyed, and I took a moment to admire the sight of him naked, spread out before me. His cock bobbed in the air, hard as a rock. I stood and walked a circle around him, stopping next to his head. He was so fucking hot. And right there, ready for whatever dirty deed my mind came up with.

Decisions, decisions.

"What now, my queen?" Nash stared up at me and licked his face. The sight of that big tongue of his flicking out decided for me.

"Do you know what every queen needs?" I peeled my panties off my legs.

Nash's eyes tracked the movement and his voice croaked, "What?"

"A throne." I smirked and straddled his face, making sure to sit facing the right way so I could keep admiring his sexy body. Nash groaned beneath me and didn't waste any time before flicking his tongue out to taste me.

"Oh, Gods!" I cried. My eyes rolled back in my head. Nash certainly wasn't kidding about having a wickedly good tongue. He licked my entire slit all at once, making my toes curl. Then he zeroed in on my clit, flicking the tip of his tongue with the perfect amount of pressure.

"That's it. Don't stop." I closed my eyes and moaned as pleasure shot through me. He obeyed, licking my clit like he couldn't get enough. But that wasn't all. He used the bottom half of his tongue and suctioned between my lips. "Fuck, yes."

I didn't know anything could feel so amazing. My body tensed, climbing to my peak so fast, the orgasm that hit me took me by surprise. I screamed, rocking on Nash's face and riding out the shudders.

When my legs stopped trembling, I forced open my eyes. Nash stopped flicking my clit, which I appreciated. It was always so sensitive after I came. But he didn't quit licking my pussy. I moaned as his tongue slipped into my channel. It was so long and thick, I quivered as he slid it in and out of me.

Gods. He's tongue fucking me—like, literally. The thought would've probably made me giggle if I wasn't so incredibly turned on.

I tipped forward, balancing myself on his hard chest and tilting my pelvis to give him a better angle. The move brought my face closer to his magnificent cock. It bobbed toward me, almost like his dick was begging me to touch it.

I licked my lips. *Don't mind if I do.* Leaning forward, I grabbed his shaft and licked him from base to tip in one slow stroke.

Nash groaned and thrust his tongue further inside me. Fuck, that felt amazing. I squealed and wiggled when he stroked his thumb on my clit. But after a second, the sensitivity faded, and pleasure jolted through me.

"Nash. Yeesss," I cried before putting his dick in my mouth. I moaned as I sucked, loving the way his ridged flesh caressed my tongue.

Nash moaned too, and his hips lifted off the floor. But I only gave him a few sucks before releasing his dick with a pop.

I cleared my throat and broke out the regal voice again. "Do you know what else a queen needs?" I didn't wait for him to answer. I climbed off his face and slid down his chest, lining his cock up with my aching pussy. Then I glanced over my shoulder and winked. "Her daily ride."

I sank down hard and fast. We groaned in unison as his dick filled me. From this angle, it felt massive—and so damn good. I peeked over my shoulder again and spotted Nash's gaze glued to my ass. I rolled my hips, fucking him slowly. Nash gripped my thighs and helped me lift and slam back down just when my leg muscles started to tire.

It was worth the burn. I'd never been one to exercise when I didn't have to, but I might have to make an exception for this.

"Zen. You look so fucking hot bouncing on my cock." Nash trailed his hands up my legs and cupped my ass.

I gasped as he spread my cheeks wider. Then one of his fingers traced down the cleft before circling my hole. I shivered as he slowly worked the bulbous tip of one of his fingers inside me. His naturally moist skin made sure it slid in easily, with only the tiniest burn.

"Fuuuccck." He groaned and slowly finger fucked my ass while I rode him.

So full... The added sensation drove me crazy. I bucked and moaned, feeling another orgasm building swiftly. Within a few more strokes, I exploded with a scream.

Nash pulled his finger out of my ass and used his hands to guide me. By the time I came down from my orgasm's high, I was feeling boneless, but Nash lifted and dropped me, steadily pumping his cock until he came with a groan. I shuddered as he spurted inside me, his thick length pulsing and dragging those delicious ridges across my sensitive channel.

"Wow, Zen." Nash chuckled as I rolled off him. "That was..."

The way he paused made insecurity flare in my mind. "Sorry. I hope that wasn't too weird for you." I covered my eyes and groaned, still fighting to catch my breath. "Gods, I just joked that you were a horse.

And then I *rode* you. What is wrong with me?" My stomach clenched, and I was too afraid to look at him. "If you hated it, just tell me."

38

Steamrolling Confessions

Nash

What was Zen smoking? I must have fucked her stupid if she thought for even half a second that I didn't like that. Watching her ride me on the living room floor just beat out catching her masturbating while saying my name for the hottest damn experience of my life.

I peeled her hand off her face. "Zen, are you kidding?"

She bit her lip and shook her head. "It's okay. I know I can be a little over the top sometimes. We don't have to do it like that again."

"Like hell we don't!" I practically shouted.

Zen's eyes bulged. "Damn, you don't have to yell at me." She wrapped her arms around herself and shivered.

"Sorry." I snagged a blanket off the couch and grabbed her, plopping her in my lap and wrapping the blanket around us both. "It's just that it would be a crime not to do that again." I smiled at her reassuringly before a sudden thought made it vanish. "Or did you not like it?"

Zenda blushed and grabbed her glasses off the couch. "Did you miss the screaming orgasm? Or how about the one before it?"

I chuckled. "Yeah, I thought so." I tilted my head. "So, why'd you think I wouldn't like it?"

Zenda adjusted her glasses. "I dunno. You don't seem like the submissive type."

I flipped Zen around, tugged her back against my chest and folded my legs around hers. "If I tell you something, do you promise not to laugh?"

Zenda cuddled against me. "I don't know. Depends how funny it is."

The little brat.

"Fine. I'll tell you, anyway." I sighed and nodded to my bookshelf. "Remember how you used to have a shelf full of those trashy historical romances?"

Zenda poked my ribs. "Hey, they're not trashy."

I rolled my eyes. "Steamy, then."

She nodded once. "That's better. What about them?"

"I was clueless when I came to Earth. I'd had a couple of girlfriends on Vorillion, but we'd never really done anything physical. So, I may have borrowed one of your books. Purely for research purposes."

"Oh, I know." Zenda's hand shot out, aiming at the bottom shelf of my bookcase. "I spotted it already, wedged between all your pulp fiction and spy novels."

"Man, way to steamroll a confession."

Zenda giggled, then clamped a hand over her mouth. "Sorry. I'll be quiet." She mumbled behind her hands.

"It's okay. There's more." I inhaled deeply, and Zenda shifted, curling her arms tightly around my stomach. With her arms wrapped around me, it gave me the strength to admit something I'd never told another soul. "I have to admit, I really liked that book."

Zenda beamed. "I told you they were good."

I chuckled. "Yeah. But it got me thinking that maybe if I acted like the guys in those books, I could make Terran women happy. It seemed easy enough. So, I did. And it worked. The girls I dated after you left liked it when I was bossy and talked dirty, like the heroes in your books."

Zenda stiffened. "So, you're telling me this to what? Blame me for turning you into a man-whore?"

"No. That's not it at all." *Oh, no you don't.* I grabbed her when she shifted, not giving her the chance to pull away before I explained.

Zenda arched a brow, but she settled back against my chest.

I barreled ahead, before I lost my nerve—or her. "See, the truth is, I always felt like something was missing. Until today, I could never put my finger on what it was. Now I think I know exactly what I was craving."

Zenda peeked up at me. "What's that?"

"Isn't it obvious? You." I tipped her face up and kissed her nose. I waved a hand at the floor. "And this. I loved everything about what we just did. It was surprising and adventurous. And so fucking hot I'm dying to do it again."

"Really?" Zenda asked. "Even the crawling?"

I chuckled. "Yeah. That was pretty sexy, wasn't it?" Honestly, it wasn't too pleasant on my joints, but if I got to watch her eyes glaze over with lust again, I'd drop to my knees in a heartbeat.

"It was." Zenda's voice dropped an octave, and I wondered if she was picturing it in her mind. She frowned. "I don't know why you thought I'd laugh at that."

I leaned back against the couch. "Maybe because I wasted so much time just going through the motions. It's kind of sad when I think about it."

Her perfect lips pursed. "Well, I hope you know you don't have to put on an act with me."

"I do." I meant it wholeheartedly. With Zen, I felt comfortable enough to laugh and play. I knew I could talk to her about anything, and explore all the facets of myself, with her by my side. She'd never judge me, or make me feel weird for wanting to try something new.

I kind of loved that. I tugged her close, reveling in the press of her soft skin sliding against mine. *I love her.*

Fuck. I'd thought the same a million times. Said the same out loud—to her—on countless occasions. You didn't have a twenty-year friendship without telling your buddy you loved them. Yet something about the words tonight felt different—more.

I think I'm falling in love with my wife.

39

The Crazy Thing

Zenda

I woke early the next morning and hopped out of bed. Nash stirred but didn't wake, even with my alarm blaring.

I smirked as I grabbed a skinsuit out of the closet and walked to the washroom. *Looks like someone's worn out.*

Not that I could blame him. We stayed up half the night in bed. If I wasn't so excited about starting my job, I'd probably have slept through my alarm, too.

I rushed through my shower and morning routine. Fact was, I was behind schedule. Professor Mueller only asked me to take care of the onboarding paperwork yesterday, but I'd put it off—to *get* off.

Chuckling at myself, I snagged a protein bar out of the kitchen, booted up my tablet, and sank down on the sofa. No harm done. I'd finish it quickly before I left and skip the trip to the mess.

I was so absorbed with the task that I didn't notice Nash until he was right behind me.

"Good morning." He kissed the back of my head and must have peeked over my shoulder, too. "What are you working on so early?"

"Morning," I replied distractedly. "Just give me a sec. I'm almost done..." I pushed send on the email to HR. "There."

Tossing the tablet aside, I spun around and kneeled on the couch, wrapping my arms around Nash in a tight hug.

"Ah, that's more like it." Nash grinned and hugged me back. It was awkward with the back of the sofa between us, but my heart bloomed at the feel of him all the same. "So, what's with the emails?"

"I can't believe I forgot to tell you." I pulled away and bounced on the cushion a little. "I got a job!"

"Really? That's fantastic, Zen. I knew you would." Nash beamed. "What did Davis find for you?"

I sank down on the couch as Nash rounded it. "That's the crazy thing. My interview wasn't going well at all."

Nash plopped beside me, frowning. "No? Why not?"

I waved a hand. "That's not important. Because right when I was sure Davis was about to tell me to get lost, Professor Mueller popped in."

Nash stiffened. "Mueller showed up during your interview?"

"Yes!" My head bobbed. "His new hire just quit. Can you believe it? He offered me a job on the spot!"

Nash groaned. "Zen. Please tell me you didn't take it."

I drew back, searching his face. "Of course, I did. Why wouldn't I? It's my dream job."

"But Mueller..." Nash dragged a hand down his face. My stomach clenched as I waited for Nash to explain his overreaction. "Don't you remember what I said about him? He'll run you ragged. I'll never see you."

I scoffed. "Don't be ridiculous. I can handle long hours." I crossed my arms. "You work long hours, too."

Nash's big black eyes traced my face. After another long pause, he blew out a breath and smiled tightly. "All right. I get it. I'm sorry I brought it up."

"Okay." I jumped up. "Shit. I better get going. I said I'd head to the lab first thing." I leaned down and planted a quick kiss on Nash's lips.

His smile brightened to something approaching normal, but I still sensed his reluctance. "Have a great first day. I'll see you later?"

"You know it." I scooped up my tablet and rushed into the hall.

Sadly, the excitement I'd felt that morning didn't return. Why did Nash have to piss on my pancakes?

My heart sank with every step I took. Was it just Mueller bothering him? Or was it something else?

Nash was so perfect last night. After that mess with Stasia, he'd said all the right things. He'd touched me with so much passion. But what if, deep down, he wasn't as into it as he'd claimed?

Maybe he'd slept on it and realized he'd made a mistake marrying me. He might even want to break up before the year was through... *I couldn't bear it.*

Fuck. I shook off the black thoughts as I approached the lab. There would be time to worry later. I had a job to start.

Nash

I marched into Uncle Prim's office, mad enough to scream. "I need your help."

"Good morning to you, too." Uncle Prim chuckled, but something in my expression wiped the humor off his face. "What is it, son?"

I paced in front of his desk. Despite being the most important person in Subralia, Uncle Prim decorated the space modestly. His desk took up half of the office, and a small loveseat and armchair sat across from it.

"It's Mueller. He's got Zenda. She hasn't been here for a week, and he's already wrecking her life again."

"Wait, what?" Prim's pen clattered on his desk. He pushed out of his chair and slung an arm around my shoulder, leading me to the loveseat. "What do you mean, he's got her?" He sat across from me in the armchair.

I sucked in a deep breath. "Mueller burst into the interview I arranged for Zen. Sounds like he snatched her up before Davis could even make an offer."

"Really?" Prim's eyes widened.

"Can you shuffle around her assignment? I can't stand the thought of her working with that bastard again."

"Sorry, son. I don't have any oversight over the research department's hiring process."

My heart sank. I'd thought as much, but I'd hoped he'd have something up his sleeve.

Uncle Prim rubbed his chin. "So, Zenda accepted? Why would she do that after what happened with her mother?"

I stared at the floor as a sick feeling spread through my gut.

"Oh. You never told her, did you?"

I looked up and met my uncle's eyes. "No."

Uncle Prim didn't chastise me, even though I deserved it. He just leaned forward, tapped my knee, and said, "You know what you have to do, then. Don't you?"

I gulped. Nodded.

"I'm proud of you, Nash."

My brow furrowed. That was the last thing I'd expected him to say after I confessed I'd been keeping a secret from my best friend for decades.

"I never thought I'd see the day you abandoned your bachelor ways and settled down." He chuckled. "You couldn't have picked a better girl to do it with." He cocked his head and scanned me shrewdly. "I knew the last time you burst in here, begging me for help with Zenda, you cared for her deeply. I only wish the two of you didn't waste so many years apart before you came to your senses and realized how perfect you are for each other."

"You've thought that all along?" Shock spread through my chest, followed quickly by shame. Uncle Prim still didn't know the entire story.

"Yes. How was the wedding? You still haven't told me the details."

I sighed. "It was nice. We had a traditional mating ceremony at Whitemist Estate."

"Whitemist, eh? How are Laytun and Siara?"

I shrugged. "Dad barely spoke a word to me. Though Mom was surprisingly nice."

"That is interesting. Hang on for a second." Uncle Prim walked to his desk and grabbed a paper off a small stack. "I spotted this a few days before you returned to Earth."

The paper crinkled in my fingers as I quickly scanned it. It was a moving application. "Wait… is this for my parents? They want to move to Subralia?"

The armchair creaked as Uncle Prim settled back down. "No. Just your mother."

I shook my head. "That doesn't make any sense."

Uncle Prim nodded sagely. "Perhaps someone else you ought to talk to, hm?"

My stomach filled with knots. It wasn't bad enough I had Professor Mueller to deal with. Now this. More drama. Confrontation. I wanted to run away and hide rather than deal with any of it.

My mother's advice rang in my ears. *"Don't make my mistake, son. Fight for what you love."*

I sighed. Maybe it was time I manned up and took it.

40

Bubbly

Zenda

I dug my knuckles into my lower back, sighing. I'd spent a long morning hard at work in the office, filing a seemingly endless mountain of Professor Mueller's paperwork.

The clock on the wall chimed, and a huge smile lit my face. Feeding time. Finally!

Interacting with the dolphins was exactly what I needed to remind me why the drudgery was worth it.

I left the office and stepped into the attached research lab. The ocean pools glistened, and I spotted fins breaching the water's surface instantly.

"I hope you're hungry in there." Mueller had left me detailed instructions on exactly when and how to feed the dolphins, but I hardly needed them. I remembered it all intimately, and my hands moved with muscle memory.

Soon I was leaning over the first pool with a fish clutched in my hands. A dolphin swam toward me, opening its mouth and clicking happily. "Here you go, beautiful." I tossed the fish in its mouth while studying the creature. The animal turned, exposing its underside and revealing its sex—female.

This beauty looked familiar... I gasped as she spun in the water and I spotted a scar on her dorsal fin.

The hatch banged open, startling me. "Oh, Professor Mueller. Good afternoon."

Mueller wandered in with his nose in a book. "Feeding time already?" He closed the book and tucked it under his arm, running an appraising glance over me. "Looks like you have it well in hand."

"Professor—"

"It's Adam. My dear, now that we're colleagues, you may call me by my given name."

I bit back the frown that fought to spread. It felt incredibly strange to be on a first name basis with the man who'd taught me for so many years. "Adam." I forced a smile. "Is this female from the same pod who we worked with when I was your student assistant?"

Mueller stopped behind me. "You have an excellent memory, Zenda. She is indeed." He pointed to the barely noticeable transmitter attached to her dorsal fin. "Test subject, F-034 is one of our most frequent visitors. Didn't you have a nickname for her?"

I grinned. "Bubbly." As soon as I uttered the nickname, Bubbly opened her mouth and uttered a series of clicks.

"I think she remembers you." Mueller planted a hand on shoulder and squeezed.

I ducked, knocking his hand off and grabbing another fish. "Here you go Bub."

She caught it midair, and the splash sent Mueller scurrying backward. I just laughed and shook the salty spray off my face.

"Well, I'll leave you to it." Mueller disappeared into his office.

It took me about an hour to finish feeding the animals. Except for the isolation tank Mueller used to help nurse sick and injured animals back to health, the research tanks had ocean access. The animals were given free rein to come and go as they pleased. Luckily, there were enough that stuck around for the free meals, like Bubbly.

After cleaning up, I returned to the office in a fantastic mood. "Professor." I winced. "Adam, I mean. I just wanted to thank you again for hiring me."

Mueller looked up from his book. "Of course, dear. Happy to have you."

I grabbed the rest of the paperwork he'd asked me to file. "I've been following your work over the years. The paper you authored in the *International Journal of Ocean Science* was so enlightening."

"You read that old thing?" Mueller leaned back in the chair. "It was nothing."

"Do you mind if I ask? How did you arrive at your conclusion? The facts seemed to support—"

Mueller held up a hand. "Sorry, dear." He waved a hand at his book. "Can we discuss this later? I have a pressing need to finish this."

"Oh. Of course." I turned aside, hiding my frown. *Weird.* Most professors I knew were happy to talk my ear off about their published work.

I settled back down to file and left Mueller to his reading. I probably should've filed everything as quickly as possible to make a good first impression, but I couldn't stop from scanning Mueller's work. It was fascinating enough to make me forget about the strange way he dodged my question.

Mueller pushed out of his desk chair sometime later. "I have a class. When you've finished with the filing, I left a list of tasks for you on my desk."

I stood with the paper I'd been skimming clutched in my hands and tingles vibrating through my belly. "Professor, I couldn't help but read a bit of this while filing. I think I might have a way to further your research, if you'll allow me?"

Mueller approached and scanned the paper in my hands. His eyes lit up. "I've been stuck working out the kinks of that project for years. If you think you have a solution, then by all means, you have my permission."

I beamed. "Thank you! I think I know the perfect person to help. Is it all right if I use your files to get the data I need?"

"Of course." Mueller headed to the door. "But see that you handle the tasks I've left for you first, hm?"

"I will!" My heart sank slightly when I found the list. *Man, Nash wasn't kidding about the workload one bit.*

I sighed, and my gaze landed on the book Mueller had been reading all day. He'd placed it in a plain protective cover, so there was no way to know exactly what he'd been reading unless... I grabbed it and flipped to the title page.

What the hell? It wasn't a scientific journal. Or anything remotely job related. Mueller had refused to answer my question because he was too busy reading a fantasy novel.

This day keeps getting weirder. Still, I didn't let Mueller's odd behavior or the massive number of tasks he'd left get me down for long.

I had my dream job. And if I was right, with a little help from a friend, I might accomplish the impossible.

Not too shabby for my first day.

Nash

I sighed as I trudged down the hall to our quarters. It had been an insane day at the office. Just before noon, we'd received word that the weekly delivery of food we'd received for the cafeteria was tainted with bacteria. I'd spent the rest of the day overseeing the cleanup, and on the phone looking for a solution.

Sure, we could rely on food processors, if need be, but with everyone so used to normal food, there might be a riot. Luckily, I'd managed to track down a secondary supplier who could squeeze us in to their delivery schedule before our industrial size refrigerators ran bare.

Now that was all over, and I could spend the rest of the night relaxing with Zen. A pang of guilt struck me. I'd originally planned to surprise her with lunch. Maybe if she hadn't eaten yet, we could swing dinner instead.

Glancing at my watch, I cringed. Maybe not. It was closer to bedtime than dinner. *Hopefully she's not asleep already...*

I frowned as I entered the living room. The lights were off, and the place was quiet. I sighed and tiptoed to the bedroom. "What the hell?" Zen wasn't in bed, or the bathroom. "Damn Mueller." I *knew* that asshole was going to overwork her.

I marched through the halls, ready to give the lazy prick a piece of my mind. After that, I was ready to spill everything to Zen.

Yeah, I'd been busy all day, but whenever I had a spare second, I kept turning over my uncle's advice in my mind. He was right. I needed to tell Zen everything. She deserved the truth. I just hoped she could find it in her heart to forgive me for keeping what happened a secret for so long.

I punched in the code to Mueller's lab and threw open the hatch. The salty scent and quiet sound of lapping water greeted me.

"Zenda?" My heart sped when I didn't see her immediately.

If she wasn't there, then who knows where she might be? Horrible images bombarded me. Mueller carting her off and demanding she divorce me and marry him instead. Her body lying at the bottom of one of those pools when she tried to swim while exhausted. If anything happened to her—

I sighed as I spotted her through the glass office window. She was asleep with her head resting on her arms atop Mueller's desk, sur-rounded by mountains of paperwork.

My stomach churned. Only Mueller would dump so much work on his new employee that they passed out. I quietly approached the desk and bent beside Zenda. She smacked her lips as I scooped her into my arms. When I shifted her to open the hatch to the hall, Zenda stirred.

She blinked at me, dazed. "Nash? Wh-what? Where am I?"

"Shh. I'm taking you home." Seeing how tired she was, I bit my tongue, though I was dying to say a few choice words about her idiot boss.

Zenda blinked a few times, then her eyes widened. "Oh, my Gods! Did I fall asleep at Mueller's desk?"

I strode down the hall swiftly. "Yes. I can't believe he expected you to finish all that paperwork on your first day. Do you know what time it is?"

"Nash, put me down." Zenda demanded.

"No," I barked, tightening my arms around her.

Zenda rolled her eyes, but she didn't press the issue. "It's not Mueller's fault I stayed so late."

I scoffed. "Sure it isn't."

Zenda slapped my chest weakly. "No, it isn't. I stayed because I had a genius idea that I needed to research." Her sleepy voice thrummed with excitement. "It's big, Nash. I can't wait for you to see—" a yawn interrupted her.

I chuckled. "Looks like the only thing we should look at is our bed." It was no wonder Zen was exhausted. We'd barely slept the night before. My blood heated as I remembered all the delicious reasons why. Maybe we could—

Another enormous yawn spilled out of Zen's lips and she snuggled against my chest, closing her eyes. "I think you might be right."

I bit back a sigh. Seems a repeat of last night would have to wait. My stomach churned as I remembered everything I needed to say.

Guess more than one thing will have to wait tonight.

41

The Surprise

The next day was much more relaxed at the office. When lunchtime rolled around, I walked to the cafeteria, hoping to find Zenda already sitting at one of the round tables. She'd been gone when my alarm went off that morning, so we hadn't talked.

I frowned when I didn't spot her anywhere. She might be on her way, but knowing her, she was probably so engrossed in her research she'd forgotten all about lunch. Still, I couldn't ignore the possibility that I'd missed her.

"Hey, Gloria." I approached one of the cafeteria workers who'd been working in the mess longer than I'd lived there. "Have you seen my wife recently?"

The old woman smiled sweetly. "Oh, you mean Portia's girl, right? What's her name?"

"Zenda."

She shook her head. "She blew through like a whirlwind early this morning. Grabbed a yogurt and coffee. I haven't seen her since."

"Thanks." I grabbed a tray. "Would you mind packing me two lunches to go? I think I'll surprise her."

Gloria grabbed the tray and winked. "Sure thing, hon. Coming right up."

Within minutes, she returned with two hot platters covered with lids and a couple of waters. "Thank you, Gloria. See you later."

Strolling down the hall, I tried my best to ignore the meteor storm swirling in my gut. I had to tell Zen. When she fell asleep last night, I swore I'd tell her in the morning, but then she'd been gone.

Fact was, there'd never be a perfect time. If I kept thinking like that, another twenty years would go by without me telling her. I couldn't let her keep going to work every day without knowing the full story.

Over lunch would be as good a time as any. I could take her to one of the empty conference rooms for some privacy.

With my mind made up, I strode into the research lab. I took one look at the scene inside and my pulse went haywire. Zenda leaned over a pool, whistling and waving a fish in the air, while that scumbag Mueller stood behind her, his filthy eyes glued to her ass.

Oh, hell no.

The tray dropped out of my hands and clattered to the floor, making both of them turn. Before I even knew what I was doing, I'd crossed the room and wrapped my hands around Mueller's neck. "Get away from her." I shoved Mueller against the glass office wall. "Keep your pervy eyes off my wife."

"Nash!" Zenda tugged my arm. "What are you doing? Let him go!"

I glanced at her and some of the fire boiling my blood subsided. But my hands wouldn't move. They'd frozen on his neck, and I was taking a perverse amount of pleasure in the way he squirmed against the wall.

"Nash, please. Professor Mueller was spotting me. I was leaning in further than was safe."

Mueller choked out, "It's true. Listen to her."

I forcibly unclenched my fingers. Mueller gasped and shuffled away, rubbing his neck. He didn't say a word, he just ran into the hall like a coward.

Zenda hissed, "What the hell was that? Are you trying to get me fired?"

"You didn't see what I did." I threw out a hand. "The only thing that creep was spotting was your ass."

Zenda crossed her arms. "Please. Professor Mueller has been nothing but professional with me."

"He *is* a pervert." I lowered my voice and tried to dampen the outrage tinging it. "You don't know what he did."

Zen's eyes widened. "Wh-what are you talking about?"

It wasn't supposed to happen like this. We were supposed to have a calm, rational conversation over lunch. I wasn't supposed to practically kill the guy.

"He's the one, Zen. He's the one who helped your mom."

Zenda shook her head and stared at the floor. "No. Why would he do that? He'd be risking his career." She met my eyes. "You must have it wrong. Who told you? Some disgruntled former employee?"

"No one told me. I was there." I pointed to the back pool where I used to swim when I first arrived on Earth. "I overheard everything. Mueller and your mom made a deal."

"What deal?" Zen backed away when I tried to squeeze her shoulder.

I stared into Zen's eyes. Tears were already gathering in the corners and I couldn't bear the thought of them falling. Or knowing I'd put them there.

"Do you remember the day your mom got caught?"

Zen frowned. "Of course I do."

"That was when I heard them. You were meeting with Mueller that day, weren't you?"

Zen paled. She nodded weakly.

"I know what you thought was going to happen. But Mueller wasn't planning to give you a job, Zen. He wanted you to marry him."

Zen barked out a laugh. "That's ridiculous."

I shook my head sadly. "I wish it was. I heard everything. Mueller made a deal with your mother. He gave her the sperm, and in exchange, he asked Portia to convince you to accept his proposal."

Zenda blinked repeatedly. I could almost see how hard she was thinking as she processed everything. Finally, her gaze snapped to mine, and she asked the one question I'd been dreading. The question that kept me up at night and made my stomach fill with knots.

"Why didn't you tell me?"

Zenda

I stared at Nash, my legs unsteady, like the floor had been ripped out from under me. "Why did you keep this from me for so long, Nash?"

All traces of the anger Nash had barely kept at bay since he threw Mueller against the wall washed away from his face. "It's because it's my fault." I shook my head. Nash cradled my cheeks, stilling the motion as he stared into my eyes. "After I overheard what they were planning, I went to my uncle. I'm the reason your mom didn't get away with it."

I gasped and backed away. "Why would you do that?"

Nash's hands fell at his sides. "I couldn't let you go through with it, Zen. He was going to offer you your dream job—but only if you married him. As soon as I heard that, I knew I had to stop it."

Shock held me immobile. I couldn't wrap my head around it. The whole sordid story was like something out of an old Earth soap.

Nash's big black eyes flitted across my face. "I asked my uncle to help. I'd hoped he'd fire Mueller immediately, but Uncle said that was impossible without proof. The work contracts the research staff sign protects them from wrongful termination. Uncle came up with the plan we followed. To retrieve the evidence from Portia and have her out him."

I sucked in a shaky breath as I remembered that horrible day. Prim had asked Mom repeatedly who helped her, but she refused to name anyone. To this day, she still insisted it was her and her alone who was responsible for my sister's birth.

"I made him promise to let you stay if she told the truth. I thought for sure your mom would come clean for you." Nash rubbed the back of his neck.

My heart twisted. *She didn't, though, did she?*

"And then after, I was sure we'd find something. One of Mueller's fingerprints on the evidence or a report he'd carelessly overlooked. But there was nothing. Just my word against his."

"That still doesn't explain why you kept this from me." My voice cracked.

Nash reached for me, but I sidestepped, dodging him. "I thought if you found out it was me who tipped off my uncle, you wouldn't want anything to do with me. I couldn't lose you, Zen."

Would I have dumped Nash as a friend if he'd confessed? I honestly couldn't say. And the fact that he took the choice away from me made nausea roll through my stomach.

"I tried so many times over the years to tell you, but the timing was never right." Nash stared at the food splattered across the floor. "I wanted to tell you last night, but you were so tired. That's why I brought you lunch today. I was planning to tell you everything."

I scoffed. "You're about twenty years too late."

Nash winced. "I know. I'm so sorry."

"You know what I don't get? If you felt so freaking guilty, like you seem to want me to believe, then why didn't you help me stay?" My heart ached from the reminder of how I'd put myself out there, and he turned me down. "Why didn't you marry me when I found the loophole? Hell, why didn't Mueller offer to marry me then, if that was what he wanted so badly to begin with?"

"Mueller told Portia he wanted someone who'd be good for his reputation. I guess you only fit the bill until your mother was caught. As for me... I couldn't." Nash's eyes met mine, and he looked so tortured in that moment that I almost felt sorry for him. "You know why."

"You're such a hypocrite! I should've never agreed to marry you."

Nash drew back like he'd been stung. "Don't say that, Zen. I know I've made a lot of mistakes, but marrying you wasn't one of them." His voice gentled. "Please give me a chance to make it up to you."

Tears welled in my eyes. I stepped away, knowing if I didn't put some space between us, I'd either burst into tears, or end up saying a whole host of things I'd regret. "I-I need to think." My back hit the hatch. I held up a hand when he opened his mouth. "I just need a little time to wrap my head around this. Alone."

"Okay. And we'll talk more later?"

I nodded and pulled open the door. "Can you do me a favor?"

"Anything," Nash replied instantly.

I waved at the floor. "After you clean up that mess, leave a note on Mueller's desk. Tell him I went home sick." There was no way I could finish out the workday with this new knowledge rattling around in my head.

With that, I turned and fled. I couldn't stand there any longer, feeling like my heart was breaking. The further I walked away from Nash, the more I wished I'd handled everything differently. Gods... why didn't he tell me sooner?

Despite everything, my promise replayed in the back of my mind. I'd sworn not to shut him out or disappear. I meant it when I said it, and I intended to stick to it. After I calmed down, we'd hash things out.

But first things first. Someone else was involved in this mess I needed to talk to, and this time, I refused to back down until she spilled everything.

42

Small Favors

Zenda

Tapping my fingers on the desk, I waited for the call to connect while my stomach churned. Usually, I'd pray for Mom not to answer. This time, I needed her to.

"Hello?" Mom's cheery voice spilled over the speaker in Nash's living room. "Portia speaking."

"Mom, it's me."

"Zenda, darling! It's been so long since you called. How are you?"

"Well, I'm—"

"Honestly, it's been too long." I scowled as she cut me off. "You don't call. You don't write. Have you been taking care of yourself?" Her already excited tone heightened. "Oh, are you calling to tell me you found a man? Are you finally dating? Please, tell me you've found someone! It would just make my—"

"Mom!" I shouted, determined to stop her rambling. "Let me get a word in, would you?"

It was always the same when I called. The unending stream of questions and complaints. I took a deep breath to compose myself—and of course she couldn't resist filling the millisecond of silence with more chatter.

"Sorry, dear. It's just that I worry about you out in space all alone. And you're not getting any younger. If you want to give me grandbabies one day—"

"Mom, please. Stop. I didn't call to talk about my dating life. I need to ask you something. Something important."

"Okay. I'm listening."

Thank the Gods for small favors. "Was Professor Mueller the one who helped you when we were expelled from Subralia?"

Silence stretched out—which was an oddity when it came to conversations with my mother, for sure, but I had to hear her say it. "Was it him, Mom? Did Mueller give you the sperm?"

"Zenda, I don't know why you're asking about this now. It's ancient history."

I pinched the bridge of my nose. "Does it matter? Look, I know you made a deal with Meuller. I know he was planning to ask me to marry him. How could you Mom?"

More silence. My stomach clenched.

Finally, a deep sigh reverberated through the speaker. "I knew our family wasn't complete. I'd been on that list for years. *Years.* I had to take matters into my own hands."

"Why would you sell me out like that? Your own daughter."

"Honey, honestly, I thought you'd be fine with it. He was a catch. And you'd get the job you kept going on and on about, too."

My heart twinged. "So, it is true." Everything Nash told me really happened.

"Can you blame me now? If I hadn't jumped on that chance, then Karsen would've never been born. You can't tell me that was a mistake. Our girl is brilliant. She's going to change the universe, and you know it."

I rubbed my temples. Mom had me there. Karsen was amazing. If Mom hadn't stolen that sperm, I'd have never gotten to meet one of my favorite people. My baby sister.

"Okay. I understand why you did it. I'll even admit that I'm not mad about how things turned out in the long run. But why didn't you turn him in, Mom?" My chest ached. "I could've still kept my job. If you'd turned in Mueller, they'd have let me stay."

"Well, at first, I thought you were about to marry the man. What kind of mother-in-law would I be if I snitched on your husband?"

Ugh. *Good thing she can't see how fast my eyes just rolled.*

She barreled on, "And then when he didn't propose, I was grateful. I didn't want to lose you. It was selfish of me, I know, but I thought if you couldn't have a family of your own, then you needed to stay with us."

I shook my head. *Yep. That sounds like the mom I know...* Karsen and I never had to wonder if Mom loved us, but she always thought she knew best.

Looking back, she might have been right—but not for my sake. For Karsen's.

I'd been an adult when Mom had Karsen, and with the long hours she'd put in at her dead-end job, she'd leaned on me heavily to help raise her. If I hadn't been there to help, not only would I have a much different relationship with Karsen, but who knows what low-life Mom would've been stuck with as Kar's sitter? The quarters we'd moved to on Mars were a small step up from the slums.

Did I resent her for sticking me with babysitting duty when I should've been free to live my life as I wished? Sure. But once again, I couldn't say I regretted it. I'd do it all again for Karsen.

"I'm sorry, Zenda. Can you forgive me?"

Mom sounded more sincere than I'd ever heard her. But I wasn't ready to let her off that easily. Not while I was still reeling from having my history rewritten. "I don't know, Mom. Maybe one day." I sighed. "I have to go. Love you."

I ended the call, trudged into the bedroom, and collapsed on the bed, completely drained. The long hours the last couple days added to the emotional rollercoaster today would make anyone tired. But I couldn't sleep yet. Not when my husband would be home any minute, and I promised not to shut him out.

Where are you Nash?

Nash

I walked through the halls aimlessly, but no matter how far I wandered, I couldn't erase the memory of Zen's distraught face. *What is wrong with me?*

I should've never kept what happened a secret. She'd probably want nothing to do with me now. It would be like the return trip home all over—but so much worse. The last few days, Zen showed me what true bliss was like. I couldn't bear the thought of losing her. Might as well rip my heart out and set it on fire.

So, there I stayed, walking until my feet ached. Then I walked some more, putting off my return home. That's when my uncle found me.

"Nash. I've been looking for you. You never came back from lunch." Uncle Prim stopped in front of me.

I sidestepped around him and continued my trek. "Sorry. Been walking."

"I see." Prim paused for half a second before catching up with me. "I think it's time for a break." He grabbed my elbow and led me to an empty conference room a little way up the hall. Once the door was closed, he pulled out a chair. "Sit."

I sighed and sank into the padded chair. Uncle sat next to me, angling his chair so he could look me in the eye.

"Son, tell me what's wrong."

Dragging a hand down my face, I met his gaze. "I told Zen about Mueller."

Uncle Prim's brow furrowed. "Ah. And she didn't take it well."

"She was devastated." I cringed. "It probably didn't help that I caught the creep staring at her ass and pinned him to the wall."

"What? Did Mueller hear you confess?"

I shook my head. "No. He ran off as soon as I let him down."

"Nash. As your boss, I must say that's entirely unprofessional."

"I know, I'm sorry." That was stretching the truth a smidge. I couldn't exactly tell my boss I'd gladly do it again.

Uncle Prim smiled crookedly. "But as your uncle, I approve. I have no doubt Mueller had it coming."

I sighed. Uncle Prim had been trying to find an excuse to boot Mueller out of Subralia for years. He was the only lead researcher who needed a new assistant every couple of months. And there'd been a handful of student complaints as well. But there'd never been enough proof to force him out of his contract.

Prim leaned forward. "So, the walking is what? Some kind of penance?"

"Zen asked for a little time alone to think." My stomach clenched. "I don't think I can go back there. What if she hates me?"

Prim patted my leg. "You can't avoid her forever. You took a good first step by coming clean. Now is the hard part. Marriage takes work."

He still didn't know. Guilt pooled in my gut. "It's not real," I blurted.

"What do you mean?" Prim retracted his hand and leaned back in his chair.

"Zen never wanted to marry me. It was the condition in the contract. In order to inherit the company, I had to marry for one year and have an heir. They had a woman picked out and ready to say I do, but I convinced Zen to marry me instead."

Uncle Prim's eyes widened. "Huh. Well, be that as it may, judging by how much you're hurting right now, I would say that your marriage is plenty real."

Uncle's words struck a chord in my soul. "I-I want it to be real. I don't want it to end in a year." As soon as the words left my lips, a sense of calm stole over me. It was as if by admitting it out loud, I was committing to Zen—not just for a year, but forever.

"You love her." Uncle Prim smiled.

I nodded. "I do."

"Well then, my boy, what are you going to do?"

What should I do? An apology didn't seem like enough in this situation. I didn't just need Zen to forgive me. I needed to prove she meant everything to me. To convince her that no matter what life threw at us, she could count on me. That I was worth sticking with for the long haul.

If only there was something I could do...

A slow smile spread across my face as an idea struck me. I met my uncle's eyes. "I'm going to make it right. Can I have tomorrow off?"

Uncle Prim sighed. "What's one more day?" He grinned. "Don't muck it up."

"I won't." Now that I knew Zen was it for me, I wasn't leaving it up to chance. And I wouldn't rest until I got her to agree to take divorce off the table.

43

Complicated AF

Zenda

I groaned, blinking my eyes open. *What time is it?* My eyes widened as I spotted the clock. It was morning already, about an hour before my alarm was scheduled to go off.

"Nash?" He wasn't in bed. In fact, his side was still crisply tucked in, like it hadn't been touched.

Maybe he slept on the couch? Yawning, I shuffled into the living room. My pulse picked up when I found the couch empty as well. *Where are you, Nash?*

I turned for the comms station, determined to track him down, but paused as my gaze trailed over the coffee table. Propped up against the fruit basket, sat a note addressed to me. I snagged the note and an apple and settled on the couch.

Zenda,

```
I'm sorry I wasn't there to wake you. I have
an important task to attend to off world.
I'll be home later today. I hope you're still
willing to talk when I get back. I love you.
     -Nash
```

A sigh spilled out of my lips before I crunched into the apple. *Looks like he's avoiding me now.* I definitely wasn't expecting that. What made matters worse was that I still hadn't wrapped my head around everything. I could really use someone to talk to.

I walked to the comms station and placed a call to the Verne. By the time I'd munched to the core of my apple, the call connected.

"Hello, Captain Arda of the Verne," Arda answered stiffly.

"Capt, It's Zenda."

"Hi, Zen." Her tone softened. "How's Subralia? I was wondering when you were gonna check in."

"It's complicated. Do you have a moment to talk? I could really use some advice."

"Sure. We're idling in orbit while waiting on a restock. I've got plenty of time."

I launched into a full recap of the last couple of days. My arrival. Nash and I getting intimate. Getting my dream job, then finding out my boss was a closet creeper. How Nash took off before I could talk to him again.

Arda whistled as I finally finished. "Wow... you weren't kidding. That's complicated as fuck."

I chuckled under my breath. "Yeah. Tell me about it. What should I do?"

"About Nash, or about your boss?"

"Both."

Arda blew out a breath. "Well, sounds like you need to talk to that wayward husband of yours. But you were already planning on that, weren't you?"

"Yeah… I just don't know if I can trust him again. How could he have kept something like that from me for so long?"

"I don't think the trust issue is a one I can help you with. That's something you have to decide on your own. Though looking at it from his perspective, I don't know if I would've said anything either."

I scoffed. "Seriously? You wouldn't?"

"Well, yeah. What would it have accomplished back then? If he'd told you when it first happened, you'd have probably cut him out of your life. Maybe even your mom too, when she refused to help. And you still wouldn't have been able to get Mueller fired."

I rubbed my temples. "That's true. My life would've turned out a lot differently if I didn't move in with my mom on Mars. I'd have never really gotten to know Karsen."

"Hell, you probably wouldn't have met me, either." Arda clicked her tongue. "As for that slimeball boss, I think we need to take him down."

I smiled. "That's exactly what I thought you'd say when I told you."

Arda chuckled. "Hey, what can I say? I don't like assholes hanging around my friends."

"The problem is how to do it." I shook my head. "The more I think about it, the more I'm sure he deserves to be fired. From searching his files, it looks like he's been pawning off his work on his assistants for years. I asked him a question about a paper he supposedly authored and he dodged it. I bet he didn't even write the damn thing."

"I'm not surprised. If he'd stoop to blackmail to land a wife, then he's probably cutting corners anyway he can." Arda went silent for a moment, then asked, "Think you can get your mom to confess? Then it wouldn't just be Nash's word against Mueller's."

I sighed. "No. She's adamant that it wasn't a mistake. I couldn't even get her to say his name out loud."

"Damn. Too bad there aren't any other witnesses."

What if there is? My legs started bouncing like they had a mind of their own. Maybe that brilliant idea I came up with the other day could save my job, and give Mueller exactly what he deserved.

"You said you're still in orbit, right?"

"Yep."

"Think you can bring Ren here? I need your help."

Arda didn't even pause to think it over. "Be there in a few. See you soon, Zen."

Zenda

Knock, knock. My heart pounded as I waited for an answer.

"Come in," a man yelled.

I eased open the door and forced a smile. "Mayor Prim? I hope you don't mind that I showed up unannounced. Your secretary said—"

Nash's uncle pushed out his desk chair with a huge grin on his face. "Zenda, of course not. You're welcome to stop by anytime." He rounded the desk and led me to a loveseat across the room. "What can I do for you today?"

I sat down with a sigh. "Well, first off, I hope you'll forgive me. I know I wasn't exactly pleasant when you greeted Nash and I the other day."

Prim sat across from me. "No need to apologize. You must have been overwhelmed with moving, and I popped out of nowhere. If anything, I should apologize to you."

How did I ever think the worst of him? Nash's uncle wasn't anything like the villain I'd worked up in my mind over the years. *Here I am trying to apologize, and he takes the blame. Who does that?*

I twisted my hands in my lap. "That wasn't it. I was still upset about being banished. But Nash told me the whole story. I realize now it was silly of me to be mad at you for upholding the city charter when Mueller was the one who got my mom in trouble. I know you were just doing your job."

"Oh, that." Prim sighed. "I'm sorry too, Zenda. Maybe if I had done my job better, I'd have found the evidence to prove his complicity."

I smiled. "I'm glad you said that. Would you mind coming with me? There's something you need to hear."

Prim looked at his watch. "I have a little time." He stood and gestured to the door. "Lead the way."

We walked through the halls in a comfortable silence. I probably should've made small talk, but my mind wouldn't stop racing. I needed this plan to work. If it did, then Prim would have his proof and Mueller would get the punishment he deserved. If not, then the chances of me being fired were pretty much guaranteed.

Soon, we arrived at the lab. Prim lifted a brow when he saw who was inside. "Captain Arda. I wasn't expecting to find you here."

Arda rose from the chair I'd set up for her in front of the main tank. "Mayor Prim. Good to see you." I side-eyed Arda as she went in for a hug. She winked at me over his shoulder. "When are you planning to invite Lux and I to dinner again? Soon, I hope?"

Prim patted her back, then pulled away, smiling. "Of course. Why not tonight?" He glanced around the room, frowning when he spotted Ren hunched over a table with her hands tangled in wiring. "Is he here with you?"

Arda chuckled. "Lux is here. He's just occupied at the moment."

I smiled and strolled to Ren. "We needed someone to keep Mueller busy so Ren could work on this." I waved a hand at the complicated-looking mess of machinery in front of her. "Is it ready?"

"It should be right,"—with her tongue poking out the side of her mouth, Ren reached deep into the mangled wiring and snapped something into place—"now."

"Excellent work, Ren. Thank you." I beamed at her, my heart racing. A part of me didn't believe she'd managed it. But Ren was a whiz with machines. We'd see soon enough if she'd achieved the impossible.

"I know it's not pretty, but I didn't have a lot of time." Ren rubbed a hand over her forehead, spreading a black smudge.

I patted her shoulder. "It doesn't matter what it looks like as long as it works."

"What is it?" Prim joined us hovering around the table.

I sucked in a deep breath. "When I worked for Mueller as a student, he taught me to mimic a few of the dolphins' clicks and whistles. I noticed when I was filing for him that the catalog of sounds he keeps had expanded significantly since I left. I asked for Mueller's permission to work on this project, which he eagerly accepted."

Arda snickered. "Bet he didn't expect it would get his lying ass caught."

Prim frowned. "I still don't know what I'm looking at."

"Allow me to show you." I turned to Ren. "It's on?"

"Yep." She leaned back in her chair with a lazy grin.

I stole a glance at the clock. It was perfect timing, too. The last two days at feeding time, Bubbly showed up as soon as I pulled the fish out of the fridge. If that was a fluke, and she wasn't always so punctual, I was about to look like an idiot. I walked to the fridge and grabbed the bucket inside.

Prim's dress shoe tapped loudly on the floor. "Does this contraption need to be fed?"

Splashing echoed in the main pool, and I exhaled. "No. But she does."

The tip of Bubbly's scarred dorsal fin emerged from the water before her head broke the surface. And just like she had each time this week, she greeted me with a series of clicks and whistles. Only this time, Ren's machine kicked in and a robotic voice boomed out from the speaker after Bubbly's clicks ended.

"Human. Give me fish."

Prim startled and his head whipped between the machine and Bubbly. "Did that thing just translate for the dolphin?"

"It did." I barely resisted the urge to jump up and down screaming.

"I didn't know that was possible." Prim shook his head.

"It wasn't—until now." I gestured to Ren. "My friend here did something similar on a run we made to the fourth moon of Triromina. I figured if she could jury-rig the ship's translator to communicate with an alien species, she could handle this too."

Ren ducked her head, hiding a blush. "With the data from those files, it was simple enough."

In the pool, Bubbly splashed, and then clicked again. "Human. Feed me."

Arda wrinkled her nose. "I didn't realize dolphins were so rude."

I chuckled as I tossed a fish into the pool. "The catalog wasn't *that* extensive. Bubbly's responses will be rudimentary for now, but with this technology working, we'll be able to expand the vocabulary quickly."

"This is certainly exciting." Prim peered over the tank's edge. "But how does this relate to Mueller?"

"It's simple." I adjusted my glasses. "You didn't have enough evidence to fire Mueller before, but what if we had a corroborating witness?"

Prim crossed his arms. "That was the plan from the beginning. Though your mother was the only one there. Is she ready to talk?"

"No. But I'm hoping someone else will." I turned to the tank and threw out my arm. "Meet your witness."

"You can't be serious." Prim's jaw dropped. "This dolphin was here that day? How can you even be sure?"

"Do you see that big scar on her dorsal fin?" I tossed another fish into the tank.

Prim's eyes narrowed as Bubbly rose to the surface to snatch the fish out of the air. "Yes, I see it."

"The day my mom was caught, Bubbly had just been moved over there." I pointed to the center tank. "We use that tank to isolate sick and injured dolphins who need a little extra care before being released. She was recovering from the injury that gave her that scar."

Prim blinked, his big black eyes opening and closing several times in quick succession. "All right. Say that's true." He eyed the machine. "This machine will let you talk to her, too?"

Ren nodded. "Yep, it can. You just need to press this button and talk into it." She gestured to the button and nodded at me. "You want to do the honors?"

Pure joy erupted in my chest. Sure, I'd learned how to mimic simple clicks like 'hello' and 'fish' way back when, but having an actual conversation with a dolphin was a dream come true. Of course, I wanted the honors.

"Thank you." I sucked in a deep breath and pushed the button. "Bubbly, how would you like some extra fish today?"

The machine spouted out a long string of clicks and whistles as soon as my finger lifted off the button. Bubbly breached the water and clicked back. "Human. You speak. How?"

I pressed the button again, a huge smile lighting my face. "We made a machine to speak for us."

"Smart human. Give me fish."

Arda and Ren started giggling. I rolled my eyes, tossed another fish into the tank, and pressed the button. "There's more where that came from. First, I need your help."

Bubbly finished gobbling the morsel. "I will help."

"I need to ask you about something that happened years ago."

Bubbly swam along the edge. "What that means?"

I rubbed my chin and turned back to the others. "Of course. Dolphins won't have the same concept of time as we do." I pressed the button. "I was thinner then. Mueller, the man who's always been here, had brown hair instead of white. You were injured and stayed in that tank. Do you remember?"

"Hurt. Stuck. I remember."

"Just before I left, do you remember what happened then?" I glanced at Prim, my stomach churning. If Bubbly said no, then my whole plan was sunk. "Can you please tell us everything you remember?"

"Then you give me fish."

Arda shook her head. "One track mind on this one."

I pressed the button. "Yes. Tell us, then fish."

Bubbly swam to the edge and spat a stream of water toward Prim. He dodged the spray, and opened his mouth, but before Prim said anything, Bubbly started clicking away.

"One like him swam in there." Bubbly pointed her nose to the back tank. "Then brown hair spoke with new human." Bubbly's gaze swung to me. "New human look like you. Everyone leave. Then you come and go in big box with brown hair." Bubbly's nose pointed to the office. "Look sad. Then you gone. Till now."

I swung my gaze to Prim. His mouth was still hanging open, and his eyes were as wide as I'd ever seen them. Was that enough proof? I racked my brain for something else that would help our case.

"Ask Bubbly if she saw Mueller give your mom anything," Ren cut in.

"Ooo, good idea." I pushed the button. "Did you see brown hair give the new human anything?"

Bubbly swam a lap of the pool before replying. "Small box. Took out of fish box."

"She must mean the fridge," Arda said. "That's got to be enough to back up Nash's story."

"I help. Give me fish now."

I lugged the bucket to the tank and dumped the rest of the fish in. "There you go, Bubbly. Thanks."

I turned back, feeling triumphant, until I spotted the pinched expression on Prim's face.

"This is incredible. The technology is revolutionary and I'm so proud it was created in our fine city. As for Mueller, I'm sorry. An animal's testimony using experimental tech won't be enough to break his contract."

Arda cocked her head and tapped on her neck. "Sorry. Call coming through. I need to take this." She ducked into the hall.

I sucked in a few deep breaths, grateful for the distraction. It was enough to stop me from doing something idiotic, like stomping my feet or bursting into tears. Sometimes the universe was an unfair place. We went through all this trouble, and it still wasn't enough to implicate Mueller.

I couldn't let that stop me. One way or another, Mueller had to go. Now that I knew this tech worked, I couldn't stand the thought of being ousted from the project again. There was no way Mueller would keep me on after Nash tried to kill him yesterday, and I tried to get him fired.

Prim sighed and glanced at his watch. "If there's nothing else—"

"No. There is." I crossed the room and opened the office door. "Let me show you the files I've found. As far as I can tell, there's barely anything in here from Mueller. If you trace the original owners of the files, almost everything belongs to one assistant or another."

Prim frowned. "I agree that is strange. But without direct proof of wrong-doing, I'm afraid my hands are tied."

The files fell out of my hands and floated onto the desk. My gaze landed on Mueller's book. I grabbed it and flipped to the title page. "Look at this. All he's done in the office this week is read this fantasy novel. Shadows That Bind Us." I lifted a brow. "That doesn't sound like research to me."

"That's enough to lodge a complaint, but Mueller will only get a slap on the wrist." Prim patted my shoulder. "I'm sorry, Zenda."

No. That was my last hope. My heart shattered. *He's going to get away with it and there's nothing I can do.*

44

What Are You Doing Here

Nash

"Come on, it's this way." I raced through the halls, heading toward the lab. We'd stopped at Uncle Prim's office only to find him missing. His secretary didn't know where he was, only that he'd left—with Zenda.

What are they doing together? I'd figured from the way Zen gave Uncle the cold shoulder, he'd be the last man she'd hunt down in my absence. I honestly had no clue where to look, either. But the lab was as good a place as any to search for them. With any luck, we'd find them there and set everything to rights.

I turned a corner and skidded to a stop just before plowing into someone's muscular back. "Lux? What are you doing here?"

I caught a flash of a white lab coat behind Lux an instant before Mueller stepped aside. "What's *she* doing here?" he asked, aghast, as his gaze settled on my companion. Eyes widening, Mueller took a step back.

"Oh, no you don't." Lux clamped a huge hand on Mueller's forearm, making him hiss. "You were about to show me your lab." Lux turned to me, smiling widely. "Care to join us?"

"What a coincidence. That's exactly where we were headed." I waved a hand, signaling the woman behind me to follow.

Lux dragged Mueller to the lab. I punched in the code on the hatch and we piled inside. Then my stomach dropped to my feet.

"Zenda," I breathed. She was inside the office, with a book clenched in her hands. Red rimmed her eyes, and her face was flushed. I took one look at her face and rage washed over me.

The man responsible for her pain was right in front of me. For half a second, I contemplated slamming him into the wall again—but I resisted the urge. What was coming next would be so much sweeter.

The door slammed closed behind us, causing everyone inside to turn and stare. Ren and Arda remained where they sat, at a table holding a strange machine beside the main pool. Then Uncle and Zenda strode out of the office.

"Mom?" Zenda lifted a brow. "What are you doing here?"

Portia stepped to the front of our group. "I'm here to tell the truth. Mayor Prim, you wanted to know who helped me steal." Her hand raised, and she pointed directly at Professor Mueller. "It was Mueller. He gave me the sperm."

Mueller's eyes bulged, and he tugged at his arm, trying desperately to dislodge himself from Lux's iron grip. "This is ludicrous. She's lying. You have no proof!"

Mayor Prim strode up to Mueller. "You would be right if it was only one word. But now it's three."

"Three?" Mueller's brow wrinkled. "What on Earth are you talking about?"

A splash sounded in the pool, followed by a string of clicks. Immediately after, a voice droned out of the machine. "Bye, bye. Stupid man."

I grinned, immediately remembering the project Zenda was so excited about the other night. This had to be it. "Zenda, you're brilliant!"

Zenda tore her gaze off her mother long enough to smile shyly at me.

Mueller did a double take. "Did that just happen?" He gaped at Zenda. "I'm going to be famous!"

"Oh, I don't think so." Uncle Prim crossed his arms. "I have it on good authority that most of the research you've been responsible for over the years has been handed off to your assistants."

"T-that's a bald-faced lie!" Mueller blubbered.

"Add to that the very serious crime of theft, and I'm afraid there's only one course of action that I'm left with." Uncle turned to me with a crooked grin. "Care to tell the professor what the city charter demands we do with thieves?"

"With pleasure." I cleared my throat. "Professor Mueller, you're fired. Don't worry about your things. I'll have them packed and sent to an address of your choosing. There's a transport waiting to take you out of the city. From this moment forward, you're no longer welcome at Subralia."

Mueller shook his head. "You can't do this to me! I signed a work contract—"

"That contract was voided the moment you stole from the city." I smirked, enjoying the panic in that lying bastard's eyes. "You've overstayed your welcome."

Mueller tried to dart into his office, but he must've forgotten Lux still had a hold of his arm. He only made it two steps before the big alien yanked him back into the hard wall of his chest.

I grabbed Mueller's other arm and lifted a brow at Lux. "Mind helping me take out the trash?"

Lux grunted. "After spending a morning with that prick? Dral, yes."

Together, we carted the crying professor out of the lab. I won't lie. Throwing the lying cheat out of Subralia was one of the most satisfying experiences of my life. Years ago, I'd sworn to bring him down, and I'd finally accomplished it.

But none of it would matter if I lost Zen in the process. I sucked in a deep breath as the door to Mueller's transport slammed closed.

Please, Zen. You have to forgive me.

Zenda

I walked to Mom as Mueller disappeared into the hall. "I can't believe you're really here." My arms spread wide, and before I knew it, I'd wrapped my mom in a tight hug. Yeah, she might not be my favorite person at the moment, but she was still my mom. And we were huggers. It was kind of our thing.

I pulled away after she squeezed me tight enough to make me gasp. "What changed your mind? The last time we talked, you were so adamant that it wasn't a mistake."

Mom patted my cheek. "Your friend Nash did. He came to find me on Mars. He told me how he got you a job here with Mueller. How he found the creep leering at you." She stacked her hands on her hips. "Why didn't you mention that when you called, hm?"

I bit my lip. I had considered it, but I didn't want the conversation to morph into something else when she realized I'd used the marriage loophole to return. "Must've slipped my mind."

"Well, that boy practically begged me to come and set things right. He arranged for a temporary travel clearance to overrule the banishment." She leaned in and lowered her voice. "Even hired a transport so fast it made him puke. He's a good friend."

Nash did all that for me? My heart expanded, sending showers of tingles shooting down my spine. "He's not just my friend. We're married."

"Yay!" Mom squealed and grabbed my arms, jumping up and down. "My baby got married! No wonder he was so determined to help you. I should've known." Mom paused, and she finally noticed the tears streaming down my cheeks. "Oh, darling. You're so happy you're crying! I know how that feels. I did the same thing when you were born." She pulled me into another tight hug.

I didn't have the heart to correct her. Fact was, they weren't happy tears at all. Because one thought kept playing on a loop, unbidden. *How can I give him up in a year? I don't want to.*

Someone tapped my shoulder gently. I pulled out of Mom's arms and scrubbed my face.

Mayor Prim stood behind me. "Sorry to interrupt. It's just that Subralia needs a new lead researcher now that Mueller's gone. I'll have to okay it with Professor Davis, but I have a feeling that once she sees this brilliant invention of yours, she'll agree in a heartbeat. How would you like the job, Zenda?"

"Really?" A fresh rush of moisture flooded my eyes. "You mean—a permanent position?"

Prim nodded. "Yes. You deserve it, Zenda."

Blood raced through my veins. A part of me wanted to scream yes immediately. But I couldn't ignore the fact that my relationship with Nash had an expiration date.

Could I live and work in the same city with him after we broke up? My heart twinged as I imagined what life would be like, seeing him but not being able to touch him. Having to go back to being just friends, when what I really wanted was what we had right now. And not for a year. Forever.

I blinked back the tears and looked Prim in the eyes. "Is it all right if I think about it?"

Prim smiled. "Of course. I'll have a formal contract drawn up. Set a meeting with my secretary when you're ready."

"Thank you." Despite my lingering doubts, I couldn't hold back the joy completely. It bubbled up in my chest, and once again, I reached for a hug I hadn't entirely planned to give.

Prim chuckled and patted my back. "You're welcome, Zenda. I hope you decide to take it." He pulled away. "Now, if you'll excuse me. I have a meeting I'm running late for." He called over my shoulder to Arda, "The dinner invitation stands. How's seven sound?"

Arda waved at him. "Wouldn't miss it!" Arda turned to me as the hatch swung shut. "I heard everything, Zen. This is amazing! Don't let me stop you. If you want this job, take it."

I sent her a wobbly smile. The thought of my sabbatical hadn't even crossed my mind yet, but having Arda's approval set my mind at ease. "You sure? I don't want to leave you in the lurch."

"You aren't." Arda shook her head. "I know this is what you've always wanted to do. What kind of friend would I be if I stood in your way?"

Tears pricked my eyes again. "You're a fucking amazing friend, that's what."

Mom cut in, "Zenda. Watch your mouth."

Ren snickered, shooting me a cheeky grin.

Arda flicked her hair off her shoulder and smirked. "Yeah, I know." Her expression turned serious. "And we'll always be friends. No matter how many light years are between us."

How the hell did I get so lucky? I had friends who would stand by my side and move heaven and earth to help me. My dream job was waiting for me to accept it. I had a family who loved me and I loved dearly.

There was only one thing missing. *I want my husband back—for good.* I lifted my eyes to the ceiling and said a silent prayer. *Please tell me Nash feels the same way, too.*

45

Be Real

Nash

Lux and I returned to the lab. My stomach filled with knots as I approached Zen. All the adrenaline from tossing Mueller out faded, and worry spread.

What if she's still pissed? We didn't grow closer until I shared the truth about my past with her. What if Zen sees this as a step back? Just another example of me locking my secrets away and not being real.

I'd have to show her that wasn't me anymore. With the Mueller business taken care of, there was nothing holding us apart any longer. No more secrets to get in the way. I'd gladly share everything with her until the day we die if she'd give me another chance.

I steeled my spine and forced a smile. "Can we talk?"

"I'd like that." Zenda's small hand slid into mine. "Let's go home."

"Okay." A burst of warmth flared to life in my chest. Home. That was a good sign, wasn't it? She wouldn't be calling my place home if she didn't mean it. *I hope.*

We said our goodbyes, and I barely registered any of it. My mind was busy plotting exactly what to say. I stayed silent on the walk to our quarters, holding tight to Zen's hand. Her touch soothed me even while my thoughts tumbled around like a ship navigating an asteroid belt.

When we made it back, I led Zen to the couch and sat beside her. "I'm sorry about Mueller. I know I should've told you from the start."

"You really should have." My heart plummeted until Zen squeezed my hand. "But honestly, when I look at it from your perspective, I get why you didn't." She added sternly, "I still don't think it was the right call."

"I know it wasn't." I rubbed the back of her hand, wanting to take my gloves off, but not willing to let go long enough to tear them off. "It's been eating me alive. Especially when I found out how much you missed Subralia. I couldn't stand knowing it was my fault you weren't living your dream. And when you found out the whole story, I knew I had to make it up to you somehow."

"Is that what made you hunt down my mom?"

I nodded. "I wish I'd done it from the start. Then maybe it wouldn't have taken me half a lifetime to find happiness. To find you."

Zen's breath caught. "Do you really mean that?"

As I stared into her eyes, the carefully crafted words I'd been planning disappeared. I didn't need that with Zen. She didn't care if I was eloquent. She wanted me to be real. So, I took a deep breath and spoke from the heart.

"I do." Shifting, I rested my forehead against hers. "You make me happier than I've ever been. You make me better. Let me be *me*—if that makes sense."

"I get it." Zen smiled softly. "I feel the same way when I'm with you."

Those words spread through my body like molten fire, igniting my blood. I leaned down and kissed her. But when I moved to deepen the kiss, she pressed against my chest.

"I have to tell you something."

Fuck. Was that good? "You can tell me anything."

She twisted her hands in her lap. "Your uncle offered me Mueller's job."

"Really? That's fantastic! You deserve it, Zen." I beamed, but when Zenda only offered me a tiny grin in return, my stomach sank. "What's wrong? Don't you want to take it?"

"No, I do. It's just... I don't know if I can." She sucked in a shaky breath and stared at her hands.

"What? Why not?" It didn't make any sense. This was her dream job. I placed a finger under her chin and tipped her face up, forcing her to look at me. "Tell me, Zen."

Zenda met my eyes and chewed on her lip. "What happens when this is over? I'm supposed to move down the hall and be your neighbor? To see you day in and day out, but not be *with* you?" Her chin quivered. "I know we only agreed to a year, but I don't think I can handle that, Nash."

Someone slap me. Did I hear her right?

"What if it doesn't have to end?" My nerves pulsed to life and sweat pooled in my skinsuit. But I wasn't about to let this moment pass me by—and this time, I was doing it right. I sank to the floor in front of Zen, down on one knee. "Zenda, will you be mine? Not only for a year, but forever?"

Zen's eyes widened, then filled with tears. I held my breath, waiting to learn whether my dreams were about to come true.

"Yes." She nodded emphatically. "I thought you'd never ask." She jumped into my arms and rained kisses on my face.

Pure joy blossomed in my heart. I could sense it radiating out of her as well, with every sweet kiss she gave me. Laughing, I held tight to Zen's waist and let her have her fill. But once she slowed, I reached up and cradled her face.

"I love you, Zenda." I kissed her mouth with all the passion burning in my heart. "It's always been you." I kissed her again, while planting my feet under me and lifting her into my arms. "You're mine, now and forever." I stood and carried her into the bedroom.

Zenda smiled. "I love you too. So much."

We'd said it before. And no doubt we'd say it a million times more. But at that moment, it felt like the first time. New and alive and so fucking vibrant it made my head spin.

We slowly peeled each other out of our clothes. By the time we lay naked together in bed, my dick was fully erect and begging for her attention. I ignored the greedy bastard, even swatting Zen's hand away when she reached for me.

That earned me a scowl. "Hey. Aren't I allowed to touch my husband?"

"Not when I have plans for my wife." I smirked, pressing her shoulders down on the mattress. I snuggled beside her and propped myself up with an elbow, admiring the sight of her laid out like a feast.

"What plans?" she asked breathlessly.

"You're not leaving this bed until I've memorized every inch of you." I splayed a hand on her belly, slowly trailing across her pale skin to her perfect breasts. "With my hands." I palmed the stiff peak, rolling her nipple until she moaned softly. "And my mouth." I dipped my head down, teasing her neck with lips. "And my tongue." I flicked my tongue out the full length and even though my face was still hovering beside her neck, I flicked her nipple with it.

Zenda gasped. The gasp turned into a deep groan that made my blood boil. I shifted, straddling her legs and giving her breasts my full attention.

Sucking. Nipping. Pinching and licking.

"Nash." Zenda writhed beneath me, but with my weight heavy on her legs, she couldn't seek much relief. "Please, I need more."

Her needy whine lit a fire in my veins. I released her nipple from my mouth with a pop and stared up at her face. She was so beautiful. Her cheeks flush, eyes drugged with pleasure. I couldn't deny her anything. I wouldn't want to.

"I'll give you what you need." Sliding down her body, I tossed her legs over my shoulders. Then I spread her lips with my fingers and sucked her clit into my mouth.

"Gods, Nash!" Her back bowed off the bed.

I groaned, loving the way her legs quivered. I pulled my mouth off and smiled at her. "Mm, delicious. I could lick this pussy forever."

Her hands landed on my head, and she shamelessly pushed me back down. I chuckled and licked her tender flesh with long, flat strokes. Zenda's hips moved, chasing my tongue. There was no guessing whether she liked what I was doing. The constant string of husky moans spilling out of her mouth made that perfectly clear.

My cock ached, needing to be inside her. To feel her tight walls pulsing around me. But I held off, wanting to push her right to the edge before I sank home.

I picked up the pace, flicking her clit harder and faster. Zen's legs tensed, and she moaned, "Gods, I'm—"

I lifted my head and climbed up her body, kissing the pout off her lush mouth. "I need you to be a good girl and come on my cock," I whispered against her lips. "Can you do that for me?"

"Fuck, yes." Zenda reached down, stroking my dick lightly before lining me up at her entrance. I gritted my teeth and thrust.

"Zenda." I moaned her name, and her eyes flew to mine. I held her gaze as I steadily rocked inside her. Pleasure zinged up my spine, and I could feel my orgasm building swiftly. "I love you, Zenda."

She gasped and the first flutters of her orgasm clenched my cock. "Love you. Nash. I-I. Fuucckkk, I'm coming." Her eyes slammed closed as her tight cunt spasmed. She screamed my name.

I couldn't hold back any longer. My orgasm hit me like a supernova, blasting plasma through every cell of my body. Cock still pulsing, I collapsed atop Zenda, breathing hard. After a few seconds, I rolled over, pulling her on top of me. She gazed at me with her bun askew and a satisfied smile on her lips. I sighed, hugging her to my chest and feeling like the luckiest man alive.

My wife. My best friend. My world. She was wrapped in my arms, and I wasn't letting go. *Never.*

46

Moving Forward

Nash

Later that night, I rested in bed, staring at Zenda sleeping beside me. I still couldn't believe it. I'd been so worried she wouldn't give me a second chance. Now that she had, it felt like anything was possible.

Maybe tonight was the night for second chances. After all, if Zen could forgive me for my past mistakes, then shouldn't I be willing to practice forgiveness, too? It'd been nagging at me that a certain someone in my life might deserve a little more empathy than I'd been willing to give.

I slipped out of bed and tossed on a robe. The living room light burned my eyes momentarily, but by the time I settled behind the comms station, they'd adjusted. I looked up local Vorillion time. I smiled. Mid-morning—an ideal time to catch my mother at home while Father was in the office.

"Hello?" Mom's form appeared on the holovid-screen. Most people weren't wealthy enough to afford the pricey tech, meaning I had to settle for voice calls—but of course my parents had it. I was grateful for it tonight. It let me see the brilliant smile that crossed Mom's face when she spotted me. "Nash? I'm so happy you called."

"Hi, Mom." Butterflies swarmed my stomach.

"Is something wrong?" she asked, brow furrowing.

"No." I shook my head and nearly ended the call without saying more than that. But then I glanced at the couch. Hours ago, Zenda had the heart to sit down and listen to me. It was time I did the same. I sucked in a deep breath and looked at my mom's projection. "I know you wanted to talk. I wasn't ready to listen then, but I am now."

A tiny smile painted her lips. "Okay. What do you want to know?"

So many things. Why did you abandon me? Why didn't you reach out before now? Did you ever love me?

I sighed, settling for something a little more recent. "Uncle Prim said you put in a moving application for Subralia."

Mom fiddled with the hem of her simple blue dress. "I did. That's one thing I wanted to tell you. I'm leaving your father. It's been the plan all along. We knew our personal issues would negatively affect the company while your father was running it, so we waited to split."

I lifted a brow. "Why would you do that?"

"For you. It's your birthright. We didn't want to ruin it before you inherited it."

"You know I don't care about running the company. Not the way Dad does." I frowned. "If you'd asked me back then, I'd have told you that. You didn't have to sacrifice your happiness to keep it running."

Mom sighed. "I understand that now. But things were different on Vorillion before you were born. In a lot of ways, they're still very different from other parts of the universe. Your father and I both made a lot of mistakes because we lived there."

"Like what?"

"Getting married, for one." Her gaze flicked down before returning to me. "I always knew your father was attracted to men, but I married him to make my family happy. He did the same for his."

That was news to me. I'd always assumed they'd shared an attraction at some point in their marriage.

"I know your father regrets the way he handled everything that day in his office." She cringed. "And I do too. I wish I'd sat you down and talked to you before sending you off on your own. I don't have any excuse except that I wasn't in a good place mentally back then. I'm sorry I wasn't stronger for you, son."

"I wish you would've told me, too." But as the words spilled out, I realized they weren't entirely true. How different would things be if they'd hashed this out with me from the beginning? I probably would have never left Vorillion. Never met Zen. When I thought about it from that angle, I was grateful things played out the way they had.

"We both wanted more for you. That's why we sent you to earth where attitudes aren't so intolerant. Your father worked to set up the company so it could run remotely." Mom clasped a hand to her chest. "I know it might not seem like it, but your father and I never stopped loving you. We've kept in touch with your uncle and watched you from afar."

"Really?" I'd have to ask my uncle about that, but judging by the tears gathered in her eyes, I sensed she was telling the truth.

"Yes. Now that the company is out of our hands, we're both planning to move to Earth to be closer to you. Me alone, and your father with his secretary."

My eyes widened. "Do you mean—the same one I walked in on?"

Mom nodded.

"And you're okay with that?"

She shrugged. "They've been in love since the day they met. Now they can finally be together. I'm happy for them. They're talking about eloping and doing a little traveling before settling down for good. I'm sure your father would love to tell you all about it—and apologize—if you're willing to give him a chance."

"Wow, that's a lot to take in." I rubbed the back of my neck. I'd always assumed I'd caught my father during a sordid fling. Knowing he was in love—had been for decades—certainly put it into a different perspective.

"I know. And I'm sorry we meddled in your love life, too. We just wanted to see you settled. For you to find someone to share your life with." She flashed a lopsided smile. "Give us some grandbabies."

I chuckled, shaking my head. "Remind me to introduce you to Zenda's mom when you get here. Something tells me the two of you will get along."

Mom's face brightened. "So, you're not angry about us moving to Earth?"

I leaned back, thinking it over. Yeah, my family wasn't perfect—far from it. They made a lot of mistakes. But hell, so did I. *And tonight's a night for second chances.* "No. I think I'd like that. I want us to move forward and be a family again."

"Oh. I'm so happy to hear that. I'd like that, too."

By the time I said goodbye, it was like a weight I hadn't realized was there had been lifted off my shoulders. A yawn split my lips as I spotted Zen in the bedroom doorway wrapped in a sheet, her long red hair spilling down her shoulders.

"Come back to sleep," she whispered, a sleepy smile on her face.

"Be right there, wife." *As for sleeping... that will have to wait.*

47

Dionus

Zenda

Six Months Later

I climbed aboard the Verne, sighing as the familiar walls slid beside me. Lux had a meeting in Subralia today, and I wasn't about to miss the chance to share lunch with my besties while they were parked in the docking bay.

I rapped on the open door before popping my head in the mess hall. "Hey, I'm here!"

"Zenda!" Arda beamed, waving me in. "Get the fuck in here, then. We've been waiting all day."

I chuckled, making a round of the table and giving hugs to each of them. First, Arda with her big blue eyes and long brown hair cascading across the shoulders of her red skinsuit. Ren's short blonde hair had grown a bit shaggier than I remembered, but she still sported dozens of stains on her skinsuit. And best of all—my little sis Karsen.

"Zen, I missed you!" A huge smile lit her face. Karsen stood, plucking me off the ground and squealing.

"Hey, you're supposed to be my *little* sis."

Since Karsen hit puberty, she'd always been bigger than me, but I swear she'd gotten even taller since I'd seen her last. Stronger too.

Ren and Arda broke into chuckles while Karsen planted me on the ground and sat back down.

"Did I tell you what happened when we picked Kar up?" Arda raised a brow.

I plunked into a chair. "Nope. Lay it on me."

Arda lifted a teacup to her lips. "I sent Lux to scoop her up. He spent an hour wandering around the spaceport looking for a redhead with glasses before Karsen tapped him on the shoulder and introduced herself."

"Did he now?" I smiled at Kar. Everyone expected sisters to look the same, but Kar and I couldn't be more different—physically, at least.

"Guess you forgot to tell him we have different sperm donors?" Kar smirked, her light brown eyes sparkling. I was positive her father had to have been a looker. Karsen was gorgeous, with flawless light-brown skin and black hair that she wore plaited in two long braids.

"So how are you liking it on the Verne? Is it everything you expected?" I asked.

Karsen smiled. "I love it. We've already been so many places."

Arda clicked her tongue. "We've barely left the system." She patted Kar's shoulder. "Trust me, the best is yet to come."

Ren sniggered. "Promises, promises."

I split a look between them. "I'm glad you're getting along. I still feel bad about leaving."

"Don't," Arda deadpanned. "We like your sister better."

I gasped. Karsen and Ren giggled. Arda's smile betrayed her, peeking out and ruining her joke.

Lux charged into the mess, panting, his long golden hair sweaty and disheveled. "I have news."

Arda cocked a brow. "Did you run here with it?"

"Maybe." He sank into a chair and placed a diskette on the table. "This was waiting for me in the Pherian diplomatic office in Subralia. Apparently, Elys sent it there when she couldn't locate us during our run past the outer rim last week."

"What is it?" I asked.

"It's the translation. Her linguist friend finally cracked it."

Arda's eyes lit up. My heart raced. It had been months since Nash and I snuck that file out of Vorillion. I'd almost given up hope that Lux's sister would come through.

Ren leaned in, her eyes widening. "What's it say?"

Lux dragged a hand through his hair. "Earth wasn't the only planet where DNA has been tampered with. It happened on Vorillon and on another planet, too. There were notes in here that point to another facility like the one we found on Vorillion. We need to go to Dionus next."

"Dionus? I've heard of that planet. They're even more leery of visitors than Vorillion. I hear the men have,"—I leaned sideways and slid my hands over Karsen's ears—"two dicks."

Karsen scowled and whacked my hands off her ears. "Please. I'm a doctor. I'm well aware that diphallia is common in some alien species."

I rolled my eyes, ready to argue, but that's when I spotted Ren. She'd paled so much I was instantly concerned. "Are you okay?"

Arda noticed too. She wrapped an arm around Ren's shoulders, her nose wrinkling. "You don't look so good. Do you need anything?"

"I-I'm fine." Ren groaned. "I may have an in at Dionus."

"Seriously?" Arda's mouth fell open.

Ren nodded. "My sister kind of lives there..."

I bit back a gasp. We'd lived and worked together for so long that I'd told Ren countless stories about Karsen. In all that time, she'd never once mentioned she had a sister. Were they estranged? Is that why Ren looked so sickened at the thought of visiting her?

"Well." Arda grinned. "I guess we're off to Dionus next."

Lux stood. "I need to go call Elys and thank her. Then I'll start logging a flight plan."

"Tell Elys thank you for me, too." Arda beckoned Lux over. He planted a sweet kiss on Arda's lips and left the mess.

I sighed. A couple of months ago, the sight of their love had been enough to make me irrationally jealous. Not anymore. Although one thing still had me slightly bummed. "I wish I could go with you. I hear the animals on Dionus are fascinating. It's a jungle world with so many species it would take ten lifetimes to study them all."

Arda spun her teacup on the table. "Why don't you tag along? Wouldn't be the first time you took a sabbatical."

I trailed my hand across my stomach. "It's not my job holding me back... it's the morning sickness."

"No way!" Karsen jumped in her chair. "You're pregnant?"

I nodded as a huge smile spread across my face. "I just found out."

"Congratulations." Some of the color seeped back into Ren's cheeks. "That's amazing."

"I'm so happy for you, Zen. What did Nash say when you told him?" Arda asked.

A bit of my enthusiasm died. "I haven't told him yet. He's been out of town all week. I wanted to tell him in person, you know? But he'll be back later today."

"He's going to be ecstatic," Arda insisted.

"You think—" A gray lump of purring flesh jumped into my lap, interrupting my question. "Smudge." I chuckled. "Hey girl. I knew you'd come around sooner or later."

Ren grinned. "It's your lucky day."

I smiled as I snuggled Lux's alien pet. *I hope Ren's right.*

Truth was, I'd never been happier. And a small part of me couldn't stop worrying that it was too good to be true. *Guess I'll find out soon enough.*

Nash

Whistling, I strolled through the halls of Subralia, nodding and smiling at the people I passed. Yeah... I was that guy. The stupidly happy guy who couldn't hide it.

Who could blame me? I was back from a week-long trip and about to see my girl. Well, not immediately. First, I'd promised to stop for dinner with—

"Oh, Nash!" A sultry purr interrupted my train of thought.

Great... just what I need. I plastered a benign smile on my face and spun around. "Stasia. Can I help you with something?"

She prowled toward me, the coy tilt to her lips and slink in her step leaving me with no doubt what she was after. "It's been so long. I thought you'd like to catch up. We can go to my place. I have a—"

"Let me stop you right there. I'm not interested."

Stasia pouted and pulled me aside. "Really, Nash? When you dismiss me like that, it hurts my feelings. I thought..."

I tuned her out as she continued to whine. The urge to run hit me hard and fast. We were in the middle of a crowded hall. I could act like I spotted someone I know, make a polite excuse.

No.

"Stasia." I stepped back, putting a huge space between us. "Let me make this perfectly clear. I'm in love with my wife. You and me—it's never going to happen. Goodbye." I flashed a bright grin and turned on my heel, walking in the opposite direction.

Stasia gasped and fell in behind me. "How could you say that to me? Me? You don't know what you're missing!" Her voice rose until she was practically screeching.

People turned to stare, but I kept walking, ignoring Stasia while nodding and waving at everyone I passed. She followed me all the way to my destination, lobbing insults and threats with each step.

Knock, knock.

The door opened, and my mom popped her head out of the hatch. "Nash, darling." She quirked a brow at Stasia and inched the door open wider. "Come on in."

"Thanks, Mom." I brushed past her with a sigh.

Before closing the door, Mom shook her head. She waited for Stasia to take a breath and cut in. "Honey, give it a rest. Desperate is not a good look on you." Then she slammed the door in Stasia's face and turned to me with a smile. "Guess we're both getting better at dealing with confrontation."

I chuckled. "Yeah. Looks that way."

"Have a seat. I'll grab us a drink." Mom and I sat down for a warm cup of melo and some homemade cookies.

She'd moved in a few months ago, and we'd started a new ritual. Every weekend, I'd stop by for a visit. Things still weren't perfect, but I think it was safe to say that we'd begun patching up our relationship.

"Where's Zenda today?" Mom asked. "I was hoping to see her."

"She'll be by soon. I spoke to her on the comms this morning. She had a lunch date with her friends, but she's planning to meet me here when she's through."

Mom clapped her hands. "Oh, good. I'll get to see her after all."

I smiled. Zen and my mom had bonded pretty quickly. I wasn't mad about it. I think Zen appreciated the company, seeing as how Zen's mom couldn't visit us without special written approval. Zen claimed it was for the best, since her mom was a 'stage four clinger'—her words, not mine. But I could sense that she missed having her friends around, and my mom helped fill the void.

"Oh, I forgot to show you." Mom pulled out a letter with printed pictures folded inside. "Your father sent me these. Look at how happy he is on his honeymoon."

My lips twitched as I flipped through the photos. "Wow. I don't think I've ever seen him smile like that."

"He's in love." Mom shrugged. "He reminds me of you in those."

I flashed a grin. "I took your advice. Called Dad."

"You did?" Mom patted my hand. "Good. I'm glad." Her eyes watered. "We're going to be a real family again."

Knock, knock.

"I bet that's Zenda." Mom popped out of her chair and hurried to the door. "Darling, you're here!" I sipped my melo while they hugged. Then Mom led Zen to the table and pulled out the chair beside me. "Sit. Have a cookie." In the kitchen, a timer blared. "Oh, the rest of the food's ready. I'll be right back."

Zen glanced at me and bent to sit.

I cleared my throat loudly, causing her to freeze. "Aren't you forgetting something?"

Her eyes widened. "What?"

"How about my hug?" I snagged her arm and tugged her atop my lap. "Since when does my mom get one and not me?"

Zenda chuckled nervously and wrapped her arms loosely around my neck. "Sorry."

Oh no. That had to be the lamest hug she'd ever given me. I tilted back as soon as she was through and stared into her face. "What's wrong, Zen? Are you okay?"

Zen shifted on my lap and nibbled on her lip. She peered toward the kitchen and lowered her voice. "I wanted to wait until we were alone, but... I can't. I have to tell you now. I'm... pregnant."

Her gaze darted across my face. With the way she was acting, I'd expected something bad, not this. "Do you mean it?"

She nodded. "Are you happy?"

"Happy?" I repeated stupidly. I grabbed her cheeks, tugging her closer to me. "Happy doesn't even come close to what I'm feeling. This is... it's everything. I can't believe you're mine." I slipped one hand down her belly. "You're both mine."

My lips crashed on hers. Zenda kissed me back, wrapping her arms around my neck tightly.

I smirked as we came up for air. "That's more like it. I thought you were dying when you tried to get away with that weak hug earlier."

She pushed my chest. "Shut up. I was nervous."

I scoffed. "Nervous? With me? Please."

She rolled her eyes. "Yeah, I don't know what I was thinking. You clearly love everything about me."

"Damn right, I do." I bobbed my head up and down emphatically.

"All right, Bobbles. Give it a rest." She leaned close to my ear as Mom emerged with an enormous platter balanced in her hands. "You're already getting lucky tonight," Zenda whispered in my ear before hopping off my lap and heading into the kitchen to help.

I chuckled, enjoying the view as she walked away. *This is it.* All I needed was Zen making jokes with me every day for the rest of my life.

And she's absolutely right. I'm the luckiest man in the universe.

About the author

Leda Palmer loves dreaming about alien worlds and star-crossed lovers finding each other. When she's not writing, you'll find her with her nose in a book or her eyes on the stars. The Cosmic Lovers series is her debut series.

Find out more about her future projects on her Facebook page Leda Palmer – Author. Or on follow her on Instagram at ledapalmerauthor

Also by

Cosmic Lovers 1 – Bloodlust Voyage

Upcoming novels in the Cosmic Lovers Series:
Barbarian Voyage — 2024/25

For early access to Barbarian Voyage, and all Leda's work, look for her stories on Kindle Vella.